UNTAMED

A BAD BOY SECRET BABY ROMANCE

EMILIA KINCADE

ISBN-10: 1530120195
ISBN-13: 978-1530120192

I never told him about the baby…

How did it come to this? Me, pregnant, with his child?

Duncan ripped through my life like a tornado through a field, and he carried me away with him somewhere amazing.

His hot lips seared my skin, his possessive hands owned my body, and his azure eyes stole my soul.

He took me, made me scream, made me his, and he never, ever stopped.

But it could never last. We were never meant to be.

I *had* to run! It was the only way!

I know he's coming for me. I know he wants his family back.

He wants to make me his again.

Only she could tame me… But then she stole my baby.

The moment I saw Dee, I knew I had to have her as my own.

I fell into her endless eyes, and her touch ignited my molten obsession.

The way she felt, the way she smelled, the way she tasted… she was always my burning need.

We had it all, had a plan. We were meant to be a family. But something spooked her, and she disappeared.

She never told me she was carrying our baby.

I know she's running for a reason. I know someone is threatening her.

I'm not letting my family go. I'm getting them back.

I'll do whatever it takes to protect them, to make her mine again.

CONTENTS

1

DEE

The sharks think him a goldfish in their tank. How wrong they are.

Clinking crystal and the hubbub of chatter and laughs are the background noises. Prideful chandeliers, and tuxedos and formal dresses are the background sights. Perfume, masculine and feminine, peaty whiskey and acrid cigar smoke are the background smells.

They circle him, lie in wait, their fins above the surface without self-consciousness. He's the object of their fawning affection, their fake friendships, but he is also their target, and they'll sink their teeth into him the first moment they get.

But he knows it. He's no fool, even if that's what people think of him by virtue of who he is, what he does.

He takes the compliments with a subdued grace and easy charm that endears him to the wicked people who scramble over each other to talk to him. It is a manner at odds with the visage of him in a steel-mesh cage, tattoo-sheathed arms laying punch after thunderous punch into a bleeding, reeling, drooling opponent.

I see scattered looks of disappointment in those that want him to beat his chest, here and now. That want him to be the cocky and aggressive creature that he is in the cage, the idiot fighter who speaks with slurred words and doesn't know not to mangle the cap of a cigar, or the difference between a merlot and a cab-sav.

Those are the people that see him as nothing but a pit bull, or a cock in a fight, a chance to make money. They want to watch the *show*, which is purple bruises, red blood, and exposed white bone.

Most of the men try to buddy up with him, shake his hand, do the fighter's double-fist-tap as if the mere gesture somehow extends the line of inclusion around them, makes them one with the fighters.

They clap him on the back, but in the same breath test him with exclusive in-jokes, or a privileged wit that he does not understand. They do their best to show that they can one-up him whenever they like, as if through words of marginalization they can tease from him some thread of insecurity, before latching onto it and pulling.

It all rolls off his shoulders like rain water.

The wives… well, they look at him differently, in a way that I don't like one bit. But I try not to think about that. I can't control what other people do. And without a doubt, I trust him.

I'm sitting at the bar in the most dangerous room in the state. Politicians, police captains, and fat cat businessmen mill about, rubbing shoulders with the bosses of every major crime family and organization in the tri-state area. At the head of it all is my father, Johnny 'Glass' Marino.

He booked out this whole hotel, a new and modern all-glass eyesore that sits like a reflective pimple on the countryside. They had to relocate all the guests at just a moment's notice, and it was only the out-of-towners who put up a fuss. But they didn't know any better.

Once they saw the cavalcade of limousines spilling out bodyguards in black, it became clear it was time to fall in line.

Dad's the man who took basement-dwelling underground cage fighting and made it the biggest money-maker in town… and the biggest money loser, for those who bet incorrectly. Dirt and grime and dusty basements are a thing of the past. Now… now it glitters.

Duncan 'Creature' Malone is the star of the show, the man whom the sharks circle. Dad's always wanted to show off his family 'pedigree', even if Duncan is not *real* family. Heck, he didn't even take Dad's last name.

Everybody else knows that he was adopted and didn't formally join the family until he was twenty. But in the interest of diplomacy, they never mention it. Dad's temper is legendary, and they allow him the useless indulgence of believing Duncan is actually his son, and actually following in his footsteps.

Wrong on both counts.

At twenty-two, Duncan handles the hostile social atmosphere, all the snarls behind smiles, surprisingly well. It's his own easy smile, those perfect teeth set within that iron jaw, and his reticence to speak too much that pulls people into the orbit of his natural presence. And when that fails to win hearts, his dark and sharp good looks, and piercing blue eyes do the rest.

There's only one person who doesn't smile at him in this room, and that's Dad. He stands apart, watches Duncan out of suspicious eyes and trembling lips pulled tight across his teeth.

At once he wants to show Duncan off, but keep him all to himself. At once he wants everybody to meet and greet his champion fighter, but his unending mob-paranoia makes him see snakes and shadows where there are none.

No, maybe that's wrong. There probably are snakes and shadows. I wouldn't trust a crook, even if he comes clothed in a *Brioni* bespoke. And for Dad… well, it takes one to know one.

But, even more than that, he wants to be

recognized as the man who discovered Duncan, as the man who groomed him into the fighter he is today.

As the man who tamed a feral street boy.

But he's kidding himself if he thinks he's tamed Duncan. If anything, Dad was a handicap, and even if he won't admit it to himself, he knows the others see it.

He's bitter. In his twisted thoughts, he thinks that Duncan is stealing his limelight. And it gets worse with each fight won, with each two-to-five million pocketed in betting profits every week.

He comes over to me at the bar. The suit jacket he's wearing strains at his shoulders. It was cut for him when he was a younger, slimmer man. His dimpled bald head beads with sweat, what I imagine a dinosaur egg in the early morning might have looked like.

For a moment he looks at the glass in my hand, as if weighing whether or not to ask me if it's alcohol, but decides not to. His gaze wipes slowly over the crowd, resting on each face for sometimes seconds at a time, before eventually returning to Duncan.

Dad grunts. "Think he's spilling our secrets? Saying things he shouldn't be?"

"Of course not, Dad," I say, not bothering to hide the contempt in my voice. How could he doubt Duncan now, after all the money he's made off the fights? Duncan's spilled red in the cage so Dad could line his pockets with green.

Dad fires an angry look at me, but I know the public setting, in front of all the other families especially, grants me precious immunity to his wrath tonight. I intend to take advantage of it.

"You should appreciate him more," I tell him. "You push him too far, and he may just push back. You'll lose your goose if you're not careful."

"What the hell would you know?" he snaps at me, before stalking back off into the fray.

Despite being used to his cruel outbursts toward me, I'm still stung by it every single time. I can't remember the last time my father said a kind word to me, and meant it.

I return my attention to Duncan. The other mob bosses rattle off questions at him: *How do you do it? What's your secret? Will you train some of my guys? Are you taking supplements? What's your training regimen?*

Duncan sidesteps every question as though he were dodging rookie jabs in the cage, and continually, as if by magnetic force, his eyes are pulled to me.

I grin at him from the bar, offer him a quick flash of my eyebrows, and sip from my pear martini. I'm only twenty, but no bartender who knows my father is going to say 'no' to me.

And I actually kind of hate that.

Duncan shoots me a strained look. It says, '*rescue me*', but I just laugh at him, shake my head. Hey, he wanted to be the best fighter, he wanted to own the cage. This is what he gets.

Mass murderers, drug suppliers, and glorified pimps competing for mere seconds of his time. Dissatisfied wives eyelashing him. Everybody wanting a piece of him, like he's just some hunk of meat to be carved up and doled out.

Be careful what you wish for.

I sigh. At least it's better than the hordes of girls who attend his fights and throw themselves unendingly at him.

All Duncan cares about is the fighting, not this

bullshit, and *I* hate the politicking even more. Mob politics are about as tortuous as it gets.

I used to think it was cool, being a mobster's daughter, having a name that 'rang out on the streets', as Dad likes to put it.

But I quickly realized that all it did was erect walls between me and everybody else. No friends, and until Duncan came into my life, no lovers…

"Your brother looks in over his head," the bartender says to me. His voice is shallow and wheezy. "I know a 'save me' face when I see one."

My brother.

I've never called Duncan that before. He's my *adoptive* brother, came into my life when I was just eighteen like a tornado ripping through a barn. He carried me off with him.

I meet the old bartender's eyes, then tilt my head to the side. He looks… familiar, but from a mental distance. I know him from somewhere.

"You don't remember me, do you, Deidre?" he asks.

"No," I say truthfully. "But your voice is familiar."

"I've worked for your old man before. I ran the bar for him at a couple of his birthday get-ups. You were just a little girl, though. Oh, it must have been ten years ago now."

"I'm sorry, but I really can't remember," I say, smiling politely. I do vaguely recall my father having birthday parties, but he stopped when I turned about ten.

"It's no problem, honey," he says. "You've grown up a lot."

"Everybody's been saying that to me."

I look quickly around the large function room. I met a lot of these people when I was younger, when Dad would take me to 'work' with him.

I used to love it when he brought me along for a ride in his limousine, what he called his 'office'. It wasn't until I found out what he actually *did* that I stopped asking if I could go.

Truth be told, I hate it here. I just wear this sham smile, maintain this pretend poise, so Dad doesn't get on my case about it later. Ironically, I'm just doing what everybody else is.

The women, of course, do it best. It takes an

especially skilled woman to survive a marriage to a gangster. These are the kind of men who can go from placid indifference to boiling rage in just half a heartbeat. These are the kind of men who are *never* wrong. These are the kind of men who all keep girls on the side.

The bartender clears his throat. "Why don't you rescue him? Duncan, I mean."

I notice that some of Duncan's easy charm is starting to fade as his patience frays. Soon he'll get bored of this.

"Nah," I say to the bartender. "He looks fine."

I stick my tongue out at Duncan, bring a big grin to his face.

Eventually the crowd around him disperses as they pick up on his signals, and he swaggers over to me, his wide shoulders swaying, and a sexy smirk prying his lips to the side.

He's got a soft but neat shadow on his face tonight, lining the iron cut of his jaw. His black, careless hair only serves to emphasize his brilliant blue eyes, but also brings out something of a boyish quality in him, something that can't be quashed by the fighting scars.

He sits down beside me, and then tucks his head my way conspiratorially. "Never thought I'd fucking get rid of them, Dee, Jesus Christ."

"You wanted this," I tell him, raising my eyebrows.

"I never wanted *this*," he says, gesturing at everything in particular.

"Don't lie to me, Duncan. You always wanted to be the best."

"In the cage," he grunts. "None of this sparkly shit. I don't need it to fucking sparkle."

Idly he fiddles with his cufflinks; he's unused to them. For his first time wearing a full three-piece suit, he looks damn fine in it, though.

The suit slims his muscular body, streamlines him, smoothes him out. It's the inversion of his usual, rougher, less refined and more boxy dress sense: An old leather jacket that highlights his broad shoulders, jeans and boots.

"You look good," I tell him. "Seriously. You should wear a suit more."

"You look better," he says, meeting my eyes. I feel zapped by energy still, every time our eyes connect. He leans into me and whispers, "You look very fuckable in purple."

I roll my eyes. "I thought you'd been working on your adjectives."

"I'm a fighter, not a writer."

"Yeah, well keep your voice down, the bartender knows Dad."

Duncan spins around, eyes the old man who asks him if he's having anything.

"No," Duncan says. "Nothing for me."

"Don't drink?"

"Got a fight coming up."

"What, tonight?" the bartender jokes.

"Alcohol affects your body for days after consumption," Duncan tells him matter-of-factly, his voice low and uninterested. "I've got a fight in days."

"Right," the bartender says, moving quickly up the other end of the bar.

"So, how are you liking your big night?" I ask Duncan.

"I never fucking asked for this. This is for your father."

"I know."

"He wants to trot me out like a fucking show dog."

"I know, Duncan," I say. I touch his arm briefly, quell the turbulent tide. "I don't want to be here, either."

"He wants to show *you* off, too."

"No he doesn't," I say, shaking my head. "He only wants me to be here because if I'm not, everybody will talk. They'll ask him where his daughter is, and he'll get embarrassed he doesn't know. Now, he knows. He can point at me when they ask him that."

"You're the brightest fucking person in this room, Dee, even if your father doesn't see it. I caught Falcone's boy looking at you."

"Shut up," I say. "Stop teasing me."

"I'm not. He was staring, had a dirty fucking look in his eyes, so I had a word with him."

"You what?" I ask in disbelief. "Duncan! You can't fuck around here."

I scan the crowd, pick out Falcone's boy, a short man with his father's cuboid head, and a neck that swallows his chin like quicksand. He meets my eyes, then catches Duncan's, and looks away instantly, ears burning.

"What the hell did you say to get him so rattled?"

"I told him not to fucking look at my sister," Duncan says in something of a growl. "I didn't need to say anything more. But that's not what I *really* meant."

"Then what did you *really* mean?"

"My girl," he says, pride in his voice.

"Shush!" I hiss, looking up the bar. Thankfully nobody is near us, and the old bartender is milling about at the other side.

"I like your dress tonight," Duncan says, looking me up and down. His tongue darts out to wet his lips.

"It feels a little snug," I say, my hand coming across my waist unconsciously. "I think I've put on a bit of weight recently."

"Don't even think about getting self-conscious, Dee." It's spoken to me like an order. "You look fucking amazing tonight. Hell, in old sweats and that soy-sauce stained hoodie, you bring me up with just a look, let alone this beautiful dress."

"Oh, wow, thanks," I say sarcastically, reaching

out to flick his chin, and not a moment's too soon snatching my hand back.

That was close.

He brings his face closer to mine, and his full, soft lips are an invitation I have to force myself to ignore.

I want to kiss him, want to feel him, want to smell him.

But not here. Not now.

It's our secret. If it ever got out…

"I want to kiss you," he whispers, his eyes on my lips. "I want to feel you."

"Stop," I say. It's too big of a risk. This is reckless, but Duncan always was like a skydiver that assembles his parachute on the way down.

"I want to smell you."

"Duncan…"

"Taste you."

"Shut up!"

"Don't you?"

I don't answer for a moment. "Not *here.*"

"You're lying," he says, grinning. "I can always tell when you lie. You definitely want to here."

"I'm not lying," I say, making a face at him. "And

I wouldn't want to do it *here*."

"You and I both know we're not talking about *here* here."

"If not here here, then *where* here?"

But he just looks at me, those supremely kissable lips pried to the side, those azure eyes on mine.

"Seriously, Dad's got a big stick up his ass today. Meeting the other bosses always makes him nervous."

He ignores my warning, and says in a low voice, "I've been thinking about you all day." His eyes travel up and down my body, linger on my every curve in hungry adulation. They settle on the skin of my neck, and his breathing quickens, and his pupils widen.

Despite my earlier protestation, I indulge him: "What kind of thoughts, exactly?"

"Oh, don't worry, nothing pure."

I shake my head and laugh.

"I haven't seen you in twelve hours. I counted."

"You can count that high?"

That pulls a deep and quiet chuckle from him.

"Why so long today, Dee?"

I sigh. "Classes ran late. And actually it's pretty normal for people to not see each other for twelve hours."

"Even couples?"

"Even couples."

"Even secret couples?"

I roll my eyes. "*Especially* secret couples."

"But not you and me," he says.

"No," I say after a pause. He's right. "Not you and me. But when I don't see you, it can be for months at a time. Or in one case, two years, though I guess that doesn't really count."

"But you left me with something in Thailand."

"What's that?"

"A reason to work my ass off."

"Why's that?"

"Did I ever tell you this before?"

"No."

He hesitates for a moment, licks his lips. "Because I knew it'd be the only way to see you again."

"So I made you a better fighter, huh?" I ask through a smile.

He pauses.

"What?"

"No, Dee. You made me a better person."

Now *I* pause.

"Come on," he says, getting up.

"I haven't finished my drink yet."

"Finish it, then."

"Hold on," I say, freely indignant. Nobody, not even Duncan, is going to rush me. "I'll drink at my own pace, and where exactly are we going?"

"The fuck out of here."

"We can't just leave. Dad will go crazy."

"Fuck your dad."

Normally, I would agree. I had enough of Dad's shit a long time ago, but tonight of all nights is not the night to test him.

"Fuck him," Duncan says, and that defiant smile and gorgeous, commanding eyes are an inch away from winning me over.

"You should be mingling with his friends."

"I don't give a fuck about his friends. I want to mingle with you." He leans forward, whispers, "Inside you."

I suppress my groan. "They're the ones who keep you fighting, you know."

"Exactly," he growls. "If you don't come with me right now, I'm going to pick you up and carry you out. Not like a newlywed bride, but over my shoulder."

"You can't!" I hiss. "Everybody will see and then everybody will know."

He smirks. "Then let's go."

We walk together, shoulder to shoulder, through the crowd. I want to reach out and take his hand, and it's a battle not to do so. I realize, with a kind of distant horror, how easy it would be to slip up, to hold onto his arm, or run my arm around his waist before dipping lower to grab his tight ass.

I do these things all the time, but in public, with people watching, with Dad watching, I have to constantly remember not to.

What if, one time, I forget? Or he does? How quickly everything would break apart!

People murmur things at us as we wade through the sea of bodies, and we reply politely, but we're bee-lining straight for the door.

I'm considering this entire hotel, booked out, empty, and Duncan says to me, as if reading my mind, "Time to go exploring."

Once we're out of the doors of the main function

room, which doubles as a ballroom or banquet hall, we grin at each other.

He takes my hand then, leads me quickly through the winding, empty hallways until I'm sure we're totally lost, and then he backs me up against a wall, pins my arms above my head, and he just looks at me.

His gaze runs down the back of my arms, and his lips part as he sweeps his eyes over my armpit, along the line of my shoulders, inward toward my chest.

He brings his lips close to my ear, whispers, "I want you right fucking now."

I grip onto his fingers tight, and his hot breath on my earlobe stirs up something inside of me. I can smell him now that he's so close to me, really *him*, beneath the cologne, and I love it.

His body is tense, hard, and I can feel the electricity in his every breath. He takes my earlobe into his mouth, bites it gently with his teeth, and then he smells my neck before laying a smoldering trail of kisses all the way to my shoulder, leaving me quivering.

"God, you look sexy with your hair like this. What do you call it?"

"It's just a braided bun," I tell him. "Don't you know anything?"

"I know how to make you feel good."

"That's just biology."

"I love it when I can see your neck, Dee." He traces a finger from my ear to my collar bone, then runs along it to the middle. "And here," he says. "I love it when I can see you here."

He meets my eyes, and I see that familiar demon in his. He takes my hand, holds it against his thigh, and I gasp when I feel him, hard as a steel bar, straining against his suit pants.

"Just like that," he tells me. "Just one smell, just one touch."

I hold onto him, rub him slowly, draw a tortured look of lust from him. "Just one man with a one-track mind," I whisper.

"No," he tells me. He takes my face in his huge hand, and I feel the heat in his palms, press my cheek into it. "Only you do this to me."

After a moment I ask him, "You going to kiss me or what?"

He smirks. "Do I really have to?"

"You assho—"

He kisses me, crushes his lips against mine, brings me up to the tips of my toes. I wrap my arms around him, heart thumping wildly in my chest as I feel his desire for me in the fervor of his kisses.

I run my hands through his hair, hold onto him, press myself against his body, as if suddenly a crack in the dam has burst. I'm as desperate for him as he is for me.

He gropes me hungrily, and I pull at his hair, and our bodies are touching all the way up and down, and I'm melting in his arms, falling into him…

"Not here," I whisper, breaking the kiss. "We're still too close."

We look around, then start walking down the hallway again. As if on cue a staff member of the hotel walks past us the other way, his eyes lingering on Duncan's crotch for a moment, a look of embarrassment stretching out his face.

I lean forward, and when I see Duncan's tented pants I cover my mouth and laugh.

"You look ridiculous."

"It's your fault."

"We are we going, anyway?"

He points up at some signage as we walk. I read it: *Indoor swimming pool.*

"Swimming?" I ask. "In what?"

"Use your imagination."

"In our underwear?"

"If you want."

"But I'm not wearing a bra."

He smirks at me. "Neither am I."

I slap his shoulder.

"Come on, Dee. Live a little."

We arrive at the pool, open the glass door, and find it completely empty. It's a heated pool, it steams, and the lighting is dim, and the pool casts shards of wavy light against the walls.

Duncan closes the door behind us, and I hear the click of a lock. He opens a digital keypad flap, touches a button, and the glass door turns opaque instantly.

"How did you know it would do that?"

"You mean because I'm just some dumb fighter?" he asks, taking me into his arms and pulling me against him.

"You are a fighter," I tell him. "And sometimes, you can be dumb."

"The button said 'privacy'. I took a chance."

"How brave of you."

I grin, pull away from him, walk up the side of the pool. It's small, meant for private parties.

I walk to a storage cupboard sitting flush almost invisibly in the wall. It slides into a recess, and I pull out a fresh towel, and lay it down on one of the deck chairs.

Duncan starts to approach me, but I stop him with an outstretched hand.

"Uh-uh," I say. I slowly take off my heels, let him watch me, and then lie down on the deck chair, get comfortable. "Take off your clothes for me. Let me watch."

He licks his lips.

"Come on," I say, daring him with my eyes. "Show me what you got, champ."

He pulls off his jacket without hesitation, folds it in half lengthways, tosses it at the deck chair next to me.

"Your turn," he says.

I shake my head at him, and so he starts at his vest, undoing the buttons one by one, his eyes never leaving mine. They're bluer than the water in the pool.

He tosses the vest, too, then loosens his tie, slides it off, his eyes ablaze with a lustful, singular intensity.

"Your turn," he says.

I take my left cap sleeve, pull it down over my shoulder, and then return my eyes to Duncan and flash my eyebrows at him.

He laughs, and begins to undo the buttons to his shirt. I watch, eyes wide, as his muscular chest comes into view first, darkened on his left side by the solid tattoo of a house silhouetted – the windows are squares of uninked skin – and on the right side a leaping tiger.

Then I see his stomach, hard, flat, cut, like any fighter's body should be.

But it just looks so much hotter on him.

He leaves his shirt still tucked in at the bottom, but runs his hands slowly down over his stomach, fingers dipping below the line of his pants for just a moment.

As he pulls it down, I see the buzz of his neatly trimmed pubic hair.

"More," I tell him.

He pulls out his shirt, rolls it off his shoulders then lets it drop down his arms. His arms are sheathed in coiling black tattoos, nothing defined, just impressions, like inked emotion. Some of those lines are sharp and severe, others calm and curved.

When he catches his shirt behind him, turns slightly to toss it onto the deck chair, I get a glimpse of the lines and lines of blessing script he has tattooed on his back.

I soak up the sight of his body, broad shoulders, narrow waist, an Adonis belt at his hips that takes my breath away, the kind that makes smart girls stupid.

God, he's drop-dead gorgeous, and it still gets me even now.

"More," I say, humming a grin at him. He doesn't move, and so I crane my neck to the side, rub a hand down it, bite my lip at him.

"You are so fucking sexy," he growls in defeat, his hands going to his belt. He unbuckles it deftly, pulls out the leather, then wraps it around one open hand until it's a tight coil, tosses it at the deck chair.

"Your turn," he says. "I'm serious this time."

I grin, reach my hands behind me over my head to pull the zip down to my dress. His eyes linger on my underarms, and he swallows, his Adam's apple jumping up and down.

"You look fucking hot in that dress, especially when it's coming off."

I pull the zip down a little, then lower my other sleeve over my other shoulder.

"Who said anything about coming off? Your turn. I'm serious this time."

The quick smudge of red-pink that is his tongue wetting his lips steals my attention, before I focus on his hands as he unbuttons and unzips his pants, pulls the flaps open to either side, and I can see his black boxer briefs beneath, his bulge.

He hooks a thumb into the elastic, slowly teases it down, reveals the base of his wide shaft. He stops, looks at me, lips slightly parted so I can see the tips of his teeth.

"More," I whisper at him.

Millimeter by millimeter he pulls down, and more

of his manhood comes into view. I gasp as he finally springs out, as he tucks his underwear beneath his smooth balls.

His eyes never leave mine, and he begins to slowly stroke himself.

"Just looking at you is enough, Dee," he groans, his body tightening.

I breathe unsteadily, let the straps of my dress fall lower.

"Show yourself to me now," he says. No, he orders.

I pull the dress lower down, and my breasts come into view, and he sucks in air, and his body goes tighter still, and he begins to pump himself faster.

"God damn I love your breasts," he growls, stepping closer to me. "Now pull your dress up."

I reach for the sleeves hung down my shoulders, but he stops me with a sharp command.

"No, not there. Lower."

"Oh, you meant there," I tease.

I reach down, and begin to pull my dress up, over my knees, and his cobalt eyes eat up the sight of my skin. Just by looking at me he makes me tingle, raises my temperature, makes me feel so sexy.

I see nothing but desire for me in his eyes.

Duncan strokes his manhood, leans back a little, crunches his stomach.

"Higher," he groans.

I pull the dress higher.

"Now spread those sexy thighs. Let me see you."

I open my legs for him, my dress now bunched around my hips, and it's like he can't take it anymore, like something snaps.

He comes to me fast, takes my lips, claims them, pulls moans from my mouth while he kisses me fiercely, while he massages my breasts and thumbs my nipples.

I grab onto him with my legs and pull his hips toward me, and I mewl when I feel him at my entrance through my underwear.

"You're so hard," I whisper at him, reaching down and holding him.

"It's you, Dee. Always."

He kisses me again, this time just my lower lip, and when I try to kiss him back, try to taste him again, he pulls away, that sexy-as-sin smirk bringing his lips to one side.

"Don't move," he says, and I obey him. He traces a finger down in between my breasts, lower still, and a soft moan escapes my mouth as I feel his hand on my thigh, coming up to my center. He cups my sex, and I gasp.

His fingers run up either side of me, and when he brushes against my clit I jolt on the deck chair. He pulls his hand up farther still, over my mound, and then slips it into my underwear, squeezes my lips down there together.

Unconsciously, I lift my hips to him, bite my lip, stare into his eyes, beg him silently to make me feel good.

He traces a finger up my sex, makes me sigh as ripples of sensation course through me, and then starts to massage my bud, rubs it in circles, makes me feel like I'm in heaven.

"Mmm," I moan. "I like that."

"Put your arms up," he tells me, and so I obey, lift my hands over my head, look him in his gorgeous eyes.

He inhales sharply, and I watch as his eyes wander over me, eat up the sight of me, from my underarms to my breasts, to my neck, to my lips.

"Come and kiss me," I whisper.

He leans into me, and just when he touches his lips to mine he pushes his finger all the way inside me, and I moan out, unable to concentrate on kissing him.

He takes my lower lip, sucks on it, bites it while he fingers me, and when he slides a second finger in, I feel stretched around him, undulate my hips, rock myself to his rhythm.

"You like that?" he asks, bringing his thumb to my clit, making me feel all kinds of bliss with just his one hand.

"I like it."

"Say it again."

"I like it," I breathe, taking his lips into mine again, pushing my tongue into his mouth.

He fingers me so deftly, brings me racing right to the edge so quickly, and I feel so tight, a coiled spring waiting to be sprung.

"Wait," I pant, pulling up, shifting my body. "Too fast. Not yet."

"Tell me what you want."

"I want to come at the same time as you."

He climbs onto the deck chair, bends my knees then crosses one over the other, and leans over me. He pulls my underwear to the side, and his tip touches my entrance, and with his arms on either side of me, he waits there, looks me in the eyes.

"Come on," I breathe at him.

He leans his weight against my knees, presses them to my chest, and then ever so slowly he inches into me.

I grip at his shoulders, dig my nails into his flesh as he stretches me, as he pushes himself so gradually into me, filling me up.

"Oh God," I pant, clamping my eyes shut, my body tensing up.

"Jesus, you're tight, Dee," he groans. "You feel so fucking good."

I reach out to his hips, run my hands up his strong waist, pull him toward me.

"Come on," I whisper, practically beg.

"Ask me again," he says, stopping.

"Come on!" I hiss, and he thrusts all the way inside me, bottoms out, pulls a cry of overwhelming pleasure from my lips.

He drives himself into me again and again, and it's all I can do to keep myself as silent as possible, God forbid someone from the party wander by outside.

With one hand, Duncan scoops up my face, tilts it up to him, and my eyes travel over his sexy lips, and I bite my teeth together, arch my body as he fucks me wildly.

He plucks strings of pleasure inside me so deep, they thrum through my body, shake me like the beat of a bass drum.

His eyes stay locked with mine, and he tangles my hair into his hand, pulls my head back, turns it to the side, and as he leans lower, he drags his tongue from my neck to my ear, an action so primal and consuming it sends me quivering.

With rough hands he turns my knees to the side, forces me to tuck them up against my chest, and then I feel his hand on my sex from behind, and he rubs my clit, and all I can do is grip onto the edge of the deck chair above me, close my eyes, and let him take from me everything he wants.

"Moan for me," he says, and he adjusts his position, and his cock rams against my front wall, and

I moan out my pleasure loudly, no longer caring that someone outside might hear.

"Fuck, I love your pussy," he growls. "I love your tight fucking pussy. I want to fuck you forever."

He speeds up somehow, and his cock swells within me impossibly more, and I'm lost in his grip, clutched by his feverish desire for me, utterly and completely his.

"Oh God!" I gasp, his fingers working my pearl like magic, his cock stretching me with each hard thrust, making me feel so full.

"Like that!" I cry, my body tightening, that ball of pressure inside me expanding. Duncan doesn't stop, doesn't slow, doesn't change his rhythm.

My mouth falls open, my tongue comes out, and I hold onto the chair with a white-knuckled grip, my body a tense snapshot of pleasure, right on the brink.

"Shit, shit, shit!" I breathe as I plunge off the edge, come hard and long, and Duncan's hand cups my face, his thumb rubs my lip, and I bite down on it as white-hot bliss sears me.

I hear him grunt, feel his body tighten as he lets go, and I swear I feel him come inside me, not just the giant swelling and twitch of his manhood.

I moan into his hand as he fucks me even more manically, as he buries himself to the hilt again and again, rubs my clit, drives me through my own blinding ecstasy, draws it out until I can't breathe anymore, until I'm tensed up, crunched up, toes curled so tight they might cramp.

And then he slows, and I'm panting, coming down, the last touches of bliss like feathers on my skin, ticklish almost.

His eyes are shut as he slowly pushes himself in and out of me, his cock jolting inside me seemingly at random. Sweat glistens on his chest, his abs, and I reach out and run my hand down his slick skin, into his buzz of pubic hair, and I squeeze the base of his shaft, still hard as if he hadn't just unloaded himself.

He climbs onto the deck chair beside me, behind me, and our bodies form the same shape as we stick to each other from top to toe, and his arms wrap me up, tell me I'm his, tell me that I'm all that he wants.

I lie there, holding onto his hands, playing with his fingers, his cock still twitching inside me, his hot breaths against my neck.

He leans up, and I take the opportunity to smell

his neck, kiss the line of his jaw, and then take his lips into mine, and we share a soft and passionate kiss that sends me quaking.

Our tongues meet slowly, our lips dance to the exact same rhythm. Our heartbeats have aligned, and if I could wish for a moment to never end, I would wish it now, and it would not be the first time I wished it.

And when our kiss breaks to the sound of voices outside the opaque glass door, we fix our clothing in unison, sharing grinning glances, until I feel the sticky sensation of all his essence globbing out of me.

"Damn. Is there a changing room here?" I ask. "You've made a big mess."

"Here," he says, leading me toward the other side of the pool.

I go in, clean up as best as I'm able to, and then together Duncan and I make our way back to the function room. As we're walking down the corridor that leads there, hand in hand, laughing and chatting, I see the double doors down the end open, and Dad sweeps out, furious eyes glaring at us.

*

2

DEE

Instantly, I let go of Duncan's hand, and watch as Dad storms up to us.

"Where the fuck have you been?" he says, his voice trembling on a tightrope.

He didn't notice!

"Relax, Glass," Duncan says. "We've just been getting some air."

"Get the fuck back inside, now," Dad spits. He turns his angry eyes on me. "Go! You're making me look bad. They ask me where my daughter is, and I have no fucking idea. Why are you always so difficult, damn it, Dei—"

Duncan steps forward, body tensing up. I take his

sleeve subtly, pull on it.

"Relax, Glass," he says to Dad, words low and spaced out. "It's no big deal. We just went for a walk."

"Have you been drinking, too?"

Duncan just glowers at him.

"You two are always ganging up on me," Dad complains, before he turns around and stalks off back toward the function room, and Duncan and I walk slowly in his fuming wake.

"What an asshole," I say. "I really don't like him. God, I wish we could get out of here."

"Then let's get the fuck out of here."

"How?"

"Easy. I'll do my rounds, and I've got a fight in two days I need to prepare for. You've got classes tomorrow, and you're my ride home tonight."

"But I'm not your ride home tonight. I didn't even bring my car. Dad had Frank pick me up in the limo. God, like I needed his limo pulling up to my dorm building with everyone watching."

"Come on, just stick with me."

"I can handle Dad myself, you know."

"I know you can, Dee," he says, stopping me, taking my hand. He presses it to his mouth, playfully bites one of my fingers.

I cast a quick look down the hallway to see Dad disappearing into the function room, his jacket flapping behind him.

"And?"

"But if we make it about me, he won't crawl up your ass about it."

"I don't need you to take the fall for me."

"He's afraid of me. I won't be taking any fall."

I sigh, pull my hand from him slowly. "I just shouldn't have to live like this. I thought moving out, leaving home, would get me out from under his shadow, but he's always over me, Duncan. He just never leaves me alone."

"Dee," he says. "Just a little bit longer."

"What are you talking about?"

"You'll see. Now come on, follow my lead."

Duncan and I walk back into the function room, and he immediately goes to the bar.

"Scotch and soda."

The old man does a double take. "I thought you weren't drinking?"

"Scotch… and… soda."

The bartender pours the drink in a hurry, puts it on the bar in front of Duncan.

He turns around with the glass, and walks into the crowd of people, and he's swaying as he walks, and he's off-balance.

He downs the glass in front of everybody, chats with a few people, shares too-loud laughs, then wanders back to the bar.

"Another scotch and soda!" he barks. The bartender obliges.

The crowd of people part, and I see Dad walking toward us, barely concealed rage on his face.

"What the fuck are you doing, Duncan? You know you shouldn't be drinking. You've got a fight in—"

"Hey, it's a party!" Duncan shouts, then almost trips, and spills the drink all over himself. "Oh, fuck!" he bellows, meeting my eyes for a moment but not once losing character. He bursts out laughing, grips onto his knees, then stumbles forward, dropping the glass onto the floor. It shatters.

I have to look away to keep from laughing.

"God damn it," Dad growls at Duncan. "You're a fucking hot-shot MMA fighter and you can't even hold your fucking liquor."

"Hell yes I fucking can!" Duncan says, slurring his words.

Dad sighs. "Go home and sleep it off before you embarrass me even more."

"I c-can't drive," he says. "Well, I probably could, but, you know, I-I don't think it's a good idea—"

"I'll have Frank drive you home."

Frank Marsh, dad's loyal protector of twenty years, his number one. A large man who keeps a sawn-off shotgun dangling down his side, veiled by his customary trench coat.

"No!" Duncan says, throwing two clumsy hands onto Dad's chest. "Frank's your *bodyguard*! He can't leave you unprotected, man." He lowers his voice into a conspiratorial whisper. "You've got enemies here. Let Dee take me."

Dad looks to me, and it's the hardest fucking thing to keep my face straight.

"Oh, to hell with it, take him to his apartment, Deidre. *Jesus H Christ*!"

Dad retreats back into the crowd, muttering strained apologies to everybody.

Duncan embellishes, throws his arm around my shoulder, leans his weight on me.

"Damn, you're heavy," I whisper at him, walking him toward the door, smiling politely at people who stare our way.

"I think I'm going to puke!" he announces to Frank as we pass him.

Once we get through the main doors, Duncan's gait returns immediately to normal, with more than his usual amount of cocky swagger.

We meet eyes and laugh as we go get my checked coat and bag, exit the hotel. The night is cool, the air chilly, and I pull my coat tighter around me.

"Dad is going to be so pissed at you tomorrow," I tell him.

"Fuck him."

"And you ruined your suit."

"Fuck it. I hate this thing, anyway."

"But you look damn good in it."

"Not as good as you look in that dress," he says, picking me up. I yelp, try to squirm from his grip but can't. He's holding me above him, and he lowers me slowly, and I find myself astonished by his strength.

He dips me until my lips meet his, and I know that I shouldn't, that we shouldn't here, but I kiss him, and he me.

Anybody could see, it's such a stupid risk to take. I don't know how he makes me do these things.

"Come back to my place tonight, Dee."

I push my lips together. "I can't," I whisper. "I've got to go into class early. It's just easier if I sleep in my dorm room so I don't have to deal with traffic in the morning. I don't even have my car."

"I'll make it a night you'll never forget," he says, smirking. "You know I'm good for it. And I'll take you to class tomorrow."

"I don't think I'll forget this night already."

"Of course you won't."

"Not because of *that*," I say.

"Yes it was."

"Don't kid yourself. You're not *that* good."

"Yes I am."

But I shake my head slowly at him. "I really need to go back to campus tonight. I'm sorry, you know I'd rather come home with you."

"It's alright," he says.

"You could come by tomorrow. I have a break at lunch?"

"Bet your fucking ass I will. Will your roommate be out?"

"No!" I say, slapping his shoulder. "We can't do that anymore, either. I think she suspects something already."

"Just open a window."

"Gross, it's not because of the *smell*! You left your watch last time."

"I was wondering where that went."

"Yeah," I say, widening my eyes at him. "See? You're always getting me into trouble."

"That's what bad boys do to good girls."

"Yeah, some good girl I am. Daughter of the most powerful mob boss in town, a man who kills people, sells drugs, and prostitutes women for a living."

"You *are* good," he says. He taps my chest.

"Here. Right here. You're a better person than I've ever known, and you're *not* your father. His shit doesn't roll down onto you."

"Unfortunately… it does."

"No." He just states it. I wonder if it is naïve denial, or if he actually believes Dad's reputation doesn't extend onto me.

"It doesn't make *you* bad," he says. "Nobody should hold him against you."

"They already do," I whisper. "Come on. Which car are you driving?"

"Same one."

"Still my mother's? Why?"

"It reminds me of you. Does it bother you?"

"No," I say truthfully. "It's just not a very manly car."

"Like I need a fucking car for that."

He takes my hand, and together we walk away from the hotel.

"Wait, don't you have a valet ticket?"

"I parked it myself." He pulls out the keys, jingles them.

I snort. "Why would you do that? They valet park here."

"I don't need some special service to park my own fucking car."

"They must have looked at you funny."

"Well, they didn't look twice."

"You can be so weird sometimes."

We find my mother's car – the one she drove before she died – looking extremely conspicuous beside all the limos and Lambos. It's just a two-door Volvo hatchback that she brought over with her from England when she moved to the States to do her west-to-east road trip.

I never knew Mom… never learned of the sentimental significance of the car. All I know is that she started in San Francisco, but never made it to the other coast. She met Dad in Chicago.

And, of course, Dad doesn't talk about her. He just clams up and shuts up every time I bring her up. Or he gets grumpy and yells at me. So I don't bring it up anymore. I've accepted that she's just going to remain a mystery.

The car just collected dust until Duncan and I stole it one night from Dad's garage for what amounted to a joyride.

"Why didn't *you* want this car, Dee?"

"It's got bad mileage," I tell him matter-of-factly as we climb in. "Hey, I'm a college student, right?"

"Right. But really?"

"I don't know. Just doesn't feel right. It's okay though, you drive it. I mean, I like the car… because it reminds me of the idea of a mother… my mother. But, you know, I can't even remember what she looks like, the sound of her voice. I mean… I don't know anything about her."

"Alright," he says. "I wasn't pushing."

"It's fine."

He starts the car, pulls us out, and we drive in silence for a while. Duncan was left on a church's doorstep, grew up in a group home. He didn't have parents… the closest thing were the social workers who went home at five. The live-in workers at the house were more like security guards than anything else, offering nothing but a jaded, harsh tongue, if even that.

And me… I never knew my mother, and Dad… well… he's never really been a father, but that's a long story.

So I forget about it, push the thoughts away even though they try to push back, try to invade my mind and threaten to ruin my mood even more.

To distract myself, I rub Duncan's thigh as he drives me back to the college campus, study his sharp side profile.

"Thanks for getting me out of there, though. Seriously. You put on a real scene."

"Don't worry about it, Dee."

"What did you mean by 'just a little longer'?"

He looks at me. "Not yet, Dee. Soon, okay?"

"You know I don't like it when you're cryptic."

"I know. Just… trust me."

"Okay," I say. "But I don't like surprises. You know that."

"I thought all girls liked surprises."

"Well, I'm not like all girls. Surprises in my life have never been good. Walking downstairs to find some poor man gagged and getting beaten up by Dad and Frank while blood leaks from his eyes is not my idea of a fun surprise."

"Wasn't I a surprise?"

"The only good one," I say.

"Just trust me, Dee. We've got a future, but it just needs a little more time."

I blink, not really understanding what he means. It's the first time I've ever really heard Duncan talk about *our* future. Together. Inclusive. A long-term plan.

When we get to the campus security checkpoint, I say bye to Duncan, give him a kiss, and then watch as he drives off.

And his words echo through my head: *We've got a future.*

And I can't help but to ask myself: *What future*?

We're a secret couple. He's my foster brother. Even if there's nothing truly wrong with our relationship – we're not blood relatives, and it started when we were both adults – Dad would never have it. He cares about his reputation too much, about what the other families might say.

So *what* future, exactly?

We can't hide forever.

It's got to end sooner or later. It's a train in the

night bearing down on us, and we won't know it's about to hit us until we hear the blare of the horn, and feel the shaking of the rails, and it's all too late.

*

A future.

That night, by the shimmering pool, our child was conceived.

If only I'd known then that my future would be keeping our baby a secret from him.

If only I'd known then that my future would be running away from him with our baby.

If only I'd known then that my future would force me to leave everything I loved behind…

But I shouldn't jump to the end.

I should start at the beginning.

3

DEE

THAILAND, FIVE YEARS AGO…

The light breaks through the leafy canopy overhead in bursts of brightness, like a thousand camera flashes are going off at once. I catch only scattered glimpses of blue sky.

The air is thick with the smell of wet soil and a dozen different flowers. There's a sourness on the air, and it reminds me of the apple orchard back home, except it hits the nose harder, has a bitter bite.

Sweat beads on my upper lip, and my t-shirt clings to my back. I should never have worn black in this heat. Even the air that rushes past us as Dad drives us through the jungle isn't enough to keep me cool.

"Where are we going?" I ask Dad, but my words are snatched away by the wind. He doesn't hear me, and he keeps driving, winding us deeper and deeper into a dark-green thicket of thin trees, dangling vines, and dense underbrush.

The jeep takes it well – at least, I imagine it does. The ride is not so bumpy, but nevertheless Dad drives slower than he does back home on the street. The sound of plant life being crushed to death beneath us fills the air, and birds stop their calling as we trundle through, only to resume when we've left their trees behind.

This was supposed to be a holiday. At least, that's what Dad said when he told me that he was taking me to Thailand. I thought I'd get to ride an elephant, see a tiger, try the non-spicy Thai foods, and experience the land of a thousand smiles.

Instead we went straight to the five-star resort full of other foreign tourists, rested and cleaned up, and then he told me to get back into the jeep with him because he had someone he wanted to see.

That was when I knew that we weren't here for a holiday.

That was when I knew we were here on business.

And even though I'm not an adult yet, I'm smart enough to know what business means. It's what Dad does… he's a mobster. Business always means drugs, women, or violence… and always dirty money.

"Dad, are we there yet?"

This time he hears me, and he turns to me briefly. "Almost, so stop asking me."

"Why are we coming out here?"

"There's somebody I need to see."

"Did I have to come?" I ask him. "Couldn't I have stayed at the hotel? They have a nice pool! Or I could have gone for a walk around town?"

"You won't be walking around town all by yourself in a foreign country," he says. "You're only fifteen."

"I'm nearly sixteen, and I can take care of myself. I'm not stupid."

Dad laughs meanly… and I know he's laughing at me, as if I've just said the most unwise thing in the world. I sink into my seat and fold my arms.

"I thought you should meet him, too," he says.

I blink. Him? "Who are we meeting?"

"A boy."

I shake my head. I don't understand. "Why?"

But he doesn't reply.

The terrifying thought enters my head: He's marrying me off!

But, after a moment's reflection, I don't really believe it.

He weaves the jeep around trees, eventually finds a dirt road, then breathes a sigh of relief and says to me, "Good thing I found the path again."

"You mean you were lost?"

"A little."

Now on the dirt path, soft from the daily rainfalls, he drives faster, and before long we come to a clearing, and I see a collection of huts on stilts. It's a small village bracketed by lush green jungle on one side, and the sparkling blue-green sea with its yellow beach on the other. The beach looks like somebody took a highlighter pen and traced the shoreline.

In the center of the village sits a wide, square wooden building without windows. It's suspended on stilts as well, but the walls look older than the houses that surround it. I see a golden elephant outside, notice the incense sticks. It must be a temple of some kind.

"Why couldn't we just take a boat?" I ask when I spot a small jetty extending from the beach.

"I enjoy the drive."

"I would have liked a boat ride."

"Deidre," he says, looking harshly at me. "Can you just shut up for a moment?"

I tighten my arms around my stomach and crease my brow, pricked by his impatience and rudeness. He's always like this, always treating me like I'm some kind of burden. Why the hell did he insist on bringing me here, then?

Damn it!

I half expect him to tell me about how he always wanted a son. He's said that to me before many times, especially when he's drunk and angry.

He stops the car at the clearing, orders me out with him with a sharp jerk of his wrist. Together we walk into the village, a wide gap in between us.

I see people working vegetable patches, spy a rickety pen of pigs, hear the hum of a generator. These people are farmers, live a simple life.

Suddenly, I feel out of my element, self-conscious. I'm here in my jeans, t-shirt and branded sneakers, whereas other kids I see are wearing hand-me-down clothing, are running around barefoot or in flip-flops that look a decade old. Their feet are dirty.

"Wait here," he says, walking off into the village.

"Dad!" I call.

He turns around. "What?"

"Dad, don't leave me alone. Please."

"Grow up, would you?"

Someone approaches him, and they talk. It's clear the man is struggling to understand him because he doesn't speak English. All Dad does is start yelling, as if that's going to help matters. Eventually the man seems to get the idea, and points toward the temple.

The other villagers pay me no mind, except for the children. They watch me from far away with wide, curious eyes. I shove one hand into my back pocket, and with the other fiddle with my wavy hair held up in a ponytail. I don't know what to do, and become more and more uncomfortable.

I go back to the jeep and get out my backpack. I rummage through it, pull out my bottle of water, but my small, pink pocket-mirror slips out. The gleaming reflection of the sun catches my eye for a moment, and then the mirror lands face-down.

Bending my knees to pick it up, I notice glass shards. I broke it.

"Shit," I whisper, looking at it for a moment before quickly picking up all the pieces as fast as I can and dropping them into my bag. I'm embarrassed... all those kids just watched me break my mirror.

I should never have come back for my water bottle. My heart starts to race, and I feel more nervous than ever. I wish Dad hadn't just left me here.

That's when I see bare feet walking toward me. The skin is tanned by the sun. I look up and gasp. A boy is approaching me, tall, topless, muscular in a stringy way. His eyes seem to glow blue in the bright sunlight, and I feel for a moment as if I'm looking into the eyes of a wolf.

Dark, jagged tattoos sheathe his arms, shoulder to wrists, and they run down the sides of his torso, too, ending at his hips.

He's smiling at me, more of a cocky smile than a warm one, and I notice that he's really attractive. It makes me all the more uncomfortable.

He looks a bit older than me, and he's definitely not from the village. His face is nice, his jaw a sharp, straight line, and his hair dark and messy, and a little too long.

"Hey," he says, his voice deeper than I expect it to be.

I furrow my brow at his accent. "You're American?"

"Yeah." He kneels down, picks up a shard of glass. "You broke your mirror."

"It's fine," I say quickly.

"Do you have another one?"

I shake my head, tell him that really, it's fine. It's no big deal. It's just a mirror. I care more that I broke it in front of everybody, rather than it being broken itself.

My heart is surging – I don't know why I feel so nervous – but I do know that I feel drawn to him. I meet his eyes for a moment, and he smiles a warm smile at me this time, and all at once his face bursts with brightness, and cute dimples dig into his cheeks, and I can't bear to keep my eyes on his any longer.

I look away.

"I'm Duncan," he tells me. "Glass told me to introduce myself to you."

"Deidre," I whisper. "You call my Dad 'Glass'?"

He shrugs. "That's what he tells me to call him."

"Do you know why that's his nickname?"

"Like he's made of glass, right? Because he couldn't stay healthy when he was a boxer."

I nod, feel his eyes burning into me. "Who are you, exactly? I mean, how do you know my dad?"

I'm too embarrassed to look anywhere but his forehead now – feel too awkward to meet his eyes, and definitely don't want to let my gaze fall down his body.

That's when I notice the scar just beneath the line of his tousled hair. It's quite fresh, still red, still scabbed.

His reply is not what I expect. In fact, I don't know what I expected.

"I'm," he says, before his voice trails off. Then he shrugs. "I guess I'm your stepbrother."

"What?" I say, stepping backward. I look past him toward the temple, and there see Dad sweeping out of it having a heated discussion with what looks like a monk. The monk, dressed in an orange garb and with a bald dome like Dad, is busy shaking his head, and together they gesture at Duncan.

"What do you mean my stepbrother?"

"Your father legally adopted me," he says. "Six months ago."

I tilt my head to the side. "You mean foster brother, then… I think. And I don't believe you. Dad would have told me."

His smile only disarms me further. He's got a perfect set of teeth. "I wouldn't lie to you."

"Why wouldn't he tell me?"

Duncan shrugs.

I look around. Why didn't Dad tell me?

"So what are you doing here?"

"Training," he says.

"Training what?"

"Thai kickboxing."

Again, I'm just even more confused. My eyes fall down his lean, muscled body, and that's when I start to see the bruises. He's got green and purple patches around his ribcage and on the outsides of his strong, defined, arms.

"How old are you?" I ask.

"Seventeen. You?"

"Fifteen. But I turn sixteen in a couple of weeks."

"Oh, yeah? When?"

"Umm, two weeks…" I make a face, surprised at the coincidence. "Exactly, actually."

He gestures at my t-shirt. "You like cats?"

I look down, see the stenciled image of two cats touching noses on my top. "Yeah, but Dad doesn't. He doesn't let me keep pets."

"We have a cat," Duncan says. He looks around. "Somewhere."

"We?"

"The village. The pets here are owned by everybody."

I grin, find that idea pleasant. "Can I see it?"

Duncan looks at me a moment too long.

"What?"

When he doesn't reply, I grow annoyed.

"Tell me!"

He laughs, and there's a flash of awkwardness in his features, a break in the confidence. "I just think you're a really pretty girl."

I flush, don't know what to say, and so try to ignore it altogether. "Where's the cat?"

"Come on," he says, leading me. "It's fine, don't worry, there's nothing to be afraid of here."

"What about snakes and stuff?"

"I'll keep you safe," he tells me. "Come on."

We walk off toward the tree line together, and Duncan starts calling out a name. It sounds like 'dye' but with an 's' instead of a 'd'.

"Just hold on, she's probably spying us."

"Spying?"

"She'll climb a tree," Duncan says, shrugging. "Sit there and watch us in secret."

Sure enough, a few moments later, a tabby cat comes bounding through the jungle, it's brown-and-black tail sticking up through the underbrush.

The cat meows, rubs against Duncan's feet, and then turns to sniff my shoes. I bend down, but the cat recoils, back arched.

"She's not good with newcomers," he says. He lifts her up gently, and then holds her out to me.

It's not exactly the world's most beautiful cat – her eyes are too small and ears too big – but she's cute nonetheless, and I pat her, scratch the top of her head, draw a purr from her.

He puts her back down, and after staring at both of us in turn for some inscrutable feline reason, she slinks off back into the jungle.

"Why does she stay in the jungle?" I ask. "Why not in the sun?" I think of all the photos of cats I've seen stretching out in sunlight.

"Oh, she'll go into the sun later. It's still early."

"Do you get wild cats here? Like tigers and stuff?"

"Not here," he says. "Not outside the parks. All tigers here are endangered and very rare."

"Oh."

We meet eyes, and I feel zapped by electricity, look away instantly.

"Why are you training out here?" I ask him, using the question as an excuse to turn back to the village. "I mean, this place specifically?"

"Glass told me that guy was one of the best former kickboxers in Thailand."

"You mean the monk?"

"Yes."

I glimpse at the man, a little confused. He's short

and small with a thin-frame. He looks nothing like what I imagine a fighter to look: Buff-as-hell and missing teeth.

"He doesn't look it," Duncan says, as if reading my mind. "But he fights like the fucking devil. Quick as shit, too. Very skilled."

"Why do you have so many bruises?"

Duncan's eyes don't leave me. "We spar," he tells me, matter-of-factly.

Dad's angry voice floats over to us, and we both turn around. Duncan puts his hands on his hips, and I find my eyes going to his naked back. Beads of sweat dot it, and they shine in the sunlight.

"What are they arguing about?"

"Payment, probably. For my training."

"But what are you training for?"

"Glass says when I get back to the States, I'll work for him. I'll fight for him in underground MMA. Until then, I need to train in different techniques. For now, it's Muay Thai. Later, I'll learn Judo, which is a defensive art, and Taekwondo, which focuses on speed kicking. When I get back to the States, Glass'll teach me to box and strike with my fists."

"You're doing all of this just so you can be a fighter?"

He turns back to me, squints against the sunlight. "Yes."

"That's stupid."

"Why?"

"Why risk yourself? You could get hurt."

With that, he surprises me with a long exhale, almost a sigh. "I had nothing before. Your father is giving me something."

"What do you mean you had nothing before?"

"I..." he begins, but his voice trails off. "Don't have any family. I... don't have a home, really."

"You're an orphan?"

"Yeah."

"So where did you live before? A foster home?"

"No. Group home."

"Oh. Like with other kids?"

"About thirty other boys, yeah. Some nights more, some nights less."

I regard Duncan, and think about what he's saying. Dad took him all the way to Thailand to train? There must be good trainers back home.

No, something else is going on. Dad is up to something. I know him well enough.

"I think my dad is using you for something. You should watch out."

To that, he says with a cocky smile, "How do you know I'm not the one using him?"

We fall into silence for a moment before Duncan turns to me. He puts out a hand. "It was nice meeting you."

I hesitate, thinking how ridiculous he is to be offering me a handshake, but then shake his hand, feel the strength in his grip, the heat in his palm. It gives me a shiver.

"You're going already?"

"Believe me, I don't want to," he says, and he nods his head toward the monk who's beckoning him. "But my break's over."

He walks away from me, hands on his hips. But he turns around, walks backward for a bit, his eyes on mine.

I give him a nervous, quick wave, and when he returns it, I can't stop the smile that erupts onto my face, can't stop my heart from racing even quicker.

But Dad's aggressive voice pulls my attention to him, and I watch as he pulls out his wallet, and he hands a folded piece of paper to the monk.

Then he walks toward Duncan, exchanges a few harsh words with him. Duncan just gazes back stonily into Dad's eyes. I notice he never once looks away from Dad, even though Dad's trying to physically intimidate him.

"Got it?" I hear Dad say as I approach them slowly.

Duncan nods. "Don't worry, Glass."

"Of course I fucking worry, boy," Dad growls, clapping Duncan over the head with an open palm.

Immediately, there's a tension between them, and they glare at each other. At just seventeen, Duncan's already taller than Dad, but there's no way he's stronger.

Duncan's eyes flick toward me.

I shake my head at him, tell him silently, No!

His eyes shine, and his tongue darts out, wets his lips. He lets his eyes linger on my own, and then seems to have to drag them off me to look back at Dad and nod.

"Good boy," I hear Dad say before approaching me, leaving Duncan standing there. Dad makes a vicious gesture with his hand, orders me back into the jeep.

I fall into step with him and ask, "Did you really adopt that guy?"

"Yes," he says.

"Why didn't you tell me?"

"It was business."

"Business?" I ask. I knew he was up to something. He didn't adopt an orphan boy from the goodness of his heart.

Dad never does anything from the goodness of his heart.

"Since when was family stuff business?"

"Are you really going to ask me such a stupid question?" he snarls.

I don't reply. Dad's looking like an overhead storm that's about to strike me with lightning.

"He's an investment, Deidre."

"But why adopt him?"

"Easier to get him a passport, get him out of the country."

"I thought they did background checks and stuff before they let you adopt someone."

"Is that supposed to mean something?" Dad's voice is a tripwire.

"Just... you know."

"If I couldn't lean on someone to get just a fucking street urchin out of the system, then nobody would know the name Johnny Marino. Jesus Christ, Deidre."

I frown. "But why him?"

"He's going to be the best, Deidre. Look at him, look at that body. Perfect fighting body. Long arms, great reach, low base, lightning fast. All his muscles are fast-twitch. Naturally low body-fat. His metabolism blazes like a jet engine. He's going to make me a lot of money."

"So you're using him," I say.

Dad stops in his tracks. "Don't judge me, young woman. He likes to fight. This is a better life than he had back in Rockford. There he was just some rat, destined to become nothing but a gutter punk. Nothing but some two-bit pissant knocking off liquor stores to feed a bad meth habit while his teeth rot out.

Look at what I've saved him from. Without me, he'd live a short lifetime of despair and drudgery. But because of me… look at my work. He's disciplined, sculpted, a mind of metal. He's going to be the best fighter in America. Maybe the world."

I frown. Duncan doesn't seem sculpted by Dad… the impression I got, in the brief time I spoke with him, was that he was always tough. He just seems that way.

Tougher than any of the boys at my school, anyway.

"But why did you have to take him out of the country?" I ask. "Why couldn't he train back home, live at home with us?"

"I don't want anybody else catching onto his scent," Dad says. "They'll try to poach him, or they won't bet against him. I want to keep him a secret."

"This is all for betting? All so you can make money?"

"He'll be an unknown," Dad says, baring his teeth at me with a nasty smile. "Everyone's going to bet against him. The underdog."

I shake my head, can't even understand why he's

doing this. I just don't get it. How can he just adopt someone, ship them off somewhere, train them, and then make them work for him? How can he expect to control another human being?

"He figures he owes me, getting him off the streets, giving him resources," Dad mentions off-handedly. He jerks his head at me, urges me to climb up into the jeep.

"What do you mean?"

"I mean," Dad says, "That he'll be easy to tame." He looks at me with that same nasty smile on his face, flashes his eyebrows. "Heel."

He starts the jeep, and we don't talk for a while.

Heel… the word echoes in my mind.

"Can you tell me how you met him, Dad?"

*

4

DUNCAN

They say I have to be taught a lesson.

To them, that means they have to kick the shit out of me.

This is how everything works in the home. The older boys teach lessons. Why they teach them, they don't know. They just use words like 'disrespect' and think that it means something.

I didn't disrespect these guys, I just didn't let them take my money. I earned that money working. It's mine, and I never let people take what's mine.

But that's not how they see it.

I don't deny that I'm afraid. I don't deny that I'm nervous. These boys are bigger than me, and they want to kick my ass, give me a beating, put me down and tell me to stay down.

They want to build their name, like a brand. They want other people to know not to mess with them, not to cross them, to hand over everything without hesitation.

They're thieves and bullies, and they think that because they're cocky and older, they have a right to do this to me.

I have no training, but I'm confident in a fight. It's not my first, and it won't be my last. I've lost before, many times, but I've won many times more. I've taken hits, kicks, and slaps. I've dished out worse.

Back me into a corner and I know I'll stop at nothing to make sure I'm the one leaving the corner walking, not crawling.

The social workers tell me that I have a violent streak. I tell them that the only other option is to let people take what's rightfully mine.

I'll never do that.

Anyway, if worst comes to worst, I can run, and they'll never catch up to me. I can go for miles, whereas they'll be out of breath in minutes.

But that's only a last resort. They'll call me names, say I'm a fucking coward for not standing and fighting 'like a man'.

But it is three against one. Running would be wisdom in the face of danger… not cowardice. If it comes to that.

I won't run if I don't have to.

You earn a name if you run.

One of the boys takes off his gloves. He's the tallest, the strongest, the oldest. His knuckles are scarred and chapped dry by winter, but his hands still shake a little.

He's scared. I guess we all are.

The difference is I *like* the fear. It gets me feeling amped, gets the adrenaline kicking through my body. I feel like my engine is revving, that I'm ready to go from zero to one-hundred instantly. My heart hammers so hard in my chest.

I… I *like* this feeling. *Really* like it. Distantly, I wonder if there's something wrong with me.

The older boy is eighteen, has got nearly two years on me and maybe two inches. He's stocky, wide, strong. He's cocky, but not necessarily confident.

He's already out. Once they turn eighteen they're on their own. That's how it is, kicked out the door. No resources, nothing but a fucking guidance counselor and a bunch of ready-made emails and bare-as-fuck resumes that, if you're lucky, land you menial work.

Nothing wrong with menial work. I clean up a tattoo parlor part time. Mopping the floor is not above me if it buys me a ticket to the movies, an hour at the gym, maybe a seat at the game, nosebleeds of course.

But these boys want glitz. They won't mop floors. They talk about fat stacks. What little help they offered him, the older boy now squaring up against me, he threw it all aside, turned to recruiting kids from the same group home he lived in to work corners for him.

He calls himself a manager. *White-collar, motherfucker.* His words, not mine.

His name is Danny, and he's got a reputation. He carries a gun, but he likes to use a knife. He likes to carve people up. It's a butterfly knife, the kind that you have to twirl open, the kind people learn to do tricks with, and if they're lucky, not lose a finger as part of their education.

That's the one thing keeping me from just wailing on him. I don't know if he's got his weapons today. If he does, it might be a short fight for me.

"You owe me," he says. "Pay up, bitch." He pulls out his gun from the front of his jeans. I tense up, but he puts it on the lid of the dumpster beside us.

"Don't worry," he tells me. "I ain't a fucking coward. I'll beat you with my fists. Like a *man*."

Like a man. What the fuck does he know about being a man?

What the fuck do any of us know?

"I don't owe you jack shit," I tell him. "You want my money, you come and take it."

It's not much. It's twenty-five bucks crumpled up in my back pocket. He's not doing it for the money – he carries around thousands, an inch-thick wad of cash that he keeps in a gold money clip. The bills are dirty, though, crumpled, once clenched in the shaking fists of addicts on their way down before they make it to him.

He likes to take it out, wave it about. Some of the boys grovel at his feet for a handout.

I don't blame them. We have nothing.

But I'll never do it. I don't fucking beg.

So it's not money he wants from me. He wants me to bend. He wants me to break. He wants to stand over me and thump his chest and shout that he was the one to beat me when nobody else before him ever could.

He's a bully. I've never backed down from bullies, and I'm not going to start now. As far as I'm concerned, the world could use less bullies.

"You better give me that fucking money," he says. "You want to disrespect me? Like Lucas did?"

He's talking about another boy from the home. Lucas disappeared after saying he was going to get Danny, going to fight back. Nobody ever found out what happened to him. That was two months ago.

Danny comes closer, and his two friends do as well. They're surrounding me. It's crazy, but I feel this thrill. It's… fun. It's like energy is being pumped into my body and I'm about to burst.

Down at the street, a limousine sidles past. It

takes forever to cross the gap between the two walls of the dirty alley we stand in. Once it's past, we hear it slow, then whine backward in reverse and before stopping at the mouth to the alley.

The limo has tinted windows. We all stare at it for a moment. It's an odd sight in this part of town, but some rich fuck in a suit isn't going to bother with us nobodies.

I return my attention back to Danny, and he to me.

There's a pause of time, the space of a blink, and then he moves. Time remains slow for me. I see his hand reaching behind his back.

I grab his arm, run forward so I've got it behind his body, and then wrap it around his back. I yank upward, slap his elbow, hear something pop, and he grabs his shoulder, grunting, and drops to the ground.

I spin with my arm outstretched, anticipating someone getting close to me from behind. My fist hits a nose, blood spurts, the boy cries and runs away.

Just one left. I drop into a natural stance, leading with my left. He tries to punch me, a wild, aimless haymaker, I slap the outside of his forearm with my palm, redirect the punch away from me across his own body.

He's jailed by his own arm now, and his side is exposed. I thump him twice in the rib cage, hard hits, too. I feel the bone against my knuckles.

The boy coughs, tries to throw another crazy swing at me.

I duck it, kick his knee out, and then when he's on the ground I pull his head up by his hair and hit him on the nose.

There are two places to hit somebody on the face if you want to stop them. One is the nose, the other the jaw. With the nose, you don't even need to hit hard to send those nerve endings exploding, to send a man reeling. With the jaw it's a little tougher, but if you hit hard enough, the brain shuts off. It's lights-out to protect you from the pain.

I know what it feels like. It sucks. My jaw didn't break or unhinge that time, but it throbbed for weeks. I came to with my shoes missing.

The boy on the ground grabs at his nose, scrambles to his feet, limps off, doesn't look back at me once.

I approach Danny, reach into his back pocket and take out his knife. It's thinner and lighter than I expected, more rectangular than I expected.

I open it up, unfold it carefully, expose a glistening and sharp blade. He obviously cleans it regularly.

"What were you going to do to me with your fists?" I growl, bending down onto one knee, holding the blade in front of his face.

"No!" Danny cries, trying to scramble away.

I put my heel on the small of his back, and press down until he goes still.

"Don't move anymore," I warn.

"No, please!"

"What do I owe you?"

"What?"

I bring my foot down hard on his tailbone. His wail of pain echoes down the alley. "I said what the fuck do I owe you?"

"Nothing!" he cries. "You owe me nothing! You owe me noth—"

"Stop it, boy."

I whip around, see a huge man standing there. Instantly my heart stops. I've been caught by an adult. The world drains away.

I'm in deep fucking shit, now.

Behind the man, I glimpse the door to the limousine standing open. He watched the whole thing.

He's big, stocky, with a bald head and a glowing gold watch. He looks mean as hell, and when he smiles I see gold teeth.

"Give me the knife, boy," he says.

I fold the knife slowly, give it to him. He takes it, holds it, tosses it to himself in one hand.

"It's good, nice weight to it. Balanced."

The man puts a hand on my shoulder, pushes me up against the brick wall of the alley. It's wet, and my clothes are getting dirty, but I don't dare say anything or push back.

You learn to tell who the mean fuckers are, the ones who are not afraid to beat up a kid… or worse. This guy is one of 'em. It's in the eyes, the peeled and snarling lips.

Then he kneels down by Danny, feels around his shoulder. He grabs his wrist, wrenches the arm, pops the shoulder back into place.

Danny's moan of pain is haunting.

"You better see a doctor," he says to Danny. "If anybody asks, you slipped on ice. If not, I'm coming for you. Don't think I don't know you and your crew work the corner at Madison and Crow. You already got eyes on you boy, some of the bigger crews don't like where you've set up shop, so if I were you, I'd relocate."

Danny's eyes fill with fear. He and I both come to the realization quickly that we're dealing with a mobster, a proper big-time gangster.

"Ice," Danny says, nodding quickly. "I slipped on ice!" He gets up, runs away, one hand clamped to his shoulder.

Ice… it hasn't been that cold for weeks.

"You," the man says, shifting his black eyes toward me. "How old are you?"

"Sixteen," I say.

"Where'd you learn to fight like that?"

I shrug. "I taught myself."

"You knew that kid was going to try and hit you from behind. How?"

I shrug again. "I don't know. Instinct."

"Huh," the man sounds. He grabs me by the back of my neck, yanks me toward him. "Take off your jacket."

My eyes widen, and I tense up. "Uh-uh, you sick fucker," I say. I turn to run, but he catches the collar of my jacket, jerks me toward him.

"Relax. It's not like that."

He rips my jacket from me, then starts feeling around my shoulders, hard presses of his thumb and forefinger.

"Good," he says. "You wearing your pants low?"

"No," I say. "On my hips."

He seems to be measuring me up.

"Show me your hands."

I put them out, and he takes them into his, turns them over. I notice his fingers are thick, rough, and his palms are calloused.

"You got good hands."

"For what?"

"For fighting."

He takes my arms, slaps them out. "Hold them straight out. Yes, like that." He steps backward for a moment, considers me.

"Good stock," he murmurs to himself. I don't know what that means, or why he would be talking about soup.

He throws my jacket back at me, and as I put it on, he guides me into walking with him. "Come on, we're going."

"Where?"

"To start your fighting training."

"Why should I come with you?"

"You want to be a pathetic drug dealer like Danny over there?" he asks me. "Or do you want to do something with your life? *Be* somebody?"

"I was never going to become a drug dealer," I say, turning to the man. I shake his hand off my neck, stare up into his eyes.

The man regards me. "You like to fight?"

I think about it. "I'm good at it."

"You want to make money fighting?"

I lick my lips. "I want to make money, period."

"Then get in the fucking car, boy," he says. "I'll make you a fucking champion."

I don't hesitate.

I get into the limousine.

"Name's Johnny Marino," he says once he's in, sticking out a hand. "But you can call me Glass."

*

5

DEE

I finish my slice of cake – black forest – and look longingly at the rest of it.

"Can I have another, Dad?"

He frowns at me, the corners of his mouth drawn down impossibly low. "No."

"Why not?" I cry. "It's my birthday."

"It'll make you fat."

I wince, stung. "Thanks a lot."

"You could stand to lose a few pounds already."

My teeth clash together, and I look away. "You're such an—"

"Such a what?" he shouts, glaring at me. "It's for your own good. Once you gain weight, it's impossible to lose, and I'm not going to be like Falcone with his fat daughter and son."

I want to cry, but bite it back. Dad hates it when I cry. He blames me for crying.

"Oh, grow up," he says. "You're going to have to take responsibility of yourself sooner or later."

"It's just a piece of cake, Dad," I say, but my protestation has all the conviction of a wilting flower.

"One is enough. Now, are you ready to unwrap your gifts?"

"Yeah," I say, sighing.

"What is it, Deidre?"

"Nothing."

"What is it?"

"Nothing!"

He straightens up, wipes his mouth with a napkin, and then helps himself to another slice of cake.

"You will tell me what is on your mind, Deidre, because I am your father and I demand it."

"Nothing!" I shout, tossing my cutlery onto my plate. I regret it instantly when Dad stands out of his chair, and I shrink into myself, wishing I could disappear.

"What is it?" he asks, spacing out the words through gritted teeth.

"I really wanted to have a birthday party this year, Dad."

He shakes his head, sits down again. "Under no circumstances."

"Why?"

"I'm not having a bunch of filthy teenagers in my house."

"Then what about the garden? What if we all just went out and watched a movie together? I wish you'd let me go out with friends more."

"I thought you said people stayed away from you at school." He digs into his second slice of cake, munches it down. I must get my sweet tooth from him.

"Did Mom like cake?"

His whole body freezes at the mention of Mom. He hates talking about her. "Sometimes," he says curtly. "The other children at school stopped being afraid of you?"

"We're not *children*, Dad."

"Like hell you're not."

"I don't know, I've got a couple of friends, I think. I would have invited them. Maria and Teresa?"

Dad just levels a blank look at me. Of course he wouldn't know anything about me or my friends.

"No," he says, shaking his head. "I don't trust children."

"Well, *you* could have been there," I say. "Or had Frank take us to the mall, or something."

"Frank!" Dad calls. He appears in the doorway, wide and round. "Give your present to Deidre."

Frank grins, and says, "Let me just get it, boss. It's in the car."

"Well hurry the fuck up."

"Right, boss."

Dad turns his eyes on me as Frank disappears out of the doorway, and says without an ounce of sympathy, "No parties, Deidre. We've got to play it safe."

"What does that even mean?"

"A few years before you were born, I was attending the eighteenth birthday party of a young man. He was the son of an associate of mine, was going to be coming into the business soon. You know, learning the ropes so he could one day take over."

"Yeah," I say. I know what Dad's talking about. Some boss' son was going to get a high rank in the organization once he came of age.

"He was shot in his own father's back garden. Blood squirted out of his chest. There was so much of it. It was like Yellowstone finally erupted. His heart must have been really going. He died, Deidre. I will not let anybody kill my child in my house. Nobody comes into my house and pulls shit like that. Nobody disrespects me like that."

I pause at the way he phrases it. My voice is icy when I say, "I'm never coming into your business."

"It doesn't matter, Deidre. They'll use you to get to me. I won't take that risk. Nobody gets the better of me."

"Gee, thanks. I never asked for this damn life."

"Hey!" he barks, pointing a finger at me. "You have a good life. You have a nice house, you eat a good meal three times a day, you have your own room, Frank drives you everywhere. How dare you complain? Do you know how many children in this world have nothing?"

"I just want to be a normal kid. Not 'Johnny Marino's daughter'."

"It's not about being normal. It's about being a guppy, or being a shark. You're either one, or the other. We're not abnormal, we're above normal. *Better* than normal. Normal people are fucking loser idiots that go through life just waiting to die. Me? I *made* something of my life, and continue to do so in order for you to have a life. I expect you to make something of your life, too. And being 'Johnny Marino's daughter' is a good thing. People will respect you. They will fear you. Your name rings out."

"But I don't want people to respect me because they fear me," I say. "I am not going to be involved in your business."

"That's fine. It's not a line of work for women, anyway."

I roll my eyes. "What a modern attitude, Dad."

"You'll understand when you're older, Deidre. Where the hell is Frank? Frank!"

He appears in the doorway again. He's got a

wrapped gift under his arm. He hands it to me, and I take it, unwrap it.

It's a book titled *Elizabeth McCollum: An Autobiography*.

Frank shuffles his feet nervously. "You said you wanted to be a teacher, right? Work with children?"

I look up at him. "Yeah," I say. "You remembered?"

"Oh, sure," he says. "I don't know nothing about teaching, but I read in the paper that this woman's book here was a *New York Times* bestseller. She taught in schools all over the country, working with all kinds of kids. Rich kids, poor kids, immigrant kids, disabled kids. She helped developed programs and stuff. You know, plans for kids with special needs. I don't mean, like, retarded kids."

"Frank," I say, cutting him off softly. "You shouldn't say 'retarded' like that."

"You know what I mean," he says hastily. "Anyway, you know, kids who need special cur…" He trails off, unable to find the word.

"Curriculums!" Dad barks. "Jesus fucking Christ!"

"Sorry, boss." Frank returns his eyes to me.

"Curriculums and stuff. Anyway, I thought you'd like it."

I smile at Frank. "It's nice, I'll definitely read it. Thank you for remembering, Frank."

"Oh, it's nothing ho—" He was about to say 'honey', but cut himself off.

"It's a good gift, Frank," Dad says. "Very thoughtful, very nice. Thank you from me, too. From the bottom of my heart." He touches his chest.

Frank bows his head slightly.

Dad continues: "Though you know with teenagers, they change their minds all the time about what they want to do."

"I won't," I say. "I want to work with children. I want to be a teacher."

"Oh, yeah?" Dad asks. "You sure about that?"

"Pretty sure."

Dad puts down his fork. "Why a teacher?"

"It's such a big responsibility," I say. "You help to shape the lives of people. I want to do good."

He scoffs. "Do good! When you grow up, you're going to be in for a shock. Nobody does good. Everybody just looks out for themselves."

"You're wrong, Dad," I tell him. "There are good people in this world. People who care about others."

"Like who?"

"Social workers," I say. I think of Duncan, growing up an orphan, being raised by social workers in a group home.

"Social workers?" Dad asks, making a sneering face. "What do they get paid?"

"It's not about the money."

"Everything is about the money," he says. "I really wish you'd learn that lesson. Maybe you want to get philosophical and all that bullshit, but I'm telling you, it's the money that makes everything keep going around nicely. It's society's lubricant."

"You're so negative."

"The word you're looking for is cynical, Deidre, and yes, I am. It's how I got to where I am now."

"Well, anyway, I want to teach kids."

"You won't once you have to deal with them. Nightmares, all of them. You were a handful when you were a child. God, you wouldn't ever stop crying. Drove me crazy."

I look between him and Frank. Frank's wearing a

distant smile, like he's slipping back into a happy memory. Dad is just scowling. One guess as to who spent the most time raising me.

We sit in silence for a while, and then Dad forces on a great big smile. "Here you go, honey," he says. He slips an envelope over the table. I open it and find two airplane tickets inside.

"What's this?"

"Paris. You and me. We can go to the *Louvre*. Do the war museum! What do you say?"

"Another trip? But we just got back from Thailand."

"I have to go for a business meeting, anyway, and I thought you'd like to join me. I'd like the company."

The way he says it, it's not an invitation. It's an order. That's Dad.

"Thanks," I say, forcing a smile at him.

"What, you don't like it?"

"No, Paris will be great," I say. It's not quite a lie… I imagine Paris *is* great. But I don't want to go with *him*. "I've never been before."

"Can you believe it? Neither have I!" Dad says through a laugh, clapping his hands together. "It'll be a good time. Frank will be joining us. Can never be too careful."

I sigh. I guess, all things considered, I can't *truly* mind. It will be nice to be a tourist. I know I'm lucky, that I have a lot of things that other girls… other people don't.

But I asked Dad if I could have my own smartphone, or even just a gift voucher so I could go shopping and get myself something. Of course, he either completely forgot, or didn't care.

"Oh, there's one more thing," Dad says. He goes to the kitchen counter, picks up a brown envelope then brings it back. "You got this in the mail."

"Who is it from?"

"No idea," he says. "The stamp must have peeled off in the rain, and there is no return address. My guess? Probably a birthday card from the school or library or something. You know, they automate these things now. Have a computer print out a card, send it to you. No personal touch!"

I furrow my brow. I doubt it was from the school or the library. I open it and peer inside.

"Well?" Dad asks.

"It's just an automated card," I say. "You were right."

"Well, aren't you going to read it?"

"No," I say. "What's the point?"

He laughs, gestures at Frank. "See, she's smart, isn't she? Knows when not to waste her time. That's my daughter, smart as a whip. Go on Deidre, it's late. Time for bed. You go get ready."

I nod, take the envelope with me, and climb up the stairs to my room. I feel something hard in the envelope. It is definitely *not* a card.

Once in my room I close the door, put a chair up against the doorknob, and I open the envelope. There's something thin inside, and I pull it out. It's a pocket mirror!

It's circular, black on the back with a cute cartoon drawing of a tabby cat. I open the envelope farther and find a letter and pull it out.

The letter is not really a letter, more like a note scribbled messily onto the top left corner of the piece of paper. It reads:

Dear Deedra: Happy birthday. I hope you still like cats.

I grin from ear to ear, almost can't believe he

spelled my name wrong. I flip the mirror over in my hand. That's when I notice that the image on the back is the kind that moves when you change perspective, a visual trick. The cat waves.

I tilt it in my hand over and over, and the cat keeps waving, paw pads shifting left, then right, then left, then right.

It's just a stupid mirror, but it's far and away the best gift tonight.

Stuffing the mirror into my jeans pocket, I walk downstairs and find Dad still at the kitchen table, on his third slice of cake.

His tired eyes settle on me, and then they go hard in an instant. "What is it?"

"Can I write a letter to Duncan?"

With a confused shake of his head, he asks, "Why?"

"My English teacher has been encouraging us to write more letters," I lie. "You know, pen pals."

"No," Dad says, tapping the table with his fingers. "Get ready for bed like I told you."

"Why not?"

He heaves a great big sigh, and it's at once

insulting and frightening. "There's no postal address there. It's a village in the middle of nowhere. And even if there were, he couldn't reply to you."

"Why not?" I ask, ever wary of Dad's waning patience.

"I don't even know if he can write, first of all," he says. "And second, he'd have to get a boat into the nearest city which is an hour away, or several hours driving. Then he'd have to buy the stationary, and then pay the postage."

I shake my head. "So?"

"Money, Deidre!" Dad barks. "Remember what I just told you? You can't do anything without money! He doesn't *have* any. Now stop asking me stupid questions and go back upstairs."

I'm hurt by his insult, but still I want to ask him why he isn't giving Duncan any spending money. Though the look on his face tells me his patience has come to an end.

I nod, climb slowly back up the stairs.

*

6

DEE

Duncan is coming home today.

I've just turned eighteen. It's been two years since Thailand.

But even after so long, I feel this silly, childish excitement. I'm eager to meet him again, to talk to him again, even though I don't know him at all. I've only ever met him once, and yet he's been almost all that I can think about.

I'm also nervous beyond belief. I couldn't decide what to wear, and in the end I settled for being comfortable. My favorite pair of dark jeans, a light-brown bomber jacket, and my favorite ankle boots.

I cast one last look in the mirror, and don't like

what I see. The ankle boots cut me off at the slimmest part of my legs, and I know I'm not model-thin so they just make me look short and chunky. But they're my favorite boots, and I'm going to wear them.

Outside, it's chilly. In Kenilworth, on the north shore of the lake, we get cold winds and the air is wetter. It makes me shiver. I sit outside in the back garden, look out at the huge plot of terraced land with its apple orchard at the back.

People at school always joke that I live in a mansion – I practically do. And all of them know where the money comes from. It's mob money. It's dirty money. It's blood money.

I hate that the suffering of others gives me this luxury. I hate what Dad does, so I try never to indulge. I reject as much of the luxury as I can.

And yet, I still live here because I have to. Sometimes, I wonder why I force myself to pay a penance for Dad's crimes.

From the back garden I can see the road, a winding, narrow path lined on either side by tall trees that squawk with birds.

I hear the limousine before I see it. Steam and exhaust wafts upward from behind green-brown hedges. My gut tightens, and my heart starts to beat quicker.

For the past two years, Dad has often spoken of Duncan's harsh training. He was going to make Duncan the best fighter ever, he would tell me.

Sure, he'd start a little later than some of the other young men who got into fighting. He'd be a little older, but his body would be more mature. His mind would be readier.

That's what Dad says. Duncan's being *incubated.*

I spot the limousine making its way slowly around the lazy bends. The windows are tinted, but it's not like I could see inside from this distance.

Standing up, I draw in breath, release it and it fogs in front of me. I straighten my jacket, check my back, and then wring my hands together. I watch the car trundle slowly around to the front, walk through the house to go and meet them.

The butterflies in my stomach are starting to flap their wings. The hurricane will hit me square in the gut.

Dad told me I had to meet them at the door. Dad told me I had to welcome my adoptive brother into our family.

But I *am* excited to see him, and I feel bad about that. Feel guilty about it. I shouldn't… anticipate it so much.

After all, he's my foster brother. He's part of the family now.

But I want to see his eyes… those crystal eyes. So clear, so blue, and yet… there's turmoil in them. Anger.

Maybe I'm projecting. Maybe I've just thought up this story in my head these past two years. Spun a narrative around him, built him up.

But I swear, when I saw him in Thailand, there was something behind those eyes.

I walk out of the front door, and watch as the limousine crunches gravel all the way up the driveway. It rounds the fountain out front, which has two cherubs with feathered wings squirting water out of their mouths.

The limousine engine stops, and black exhaust no longer belches out of the back. I hold my breath, wait for the door to open, but it doesn't.

Frank steps out, waddles around the front of the car. He smiles at me, gives me a small wave, and I wave back, glad to see him.

He goes to the passenger side door, and opens it. Out steps Dad. He doesn't even look at me. Instead, he turns around and continues talking into the car. I don't know what he's saying, and I don't care. I'm eagerly trying to look past him, trying to glimpse Duncan.

I see a head of neatly trimmed dark hair. Then, from inside the car, I see those eyes. They seem to shine, reflect the waning sunlight. I'm taken aback. They're sharper than ever, and again I'm reminded of a wolf's eyes, and when he climbs out of the car, I gasp.

He's grown… so much. He towers over Dad, and Dad is an even six-feet, and his shoulders are so broad he makes *Dad* look small. And I would never have described Dad as being small.

Duncan looks at me, and as I drag my eyes up his body to meet his again, I'm jolted, shocked by electricity. It's a zap that forces me to instantly break eye-contact, look at a spot above his head instead, and I feel that hurricane acutely now.

He's so good looking. His jaw looks cut from steel, and his lips are full, generous, untouched by the last of the winter dryness. His cheek bones are high, giving him an angled, almost pretty look.

I see a smudge of pink. His tongue darts out to wet his lips. I'm taken back in time to Thailand. He did that then, too. It must be a habit.

He's wearing jeans like me, with black boots, a white t-shirt, and a faded leather jacket. He looks… great, if in a timeless way.

"Deidre, come here," Dad says, beckoning me impatiently with his hand. His gold watch catches the setting sun, beams it straight into my eye. I feel like it's a spotlight. Everybody is watching.

I chew on my lower lip, walk toward them, take my steps carefully. Knowing me, I'll probably trip on nothing and make an ass of myself.

My eyes are on the ground, but Duncan's eyes are on me… I know it. I *feel* it. They sear me.

"I think an introduction is in order. This is Duncan Malone."

I look up, and sure enough Duncan is looking right at me, nowhere else. Not at the big house behind him, probably bigger than any he's ever seen. Not at the fountain, or the gardens that you can spy from the front. He's looking right at me.

"Hi," I say. My voice is just a shaky whisper.

He puts out a hand; I see the beginnings of his tattoos on his wrists. I slip my hand into his and shake it. He makes me feel physically tiny. His palms are soft, hot to the touch, as if he's been holding them against a fire.

It's just like when we shook hands in Thailand. I think it's so absurd, that we're *shaking hands* again. I want to grin, laugh even, but in front of Dad I'm a nervous wreck. I don't know how he expects me to behave.

And Dad has many expectations for me.

"Duncan," he says. "This is Deidre Marino, my daughter."

"We've met," Duncan says, not turning to Dad. "I remember."

"Oh, yes," Dad murmurs. That memory has obviously escaped him.

Now I smile at Duncan, and when he returns it, it only makes mine grow wider.

God, Thailand two years ago! We stood together and watched Dad make an ass of himself. Watched Dad bully the village people, argue over money.

My smile fades.

"Yeah," I whisper.

Duncan's eyes don't leave mine. I feel like he's looking straight through me, like he can see exactly what I'm thinking, see how attractive I find him… how drawn to him I am. How nervous I am.

"You look great, Dee."

I laugh at the out-of-place compliment, but the tension only grows thicker. I can feel my cheeks burning.

I only catch it a moment later that he called me *Dee.* Nobody has called me that, not even at school.

"Thanks."

My heart is racing so quickly, and I tug my hand from Duncan's, watch as his long fingers close around empty air.

Dad is oblivious to our exchange. He claps Duncan on the back, grips his neck and guides him around me. I watch as they walk into the house.

Dad is announcing that he'll give Duncan the grand tour, that this is his house now, too. I hear him saying something about them leaving for a trip tomorrow, but I can't make it out.

But as they climb the steps up to the front door, Duncan turns over his shoulder and looks at me, and I look at him. We don't break eye-contact until he disappears inside the house.

When he's finally gone, I lean against the side of the car, fold my arms across my chest, and chew on my lower lip.

"Don't worry, Deidre," Frank says, walking up to me with wide duck-steps. "He hasn't forgotten you."

I blink, crease my brow. "What?"

"He's just trying to be good to Duncan, you know? Show him the ropes. Welcome him into his home."

I smile at Frank. He's got some heart, but I'm grateful that he's missed the mark by a mile.

"Thanks, Frank," I tell him. "It's cold out. Come inside for a cup of coffee or something?"

He purses his lips, shakes his head. "Oh, no, I'll wait out here."

"You can come in, you know."

"If your father wants me inside, then I'll come inside."

"But it's cold."

"Deidre, you're old enough to understand." He implores me with his eyes not to make this any more difficult.

"Dad's the boss," I say.

"That's right," Frank replies. "And he hasn't invited me in."

"Right," I say, nodding my head.

"You go in, though, honey. Don't catch a cold."

"See you, Frank," I say, sighing.

I wonder what life is going to be like, now, living with Duncan.

*

7

DUNCAN

It's the same limousine I first climbed into two years ago.

It's the smell I remember first. The sticky leather… it makes me feel sick instantly. It's a wet smell, something that coats itself to the inside of my throat. Something I can almost taste.

I guess I'm just not used to luxury.

Glass hasn't changed a bit. He's still got those crooked, smoke-stained teeth bracketed by gold ones, the gold watch, the completely bald head, the hard, mean eyes.

I don't let my guard down for an instant, and I won't ever around him. I didn't trust him as a kid, I just didn't know it at the time.

Now… now I understand the trepidation I felt when I climbed into that limousine. I was faced with the choice of taking something given to me, and then finding out how not to be controlled by it. Glass is a serial controller.

Or I could have returned to my life as it was… destined for nothingness.

I hate the idea of being nothing, of being worthless. I have worth.

They used to say that every human being, inherently, had worth. But even as those words left the social worker's mouth, I could sense that they were empty. She couldn't hide her true, sad thoughts behind that well-practiced smile. A warm smile in the winter wind. She may as well have said nothing.

But bless her. Bless all of them. They stand in the way of the storm, try to block it with words and compassion and sometimes, in rare cases, even love.

It won't work. It will never work… not in this God damned world.

But rare is it that the cards you're dealt can be exchanged. That's why I climbed into that limousine.

That's why I followed a man like Glass who just stank of something rotten.

I got to turn my cards in, get dealt a new hand. How many times can people say that?

"I've set up a gym for you in the back of the house. It's my old one, but I've got all-new and modern equipment. We're going to get you on a proper diet. I've got the best supplements, some experimental ones too, testosterone boosters, everything."

I nod at Glass, lick my lips.

"And I've got a trip set up, we leave tomorrow. We're going to talk to Jim McNamara in Omaha. You ever heard of him?"

I shake my head.

"Well, he trained some of the best boxers this country has ever seen, and he owes me a favor. He's got a compound a ways away from the city. You'll live there, train with him and the other boys. I'll stay with you, spar with you, show you the ropes, show you my best moves."

"Got it," I tell him. "For how long?"

"Around six months. You're going to be the best,

boy," he says, gripping my shoulder, squeezing it tight. "A man like you is welcome into my family."

"Thank you," I tell him.

The truth is, I do feel gratitude, but I also recognize the tongue of a snake. That was my education; learning how to tell the good people from the bad. I suppose that's everybody's education, really, but in my life, when you see bad people all the time, you start to notice patterns.

It's always the promises… the promise of greatness, success, money, whatever. You learn to tell that they aren't promising *you* these things… they're promising *themselves* these things.

You're just the tool, the instrument.

Well, I'm no tool, though I've been called one before.

"We're fighting strictly underground in the beginning," he says. "Nobody will know you. They'll think you're easy pickings, bet against you. I'll sell it. Don't worry boy, I'll play my part."

"Your part?" I ask.

"Yes. We all have a part to play. Life is a stage, don't forget that, and we all have roles. All my men understand this. My daughter understands this. Play your part, I'll make you rich. I'll make you the underdog nobody wants to back. I'll sell you short."

I don't say anything.

"Does that bother you?"

"No," I tell him truthfully.

"Good. You'll be the guy who is *supposed* to lose. You understand, Duncan, you'll need to sell it. Look like you're getting beat, then wham!" He claps his hands together. "Then you fucking take them down and submit them."

"So you want me to take a beating," I say.

"Precisely. I knew you were smart the moment I saw you," he says. "You got a good head on your shoulders, Duncan. You'll go far in this business."

"What happens when everybody knows who I am? What happens when you're no longer taking bets against me?"

"We shut it down. Nothing lasts forever. You go pro."

"Pro, huh?"

"UFC, whatever. Then we go big on a national stage, international, even. The money there will be amazing. But you need a reputation first, and we'll build it in the underground cage. Your name will echo."

"You've got it all figured out, huh?"

"Damn right I do," Glass says. "How the fuck do you think I got to where I am? How the fuck do you think I ride around in a limousine all day? Drink only the best whiskey? Own a house like the one that I do?" He gives me a big grin. "We're going to make a lot of fucking money. I know it."

I narrow my eyes at him. "We?"

"You'll get your cut, boy, don't you worry about that. Five-percent of the pot, non-negotiable. I expect the pot will climb to over ten million some fights, so you'll be good. Don't ever say I wasn't a generous man. I take care of my own. Just ask Frank. Frank! Frank!"

The intercom hisses to life. "Yes, boss." Frank's hoarse voice is made scratchier by the static.

"Don't I take care of my own, Frank?"

"You do, Mr. Marino."

"See?" Glass says, looking at me.

I swallow, nod again. Promises. But maybe Glass

will be good for them. There's more to me being a good fighter than simply him making his quick buck. I've been a years-long investment.

There's emotion behind this whole thing. This is more than just *business*, even if he claims the contrary.

"You want me to be the fighter you never were," I tell him. "You want to live through me."

The words silence him, still him. I call it how I see it.

"I won't lie to you, Duncan. We're family, and family don't lie to each other, right?"

"Right."

"I've treated you like my own son. I've given you a life. I want *you* to carry *my* torch." He slaps my chest, holds his hand there.

His torch. The one he never held.

Glass continues: "You don't know what it's like having my body, being robbed by my body. This piece of shit!" He thumps his hand against his own chest. "This stopped me from being the best. Brittle bones and inelastic tendons. Genetics." He scrunches up his face in disgust. "I hate my body. But you… you have it all. You were blessed. Your name may still be Malone – and I'm really fine that you kept your own – but legally you're my son. You are Johnny Marino's son!"

He shouts it triumphantly, like a trumpet blaring in victory.

I just nod at him.

"You'll make me proud, won't you?"

"If you mean that I'll fight to the best of my ability, yes."

"Good, good."

"I don't like to lose," I tell him.

"You and I are similar," he says, clasping me around the shoulder, pulling me into him.

No we're not, I think to myself. But this is an opportunity, not one I'm going to turn down.

Not to mention, I've got another motive for being diffident toward Glass, one that I'm sure he wouldn't like.

"We're nearly there," he says. "Frank, go a little faster would you?"

The speakers in the back of the limo crackle to life again. "Right, boss."

The car speeds up, and we take the bends breezily.

"There," Glass says, pointing out the window. "That's your home now."

I see a huge house, three floors high with a… I don't know the word… layered back garden. I see trees, like a small forest, and sitting on a bench I see a lone girl.

Dee.

My heart starts to quicken, and I swallow. The last time I saw her she was just a little girl, all of fifteen, nervous, insecure.

But even then she was pretty. It was plain as day that she was going to grow up to be a beautiful young woman. Those generous lips of her small mouth that sits above a soft chin, those big, black eyes, that voluminous, wavy hair, a light shade of brown, pulled back tight into a ponytail.

I blink myself out of the past, distantly wondering if my thoughts are wrong. I'm not insecure about what I think – I think what I do and I won't apologize for it – but sometimes I still wonder. Was she too young? Was I too old?

It doesn't matter. We're both adults now.

"Your room will be upstairs, next to Deidre's,"

Dad tells me. "The third floor is off-limits, though. That's where my office and bedroom are."

Fair enough, it's his fucking house.

"Now, do you have any questions?"

I think about asking him if I should stop wanting to fight, then what? But he strikes me as the kind of person who would inform me that I only stop fighting when *he* tells me to.

It's better not to ask the question. When I'm ready to quit, I'll do it and leave. It doesn't escape me that he's simply using me, and so I'll use him in return, leave on my own terms.

I think about Deidre in Thailand. She said those exact words, that Glass was just using me. I make a mental note that she's smart. She was right on the money. She saw straight through her father. She saw it before even I truly did.

Better play it straight with Dee.

I started calling her Dee in my head the moment I tried to write her that letter and realized I didn't know how to spell her name. I tried anyway, knowing fully well I probably got it wrong.

There's conflict in me, a kind of still storm. I

haven't stopped thinking about Dee, her face, her voice, her shy smile.

All this time, for every punch I took, for every kick I skipped over, for every jab I slapped away or took above the eye, she was in my mind. Not always consciously, not always right at the forefront, but still there.

If I wasn't consciously thinking about her, I was definitely subconsciously doing so. Sometimes I'd wake up at night having dreamed about her.

I wondered what her life story was like, tried to piece it together from just the bits and bobs I had gleaned that day we met. An overbearing, asshole father who is a mob boss no doubt played a huge influence in her life.

But no sight of her mother. I guessed that that meant she didn't have a mother, because I can't imagine a mother not being there to protect her daughter from Glass.

He's a capable man, of that I have little doubt. But his responsibilities do not lie with his daughter… of that I have even lesser doubt.

But in the end I realized I'd never be able to put

together her story. The only way to ever truly know it was to meet her again.

And the only thing standing in the way of that was doing what Glass wanted. So I wasn't just training to be the best fighter, I was training to ensure that I didn't let down Glass, that I got glowing reports from my instructors.

Because I knew he would take me back to the States.

I knew, through him, I would get to see her again, learn more about her.

She's become an obsession.

The limousine vibrates as we start crunching over the gravel of the driveway, and eventually we round a fountain with winged baby angels spitting water.

I can see her, standing there, hands in her pockets, looking awkward. It makes me smile. She's grown more beautiful, more mature. It's the only way I know how to describe it. She looks more like a woman now.

And I just can't take my eyes off her. She makes me feel a kind of tense anticipation in my gut, makes my temperature rise. Just the brief glimpses I get as the car rounds the fountain, and I feel like I'm ready to burst.

We slow to a stop, Frank lumbers around, and as Glass gets out I struggle to look past him, to see Dee.

I finally catch a glimpse of her big, black eyes. I'm lost in them in an instant, swimming in her gaze, feel like I'm pulled to them by some magnetic force.

She breaks eye-contact, looks down at the ground, doesn't look back up at me until we're reintroduced by Glass.

I can't take my eyes off her, and my heart hammers in my chest as we shake hands. I don't want to let hers go, but she pulls her shy fingers from mine. She leaves my skin tingling.

Glass guides me into the house, but I keep looking at her over my shoulder. I smile at her, and for a moment she smiles back at me, and it's like I'm shocked by the electric paddles doctors use to save lives. It hits me right in the chest, takes my breath away.

She leaves my world reeling as we walk inside the front door.

Glass takes me on the grand tour. I don't pay a lick of attention.

Then we get to the gym. It's first-class, better than anything I've ever seen, even on gym advertisements on the television.

I'm actually impressed, and when I see Glass grinning at me I can't help but to smile back.

"It looks good," I tell him.

He laughs, claps me on the back, then puts an arm around my shoulder.

"We're going to make a lot of money," he says. "And a legacy. You're not my real son, you're not my blood, but legally, you *are* my son. I expect, if you have any children of your own, they will carry the Marino name."

I meet Glass' eyes, and tell him slowly, "Children are a long way off for me."

"Right, right," he says, before hastening to add, "But make sure they are a consideration. Find yourself a woman, someone who will listen to you and not make trouble. Someone who'll be happy if you just give her a child. This is important to me, Duncan, you understand?"

I make sure not to show any expression on my face, even if I find what he says outdated and disturbing.

Slowly, I give him a non-committal nod.

"Good, good."

I keep my eyes level on his own. We stay locked for a moment, like two fighters measuring each other up before sparring.

"Right, well, this is your home now. Do as you please. But tomorrow we set off, remember."

"Yeah," I say.

"We'll teach you how to fight old-school."

"Got it, Glass."

"You're going to be the best, boy!" he says. He can barely contain his excitement again. I picture him rubbing his hands together like some cartoon villain staring at a stack of cash. "I've got some business to attend to."

"Okay."

"I'll take you out tomorrow and we'll get you some clothes before we set off. It'll be a long drive."

I laugh. "Yeah, I'm wearing everything I own."

"You wear it better than me," Glass says, rubbing

his belly. "See you tomorrow morning."

"Right."

He walks off, and I stand in the gym alone for a moment, gazing around. Free weights, machines, treadmills, bikes, punching bags, supports for calisthenics, tires, medicine balls… it's fully loaded.

It's a God damn paradise for anyone who needs to train.

I need to train.

I turn around, leave the gym.

Find a girl, he said.

So I'm going to find Dee.

*

8

DEE

"Hey."

I'm startled, turn around and see Duncan standing in the doorway. We meet eyes, and when he smirks at me, I can't help but grin back.

"Dad give you the *grand tour*?" I ask, not bothering to hide the sarcasm in my voice.

He hooks his thumbs into his belt. "Yup."

"Well, he likes to show off."

"I've noticed."

We look at each other for a moment, and once again my heart is sent into overdrive. I feel a shiver, and try to distract myself by offering him a cup of tea.

"No thanks. No caffeine."

I furrow my brow. "Why?"

"Messes with my rhythm."

"Really?"

He nods, comes into the kitchen, rubs a hand along the marble counter. "Yeah, really."

"Why?"

"Caffeine increases your heart rate and blood pressure," he says. "Even if just a little bit. But timing is everything in a fight. One heartbeat too late… and you're locked up."

"But you're not fighting now."

"Wouldn't want to like it, then have to give it up."

I consider that. He *does* seem like a kind of spartan person… someone with only a need for simple pleasures.

"You mean you've never had a cup of tea before?"

"Not since I was young."

"No coffee?"

"Not since I started training."

"Huh," I say. The gulf between us seemingly has grown wider. There's a moment of silence, and I feel awkward as hell. "Where did Dad go?"

"Said he had business to attend to."

I roll my eyes. "Right. *Business.* You know what he does, right?"

Duncan sits down beside me, looks straight at me. His eyes catch me off-guard again.

"Of course I know."

"Then you know what business means."

"And you?"

"What do you mean?"

"Are you… in business?"

"With Dad?" I ask, snorting. "God, no. I'm still in school."

"High school."

"Yeah."

He nods. "So it must be your last year if you're eighteen."

"That's right," I say. "I graduate in a few months, actually. What, you keeping track?"

"You told me when your birthday was."

I suck on my bottom lip. "Thanks for the mirror. I still have it."

"Yeah?" His smile becomes more genuinely joyous, and it brightens up his whole face.

"Yeah. How did you even get my address?"

"Took it off the back of the check Glass gave my kickboxing instructor."

"What about the cat? Um, Sai, was it?"

"Oh, she's still around somewhere, I'm sure."

"Do you miss her?"

"Yeah, a little. So what happens after you graduate?"

I blink. "Well, then I go to college," I say. "Why?"

Duncan shrugs. "I don't know," he starts, but doesn't finish the sentence.

"Don't know what?"

"Anything about your life, I guess. About what people like you do."

I frown. "People like me?"

"People not like me."

"You could go to college if you wanted. All you'd need to get is a GED. I mean, you wouldn't get into a top-rated one, but it's possible. Or there's community colleges, vocational schools."

"Never was much for school." His expression is almost mischievous, and at once makes him look a little younger. It's infectious, makes me smile.

"Let me guess, you never went to school. Truancy police ever come after you?"

"They tried," he says, then he laughs. His Adam's apple bobs up and down. "They couldn't keep up with me."

"Bad boy, huh?"

"Just didn't see the point."

"Why?"

"What was I going to do?"

"Get good grades? Go to college? Get a job? Isn't that what we all do?"

"Well, not all. Besides, I was behind already… and at the home, it's not like we had anybody to ask for help. If you were caught doing homework…"

"What?" I ask, genuinely curious.

"Well, you made yourself a target for bullying. Having a book open was an invitation."

"You don't seem like somebody who cares what other people think of you."

"Everybody cares what somebody thinks of them," he tells me.

Somehow, I suspect he's hinting that he cares what *I* think of him.

"Well, don't worry," I say. "I won't judge you. Did Dad show you the garden?"

"No."

"Want to see?"

"*You* going to show it to me?"

"Yes," I say a little slowly. "As long as you want to."

"I want you to."

I'm puzzled by his weird phrasing of it, but nevertheless take him outside, and together we walk through the garden, all the way down to the orchard.

Our shoulders rub now and then, and I feel sparks of energy, nervous energy. I've got my hands in my jacket pockets, and he's got his by his side.

"So you're going to be some big-time fighter, huh?" I ask.

"One day."

"You want to fight?"

Duncan shrugs. "It's all I'm good at."

Somehow, I doubt that.

"What do you want to do?" he suddenly asks me.

"I want to be a teacher."

"Really?" he asks, his interest obviously piqued. It

seems curious to me. Why would *he* give a shit?

"Yeah."

"Like, high school?"

"No, younger. Kindergarten or maybe elementary. I want to work with children."

"Why?"

I shrug. "I just like the idea. It's important."

"I agree," he says.

"You do?"

"Sure. Teachers shape the children they teach. It's a big responsibility."

"That's exactly what I said!" I blurt out. "Dad thinks it's not a good job, though."

"Why?"

"Well, you don't earn much."

"Depends on what it is you think you're earning."

I grin at him. "Exactly. Dad doesn't understand that at all. But I guess it's hard for him, you know?"

"I don't know what you mean."

"All he's got to measure himself by is his empire. And *that's* all about money."

"He's got you."

I snort, wave off Duncan's words with my hand.

"Please. You don't even know me."

"You're very attractive."

"It's not like Dad played any part in that," I say, blushing, looking unfailingly at the ground before us. "And I don't."

"Brave as well."

"How do you even figure that?" I challenge. "You just, what, have a talent for sensing people?"

He smirks. "Maybe. Just an instinct."

"How do you know your instincts are right?"

"Had to rely on them up until now."

"Well, you guessed wrong with Dad, you know, following him."

"But following him led me to you."

Now I *really* stop. "What are you doing?"

"What do you think I'm doing?"

"Something you shouldn't be," I say, but his grin is infectious, and I can't help but return it. "And whatever it is you're doing, you're not very good at it."

I suck in air as he steps a little closer to me. Despite the brave face I put on, on the inside I'm all wobbly and nervous.

Why would he do this? Drop hints that he likes me like it doesn't matter at all that he's technically my brother, that we're both living under the roof of an insane and violent man.

"You seem like the kind of person who gets into trouble a lot."

He shrugs. "I do what I want."

"Well, you can't anymore, and that's a childish attitude anyway."

"Why can't I?"

"Well, for one, Dad will—"

"He'll do nothing."

I laugh softly. "You're wrong. You are so wrong. Trust me on this, I know better than you."

"Then we just won't tell him."

I put my hands on my hips. "Tell him what, exactly?"

"Whatever it is you don't want him to know."

"There is nothing I don't want him to know."

"That's not true."

"It is!"

A third voice bursts in: "There you are!"

I snap my head toward the house, see Dad

storming out into the garden. Duncan just smirks at me, like this is all a game.

"You really don't want to be pissing my Dad off," I say to him quickly. "I mean, about anything at all. He's got a temper."

"I can handle your father."

"Duncan!"

"Yes, Glass," Duncan says, turning toward Dad, his voice more than a little bored.

"Get inside! Let's spar."

"I thought you had business to attend to."

"Well, it fell through. Come on, show me what all my money has bought me."

Duncan looks back at me for a moment.

"You'd better go," I whisper at him.

"I'll see you tonight, Dee."

"Yeah," I say. "Good luck."

"Don't need it."

He swaggers off toward Dad, who glares at me for a moment – as if I'm somehow responsible for his rotten mood – and then walks with Duncan back toward the house.

Again, I catch Duncan looking over his shoulder at

me, and I look at him.

And I'm terrified at how their sparring session is going to go.

I know Dad hates to lose, and I have no doubt that Duncan can win.

I just wonder if he'll be smart enough to not win so convincingly.

*

9

DUNCAN

Someone I have never seen sets down a bowl of steaming soup in front of me. I turn to the woman, short, round, eyes-down.

"Thank you," I say.

"Thank you, sir," she says immediately, her voice quiet, before disappearing out of the door.

"Who is that?" I ask.

Glass clears his throat. I look at him, see the bright purple welt on his forehead, and the dark line of his split lip. Unconsciously, my hand goes to my own face, where I run over the slight swelling at the side of my jaw.

It was a good sparring session. I won, but he surprised me for an old man.

"That's Susan," Glass says irritably. "She's on my staff, forget about her."

Forget about her.

He just treats people like disposable things, even the people who work for him.

I turn to Deidre, sitting opposite me along the lengthy, narrow table. She doesn't meet my eyes, and instead looks down at her soup.

"Well, what the fuck are you waiting for?" Glass growls, and when I snap my head to him, I notice he's staring angrily at Deidre.

"Glass," I say, pulling his attention away. "What was that move, you spun on your heel, like a pivot, but it was a fake, you bounced off and went the other way."

He grins at me, slurps soup off his spoon. "I came up with that."

"Yeah? It was good." I rub my jaw, sell it. "You got me good."

"Damn right I did, boy. I'll tell you about it tomorrow, we don't talk about work at the table."

But now his mood has lightened, and I look at Deidre, and her eyes are on me.

We all drink our soup in uncomfortable silence.

"Excuse me," Glass says after a moment, as if unable to bear it any longer. "I have to make a telephone call."

He exits the dining room, and once the door is closed, Dee says to me, "Oh my God, did you do that to his face?"

I nod at her. "Yeah, but we were wearing padded helmets. Is he always like this at dinner?"

"Yeah."

"Does he always get on you?"

She nods slowly.

Distantly, through the heavy wooden doors we can hear his angry voice shouting on the phone.

"Does he always do business during dinner?"

"We haven't had an uninterrupted dinner in years," Dee tells me. "Not that I mind. It's not like we talk."

"Why not?"

She frowns, bristles almost. "How the hell should I know? He's just a prick."

"You shouldn't let him push you around. He's a bully."

"He's my father."

"So?"

"You wouldn't understand."

I set down my spoon. "What do you mean?"

"You didn't have a father."

"Yeah, but there were plenty of bullies in my life."

"You just joined this family," she says. "Don't think you understand how it works."

"So how does it work?"

"Not the way you say it does. I can't just push back."

"Why not?"

"He loses his temper."

"Does he hit you?"

Her spoon clinks against her bowl. "No."

"But he shouts at you."

"Yes. Can you stop asking me these questions?"

I let out a slow breath, look briefly toward the door, then back at Dee. She looks haunted by these questions, and is no longer meeting my eyes.

"Dee," I say, and I tap her foot under the table

with mine. I see the flash of a smile, but otherwise nothing. "Dee," I say, doing it again.

"What are you doing?" she asks, failing to hide the same smile. She kicks my foot back.

"There's been something on my mind."

"What?"

"It's going to sound weird."

"Just as long as you don't ask me about Dad anymore. I'd rather not think about him."

"No, it's not that."

"Then what?"

"It'll make me look stupid."

"How do you know you don't already look stupid? After all, you climbed into that car with Dad."

"Ouch."

She lifts her spoon, points it at me. "Don't play with fire, I'm your only ally in this house."

There's a certain truth to that, I'm sure.

"Well, go on, ask me."

"How exactly do you spell your name?"

There's a space, just a pause of time where we grin at each other, where our eyes meet, and it's like we're transported somewhere else.

At least, that's what it feels like to me.

And then she looks down, laughing a little, shaking her head. "I forgot about that."

"Did I get it wrong?"

"Very wrong. It's D-E-I-D-R-E."

"Huh," I say. "I would never have guessed."

"That's what you get for skipping school."

"It's not exactly the most common name."

"Common enough," she fires back, "To know how to spell it."

At that moment Glass bursts back into the room, and at once blankets the mood with his own.

"Get up, Duncan."

I frown. "Why?"

"I've got some things to handle tonight, so I need to get your measurements and vitals down first. You can have dinner later."

I consider resisting, but when I see his angry eyes flick to Dee, I immediately say, "Okay, Glass."

I get up, leave the room, cast one last look at her.

"It's okay," she whispers, and she starts to sip soup from her spoon, as if eating alone in the large dining room is completely normal for her.

Maybe it's just me who is abnormal. Back in the home, we never ate alone. It was fifteen or twenty boys spread down a long steel table, each guarding their food, wolfing it down as fast as possible. In Thailand the whole village ate together in a communal dining hall.

I don't think I can remember the last time I ate alone.

That image of her, by herself, somehow unnerves me.

I realize I'm standing in the doorway looking at her. Glass has walked off toward the gym, and Dee is paying me no attention.

"Don't keep him waiting," she says. "Trust me."

"You eat alone a lot?"

She shrugs. "Pretty much every night."

"What about Frank?"

"Dad doesn't invite him in much."

"You mean he waits outside in the car?"

"Yeah."

I lick my lips. "What are you doing after dinner?"

"Homework, and then going to bed," she says, as if it's the most obvious thing ever.

I nod.

"You?"

"Probably get some weights in, then go for a run."

"So your own homework."

I grin. "Yeah."

Glass' voice booms through the house: "Duncan!"

"Go," she says.

It's so hard to drag myself away from her, but I do, jog toward the gym.

When I get there, Glass is waiting. He's set up a bunch of testing equipment and measuring equipment. Height, wingspan, vertical jump, standing reach, weight, body fat percentage by caliper – which is unreliable – blood pressure, heart rate, and some other machines I don't recognize.

"I'm going to need to take blood," he says.

"Why?"

"I want to see your resting oxygen saturation."

I realize there is a lot I have to learn, and for now, I hate to just have to blindly trust him. I don't much like that.

"What do you need all this for?"

"You've got a great body but it's not mature yet,"

he says, patting me on my chest. "You're hard, I know, low body fat, that's good. But we need to get more weight on you, especially here," he says, and he slaps my ass, and then my thighs. "You need lower body strength."

"Right."

"So these measurements will help me determine how to train you. McNamara will help us as well, he's got a team of doctors on his staff."

He pauses for a while as he sets up the equipment. "What do you think of my daughter, Deidre?"

I'm caught off-guard by the question. At first, I think he's going to issue me a warning, but the look in his eyes tells me that is not the case.

"She's seems smart."

He smiles. "She is. Very smart."

"Mature beyond her years."

"She always was precocious."

"Beautiful."

"She takes after her mother, but she could drop a few pounds."

"She doesn't need to," I say.

Glass flicks his eyes up to me, narrows them.

"You don't think so?"

"No, not that what I think is important. What *she* thinks is important."

"Learn a lesson from me, boy," he says, lifting a finger. "When you have kids of your own, you got to teach them how to think, or they'll pick up all the wrong shit."

"You can't force your ideas into someone else's head."

"You can."

"You shouldn't."

"That's philosophy," he says. "But if you can guide them down the right path, shouldn't you?"

"Do you guide Deidre?"

"I try to, but she is resistant to me. Always has been."

"Do you know why?"

"How the hell should I know?" Glass barks without an ounce of self-awareness.

I don't emote. It was the answer I expected.

"Now come here and stand against the wall, I need to measure your height."

"I'm six-three I say."

"I need exact measurements."

I shrug, do as he says, my mind on Dee for the whole time.

But when we're finally done, and I go looking for her around the house, I see that she's already gone into her room, already showered judging by the steam on the mirrors in the bathroom, and the lingering smell of shampoo and shower gel in the air.

So I shower, too, clean up, realize I have nothing to wear outside of a few pairs of new compression shorts Glass gave me to spar in. They were still in the wrappers, to my relief.

With no other choice I put them on, crawl into an unfamiliar bed, and instantly feel uncomfortable.

It's the softest fucking bed I've ever been in.

I get out, throw the pillow onto the carpeted floor, drag the sheets down with me, and lie down there instead.

This is more like it.

*

10

DEE

The screams keep me awake.

It's past midnight, and I have school in the morning, but I keep hearing the screams.

I hear shouting and crying. Dad's voice is shouting. Someone else's voice is crying. Someone's voice I don't recognize, but I do know it's a man's.

Then it stops. Finally, my heart can slow down. Finally, I can stop imagining what's going on downstairs.

But then I hear the footsteps. They stomp up the stairs, and I wince when I hear Dad's harsh voice call my name. Then he calls Duncan.

"Get down here, now! Both of you!"

I climb out of bed, put on a night robe, slip my feet into warm slippers, and open the door, squinting into the bright hallway.

"What is it, Dad?" I mumble, rubbing my eyes. I look down the hallway and see Duncan standing in nothing but tight spandex shorts, the kind cyclists wear, but they have a built in, padded crotch. On Duncan, it bulges.

I snap my eyes up from his center. The lights cause dark shadows to form along the lines of his muscles. He's got a really great—

"Put on some fucking clothes!" Dad yells at Duncan. "Then you and Dee come down to the living room." He storms off back downstairs.

I go toward Duncan. He looks concerned. "This isn't going to be good," I whisper, pulling my night robe tighter around me. My eyes linger on his chest for a moment before I force myself to look up, to meet his eyes.

"You should stay up here."

"No," I tell him. "Dad will shout at me. I don't want to deal with his bullshit."

"I'll deal with your father," Duncan says.

"Hey," I say, growing indignant. "I can handle myself. I don't need you to protect me. You've only been here one day!"

Duncan regards me for a moment, then disappears back inside his room. He comes out wearing his t-shirt and jeans, and together we walk toward the steps.

It's all dark downstairs except for the light pouring out of the corridor into the living room. I can hear whimpering.

I slow down on the landing, and my hand touches Duncan's by accident. He grips onto it, holds it, and it's like electricity shoots straight into my arm.

We look at each other. There's no more screaming anymore, there is only sobbing.

I pull my hand out of his, and my skin is left burning. "Come on, Duncan, we have to go down. Stop trying to protect me, I don't need it."

"He's been drinking. I can smell it."

"I know."

"He just wants to use you to make a point, Dee."

"Isn't that what he's doing with you?" I ask. A few seconds later I wish I hadn't. The bite was unnecessary, even if he didn't flinch. "Come on. Let's get this over with."

Together we walk into the living room. Dad is sitting in the sofa looking toward the fireplace.

Just in front of the fireplace is a man on his knees. He's got his head bowed, and there's something dripping off his chin.

It's blood.

"Frank," Dad says. Frank, behind the man, lifts his head up by his hair. I gasp when I see the bruised and broken face. It's completely misshapen, split open on both his cheekbones, and his eyes are swollen shut. I look away immediately. My hands start to shake.

"This is my family, Mr. Jung," Dad says. "This is who you are hurting."

"Please," the man says, shaking his head. "I didn't hurt anybody."

"When you don't pay me what you owe me, you hurt my livelihood. My livelihood is my family's livelihood. Now, you're an eastern fella, aren't you? Aren't you all always talking about family, tradition, all that? Isn't it strong in your culture over there? I trust you'll understand how important family is. My family is important to me."

"Please," the man says.

I grit my teeth together. I hate my father. I hate being in his family. I hate all this bullshit.

I look up at Duncan, but all he's doing is staring blankly at the man. How can this not affect him?

"You see my beautiful daughter," Dad says. "She's going to be a teacher. And my son, he's going to be a champion fighter. They are who I care about most in this world."

I roll my eyes. Dad only cares about himself. Duncan only *just* got here. It's all a show. It's all dramatics.

"Please," the man says. "I'll get your money. I need more time."

"When you come into my town," Dad continues, waving his hand. "And open your fucking little shops, your laundries, your fucking liquor stores, then I get to tax you. This is how it's always been. This is how it always will be. If you don't pay your tax, then you don't get to run your God damned fucking business! If you don't pay your tax, my family suffers!"

Dad's breathing hard, snarling. He's rabid… I can almost imagine saliva dripping from his mouth.

"I don't have it yet!" the man cries, his voice a dribbly slur. He can barely enunciate anymore, his lips are so puffy. "Business is not good."

"That's on you!" Dad roars. "Go to business school! I don't fucking care, that's not my problem. My problem is you have not paid me what you owe me. You are two weeks overdue. I expect it by Friday."

I grimace. Dad is just one big bully.

"That's not enough time," the man says. "I can't get it to you by then."

Dad looks at Frank, who nods and then thumps the man in the gut, drawing a howling moan of pain from his lips. He hauls him up to his feet, then slaps him across the face, dropping him back down to his knees.

"Look at my family," Dad says. "Look at them!"

The man looks up at me. My eyes are red. I know I shouldn't cry but I can't stop the tears from forming. I feel nothing but compassion for him, and wish I could make it end.

"I will be very angry if you hurt my family's livelihood again. Now get the fuck out of my house. You're getting my carpet dirty."

Frank hauls the man up, pushes him out of the room. I hear the front door open then shut.

"That is what fucking happens when you don't follow the rules in my fucking town!" Dad belts out, casting angry looks at us. He pours himself a big glass of something brown, and drains it in one gulp. Then his eyes settle on me.

I shrink as he approaches me. I don't miss that Duncan straightens his back, steps a little forward and in front of me.

"Are you crying?" Dad asks me.

I shake my head.

"Are you crying, damn it?"

"No," I say, my voice barely a whisper.

"You'd better not fucking be, not in front of anybody else, you got that? I can't have you crying in front of anybody. It's a bad look."

"What you did to him looked worse," I say.

"Oh, now you're going to get all sanctimonious on me? How do you think you have the life you do? Damn it, Deidre, why are you always so difficult?"

I shake my head. "You're a monster."

Dad opens his mouth to shout at me, and I wince, shutting my eyes, recoiling, taking a step back. I know it's going to be bad.

But the shouting never comes. I open my eyes to see Duncan's hand on Dad's shoulder. He's not saying anything, just staring at Dad.

Dad's eyes flicker between us, and then he fixes them on Duncan. "You better watch and learn," he says, his voice lowering. "You need to know how it works."

"It's late," Duncan says. "Don't we have an early start tomorrow? Long drive?"

Dad straightens his back, rubs a hand rapidly over his dome. "You are correct," he says.

Duncan's hand comes off Dad's shoulder.

I'm just shocked. I've never seen something like this before. The whole atmosphere changed. The air between us three has gone ice-cold.

"Had a bit too much to drink tonight," Dad says,

joking. "It's the good stuff. It was a gift from Mr. Jung."

Dad holds up a bottle of what I can now see is brandy. "Them Chinese fellas love their brandy, don't they?"

"Jung is a Korean name, Dad."

"Whatever," he slurs at me.

"You should go to bed," Duncan says, his voice even. "You don't want to be hung-over tomorrow."

"I haven't been hung-over in two decades, boy," Dad fires back, some of his nastiness returning. He pushes past Duncan, and starts climbing the steps, hanging precariously onto the railing. "Tell Frank to lock up on his way out. I expect to see him at seven tomorrow morning."

"Right," Duncan says.

We both watch Dad climb up the steps, wait until he disappears up to the third floor. We hear his bedroom door slam shut.

I look at Duncan, and he meets my eyes. I see… anger in his. He turns around, begins to walk away.

"Where are you going?" I ask.

His steps stop. The features on his face soften,

and he comes back to me, grabs my hand, and pulls me with him.

"Where are you taking me?"

But he doesn't answer. He pulls me through the house, and into the gym. A hard slap against the light switch, and the room buzzes into brightness.

Immediately, he's setting something up; the frame and the punching bag.

"You feel angry right now?" he asks me when he's finished setting it up. His eyes, now a blazing blue, are hard on mine.

"Yes," I tell him. "Angry… and sad."

"Do you feel powerless?"

I tilt my head to the side. That's a strange question. "I guess so."

"Come here," he says. I step toward him, and his fingers go to the edge of my robe.

"Hey."

"You can't wear this."

"What if I'm not wearing anything underneath," I say, pulling away from him.

"Aren't you?"

"I am," I say. I take off the robe. Beneath it I'm

wearing my pajama pants and a t-shirt. "But you can't just go taking off my clothes like that."

From the equipment cupboard, he produces a pair of gloves. "These are a bit big."

"What are we doing, Duncan?"

"Trust me," he says. "Okay? Will you please trust me, Dee?"

I shrug. "Fine, okay."

He takes my hands into his, and begins to wrap a bandage around them, delicately, but tight.

"What's that for?"

"Prevents injuries. Keeps your fingers from bending in ways they shouldn't. And your wrists."

He wraps it around, precisely, methodically, in a crisscrossing pattern he's obviously committed to memory.

When they're tight, he motions for me to ball my fists, and so I do. He slaps each of them, grips onto them, shakes my wrists.

"Good," he says before fixing the boxing gloves over my hands. They're bright blue, big, cushioned, surprisingly snug on the inside. And very warm.

"You're right handed," he says. "So you lead with

your left hand and your left foot. It may feel a little weird at first, but you want your strong arm in the back, not the front."

He bends down and grabs onto my thigh, and I yelp as he places it in position.

"Your left foot here," he says.

"Okay," I say, nodding.

"Okay, like this. Jab, yeah? With your left. Yes, just extend your arm quick, straight out in front of you, then pull it right back in."

I do it.

"Faster."

I do it faster.

"Watch," he says. He demonstrates it for me, lightning fast. He whacks the punching bag, his arm is out and back in an instant, like a snake striking. The thud against the bag is so loud it shocks me, and the chains rattle.

"Go on, you do it."

I jab, and my fist hits the bag. It thuds.

"Like that?" I ask.

"Pretty much," he says. "Do it again."

"Why?"

"Trust me."

I hit the bag again, listen to the thud, the chains rattle.

I hit it again.

Thud.

Rattle.

Again.

Whack.

Thud.

Rattle.

Again.

My hits become harder, faster. I become better at it in a matter of moments.

"Okay. Now, use your left foot to pivot." He holds me by the waist, turns me. I keep my left foot in place, but rotate my right foot around until I'm facing the other way. When his hands leave me, my skin is left tingling.

"Good," he says. "This is where you get your power from. It's not in the arms, it's in the hips and legs. This is a one-two. See? I jab with my left." He extends his left arm straight out. "But it's a fake or a test. He'll counter, dodge or slap it. Then I cross with my right." He throws a punch across his body with his right, at the same time pivoting on his left foot, getting his body behind the punch. "Your legs give you the power. It's a combo. Try it."

I do it slowly first. I jab with my left, straight out, then I pivot my weight, cross with my right with more power.

"Again," he says.

I do it again.

"Harder," he says.

I hit harder.

"Faster."

I hit faster.

Again.

Again.

I hit the bag, jab, pivot, cross, pivot, jab, pivot, cross, pivot.

The chains rattle constantly. The bag thuds with each of my hits. My hits get harder, faster.

Jab, cross.

Jab, cross.

Jab, jab, jab, punch, punch punch, punch…

I wail on the bag, hitting it as hard as I can, throwing my whole weight into every punch. I hit it and I hit it and I hit it until I realize that my eyes are wet, that tears are streaming down my face.

I keep hitting it, harder and harder.

I hit it so hard it shakes the bones in my body.

I hit it so hard my hands ache.

And then I hit it some more.

And then I kick it.

I kick it, and I kick it, and I kick it, and I scream as I beat on the bag, again, again, again, again.

And then I'm spent. It's over. I'm sweating, heaving, panting. I'm no longer crying. Somehow, I feel better.

I fall backward onto the mat, landing on my bum, and I hold onto my knees, sucking in oxygen. I glance up at the clock and see that twenty minutes have passed.

Twenty minutes!

I wipe my no-doubt red eyes, turn them on Duncan. He sits down opposite me, crosses his legs. He takes my right hand and begins to undo the glove. He takes them off one by one, then starts unwrapping the bandages around my fingers and wrists.

His fingers are so soft, so gentle with me. I just watch as he tends to me.

“You’ve bruised your knuckles a little,” he says quietly, holding my right hand and running his fingers over the knuckles. His touch sends sparklers sizzling through me.

I close my fist in his hands, squeeze, feel the pain of the bruise in my knuckles as the blood rushes there.

His hands close around mine, and then I unball my fist, and our fingers link at their tips.

“Is this what you do?”

He nods. “It works.”

“I never knew.”

“The bag is designed to be responsive. Your mind does the rest. I find it therapeutic.”

“I hate living here,” I say. It just slips out of me. “I hate everything about this place. About my life. I hate seeing all this shit. It’s not the first time I’ve watched Dad ‘teach a lesson’, and I know it won’t be the last. I can’t stand how he treats people.”

“I know,” Duncan tells me. “You’ll be able to move out soon. Once you go to college, right?”

I take in a deep breath. “Yeah. But *you* won’t.”

*

11

DEE

Duncan shrugs.

"Before this, I had nothing. Now, I have something." He looks at me, holds onto my hand tight. "I'll get out eventually. This won't last forever."

Our fingers entwine, and my breath hitches, and I want nothing more than to push myself into his arms. As if reading my mind, he scoots forward, captures me in his strong arms, and pulls me toward him. His hand is huge on the back of my neck, hot, and he tucks hair behind my ears, presses his forehead to mine.

"Are you okay?" he whispers.

"I'm fine," I say.

"You got a good workout in."

"Yeah," I say through a laugh.

I press myself into him more, and then turn, let him wrap me up from behind. I'm embarrassed that I've cried in front of him, and I don't want him to see my puffy eyes.

He holds me tight, his chest against my back, my fingers in his, and I'm thinking to myself that this is insane. What is going on? Why am I letting this happen? Why do I want this?

It would be a big mistake. It could never work, *never*! Not with Dad in the picture…

I feel his breath on my neck, and I lean back against him, growing more comfortable by the second, yet my heart only beats faster.

There's a voice inside me screaming: *Don't do this, Dee! You're a smart girl. What if Dad comes down?*

But I want to do this. I've wanted to be close to him since he first stepped out of that limousine… or maybe it even went back to Thailand.

"I never stopped thinking about you, Dee," he says quietly.

I don't reply. I don't know how to. All I know is that I thought about him too… often.

"You shouldn't have come here," I whisper, playing with his fingers. "You're trapped now, like me."

"Then I would never have seen you again."

"Dad will use you until you're broken, then throw you away."

"No he won't."

"He will."

"Dee, don't think about that anymore."

But I can't help it. "I feel so alone here."

I hear him suck in a breath of air as if my words somehow hurt him.

I pull his hands tighter around my body, and that's when I feel the tip of his nose by my ear. Unconsciously, I press myself to him, tilt my head to the side, and when his lips touch my skin he sets it on fire.

My breathing quickens, my heart starts to thump in my chest, and I hold onto his hands tighter as he kisses me again beneath my ear, and then again.

I turn to him, look into his gorgeous eyes, look at

his soft lips set within that granite jaw.

Now I say it: "I thought about you, too. All the time."

He kisses me, and I melt into his arms, fall into him as he claims my lips. It's the first kiss I've ever had with a boy, and I have no idea what I'm doing, but he kisses me so softly, so gently, as if guiding me with his own lips.

And I love the feeling of it, his lips on mine. It makes me tingle, makes me feel this building storm of anticipation in my belly, and butterflies… so many butterflies.

"Dee," he breathes, holding onto my face, kissing me harder. I fall into him more still, turn myself around, clamber on top of him so that I'm straddling him, and I hold onto his face, run my hands through his hair, kiss him harder, faster.

There's an urgency coursing through me, something I've not felt before. I press my body against him, imagine our heartbeats aligned as one, and his hands hold onto me, touch my neck, my collar bone, touch me lower still.

His fingers love my body, and in a hurried flurry I

take his t-shirt and pull it up. He gets it up over his head, throws it away, and I push against his shoulders, guide him down onto the mat. I look down his gorgeous, muscled, and tight body, feel my temperature skyrocketing, and then I'm on top of him, kissing his lips, and I feel the touch of his tongue.

My heart surges, and I push my tongue into his mouth, meet his, dance with his, and I love it even more. I never imagined it would feel this good, but somehow it does, and I can barely breathe, but I don't care. I never want him to stop kissing me.

I touch his hard chest, his tight body, but a moment of panic seizes me, and I break our kiss, lean up from him, my hair falling down around his face.

"I…," I begin, before trailing off. "I'm all sweaty."

Duncan smirks. "It's really sexy."

"I've never… you know."

"Don't be scared. I won't do anything you don't want to."

His tongue comes out, runs across his lower lip for a moment, and I have the sudden urge to lean back down and taste him again, but instead I get off him.

"Come on," I say. "We can't stay here."

Together we go upstairs to my room, and there he takes my hand, turns me, presses me against the wall, and kisses me again.

I latch onto him, link my arms behind his neck, and then I feel his hands on my thighs, and gasp when he lifts me up easily. I quickly latch my ankles around his waist.

Above him now, looking down on him, I kiss him feverishly again, and he carries me into my room, kicks the door shut behind him.

Our teeth bang into each other, the kiss is rough, not at all delicate, and I'm panting, my heart is racing, blood is thundering in my ears.

I'm so nervous, but so excited. I'm scared, worried that I won't know what to do, or what we even will do.

Here I am, inexperienced, a virgin, making out with my foster brother, and my hands are on his hard chest, and it's like I can feel electricity arcing into my body.

I moan onto his face, bite his lip, feel this intense

energy growing inside me. It washes the world away, and it's just Duncan with me here, and nothing else matters. Nothing else matters.

His hungry hands devour my body, grope me, squeeze me, knead me. I feel his palms on my ass, my thighs, run up my sides into my armpits, making me shiver, feel warm, then hot.

I can feel his desire for me pressing through his pants, pressing against me, and I hold onto his neck with just one arm and send the other in between us, down his sculpted body, to cup him through his jeans.

His heated eyes tunnel into mine, flick down to my lips, and he captures them again, like he needs my lips to live.

I feel so wanted, so desired, it's nothing I've ever felt before.

He sets me down, turns me around, then lifts my arms above my head. His fingers hook beneath my t-shirt, and he pulls it up over my head.

From behind me, he runs his hands tantalizingly down my body, cups my breasts, bites at the back of my neck and shoulder. He squeezes me, rolls my nipples softly, and I reach my hands over and behind me, run them through his hair.

He comes around my body, holds my hands behind my head, and he looks at me, my bared breasts, my body on display for him, and in his eyes I see a growing storm of desire.

Slowly, on my right arm, he kisses me from my elbow to my armpit, down my side, the wet dab of his tongue now and again setting my skin on fire.

He crouches down, and I lower my arms, grab onto his hair, watch and laugh as he takes the elastic of my pajama pants into his mouth, and he pulls it down slowly, his gorgeous eyes never leaving mine.

When I see my underwear, I say hastily, "Wait."

He stands up, and I put my hands on his chest, not knowing how to say it. I figure I should just come out and say it.

"I'm… you know, it's my first time doing something like this."

"I won't hurt you," he says.

"I know you won't. But… I guess I just don't know what to do." I feel so awkward and embarrassed saying it, so silly and stupid.

"Hey," he says, taking my face into his hand.

"Only do what you want to do."

I nod at him, bite my lip. "I do want to."

"Yeah?"

"But you should take charge."

He grins. "I can do that."

Duncan leans down, takes my lips in his again. I find myself surprised all over again at how soft they are, how gentle and yet forceful.

He guides me with his kiss, teases my tongue out, and our tongues dance and I wrap myself around him, feel the fire between us start to ignite again.

I love him holding me so close to him, feeling his body heat, the warmth of his breath, the touch of his fingers.

He moves me toward my bed, and I fall into it, and him on top of me, and he takes my arms and holds them above my head, leans up and looks at me for a moment.

My eyes travel down his body, sexy, tight, back up to his lips, his eyes.

"You're so fucking sexy," he tells me, and the way he looks at me makes me believe it. He leans down, kisses my neck, along the length of my collar bone, and his hands sweep up my body to knead my globes, before lowering himself to my stiff nipple and taking it into his mouth.

I grip the sheets behind me as he licks my nipple, as he sends shivers of sensation shooting up and down my body.

I bring one arm down, hold onto his head, run my hands through his hair, pull it, pull him down harder on me.

His tongue teases, and then I feel the press of his teeth and I suck in air. He moves to the other, teases me there, rolls my nipples in his finger, licks the skin in between my breasts.

And then he's moving down, his hands, fingers working my body like I'm an instrument, pulling soft sighs and moans from my lips.

I arch my back, stretch out on the bed as he kisses me around my navel. It tickles a little, but only a little, but it makes the hairs on the back of my neck stand up, makes me quiver.

He teases my pants off, leans up to look at me reverently, and then he's kissing around my navel, hooks his teeth into the elastic of my underwear, and pulls it down my legs.

And as I lie there, on the bed, looking at him, I know I'm feeling lustier than I ever have, and I know he can see it in my eyes.

He opens my thighs gently, slowly, a hand on each knee, bares me to him, displays my most private place to him.

Of course I feel the sting of modesty. I'm not clean-shaved – I don't think I should have to be – and I'm afraid he won't like me.

But he does. He leans down, buries his nose on my mound, smells me, and then I feel his warm tongue run up the side of my sex, and he makes my body tremble.

"I love that you don't shave," he growls, and he teases me, plants soft kisses around my center, every now and then touching my clit with his tongue.

I press my head into the pillow, run my hands over my breasts, down my body, find his hair and I thread my fingers through it, feel him, and then I push him onto me slowly.

His tongue presses against my folds, pulls up my

sex, and I let my eyes fall closed, raise my hips off the bed to meet him.

He starts to lick me, settles on my clit, flicks it left to right, and he goes so nice, so fast, I'm almost instantly in heaven.

I stretch out, undulate my body, grasp at him tighter, bring my hips up higher.

"Yes," I whisper, and his finger goes to my entrance, and he rings me, teases me, and I angle my hips down so his finger tip dips inside me.

I groan, tighten up at the sensation, and when he pushes his finger all the way inside me I can't help but to moan loudly at the sudden influx of feeling.

I feel like ink in water, coming apart, twirling about, and he licks me like he starves for me, thirsts for me, laps me like there's nothing else on Earth he'd rather be doing.

He angles his finger upward, rubs my front wall, and I grab hold of my breasts, breathe out some incomprehensible sound.

When I feel his lips wrap around my clit, suck it while still flicking me with his tongue, it's all I can do not to cry out. My temperature is rising, and he slides a second finger into me, pulling a long groan from my mouth.

He starts to finger me faster, lick me to the same rhythm, and I'm his captive, at his mercy, letting him drive me.

"Just like that," I tell him, though I know he needs no instruction. His fingers and tongue play me like an instrument.

"Fuck, like that," I breathe, my voice hoarser, deeper. "Like that, oh, God, yes!"

I lift my whole lower body off the bed, and I'm shaking and buzzing and gone all electric.

"Don't stop," I beg, I mewl. "Don't stop!"

He brings me racing into orbit, sends me soaring, and pleasure crashes over me, radiates outward from my center, sparkles down to my toes.

I grip at him hard, mash him into me, moaning and trembling and writing and squirming. I then squeeze, freeze, muscles tight, stomach crunching, stuck still in bliss.

And then I'm coming down, on the other side, panting, seeing stars, dizzy, and smiling.

"Fuck," I whisper, putting my hand to my head,

staring up at the ceiling, waiting for the world around us to slowly fill back in.

I pull him up my body, bring his lips to mine, kiss him, taste myself. I send my hands down urgently between us, unbutton his jeans and rip apart the flaps. I stick my hand down his compression shorts, grab onto his cock, start to pump him wildly.

I reposition myself on the bed, sit up against the headboard, with one hand grab his ass and pull him forward over me, his leg on either side of me, so that is manhood is closer to me.

With some difficulty, I pull his compression shorts down, and his jeans with them, and I jerk him, a kind of feral need to give him pleasure like he gave me pleasure thrilling through me.

I take his tip into my mouth, and I suck on it and swirl my tongue over it, taste his pre-cum, a little bit salty, a little bit sweet.

He leans back, groans, runs his fingers through my hair, pulls my hair toward him, makes me take him deeper down my throat.

I'm urgent with lust, don't even know if I'm doing it right, but at this point all that worry has all but drained away.

I work him as hard and as fast as I can, run my tongue up the back of his tip, bob my head to the movement of my hand.

It takes me only a short while to realize that he likes it when I press my tongue against the back of his tip, and so I focus on it, and I feel his thighs tighten, feel his body tense, and his hands grip my hair harder, and he groans hoarsely, "Shit, Dee, you're going to make me come."

I want to make him come, and so I go faster still, and soon he lets out a sharp sound of pleasure, and I feel his cock twitch in my mouth, feel him fire down my throat.

I struggle to swallow it all, but there's so much it dribbles out, runs down my chin, but I keep pumping him, keep milking him, keep wanting to make him feel good.

And then his hands loosen their grip of my hair, and his eyes, previously shut tight in pleasure, open, and he looks at me, and his blue orbs have turned a darker shade, full of desire.

I let him out of my mouth, wipe my chin, swallow the rest, thinking to myself that it doesn't taste nearly as strong as I'd imagined it would.

His lips come hungrily to mine, and he pushes his tongue into my mouth, kissing me, and I reach out and point to the bedroom drawer, tap on it.

Duncan leans over me, opens it, and then looks at me. I nod at him, and he pulls out a pack of condoms, tears one open.

He starts to take off his jeans the rest of the way, but I stop him, instead doing it myself, and I work them off his feet one at a time, my eyes never leaving his unsoftening manhood.

"Can I put it on?" I ask him.

I'm curious, anyway, and so I take the packet, pull out the slippery condom, and pinch the tip, and unroll it down his cock. It's hard to, he's so thick and long, and it doesn't reach all the way down to the bottom.

"Is it okay like this?"

He nods at me, climbs back on top of me. I love the way he kisses all over me. It's like he wants to take every inch of flesh into his mouth, every last sliver of my body. It's like he wants to taste me *everywhere*, as though there is nothing else in the world he could ever want more.

It seems naïve, thinking like that, but it's really what it feels like.

In between us, his manhood juts up, and I reach down, hold on to him. He's so hard for me, and he squeezes some muscle I never knew existed, and his cock jumps in my hand, grows even thicker, his tip swelling some more.

A drop of pre-cum oozes out – I can see it through the condom, and I rub my thumb over it, spread it over his tip through the lubricated latex, massage the back where I know he's sensitive.

I see his face ripple with pleasure, and his lips part, and his breathing quickens, and it turns me on so much to see him like this.

He strokes my thigh, guides it apart a little father, and then he lowers himself down to me. I look him in the eyes, and then I suck in a breath of air, bite my lip.

"Okay," I whisper.

I gasp when I feel his tip at my entrance, and I ring my arms around his neck, shutting my eyes, clenching my teeth as I feel him stretch me with the head of his manhood.

"Shit," I hiss, throwing my eyes wide open and groaning as he inches inside me.

I've never felt anything like this before. He stretches me, and for a fleeting moment I feel a hint of a sting, but then it dilutes in the overwhelming sensation.

"Slower, slower," I pant, and so he goes slower, slides into me gently.

My breathing quickens, I look at his lips, and he senses what I want, leans down, his hard muscles not shaking at all as he holds himself up while kissing me.

I pull his head harder on mine, lock my lips with his, and groan into his mouth as he inches inside me bit by bit.

He fills me up so completely, makes me feel so full on the inside. It's… amazing. It's overpowering.

I'm squeezing randomly around him, my whole body is shaking, and already I can feel that pressure again in my belly building up.

I reach down with one hand, clamp onto his hard ass, and I push him into me. He slides in all the way, bottoms out, draws a sharp moan from me.

"Wait," I say breathlessly. "Just wait a second."

He kisses me slowly, licks my lips, sucks on my tongue, and then when I run my hand across the side of his ass, to his hip, guide him up, he starts to pull out of me.

All at once I'm blinded. My body goes tight, and my mouth drops open, and I clamp onto his skin with my nails as he pulls himself all the way out of me.

It feels so damn good, so much more than just fingers which is all I've ever experienced before this.

As he pushes inside me again, I grow used to the way it feels, and I wrap my legs around his ass, push him down harder.

"God, you're so tight," he growls. "You make me feel so good."

He starts to slowly thrust in and out of me, and I control his speed with my legs, push my hands against his chest, feel his hard, tensing muscle.

I lean my head back, and his tongue sets the skin of my throat on fire.

"Oooh," I moan, overcome. I hold onto the headboard behind me as he fucks me, push down from it, raise my hips to meet his thrusts, utterly lost in the blissful sensation, in heaven.

"Faster," I gasp, and he goes faster, and in no time I'm writhing beneath him, eyes clamped tight, at the mercy of the pleasure he grants me.

I'm lost, so utterly lost, and as his lips hungrily claim the skin on my neck, by my ear, along the stretch that leads to my shoulder, I shiver, hum, smile, moan.

He slows down, and I grip onto him tight, feel his hard body, and then he pulls himself out of me, gets up, takes me by my hips and flips me over on the bed.

I try to get to my knees, but his hand goes to the small of my back, guides me back down.

"Lie flat," he tells me, and so I do, waiting, wondering what he's going to do.

I feel his fingers on my sex from behind, and he rubs my clit, kisses me down my back. Then I feel his tip at my entrance again. He pushes my thighs together, and then slowly enters me.

I gasp out loud, grip the bed sheets. I feel so much more this way – he feels so much bigger inside me – and I'm just floating in oblivion.

He eases into me, slowly, gently, giving me time to

get used to it, and then he takes my hair into his hand, twirls it around, pulls it.

A groan slips from my lips, and then he starts to fuck me from behind, and his cock is right against my front wall, and I feel better than I ever have before.

I feel fingers slip around my hip, in between my body and the bed, on my clit. He rubs me as he fucks me, and every nerve ending inside me is on fire.

He leans down, I feel the bite of his teeth on the back of my shoulder, and I know that I'm all his.

"Shit," I gasp, my breathing growing faster. It feel so good like this, so amazing, and his fingers working my clit so well, it's just too much.

I can feel that pressure inside me again, the climb upward toward the crest. His fingers are like magic, and the sting from how he pulls my hair is so hot, mixes in with all of it.

"Don't stop," I gasp at him, as I hear his breathing quicken behind me.

"You feel so good, Dee," he groans. "God, I love your tight pussy."

"Don't stop!" I cry again, my body pinching inward, the world draining away. "Like that, like that!"

I'm right there, right at the edge, already feel all my muscles crunching, my toes curling, this ball of pleasure inside me about to—

"Shit, shit, shit, oooohhh," I cry, pushed off the edge, for a moment in between two worlds.

Then ecstasy comes crashing down onto me, so intense it stops me breathing, and I squeeze around him, quake in bliss, and he drives me through it, keeps it going, and I buck back against him to each of his thrusts as I fly so high.

I'm somewhere wonderful, somewhere perfect.

"Come for me," I groan at him, the only words I can get out.

His thrusts get faster, I feel him get harder, feel him tense up. It's even more crazy, makes me feel even better, and then I hear him groan behind me, and feel his cock flex inside me again and again.

He lets out a long sound of pleasure, bottoms out one last time inside me, and I know he's emptied himself.

He lets go of my hair, lowers himself onto me, kisses my back while I pant, while my own pleasure ebbs away, leaving me tingling and satisfied.

"Oh, God," I whisper, lying my face down flat against the mattress. He's still inside me, still so big, and every time I feel his cock twitch I jump at the sensation.

He begins to retreat, and pull himself out of me, and I gasp, rolling over, looking up at him. He positions himself above me, leans down and kisses me.

I hold onto him, clamp my legs around him, bring his body down to mine. I get the covers, pull them up over us, and I keep kissing him, our tongues keep dancing, and I can't get enough.

And then we lie together, under the covers, and I'm grinning at him, thinking about all the horror stories I'd ever read about first times, and thinking how this was nothing like that.

I lie with Duncan in bed, in his arms, feeling his warmth beneath the covers. He's playing with my hair, stroking it, smelling it.

I feel worshipped.

His fingers trace buzzing lines up and down my body, still exploring me, as though he wants to commit the curves of my body to memory, so he can never forget me.

We meet eyes, and he smirks at me, and I smile back, push my face into his neck, smell his smell, feel his heat.

His insatiable fingers roam over my breasts, dip in between them, before sidling down my body. I feel them thread through my pubic hair, and then two fingers slip down each side of my sex, and he squeezes them together.

I'm not so sensitive anymore, and so I let him touch me, let him touch me while he kisses me. His body is hard, tight against mine, and I feel like I'm in a safe place.

His fingers move to my pearl, and there he finds my stub still hard, and he begins to rub me. At first, it's almost itchy, awkward because I'm still a little sensitive, but he rubs me slowly, so slowly, teases me, and I feel those threads of anticipation again worm through me.

I lie flat, open my legs for him, look up at him and beg him with my eyes to kiss me on the lips again. And he does, claims my lips as his, and he kisses me and rubs me until my body is hard and tight, until I'm right at the edge again.

And then he pushes me off, and I jolt and shudder at my orgasm, tense up and grit my teeth, and then I suck on his lower lip, bite it while I come, and then I'm coming down again, exhausted, utterly exhausted.

I hum into his mouth, grin, feel the wet press of his tongue on my lips.

Without speaking about it, I know he's going to stay with me tonight. We get out of bed together, and I watch as he pulls off his condom, full of his essence. He drops it into the waste paper basket in my room, and together we go out into the hallway, naked, shivering at the cool air, rushing and laughing, the thrill of being caught breathing a kind of excited, playful energy into us.

He slaps my bum as we go to the bathroom, pinches me, stops me and gathers me up, presses me against him.

We brush our teeth together, take turns peeing, and then we go to back the room together. But even as I lay in his arms, his huge, warm arms, his breathing slow and steady on the back of my neck, his nose pressed against my head, his thigh over my legs like he thinks I belong to him, I can't fall asleep.

And neither can he.

*

12

DEE

I lie with my head against Duncan's chest. I like listening to his breathing. It's so slow, controlled. I swear he breathes slower than I do. There's something relaxing, hypnotic even, about the movement of my head on his chest as it rises… then falls.

"Your heart," I whisper all of a sudden, frowning. "What the hell?"

"What is it?"

I gaze at my clock, watch the seconds hand tick by.

"It's really slow."

"Last time I measured, my resting rate was forty-five."

"Forty-five?" I echo in disbelief. I think the last time I measured, my resting was in the eighties.

Sometimes, as I listen, I think that his heart has stopped, but then I'll hear the beat, that one huge thud in his chest.

His skin is so warm, like he's got a burning furnace inside of him. His body heat radiates into me, and when he wraps me up in his arms, I feel so safe, so comfortable, like I've escaped from everything I don't like about my life, from the world altogether.

It's just me and him, together, alone, without a worry in the world. I've got school in the morning, but fuck it, I want to stay up. We shouldn't be in here together, lying naked like this, but fuck it, it's what I want to do.

I feel immature thinking this way. I feel like a caricature of a young adult rebelling, but I can't help it. It's just the way he makes me feel.

I run my hand over his stomach, feel the bump of every abdominal muscle. His body is so tight, so trained. I know it can't have been easy to get it like this. The discipline… it's attractive. He's in control of himself, and I like that.

"Duncan," I say, trailing my finger up his chest to where the deep black tattoo of a house is on one side. "What is this of?"

He shifts a little under me. "It's from a photograph," he says.

"Of a house?"

"The group home I spent the most time in."

"Why did you get a tattoo of it?"

"Have to remember where you came from."

"Sometimes some of us want to forget," I murmur.

He strokes my hair, fiddles with it, plays with it. I know he's going to make knots that I'll have to brush out, but I like that he does it.

"Was it like what you see on television? Living in a group home I mean."

"I don't know," he says. "Our television didn't work half the time."

"I mean, like, violence, drugs, kids skipping school, that kind of thing?"

He laughs. "I didn't go to school for three-quarters of the year."

"You didn't get in trouble for that?"

"Who would get me in trouble? The truancy officers didn't *really* care, they were just there for a quick buck. The teachers at the school focused on what they could: The kids who *did* turn up. Sand always falls through the cracks in your hand."

"What about social workers at the home?"

He delves into his memories. "There were other boys who took up all their time, constantly getting into fights, getting into trouble with the police. Shoplifting, usually, but some started working corners real early. Or doing drug runs on bicycles."

"Did you ever shoplift?"

"Yeah, every winter for nice jackets."

"How did you even get out of the shop with a huge coat?"

"We'd run a whole system, you know?" he says, a kind of half-guilty, half-mischievous grin tugging at his lips. "One boy distracts the staff, the other pretends to fall over and knocks some stuff over. A few of us walk in, grab, and run."

"Did you ever get caught?"

"Caught, no. Chased, yes." He sighs. "It's not like I'm proud of it. Half the time during winter we were never warm enough to spend a long time outside, and we always preferred to be outdoors than in the house."

"Why?"

"It was brighter. We'd fool around, you know? Spit at cars from a bridge, throw ice at people… that kind of thing. It was better than being in a shitty house that was barely warm enough and hardly clean enough."

"Was it tough?"

He shrugs. "I got used to it. There's a way things work like with anything in life."

"I read about it," I say. "It was in a book Frank gave me for my birthday before, written by a teacher who worked with kids like…" I trail off.

"Like me?"

"Yeah. Sorry, I don't mean it in a bad way."

"What's bad about it? I'm not ashamed of who I am or how I grew up."

"Anyway, the writer said violence is a big problem."

"Yeah, there are bullies. Nothing I couldn't handle, but some kids had it bad."

"How bad?"

"They just weren't tough up here," he says, tapping his temple. "That's what it takes. You don't have to be big or strong, you just got to be tough, not back down, not be afraid. They're only other boys just like you, you know? Other kids who are also scared. We were all rejected, unwanted. Kids take it out on each other, that's nothing new."

"Yeah, I read about that, too, but the teacher was writing from a girl's perspective. She said the toughest thing to deal with was constantly being reminded that you were unwanted, almost forgotten, you know? Like, it's something that's really easy to dwell on."

"When you're younger, yeah," Duncan says, and I swear I hear a hitch in his voice, just a momentary break in that hard, outer shell. "You stop thinking about that shit as you get older. And then maybe, once you get older than that, you start thinking about it again. But I'm not there yet."

"I read that in some group homes, the staff aren't even allowed to hug the kids. Every kid needs hugs, right?"

"Hugs?" Duncan echoes.

"Yeah," I say. "Affection. Otherwise they never learn to show it themselves. Group homes don't prepare kids for normal adult life. They…"

My voice trails off. I'm embarrassed to have said that.

"I'm sorry."

Duncan shrugs. "Like I said, I don't think about that shit."

But I don't believe him. Otherwise, why would he get the tattoo of the house? It doesn't make sense.

"I got this just to remind me, you know."

I blink. It's like he can read my mind.

"If you were wondering."

"I was." I decide to change the subject. "What about this?" I say, tracing the outline of his other big tattoo, a leaping tiger. It's not snarling ferociously or anything, but it seems to be leaping over the house. It takes up the whole other side of his chest and stomach.

"I got that in Thailand," he says. "Result of a drunken night out."

"You went out drinking?"

"Yeah. Me and another kid from the village would sneak out, go into town, hit up the bars. It was always good for a laugh, all the foreign tourists making asses of themselves. Sure, I mean, I wasn't Thai, you know, so I still was not one of them, but I mean, I caught on quick. Some of these guys, just embarrassing. They'd be falling off barstools, getting cleaned out by all the waitresses and dancers who knew an easy mark when they saw one."

"Sounds fun," I lie, not bothering to hide my distaste in my voice.

"You don't like it."

"I know the reputation Thailand has. I mean, the red-light reputation."

"It's not all like that," he says, gently stroking my arm. "Actually, for the most part it's pretty straight forward these days, but yes, there is a rep. Hey, it's a poor country, and tourists bring their money in."

"I don't like it," I say, knowing that maybe I'm being harsh, maybe I'm being judgmental. "Dad has pimps out here working for him, and they force the girls, give them no choice. I know it, and I hate it, and I bet for a lot of those girls over there, it's the same."

"I bet it is, too."

"So why the tiger?" I say.

"Well, to be honest with you, it was the kid's idea."

"The kid?"

"Yeah, the other boy from the village. He was the closest one to my age, younger than me by a year I think. He said the tiger symbolized unconditional confidence and discipline in Buddhism, which was their faith… philosophy. He said the bald white man – what they called your Dad – was trying to make me his pet, and only through unconditional confidence in myself, and mental discipline, could I resist being enslaved."

He shrugs.

"Why over the house?"

"I have to be confident about who I am, and that includes where I came from."

"Huh," I say. I didn't actually expect the tattoo to have that much sentimental significance, though I don't know why. Dad's always hated tattoos, but now that I think about it, he hasn't mentioned them with regard to Duncan once.

"What about these?" I run my hand over his

shoulder, over the intricate script that adorns it, stretches around onto his back. It's weird, because on his arms, he's got tribal-inspired lines as well that run even on the underside his arms and down his ribcage and waist. It's two totally different styles.

"The older ones, the tribal stuff, that was when I was a kid. You can see it's all stretched because I didn't hit my big growth spurt until I was about seventeen."

"You got them before Thailand?"

"Oh, yeah. Worked for a tattoo artist briefly, helped to clean up and watch the shop when he was too blazed out of his mind to come into work. He did these for me for free."

I trace the jagged, flowing lines, am reminded of a serrated edge… maybe a dragon's tail.

"And this stuff? The script?"

He rolls over, shows me his back. There I see lines upon lines of script, with some illustrations inlaid, like a magazine article or something. It covers his entire back.

"That's Thai, a blessing from a Buddhist monk."

I peer at the illustrations, try to make them out.

He's got four animals on his back, a tiger, a dragon, a fish, and something that looks like a bird. They sit at four points of a square, and inside is a depiction of a temple, surrounded by lines and lines of those flowing, liquid words.

"What does it say?"

"I don't know," he says. "They don't tell you, and I never asked someone to translate."

"Why not?"

He pauses, seems to think about it for a moment. "Because now it can say anything I want it to, I guess."

"Was it the same monk who trained you to fight?"

"No. I had to go to a temple in the hills. My instructor took me. It was something he insisted on, and I saw no real reason not to. He said the ink they use is imbued with magic properties, and contains venom of a snake."

"Really?" I ask, doubtful.

He shrugs. "We had to line up for three days, just waiting outside the temple. I wasn't too interested, but he said it would protect me, make me incorruptible."

"Did it hurt?"

"A little."

"I kind of want a tattoo."

"Do you know what of?"

"No," I say truthfully. "Not really." I laugh. "I don't know, I like the idea, you know? It makes me feel kind of bad."

"Get one if you like. It's your decision."

"It's harder for girls to get tattoos."

"How so?"

"We're judged more."

He turns a raised eyebrow at me, shakes his head.

"Think about it. There's no equivalent for the word 'tramp stamp' for men's tattoos, right? It's just not the same. It's cool when a guy has tattoos, but if a girl has it, she's 'alternative' or whatever. Or going through a 'phase'. Or people just assume it was a product of a drunk-night-out, you know? Or they think it's 'slutty' or 'skanky'."

"Who cares what people think? You can't control that."

"Easy for you to say."

"If you ever decide you want a tattoo, Dee, I'll

support you. I'll come with you."

I smile. "Thanks, but I don't think that I ever will. Dad would hate it."

"Don't let him know."

"Are you kidding me?" I cry. "God, I'd get an earful. He'd never stop."

Duncan's tongue wets his lips. He rolls onto his back again, and I lie in his arms.

"I'm not tired," I tell him.

"Neither."

"I can't stop thinking about that guy, his swollen eyes… God, I hate living here."

"You want to get out of here?" Duncan asks. "Tonight, I mean."

"Go where?"

"Anywhere."

"Why?"

"Well… we could just say good night and go to sleep," he says. "But I don't want tomorrow to come. Tomorrow, I leave… and I don't know for how long."

"To train," I whisper. "With one of Dad's old boxing buddies."

"Yeah."

"I don't want tonight to end, either."

"Come on, then. Let's go."

"But where?"

"Fuck it, we'll go anywhere."

He gets up, and I look at his naked, athletic, strong body, and then see that he's caught me checking him out.

"Can't a girl look?" I ask him.

"Look all you want. I want you to look."

He starts to pull on his clothes, then extends an arm out to me. "Let's go have some fun."

I pause, then shake my head. "We shouldn't. What if Dad catches us?"

"Fuck him, he's out cold," he says. "Come on, Dee. Live a little."

I look at him for a moment, and it's like a light switch just flips in my head. Why not, right? Why not be bad for once? Why not break the rules for once?

I get dressed with Duncan, ask him to empty my trash can into a plastic bag so we can take it out with us and chuck it. I don't want to leave a condom in my room.

I tell him that I know a place we can go, a mall I used to go to as a kid.

"A mall?" he asks, a look of puzzlement on his face.

"We can go to the ice rink," I tell him, grinning.

*

13

DUNCAN

I put on a jacket, wait for her in the corridor, and she emerges wearing a black hoodie and dark jeans. She's got her hood up, the cords pulled tight so that it wrinkles in a circle around her face.

"Why are you laughing?" she asks, as if she's accusing me of making fun of her.

"Nothing," I say.

"Tell me," she says. "Or I won't go with you."

I see the flicker of a smile on her face, and say, "You just look like you're about to rob a store or something."

She fingers the rippled edge of her hood, grins. "Is there a dress code for that?"

I shrug. "You tell me."

We share a small silence, and I put my hand out. She looks at it for a moment, and there's this… stoppage of time, as if someone has pressed the pause button on our lives.

We look at each other for what feels like an eternity. When she takes my hand, holds it, it fills me with some crazy kind of feeling, like I've got bubbles inside of me, floating me up.

I've never felt this before.

"You ready?"

She nods. "Sure."

We creep down the hallway together, even though we have no real need to. Frank is long gone, the staff has left, and Glass must be in a deep and drunken sleep.

We slink to the garage, adjacent and unconnected to the house, and open a door with squeaky hinges. I spot the silver key box on the wall, open it and look through the sets of dangling car keys.

"Which car is your favorite?" I ask, looking out at the cars parked. There's a Ferrari, a BMW coupe, a Camaro, a boxy SUV I don't recognize, a… it dawns on me that outside of the SUV, there isn't really a *family* car in here. Just two-door sports cars.

"I always liked this one," she says, pointing to a small, old-ish hatchback hiding behind the SUV. It looks like it hasn't been driven in a while.

I look for the corresponding key, take it, and open the driver's side.

"Wait, I thought I was driving," she says. "Do you even have a license?"

I blink. "Yeah, actually. We got driving lessons at the home. They even had somebody come down every day, and if we were old enough we'd take turns. Glass had me do a bunch of hours in Thailand at the best school they have there, then had my license converted for here."

"Oh," she says. It's this bizarre moment, like we've just come face-to-face with the fact of how little we actually know each other.

As we get into the car, I'm suddenly pulled back into an old memory, one that makes me grin at the stupidity of it, but also makes me cringe at the stupidity of it.

"What's so funny?"

"I was just remembering something."

"What? Tell me."

"Before I went to Thailand, sometimes the boys at the home and I… we'd, well, we'd go for joyrides. We could boost a car in fifteen seconds."

"You stole cars?"

"Borrowed them."

"What do you mean?"

"We usually left them somewhere nearby where we took them. We just did it to drive around at night."

"You never got caught?"

"Sure we did," I say. "Squad car rolls up, all flashing red and blue, and we split in different directions. They never get us. Half the time they weren't even up for a proper chase even in their cars, let alone on foot."

"I had no idea it was that easy to steal a car."

"Sure it is," I say. "How many cars are stolen per year? I'd bet fucking loads. You think every car thief is a genius?"

Dee puts out her hand, and I furrow my brow, shake my head.

"The keys," she says. "Give them to me."

"Why?"

I see a playful grin spread her lips. "Prove to me what you just said was true."

"About boosting cars?"

"Yeah. In fifteen seconds."

"Alright," I say, returning her smile and dropping the keys into her open palm. "Are you going to time me?"

"Just do it already."

I shrug, and say, "I'm going to need the keys, though."

She just tilts her head to the side.

"Actually," I say, digging through my pocket. I pull out my set of house keys that Glass gave me. "It's fine."

I peel off the plastic seals covering the screws on the steering column, use a key to unscrew them. I crack it open, find the wiring harness connector, and pull out the battery, ignition and starter bundle of wires. I use my key to strip them, twirl the battery and ignition wires together, and then spark them with the starter wire.

The car rumbles to life, and I rev the engine to prevent a stall.

All in all, it took about thirty seconds, but I'm out of practice.

"Holy shit," Deidre breathes. "I didn't think you'd actually do it."

"Good thing you picked this car," I tell her with a smirk. "Only works on older models."

"Can you fix… it?" she asks. "So Dad won't know?"

"Don't worry, I'll deal with your father if he finds out. I'll just tell him I borrowed the car, but didn't know where he kept the keys."

"He won't like that."

"Seems like nobody has driven this car in a while, though."

"You're right," Dee says. "This was Mom's car."

I lick my lips as realization oozes all over me like lava. *I just vandalized her dead mother's car!*

I look at Dee. The atmosphere has grown somber in just an instant.

"Oh, don't worry," she says quickly. "I don't care about the car."

"What happened to your mother, Dee?" I ask her gently.

"She died when I was young. That's all I know. I don't know how or why. Dad never talks about her."

"I'm sorry."

"Me, too. I can't even remember what she looks like, and Dad doesn't keep photos around the house. Sometimes that bothers me, you know? But most of the time, I just don't think about it." She turns to me. "Do you know what your mother looks like?"

I shake my head. "She left me on a church doorstep as a baby. Never met her, never seen her, never heard her. Well, not literally never, just nothing that I can remember."

"Would you want to? See her I mean… hear her?"

I suck in a breath of air. It's a question I've thought about for a long time. "Sure," I say eventually.

"But why? She just abandoned you. She wasn't there for you."

"People do all kinds of shit," I tell her. I don't know how to put my thoughts into words. "I do what I want, and I don't *want* to hold a grudge against my own mother. Even if her reasons were stupid, or bad, or whatever… how can I stay bitter?"

"But your life could have been so different."

"It could have been worse," I say. "She wasn't a stable person, and had a drug habit to boot."

Dee fidgets. "Really?"

"That's what I was told."

"By whom?"

"She was seen leaving me. People around the area knew her, everybody knew what she was about. *I* found out from a social worker who lived in the area and worked in the home."

"Is she still alive?"

I shrug. "I don't know."

Dee pauses for a moment, then asks me, "But wouldn't that mean that when she was pregnant—"

"Obviously she stopped using during that time," I say. "That must have been hell for her. But for that, I'll always owe her one."

"Owe her one," Dee echoes.

"Yeah," I say. "My life, probably."

"Come on, let's go," she says, looking straight

ahead. "And change the subject. Let's not talk about our parents."

I put the car into gear and drive us out of the garage. The doors are automatic, don't require a signal. Nobody breaks into Johnny Marino's house and steals his cars. Not unless they want to end up floating face-down in the river.

"Tell me where to go," I say.

Dee gives me rough directions, and after a bit of searching, we come to the mall. I park the car beneath a tree, shield it in the shadow, and together we climb out and walk through the near-empty parking lot.

"This way," she says, taking my hand. "There's something eerie about walking through an empty mall at night, don't you think?"

We pass by a guard post, and I spy that he's sleeping, slumped into his chair, newspaper on his chest. I stop, peer at him, measure how deep he's sleeping. His breaths are very slow; he's been out for a while. Coffee sits cool in a paper cup, untouched, not steaming.

"What are you doing?" Dee hisses at me, but I put

a finger to my lips. I kneel down, turn the doorknob carefully, pull open the door, wincing as it creaks.

The guard doesn't move. I reach out, unclip his keys from his belt, clasp them in my hand so they don't jingle, and then shut the door.

"Damn it, Duncan!" she breathes as we walk away. "Tell me before you do shit like that."

At the main entrance to the mall, I unlock the door inset into the steel shutters that have been pulled down, and we weave our way through dark hallways.

"Here," she says, leading me down a set of steps until we come to a wide double-door. I test the door, find it unlocked, and we walk in, and instantly feel the cold of the indoor ice rink.

Dee guides me to the seats that surround the rink, and sits down, puts her feet up on the chair in front, and holds herself, shivering.

I sit down next to her, wrap my arm around her, and ask her, "Why did we come here?"

"Frank used to take me. I spent more time with him growing up than with Dad. He… well, he kind of raised me. I mean, he wasn't a surrogate father or anything," she says, scoffing at the thought. "In fact,

I'm not sure he should *ever* be a father. But… he was there for me more than Dad was."

"Do you like him?"

"I used to… a lot. We got along, you know? I found him funny, and he seemed soft and less threatening than Dad. Frank's like a teddy bear, and compared to Dad who is more like a… I don't know, a cannon ball or something, it was just easier."

"Frank may look soft, but I'd guess he isn't at all."

"No," she says. "He can handle himself. Anyway, then I found out what he did regularly… like what he did to that poor man tonight."

"And you stopped liking him."

"Not really… I don't know how to explain it. I just like him less, but I still like him. He's always kind to me. He's pretty thoughtful, actually, for a man so utterly devoted to my father."

"Huh. I haven't really had a chance to speak with him."

"He's alright, but he's a slave to Dad. He's super loyal, that's why Dad keeps him around. You need loyal people."

"Especially if he's your driver and bodyguard."

"Exactly."

After a moment, I turn to Dee. "Let's go ice skating."

"How? The ice is covered."

"Come on, I'm sure we can get it off."

I stand up, take her hand, and together we amble toward the office and booking area. I see the control panel, find the corresponding key on the guard's chain, and unlock it.

There's a bright green button with a stenciled label beneath which reads 'Cover'. I press it, and there's a loud humming, a grinding of gears, and then the cover is pulled back across the ice, and into a recess on the long, closest side of the rink.

The ice glows in the darkness. I know it's just a reflection of the moonlight streaming through the windows, but it looks unreal. From here, it's too dark to see all the seats surrounding the rink. We might as well be standing alone together on an ice berg.

With Dee, I go to the shelves where they stack the skates, pick out my size, then help her find hers. We put them on, waddle onto the ice, and skate for what feels like hours.

We chat, hold hands, and she shows off some kind of ballerina-style spin which I could never hope to mimic. I try, of course. I'm never above trying.

But I fail hard, and land on my ass.

We race, go as fast as we can, laugh, and then eventually just start skating around in circles, hand in hand, again and again as if we were rehearsing for *NASCAR On Ice*.

I never want this night to end.

But a bright beam of light washes over us, and I jerk my head toward the entrance, see the door open. A guard is descending the steps, flashlight aimed at us.

"Fuck," Dee whispers.

"It's fine," I tell her. "Nothing will happen."

"You two!" the guard shouts. I can't see what he's doing; the light is blinding. "Off the God damn ice!"

We exit the rink, and then the guard draws up close to us. I hear the click of his radio, and know he's thumbed the transmit button. He's going to call it in.

"Wait," I say. "We were just messing around."

His flashlight beams at my face, then moves to

Dee's, then lingers there for a moment.

"You," he murmurs at Dee, who just frowns in response while shielding her eyes. "I know you."

He lowers the flashlight, and I have to blink rapidly to adjust to the darkness. I see the same guard I took the keys from. He must be in his sixties, and he's got a white mustache and looks frail and weak.

"Here," I say, handing him his keys.

He chews on his mustache for a moment, but doesn't say anything to me. That catches me off-guard. Something feels off.

"Do you remember me, young lady?" he asks after a moment, straightening up.

Dee shakes her head. "I'm sorry, sir, I don't."

"Well, I remember you, from when you were just a little girl… and I know who you are."

The guard looks caught between a rock and a hard place. He shuffles on the spot for a moment, then flaps his hand at us.

"Oh, it's not worth it. You two stay here for however long you like."

"Wait," Dee says.

"Now, I don't want any trouble," he says, recoiling

from Dee. He steps backward, palms up. "You do what you like."

"Who am I?" Dee asks.

"Why, you're Johnny Marino's daughter," he says, stumbling over his words.

There's a still silence, and then Dee just sighs.

"It's okay, we're leaving."

"You can stay as long as you like, now. I won't stop you."

"We're leaving," Dee says, and she steps forward, and touches the man's shoulder. "Don't worry. Don't be afraid."

"N-now, I'm not kicking you out. You want to skate, you can—"

Deidre's voice is soft, calming. "It's okay," she says. "We were going anyway. Don't worry. I'm sorry we snuck in here. We were wrong, and you're just doing your job. I won't tell a soul."

The guard grumbles to himself, but acquiesces.

I look at Dee, a new admiration for her growing. She read him perfectly, calmed him, reassured him when she didn't have to.

She could have brandished that power her name

gave her, wielded it, but she didn't.

She's nothing like her father.

"I'm sorry if we've caused you trouble," Dee says, taking my hand. "We'll make sure everything is put back properly."

We're true to her word, stack the skates back, re-cover the ice, and then she tugs my hand, says, "Come on, let's go."

We leave the building, walk out of the mall back to the car.

"Does that happen a lot?" I ask.

"Yeah," she says with a sigh. "Can you imagine how hard it is to make friends when everybody around you walks on eggshells?"

"It bothers you," I say.

"Sure it does. I don't *want* people to be scared of me. I'm not scary!"

With a kind of imprisoned frustration, she climbs into the car, shuts the door hard. I get in after her, start the engine by sparking the exposed wiring again, and then drive us back toward her home.

The mood has changed, and she stares out of the window, chewing her nails, so I don't talk. She doesn't seem to want it.

"Sorry," she says after a while. "I just hate it when shit like that happens."

"Don't sweat it."

"I wish you weren't going tomorrow," she says. It's a thump right in my gut, one that is harder than any hit I ever took in a fight.

"Same."

"But you have to, don't you?"

I grind my teeth together for a moment. Now *I* feel caught between a rock and a hard place. "Yeah," I say. "I think I do."

"I know you do," she says, looking away from me again out of the window.

We drive in silence the rest of the way, and when we get back, park the car, sneak inside, she tries to go to her room without saying a word, but I ring her wrist and tug her toward me.

"I'll be back, though," I say.

"Not for six months or however long Dad wants to train you for."

"But I'll be back."

She doesn't reply, just slips herself from my grip,

and leaves me in the hallway, so that all I have is her faint, lingering scent, and her look of disappointment burned into my mind.

*

14

DUNCAN

It is surprising how quickly time flies when you're looking ahead to something.

I look ahead to seeing Dee, every damn day.

McNamara and Glass train me individually day after day, the former in the morning, the latter in the evenings. In the afternoons I work on my conditioning with the other boys at the camp. We skip rope, run sprints, and then do calisthenics, the kind most people would find extreme.

We fall down from a standing position into a push up, and then push ourselves up into that standing position. We do handstands with no support, then dip down until our heads touch the floor, before straightening out our arms. Then we do it again balancing weights on our feet.

Even with the blood rushing into my head, my face no doubt a swollen red, and my shoulders and triceps shaking by the time I get to my fiftieth repetition, all I'm thinking about is Dee.

I think about how we went ice skating, how when I looked back as Glass drove me away I saw her in the window, waving. That smile… those eyes.

I think about her lips, our kiss, the feel of her hot breath on my face, being so close to her, so intimate.

Glass thumps me in the gut, and I fall over in a heap. I growl, get to my feet quickly, angry at the unprovoked attack, but he just stares at me.

"Look down."

I look down, and am a little embarrassed to find I have an erection.

Glass slaps my head, and I strike out instantly, stop my fist at the last moment hovering millimeters from his face. He's winced, leaned back, recoiled.

I pull back my fist. "Reflex," I tell him bluntly.

He points a finger at me, tells me to focus. "I know what it's like to be your age, but focus. Stop thinking about girls. You're a fighter now, an athlete. Girls will only unravel you. They will only prevent you from becoming all you can be."

He walks stiffly on, and I become aware of the other boys in the camp gazing at me. I meet their eyes, and we all share a cheeky, childish snicker, and then I get myself into a handstand again, and start dipping.

Girls. Glass wasn't too far off the mark, but he was wrong enough. I wasn't thinking about girls in the plural. I was only thinking about one girl.

The days blur together. Glass and McNamara teach me old-school moves, and new-school ones, too. They teach me how to feint, how to feint like I'm going to feint, and then how to feint that I'm going to feint that I'm going to feint.

Fighting's not just two brutes wailing on each other in a cage. If you're a moron, you'll never be good at it.

I learn how to chain moves together. You don't reset after each punch, kick, or block. Fighting is fluid, flows like water taking bends in a creek. You read and adapt. Read and adapt. You bend like water. Obstacles don't stop you, you just go around them, over them, under them.

Opponent jabs, I dodge, use my momentum, turn it into a kick. Opponent ducks the head kick, I spin into an elbow. Opponent slaps the elbow away, I duck into fast gut punches. And so on. All moves strung together, no pauses, no stops, no resets. You think on the fly, and you *have* to think.

People fancy that boxers, that MMA fighters, that kickboxers are stupid, fools, idiots. Just men who get hit in the head too much that they slur their speech.

They don't understand that fighting is like chess – not that I've ever played it – but you know what they say, always be thinking so many moves ahead.

Before I know it, three months have passed, and I know that I'm over the hump, on the downside of the hill now. Now, I see Dee in fewer days than I've been away from her.

We've not been allowed any contact with the outside world. In here, there is one thing and one thing only: Training. Sure, the other boys and I shoot the shit. A lot of them are like me, just looking to do something with their lives.

It burns me that I can't contact Dee, can't even call her. No phones on the camp, no computers, no internet. No kid has a mobile phone. There is only a payphone five miles away – I snuck out there one night, ran the road, to call her. The payphone was busted, looked like it hadn't been used in years.

So every day I wonder how she is. I wonder if she does well at school… she seems like she would. I don't get the impression she works her ass off, but I think she's a good and smart student.

I wonder what she does day to day. How different are our daily schedules? And then I think of her eating dinner alone, every night. Heck, she probably prefers it. She has a laptop, and there's the huge television, and then there's the library in the house, and all those books…

Books. I don't think I've ever finished a book… at least not one that I can remember.

The second half of my training involves endurance. Not fitness, not motor, not how long you can go for, but how much you can take.

Fighting's not about how hard you hit. You don't have to hit that hard to knock someone out, to force the brain to fire synapses that pull a person into unconsciousness as a protective mechanism.

No, fighting's about how hard you can get hit. Fighting's about pain threshold, toughness. These are things that can be trained, and we train them.

I take hits from Glass and McNamara. To the face, to the arms, to the shoulders, to the chest, the trunk, the legs, the calves.

They kick me and punch me, and I come roaring back for more. I swear at them, shout at them, unable to hit back. I bellow curses at them, and when they think I've had enough, I taunt them, ask them if that's all they've got.

But then I get used to it. Then I take it silently. Kicks, punches, slaps. Every night I have new bruises, and every day we do it again.

Desensitization, and mental discipline. That's all it is.

It's these last few weeks that pass by quicker. For every punch I endure, I think of Dee, and threaten to smile. If I smile, Glass just hits me harder.

Sometimes I smile. I'll take the hit.

By the end of it, we're in full-on sparring matches.

Glass can't keep up with me, so I spar with McNamara. He's got that old-man strength you can never underestimate. It's not muscle mass at that point, it's central nervous system.

He's got that old-man endurance, too. He doesn't even *feel* pain.

We spar twenty times in twenty days, pure boxing, no MMA, no take-downs. I win sixteen times, five times by knockout, the rest concession. The four I lost, McNamara surprised me with them old-man tricks.

After our last fight, Glass comes to me, grinning widely, his eyes shining. "God damn it, boy," he says, throwing an arm around my shoulder and squeezing me into him. "You're fucking magic, baby."

I take off my gloves, unwrap my hands, and then go to McNamara, still on the ground, holding onto his eye. Blood streams down the side of his face, but he takes my arm and I help him up.

"Good fight," I tell him, and we tap fists.

"Wasn't for me," he jokes. "It's been good having you here, Duncan. You did good. I'm sure fucking glad you're done here, because I don't think I can take any more of this."

"Sure you can," I say, nodding toward his trophy cabinet. "They once called you champ."

"You'll earn that name soon," he tells me, slapping my shoulder affectionately.

We leave later that afternoon. During the drive back – we take turns – he talks about how much better I look. I've put on weight, maybe twenty-five pounds of lean mass in the last six months, without losing any speed or agility.

They fed me five thousand calories a day at McNamara's fighting camp, and when you're not eating junk, you really come to appreciate just how much food that is.

Boiled chicken, brown rice, and broccoli six times a day, basically. Full-sized meals. On top of that were the multitude of supplements, and the post-workout protein milkshakes blended with egg whites.

I stayed away from the stimulants, though. Some of the other's liked it, yohimbine, caffeine, even just green tea extract. But I can't take it. It fucks with my rhythm.

Glass slaps the steering wheel in excitement, then looks and me and laughs. "We're going to give all those fuckers a real surprise with you, boy."

Those fuckers. The other mob families and groups he hopes to swindle by selling me as an underdog so they bet against me.

It won't last for long, but at the start, he'll make a killing.

And I'll get my share.

And yet… all I can think about is what *Dee* will think about that.

Will she begrudge my taking part in her father's plan?

I know that I am going to fight, and I know that I am going to make money, and I know that I am going to be the best.

But I haven't thought past that. I could go pro at some point like Glass will want me to, but dealing with the politics and intricacies on that stage doesn't particularly interest me.

No, the more appealing idea is to just walk away when I've had enough, take my money, and go.

But it's only more appealing if I have Dee going with me.

I suck on my lower lip for a moment, then engage with Glass who's chattering animatedly about his plans.

I need to stop looking so far ahead with Dee.

There's no telling how much she may have changed in these past six months, whether our last night together will mean as much to her as it still does to me.

And beyond that, there's no telling about our future, about how things will play out.

Shit, everything could go to fucking hell.

I try to imagine the worst situations, the ones I hate the most, and find that in all of them, Dee and I are not together.

*

15

DEE

It's graduation, and of course Dad's not here. I don't know when him and Duncan are going to return home. He hasn't called once, and I'm sure that he's the reason Duncan hasn't called, either. I thought I'd at least get a postcard or letter, but nothing turned up.

If I had to guess, it'd be that Dad's kept Duncan locked up like a princess in a tower. I have to *rely* on that assumption, because I don't want to think about the idea that maybe… maybe Duncan just chose not to call.

For six months it's just been Frank and I at home. He tried to cook meals, but it was usually some variation of eggs on toast or tinned food. Not exactly healthy. I ended up cooking for *him*.

I sit in my gown, watch on as several people on stage make speeches, but I don't really listen to any of them.

I grow hot and bored, feel my dress under my gown clinging to my back. The sun is warm overhead, and I'm frustrated, so that just makes me even more uncomfortable.

I don't care that Dad's not here, anyway. I'm still angry at him because he specifically ordered Frank not to let me go to prom. His reason? It was too big of a *risk*.

Right, like a bunch of high school students dressing up and dancing in a rented ballroom of some three-star hotel is too great of a risk. He's just a control freak, wants to control every aspect of my life, even when he's in a different state.

It doesn't matter that I heard prom kind of sucked. The rumors were that nobody spiked the punch bowl, that the music was too quiet, that the room was poorly ventilated, that the carpet wasn't washed, and that it smelled like old gym socks… but I would still like to have been there myself rather than learning about it through the photos and comments everybody else uploaded.

I sigh. This speech is dragging on.

I look around the football field. I'm just one of a few hundred students graduating, buried in a column of chairs. All of us are wearing our gowns, all of us look so uniform.

Parents and family are scattered about in the stands, and as the valedictorian finishes her speech, offering some cliché remark about how bright our futures are and about how much we've already accomplished – it's *only* high school, geez – everyone bursts into applause and cheering. Some people throw their hats up, but I don't. I don't want to lose it or have someone trample it.

I look around, see everybody chatting, hugging, going to see their family members, celebrate with them. Me? I'm under orders from Frank to catch a cab straight home. He couldn't even be here today, said he had business to attend to.

I continue scanning the crowd, and my eyes dart past the dark mouth of the tunnel that leads to the changing rooms. I see a figure there, leaning against the wall.

I squint against the sun, and then grin from ear to ear. I feel this explosive surge in my chest, a mixture of happiness, confusion, relief.

He came! I can't believe it. I'm not alone at my graduation.

I rush toward him, beaming, put my cap on, and when I see him open his arms, I throw myself at him, and we hug so tight, and I feel his huge, hard body, his heat, and I'm in his arms.

Duncan pulls me back into the tunnel, pins me against the wall, and he kisses me. Soft at first, gentle, but his lips grow hungry so fast, and I feel an overwhelming urge to kiss him back harder.

I run my fingers through his hair, clamp his lips to mine, and I kiss him for so, so long.

My heart is racing, my breath is quick, and I don't even care that everybody on the football field… they could all just walk past the tunnel and see us, see me, like this.

Our kiss ends, and I hold onto him, hug him, and

he holds me tight, and I bury my face in his neck and I smell him.

"I fucking missed you," he tells me, one hand on the back of my neck, the other running down my back, making me tingle.

I laugh. "Me, too. I can't believe you came!" I feel almost delirious with happiness and relief. It strikes me how much it means to me that he came. I'd assumed that all day I'd be alone, and graduating – even if I didn't do so as an ace student – means a lot to me.

Our embrace fades, and I look him up and down. He's wearing slacks and a dress shirt, black shoes. He looks amazing.

"Congratulations," he says.

"Why are you so dressed up?"

He gives me a sheepish smirk. "I thought it would be more formal." When I make a face, he says, "It's not like *I* ever graduated. I didn't know if there was a dress code. That girl just went on and on, didn't she?"

I roll my eyes. "Yeah. That's Jenny Halbrook.

She's so stuck up, thinks she's the smartest girl in the world."

"Glad it's over?"

I nod. "Yeah."

"Want to get out of here?"

I grin. "Definitely! Where to?"

"You tell me."

I narrow my eyes at him. "When did you even get back?"

"We got in early this morning, but you had already left."

"I volunteered to help set up here. Did Dad come back with you?"

"Yeah."

"Figures," I say, looking away. I'm not even surprised he didn't turn up. "So, that's it, all your training is over?"

"Pretty much. First fight is tonight."

"Tonight?" I echo in surprise. "That quick?"

"Yeah, Glass is busy setting it all up now. He wants to get started as soon as possible."

"And you're fine with that?"

"Got to start sometime, right?"

"Then aren't you supposed to be preparing for your fight?"

"I worked out this morning, got some reps in, took a nap. Now I've got to eat a little and hydrate, really. It's nothing."

"Hydrate, huh?"

"That's right."

I pull off my gown, and then nervously smooth my dress. It's a black, sleeved midi-dress that I had altered so it ends right above my knees, rather than half-way down my calves.

I still feel frumpy, though, and I look toward some of the other girls who wear their tighter, shorter dresses so much better than I wear mine.

"You look beautiful, Dee," Duncan says, pulling my eyes back from the other girls and up to him.

"No I don't."

"You do. God fucking damn it, you do. You're hot as hell."

Feeling awkward, my face going red, I turn toward the columns of chairs. "My bag."

"Let's go together." He puts out his arm. "Nobody knows who I am, right?"

I shake my head.

"Come on then," he says.

"Somebody has a big head."

He smirks. "I know I make an impression."

I take his arm, and together we walk back toward the chairs. Some of the girls notice us – or rather, they notice him – and before long all eyes are on us.

God, this is so stupid, but as we pass people I hear the whispers, and suddenly I feel like I'm walking down the red carpet. They're all asking who this hot guy is, is he a gangster like my father… they're all asking why he would be with *me*.

Little do they know that Duncan and I… well, there's something going on between us, that's for sure.

Little do they know that he's my adoptive brother.

It's all so… risky.

It's kind of… exciting.

It's also reckless, but I'm not in the mood to care right now. I feel like I've tossed my parachute out of the plane first, and now I'm diving down to collect it.

Live a little.

We get to my chair, he takes my gown and hat and

I pick up my bag. Together, we walk off the football field, past teachers who dare not speak to me because of my dad, past students who were never my friends because of who my father was.

Finally, I wasn't alone in school, even if it was, for all intents and purposes, the very last day.

Idly, Duncan rolls up his shirt sleeves. He shows off his tattoos, and I can't hold back my laugh. He's really putting on a show, he's really milking it.

The girls are all wondering who that tall guy is, with the broad back and tight body and the tattoos.

The boys are all wondering who'd have the balls to date a mob boss' daughter.

I feel like we're in a cheesy high school movie.

When we get outside the school, and start walking toward Duncan's car, I laugh, slap his shoulder. "That was bad," I say.

"They'll gossip for weeks," he says. "The whole summer, maybe."

"No they won't," I tell him. "You're not *that* hot. Hey, thanks for coming. I… I'm really glad you did."

He turns to me, and then without warning leans down, scoops my face into his hand, and kisses me.

It's a gentle kiss, lingering, on his hot lips the promise of more, but we just can't do this in public! Not this level of affection, and not out on the street.

"Duncan!" I say, pushing off him. "No, Frank could be watching."

He shakes his head. "He's not here. He went to meet your father."

"Well anyone of Dad's guys could be watching now that we're out here. No."

He just smirks, and we climb into the car together.

"So, where to?"

"I want to watch you fight tonight."

"I'm down with that. I'd like you there."

"So, do you like, need to do any more preparation?"

He licks his lips, thinks for a moment. "I'll need to warm up."

"Let's do that," I tell him.

"You're sure?" he asks. "You want to come with me and watch me prepare? It'll be boring for you."

"You've got to, anyway, and I'm going to be there to support you. We may as well get started. Maybe I can help somehow."

"Just being there will help me."

"Why?"

"Motivation."

"There's just one thing, though…"

"What?"

"Frank told me Dad wants me to go home straight away after graduation."

"No offense, but fuck your father. Do what you like, you're your own person. Do you really care what he'll think?"

I shrug. "Not really. He'll just shout at me for not being the good girl or whatever."

"You want to be the good girl?"

"No," I say with a shake of my head.

"Then…?"

"Let's go," I say. "Fuck what he says, I'm not going straight home. It's time I stopped letting him push me around."

"Fucking right," Duncan says. It's almost a growl, catches me off-guard.

He starts the car, guns out of the parking spot and around the bend. I'm thrown into my seat by the acceleration, love the feeling of it. Dad always has

Frank drive the limousine so slowly.

Duncan drives me to the location, a restaurant that only exists as a front. As we get out of the car, I see Dad sweeping out of the door, and he's pointing at us.

"What the fuck are *you* doing here?" he bellows at me.

*

16

DEE

"I want to watch Duncan," I say, folding my arms. "I'm here to support *family*. Isn't that the most important thing, as you're so fond of saying?"

Dad sighs, runs a hand over his smooth head. He turns to Duncan, says, "You brought her here?"

Duncan meets Dad's eyes. "She wanted to come."

"You should have told her not to."

"I'll never tell her she can't do anything."

"God damn it, don't you two start ganging up on me. Where the hell have you been?"

"At your daughter's graduation," Duncan says.

I wince when I see Dad's expression.

Dad looks at me. "I had to prepare for the fight tonight, sweet—"

"I know," I say coldly. "*Business.* I'm here to support Duncan, and you can't stop me."

"Deidre, this is no place for a young woman."

I laugh, shake my head. "You really want to have an argument with me in front of all your friends?" I gesture with my head at the restaurant. "Because of my *gender*?"

Dad turns around, sees everybody standing at the window, watching us. Other families and organizations, all dressed in their expensive suits, and all wearing glinting gold jewelry. Frustration ripples across his face.

"We are going to talk about this when we get home," he says.

Duncan steps forward. "Deidre just wants to support me," he says, flashing a charming smile.

Dad grumbles. "You really want to be here?" he asks, looking at me.

I nod at him. "I do." As the words leave my mouth, I wonder if it's the truth, or if I'm just trying to stick it to Dad. He doesn't want me here because he's scared I'll embarrass him.

I catch Duncan's eye, and we exchange a glance. With Dad in front of us, I trail with Duncan. He's got a cocky gait, with his hands in his pockets, like he hasn't a worry in the world, and each time he smiles at me, he injects me with confidence.

"Don't worry," he says as we cross the street and enter the restaurant. "But I want you to stay with me."

"Why?"

"Just stay with me every moment you can."

"Do you think something is going to go down?" I ask, furrowing my brow.

"No," he says. "But with people like this, you never know. So just stick with me, okay?"

"What, you going to protect me?" I ask, teasing him.

"If I have to."

We walk through the restaurant. All the chairs are upside down and resting on the tables. There are no table cloths, no linen or cutlery. I'd guess the restaurant hasn't been used for its apparent purpose in years.

Dad introduces me to all of his friends, and then Duncan as his fighter. I run the gamut of '*haven't seen you since you were a little girl*' and '*what a beautiful young lady you've become*', and I wear a fake smile, and pay everybody the proper respect.

Even if I'm feeling rebellious toward Dad, there's a part of me that knows I have a role to play in this little gathering, and if I don't play it, then I'm only going to make things difficult for him.

He leads us through a back door, past the kitchen, and then down some steps into a wide-open basement, spacious, dusty, the smell of mildew on the air.

In the center of the room is a cage, illuminated by some construction-site lights. More men mill down here, smoking cigars and cigarettes, sipping from beer bottles or shot-glasses of spirits.

I realize I'm the only woman here.

"Your private changing room is back there, Duncan," Dad says. "There's bikes for you to warm up on, treadmills, free weights. Everything you need is in your locker. It's for you, only. The other fighters have their own rooms."

"Alright, Glass," Duncan says. He looks at me, and beneath Dad's suspicious eye, we both walk to the back room. On the way there, I almost instinctively grab Duncan's hand, but pull back at the last moment.

Close, I think to myself. Managing this secret is only going to get harder and harder.

The back room is larger than I expected, and I realize the basement expands to the building next to the restaurant, and even the one after it.

The whole street is mob-owned, and this whole block is one giant front. But we're not in Dad's part of town, which probably explains why he's acting a little nervous.

Duncan walks around, checks under the benches, on top of the lockers.

"What are you doing?"

"Just being paranoid."

"For what?"

He shrugs, then turns to me, grins.

"Is it everything you hoped for?" I ask, laughing. Even though there's lots of equipment back here, it's pretty dark and dingy, not glamorous at all.

I wonder if this is what Duncan had in mind when he envisioned becoming an underground fighting star.

The glitz and glamor won't come for a while yet. When I tell him so, he just nods, gives me a small grunt, like that doesn't really matter.

"I thought you wanted to be the best?"

"I don't need it to sparkle."

He begins to take off his clothes, and immediately I look away without knowing why. It's just... *awkward.* It's been so long since he and I—

"You don't have to turn around," he says.

So I don't. I watch as he unbuttons his shirt methodically, calmly, then peels it off his muscular body.

In the dim light he looks more cut than ever, and then his fingers go to his belt buckle.

I swallow, feel my blood start to surge, thunder in my ears. My face grows hot.

He pulls off his underwear, and I gaze at him, eyes wide as his naked body comes into view. He catches my eye, and says, "I'm glad you came," while approaching me. He takes my hands, places my palms on his chest.

I start breathing quicker, feel a rush of excitement, of thrill. His chest is so hot, firm, and I swear I can feel his heartbeat thumping underneath.

He holds my face in his hand now, tucks my hair behind my ear, and then he leans forward, puts his lips right below my ear, and kisses a smoldering trail down my neck.

"Oh, I want you right now, Dee. Right fucking now."

I suck in air, feel a tension in my thighs that pulses right down to my toes, and I shiver, goose bumps exploding all over the tops of my arms, my hairs standing on end.

"You smell amazing," he tells me, and I feel the press of his teeth against my skin, and it only makes me shiver more.

His hard chest is inviting, and slowly I run my hands down his torso, across the undulation of his tight stomach.

I slide my hands around to grip his strong waist right above where it dips into his Adonis belt. He takes my hand, sidles it around his front, through the buzz of his pubic hair. I grip onto his shaft, my breath hitching, a ball of desire growing in my belly.

But then nervousness takes ahold of me. We can't do this here. What if Dad walks in? What if someone else does? It's too dangerous… and I step backward, flustered. "You know that this… is impossible."

"What is?"

"I don't know," I say, growing frustrated. "Us?"

"Why?"

Without warning he rings my wrist, tugs me toward him, catches my lips in his, kisses me hard. I don't push off him, I let him kiss me, shut my eyes, run my hands through his hair.

I feel his hardness against me, instinctively press my body against it, but then there's a knock at the door and we separate instantly.

"One minute," Duncan says, pulling on compression shorts and then his fighting shorts.

Dad pokes his head in after a moment, looks at both of us slowly.

"Let's go, Duncan," he says. "Round one. You're up. They want to kick off early."

"I haven't warmed up properly yet," Duncan says,

standing with his back to Dad. I put my fingers to my lips, struggle to keep my smile from forming. He's hiding his boner! At once it's funny and dangerous… a heady concoction.

"You'll be fine, your first opponent is a nobody."

"Just give me a minute."

Dad disappears, and Duncan turns down to me, takes my lips in his again. He kisses me urgently, his breaths quick, his body-heat seemingly doubled.

He presses me up against the lockers, pins my hands above my head, and kisses and bites a swathe of skin down my neck.

"We want what we want," he tells me. "So live a little."

He takes my hand, pulls me toward the door. Just as he opens it I pull my fingers from his grip, and he walks out, his gait all business, all swagger, his shoulders swaying. He doesn't even look at Dad, but he looks at me once more, smirks.

Our eyes meeting is like our own private conversation. I've got tunnel vision. All I can see is his crystal-blue orbs.

Win this fight, I think to myself, looking from

Duncan toward his opponent already in the cage. *Beat his ass.*

Duncan climbs into the cage, puts his mouth guard in, greets the referee then taps fists with his opponent.

A bell dings. The fight starts. Duncan lunges.

*

17

DEE

One charge, a flurry of punches, and Duncan's opponent is reeling. Each hit is a loud thump that makes me wince. It's like the beat of a bass drum.

The aggression I suddenly see in Duncan shocks me. He's turned into a creature in the cage. He's right up on his opponent, crowding him against the chain-link barrier, landing punch after super-quick punch into his gut, side of his head, mouth, neck.

His opponent blocks one fist, Duncan swings with the other. His opponent flails wildly, and Duncan easily slaps the errant hook, lands his own counter straight at the man's eye.

Finally, when his opponent drops to his knees on the ground, Duncan wraps his arms around his neck from behind, pushes his knees into his lower back, and bends him backward, using his own bodyweight to choke him.

It's not long before he's tapped out.

Duncan gets up the winner, pulls the loser to his feet, slaps his head with the kind of affectionate camaraderie I only expect fighters to have, and then is out of the cage, storming past Dad, who looks on in wide-eyed surprise.

The whole basement has fallen silent. The aggression, the violence everybody just witnessed has shocked them speechless.

A bunch of fucking mobsters and gangsters who kill and prostitute people for a living are beyond words.

And so am I.

I turn toward the changing room, see the door swing closed.

I go back there, see Duncan on a stationary bike.

"Lock the door," he tells me, and without hesitation, I do.

He looks at me, almost as if he's worried I disapprove, but then starts pedaling faster.

"That was insane," I tell him.

"I saw it in his eyes."

"What?"

"He was all about the show," he says between pants. Sweat drips off his chin. "Expected us to test each other, dance before we fight. Embellish. He's a show fighter."

"And?"

"So I got up on him hard and fast. Overwhelmed him."

Duncan's voice is completely neutral. He explains it to me matter-of-factly, as if recapping last night's news.

How the hell can he divorce that kind of aggression from his natural emotional state?

He wipes blood off his knuckles, and I go to him, brow pinched together, a surging worry in me. "Are you bleeding?"

"Yeah," he says. He lifts his knuckle up to me, shows me, and I gasp, covering my mouth.

"Oh my God!" I cry, stepping back. There's a

tooth lodged in between the knuckles of his middle finger and forefinger.

"Idiot didn't wear a mouth guard," Duncan says, and he pries the tooth from his flesh, pushes a towel against the open wound that immediately bubbles blood. The sound of the loose tooth dropping against the floor is just a dull clack.

"Does it hurt?" I ask, feeling stupid the moment the words leave my mouth. *Of course it hurts.*

"Yeah," he says. "It's fine, though."

"Did that guy even get a hit on you?"

"No."

I take a trembling breath of air, then calm myself down. I guess I'd never expected it to be that brutal. I guess I'd expected it to be more of an artistic dance, like martial-arts movies, than a tooth embedded in a fist.

"How long before the next round?"

He glances up at the clock. "Fifteen minutes."

"Are you serious?" I ask. "You don't get to rest?"

"Better that way. Won't cool down."

He hops off the bike, digs into his locker and pulls out a jump rope.

I feel so awkward just standing there, watching him do his jumps, cross the rope over effortlessly, reverse his swing so he's going backward.

His timing is damn-near perfect, and he's skipping faster than I ever could. Better than I ever could in gym class.

When he's out of breath he throws the rope against the bench, almost violently, puts his hands on his hips, sucks in huge gulps of air.

There's a knock at the door, and Duncan walks toward it, slides open the rusty deadbolt.

Dad's head pops in again. "This guy is Falcone's fighter," Dad says. "Quick hands."

"Right."

Duncan shuts the door, turns to me, wipes his face with a towel.

"Kiss for good luck?"

I frown at him, make a face. "Are you serious?"

But just as I finish the sentence he's closed the distance, grabs me by my waist and kisses me. I'm caught by surprise, let out a yelp, and when he sets me down I slap his sticky chest, a little grossed-out by the thought of his opponent's sweat being there, too.

He looks into my eyes for a moment, as if searching them.

"What are you doing?"

His tongue darts out to wet his lips, and he tells me, "Wish me luck."

"Good luck."

He nods.

"Kick his ass."

Duncan's face hardens, all emotion and softness drain from his features. He becomes an iron statue, almost lifeless.

He turns around, leaves the changing room a charging hurricane.

I watch from the doorway of the changing room as he climbs into the cage. The referee starts the fight, and this time his opponent immediately gets up on him, throws a quick punch and Duncan takes one above the eye.

I see the spill of crimson, but the ref doesn't stop the fight. I turn my eyes to Dad and he just shrugs.

They dance for a while, tip-toe around each other, size each other up, but again, in a flurry of fast and hard movement, Duncan lands hit after hit, thumps the wind out of his opponent before going for a mid-waist takedown and locking his knee.

The guy taps out just when I think his lower leg is going to separate from his upper leg.

Duncan stands, doesn't gloat, doesn't show off. He just throws open the door to the cage, storms back into the changing room past a once-again silenced crowd, and hops on the bike.

I lock the door behind him.

"I feel like your trainer or something," I say, offering him a smile.

He returns it, and warmth floods back into his features.

It's like he's a different person in the cage. I guess he has to be.

"Two down," he grunts at me. "Three to go."

"Is this how you always fight?"

He stops, then, stops pedaling. I feel like I've touched a nerve or something, but I don't know what.

"I've never fought like this before," he says slowly.

"What do you mean?"

"Organized, pitted against someone like a fucking dog."

I hear some anger in his voice, feel its sting. Is he regretting this?

"You don't have to fight, you know."

Duncan shrugs. "What the fuck else can I do?"

He lowers his eyes to the digital readout on his stationary bike, and starts pedaling harder.

Another knock at the door: Dad's voice floats through.

I slide open the deadbolt, and Dad pushes in, looks at me. "Why the hell did you come if you're just going to spend all night hiding in here?"

I'm taken aback, don't know what to say, but Duncan is off the bike, walking toward us.

"Get out," he says to Dad.

"You're winning too quickly," Dad protests.

"Get the fuck out, Glass, I need to concentrate."

Dad looks between him and me. "What about her?" he asks.

I'm surprised by the tone of his voice. It was almost… petulant.

"She's helping me."

"How?"

"You want me to win these fucking fights for you or not?"

"Yes, of course, but—"

"Then I do it my way. I'm not here to put on a fucking show for you."

"Yes, you are, boy," Dad says, his voice rising.

Duncan immediately starts to unwrap his wrists. "Then I'm done."

"Wait, wait, wait no. That's not what I meant."

"I fight my way, or I don't fight."

There's a standoff between them. Duncan's so deftly turned Dad's anger that was once originally aimed at me straight onto him.

It's not like I don't know how to handle Dad, but I appreciate it.

Dad puts on a stony front, but slowly he retreats.

The only person I've ever seen Dad retreat from is Duncan. It's honestly shocking, and a little confusing.

Duncan slams the door shut, slides the deadbolt across, then looks at me. His Adam's apple jumps up and down as he swallows.

"I don't need you to protect me from him," I say

to him. I add, "He's such an asshole, but I can handle him."

"I don't like the way he treats you."

"Neither do I."

"Then you and I are on the same side."

"I don't want to take sides against my Dad," I tell him truthfully. "Not really, anyway."

"It's too late for that, Dee. Protect yourself, first and foremost."

"You don't need to get in between us."

He shrugs. "I do what feels right."

There's a pause, and we look at each other.

"We're a team now, Dee."

"What, like brother and sister? Ganging up on Dad?"

"Maybe. You want to come outside and watch the next round? Be where I can see you."

"I do," I say truthfully. "It's a little exciting. But…"

"But?"

"Everyone else…"

"So?"

"I don't know."

"Show them what you're made of."

"They intimidate me."

He spaces the words out, almost savagely. "Shine brighter."

A bell dings, he throws open the door and goes toward the cage.

I watch him for a moment before taking off my coat, and walking out as well. I do as he says, walk my best walk. I realize, belatedly, that as many eyes are on me as they are on Duncan.

I go to Dad's side. He regards me with little more than a grunt, but I stand there, and when Duncan looks at me from inside the cage, I meet his eyes.

We share a look, and nobody in the room misses it.

We're a team.

In this big old fucking boy's club, I'm the one he looks at.

He beckons me to the cage, and so I go toward it. He falls into a squat, checks the wraps and tape on his hands and wrists. Then he pushes his fingers through the cage.

I take them quickly, give them a quick squeeze. I

don't care who is watching now.

"I prefer you out here," he whispers.

"Why?"

"Because losing in front of you is unthinkable."

He jumps up quickly, and I step back, falling in line with Dad again.

We watch, everybody, the whole crowd in anticipatory silence. The ref starts the fight.

Duncan and his third opponent begin their dance.

*

18

DUNCAN

Legs like tree trunks, short, low center of gravity. He's a kicker, but not a high-kicker. He'll go for torso-kicks and thigh-kicks. He'll try to tire me out then take me down. On the mat, in between those legs… that's a position I must not find myself in.

I look toward Dee. She's absolutely shining. She brightens up the whole room. She fills me with a crazy motivation. I don't even want to take a hit with her watching. And when you're a fighter, you're expected to take hits.

The referee tonight is nothing but a safety release. He's short, too, but big, strong, and he's there to make sure the fight doesn't end in a death.

I have no intention of taking a life in the cage, but I can't say the same for the man I'm about to trade blows with. He looks at me out of wild, undisciplined eyes. My guess? He out-violences people in the cage.

It's the wrong way to fight. You can never rely on anger. So he won't submit me tonight.

Definitely not with Dee watching.

It's odd to me, this feeling of not wanting to lose in front of someone. Before, it used to just be my own self-respect, but all that buys you is immunity against cowardice, and for some men, not even then.

But with Dee looking on, her dark, endless eyes on me, suddenly there's more to fight for. Now it's no longer appeasing whatever selfish instinct I have to uphold a personal sense of greatness or achievement or some bullshit like that.

Now… now I feel like I'm fighting *for* her.

And I'm not ashamed to admit… I don't want her to see me lose.

She doesn't know it, but she gives me a reserve of strength, determination. It'll make me work harder, faster, better. Without realizing it, she makes me a better fighter.

The ref starts the fight, and I extend my fists. My stocky, square opponent – 'Beefcake' in my head – doesn't tap my fists.

I grin at him, wink as we back up. He seems to take offense at that, and it riles him up.

Good, got to get him off-balance to make this easier.

The ref slices the air between us, and we dance, circle each other, size each other up. He's a righty, strong base, can push off hard and take you down mid-mass.

I glance to my left, see Dee's face, see her chewing on her lower lip. She looks nervous.

Beefcake tries to use that moment, lunges for me, goes straight for the take-down. I spin out of his way, a fast pivot on the heel of my right foot, and he goes sailing past me.

I catch him mid-move, wrap up his neck into my arm, twirl him into me like we're doing some kind of fucking modern dance, use it as leverage as I pull my weight around, jump off the mat, and latch onto his back.

I knee him in the thigh, send him off-balance, then

kick him in the back of the calf. He drops to one knee with a grunt, and I launch myself higher up onto him still, sit on his shoulders for the briefest of moments before I coil my legs around his neck and straighten out my body, jerking backward.

Both our backs slap the mat hard, wet, sweaty, sticky, and he's gripping at his neck. I twist him with my legs, bring his neck into the pit of my knee, and grab hold of my own foot, and pull.

He tries to punch above him, and I catch his arm, twist it, use it to leverage him against any movement.

It's only a matter of time now.

He's a fighter, that's for sure.

Tap out motherfucker.

Tap the fuck out!

He doesn't. He keeps going, face beet-red, lips now blue. I've cut off his windpipe, his major arteries. The split second he loses consciousness I need to let him go, or I risk permanently damaging him.

"Tap out you dumb motherfucker!" I growl, twisting his arm some more. He lets out a strangled cry of pain, but still he does not tap.

Slowly, his light fades. In maybe fifteen seconds, he's out, and I let his limp body go. I scramble up to him, roll him onto his side, check his throat.

He's still breathing.

The ref races toward me, pushes me away, inspects Beefcake, then declares me the winner.

Another fight over in under five minutes.

I leave the cage, pass Dee's father first. Glass's expression is that of something approaching arousal, but I expect nothing less from him. And nothing more.

I seek out Dee, and she just looks at me wide-eyed.

I retreat to the changing rooms, go to get back on the bike when I hear a rising murmuring behind me. Dee quickly comes in after me, shuts the door.

"They've cancelled the rest of the fight," she says.

I crease my brow, look at her, and then rush to the door and slam shut the deadbolt.

I press my ear to it, hear shouting, arguments. Glass is defending himself against accusations of bringing in an ex-pro.

"Fuck," I say, pinching the bridge of my nose.

"We need to get out of here," Dee says.

She's absolutely right.

I scour the changing rooms, past the shower, past the toilets, past the workout equipment, and see a fire escape.

Returning to her, I can already hear the shouting escalating. She slips her hand into mine, and together we weave through the room, out the fire escape which takes us to street level around the back.

It's fucking freezing, and I realize too late that I'm still just in my fighting shorts.

We rush around to the front of the building, and there see Frank sitting on the hood of the limousine.

"Frank!" Dee calls, pointing toward the restaurant. "Dad needs your help!"

He flicks his cigarette, reaches behind him and pulls out a large silver pistol. "Get a cab, you two," he tells us, waving us off, and he waddles into the building, his dark trench coat flapping in the wind behind him.

Dee flags down a cab, and we climb in together.

"Think my Dad will be okay?" she asks.

I nod, but I'm angry with myself.

It had never even occurred to me, not even once.

Why couldn't I see that fighting at my best would put Dee in danger?

*

19

DEE

"What the hell is the matter with you?"

Duncan's been broody and silent the whole cab ride home, and when we finally walk up the long driveway, he refuses my coat, and instead wraps an arm around my waist as if shielding *me* from the cold wind.

And all he's wearing his is fucking fighting shorts. He looks ridiculous.

Boys. Always got to be the tough guys.

We go inside, and Duncan climbs the steps two at a time, and I hear the old pipes shudder to life. I walk up after him, see the bathroom light spilling out into the hallway.

I hear the sound of splashing; a sink full of water, then some of it splatters to the floor.

I push the door open. Duncan is washing his face, then peers at himself in the mirror.

"Did you get hit?"

"Just here, above the eye," he says. "It's stopped bleeding."

I examine it in the mirror, see a thin line of split skin.

"Damn," I say. "It was close. I'm surprised you didn't get hit more."

He growls at me, "That's the fucking problem."

I'm taken aback by the tone of his voice, step out of the bathroom. He tears off his shorts, squeezes past me and goes into his room. He comes out later wearing jeans and a t-shirt, and then walks past me without meeting my eye.

"Why the hell are you giving me the cold shoulder?"

He stops at the top of the stairs, turns around, tongue on his lips. He heaves out a breath of air, and then frowns. It almost looks like he's struggling to find any words.

"You can tell me," I say, going to him. He's so wound-up, I want to help him calm down, but I don't know how. *I don't know how!* I wish I did, I wish I could help him.

But I don't even know what he's so fussed about! He won those fights only taking a single hit. I don't know anything about fighting, but I don't think that's typical. It sounds like a pretty good showing to me.

"You fought really well," I tell him. "That last move, it looked like it was all choreographed for how smooth it was."

His eyes narrow a little. "Dee, I put you in danger," he says, not breaking eye-contact with me. "I was stupid. It won't happen again."

I push my lips together. "What are you talking about?"

"God damn it," he begins, running his hands through his hair. He opens his mouth to elaborate, but the front door downstairs bursts open, and I hear Dad walk in swearing with Frank.

"Deidre? Duncan?"

"Dad!" I call.

"Get the fuck down here now!"

Duncan and I meet eyes, then slowly descend the stairs.

Dad's huffing, looks at Duncan first, then at me.

"Good job getting out of there," he says to both of us, and starts to calm down. "That got close. They thought you were a fucking ex-pro. Thought I was playing dirty. They didn't believe you'd never fought a match in your life."

I glance at Duncan, but his mouth is just a thin, grim line.

"And you, Jesus Christ," Dad says, turning on me.

"Glass," Duncan says, stealing back his attention. "What did you offer them?"

"What?"

"They didn't just let you walk out."

"Do you know who the fuck I am, boy?" Dad asks, his temper flaring instantly.

"Don't fucking do that," Duncan growls, silencing the outburst. "Don't you dare fucking start that shit up. Tell me the truth."

My eyes grow wide. I've never heard anyone talk to Dad like that. He seems totally checked by it.

"Those men in there thought you cheated them

tonight, and they put money down. It might not have been much, but I know what the fuck you all are like. Can't even stand to lose a dime if it offends your warped sense of honor. So you had better fucking tell me what fucking deal you made."

Dad starts stammering, and Duncan pushes out a forearm against his neck, backs Dad up against the wall.

"Duncan!" I cry, but he pays me no attention.

"What deal did you make, Glass?"

"I said they could bring in anybody they wanted to," Dad says. "To fight you. Double or nothing on all losses tonight."

"Anybody," Duncan says, shaking his head with what seems to me to be disgust.

"What do you mean?" I ask, looking at Dad.

"Ex-pros, people with proper training and experience is what I mean," Dad says. His eyes snap back to Duncan. "But don't worry, you're fucking magic in the cage, boy. I'm not afraid of anybody they bring in. They couldn't find a fighter on this continent that could match you. It'll be a cakewalk, and we'll win our money fair and square."

"Huh," Duncan says, and he grits his teeth together for a moment.

"Don't act like you didn't play a part in this," Dad says. "You could have milked the fights a little longer!"

Duncan turns around, hands on his hips, breathing quick.

"The other families are pissed at us?" I ask Dad, and he nods slowly at me.

Duncan looks at me, and his eyes grow sad. They lose their shine, their blue energy.

"Fine," he says to Dad. "For now."

"You'll have to put on a show," Dad warns.

Duncan just waves him off, and starts climbing back up the stairs.

I turn to Dad. "Put on a show?"

"He's going to have to take a beating. Make the fights last."

"What! Why?"

"It's a cock-fight," Dad says. "We want to watch the cocks… fight. If people think he has a chance of losing, then they'll put down money."

I shake my head slowly. I don't know what to say to that.

"Frank and I will be gone for a while," Dad says. "Still some smoothing out to be done. Congratulations, Deidre."

I blink, confused. "For what?"

Dad looks taken-aback. "For graduating, of course."

I blink again.

What a long and crazy day it's been.

*

20

DEE

The walls rattle, and I hear the familiar sound of the house's old pipes groaning to life.

"Duncan?" I call, walking upstairs. The bathroom door is open, and a straight column of light partially fills the hallway.

I walk past the doorway, see him standing behind the fogged up glass of the shower. His body is blurred by all the steam, but I can see that he is running his hands through his hair, like he's stressed out to hell and back.

"You okay?" I say, feeling a little silly for even asking it. It could very well be that he is not okay after hearing what Dad just told us, that he's going to be facing the best of the best as nothing but a rookie fighter, even if he is exceptional already.

But I have to ask it… I realize I genuinely care. I want to know if he's not okay. I want him to tell me so.

I don't get a reply, though, and so I figure he probably wants to be alone. I decide to leave him to himself for a bit, let him shower in peace.

But as I turn to walk away, I feel wet fingers on my hand, and he's right there, naked, dripping, and pulling me into the bathroom. His fingers are on the zip of my dress pulling down, and then he's slipping the dress over my shoulders, and sliding it down my body until it's just a puddle of fabric around my feet on the floor.

He flicks apart the clasp of my strapless bra easily, lets it drop. His eyes are on mine as he pushes his fingers beneath the elastic of my underwear, pulls it down my legs. I step out of them, and for only the second time ever I'm naked in front of him, bared to him.

His eyes travel slowly up and down my body, and a moment longer I might have gotten nervous or insecure, but he doesn't let it go that long. He wraps me up into his arms, pulls me tight against his slick body, his hard manhood pressed up between us, and he whispers into my ear, "I've missed you so fucking much."

I let him guide me into the shower, and once we are both under the hot stream of water, he worships me.

His lips run a fiery trail from my chin to my ear, down my neck to my shoulder, and across my collar bone. His hands and fingers touch every inch of my body, savor my curves, knead me and caress me, get me all wound-up.

I find his lips, seek his kiss, and he claims mine, a kiss somehow both tender and powerful, as if he means to tell me that he'll treasure me, but that I'm also his, and his alone.

His lips are so soft against me, but every now and then I feel the press of his teeth, just a teasing, gentle bite, and it makes me smile, makes me hum.

But then he breaks the kiss, and he does something really strange… strange to me, at least. Something I would never have expected.

He begins to wash my hair. He does it with a kind of determined concentration and care, making sure that no shampoo gets into my eyes. It's the most thorough wash I can remember, and when he conditions my hair, he rubs it into every single strand of hair methodically, and I am reminded of calculating way in which he wrapped my hands with the fighting tape.

I find it strange because it is so totally at odds with what I know of him so far. What I see on the outside is a hard, tattooed body of someone who does what he wants. I see a cage fighter, someone who beats other people up simply because he's good at it.

I never expected that he could be like this. I feel like something delicate in his large, strong hands, something small, but I feel safe. His hands are not rough with me, they are only caring.

"It'll all be okay," he tells me, as if *I'm* the one who just found out that all the other bosses would be bringing in their best fighters to try and break me. As if *I'm* the one who has to climb into that cage and fight a man who is going to stop only two inches short of snapping my neck.

He rinses my hair, and when I shut my eyes to stop water from getting in them, I feel his lips close around my lower lip, and he bites it.

I grin, try to kiss him back but he pulls away, and then when I'm not expecting it he takes my lip again playfully, kisses me again.

I fall into him, wrap my arms around him, determined not to let him pull away again, and his kiss grows hungry, urgent, and our tongues dance, and the shower washes away the taste of him to my dismay.

We kiss for ages, holding onto each other, and with my confidence growing, I reach down in between us and grip onto his manhood, start pumping him.

"What are you doing?" I breathe as he turns me, wraps me up from behind. My back is against his chest, and I can feel his hard body, his heat, and I hold onto his powerful arms, let him kiss the back of my shoulder, right where it touches my neck.

I feel a longing for him in my belly, and when his hands run up my sides, over my curves, roam my body, I arch my back, turn my head up toward his chin and neck.

In his arms, I let him touch me, run his hands up and down my body, roll my nipples and squeeze my breasts, bring me to the tips of my toes.

"You're so fucking sexy," he says.

His hot breath on my neck makes me feel so wobbly, and constantly in my mind is the thought that I can't believe we're doing this, here, now. Dad and Frank could come home at any minute!

His hand runs over my belly, and my longing for him grows, and I feel hot beneath my skin, hot down there.

His fingers sidle slowly south until he reaches the bulge of my pearl. I'm breathing hard against him, and I reach behind me, grip onto his hardness, hold him, feel his desire for me. His breath quickens, the movements of his chest speed up, and I slowly start to rub him through his jeans.

"Fuck, Dee," he growls. "I want you so fucking much."

His fingers dip into me for a moment, and I feel how slick I am, how swollen I am for him. It's fleeting, a hint of pleasure, and then he pulls his finger up, pulls a moan from my mouth, and starts to rub my clit.

My hand stops moving, I can't concentrate anymore on him. I relax against his body, let him touch me, let him own me, let him do what he wants to me. I know he's going to make me feel so good.

But he just teases me, and somehow it's both sexy and frustrating. His finger moves slowly, and I crane my neck to the side, look at the side of his dripping face.

"Come on," I tell him breathlessly.

He leans forward, takes my lips in his, kisses me, and at the same time he rubs me faster, just the way he knows I like it.

I moan into his mouth, shut my eyes tight, stay lip-locked with him. I clutch onto his thighs on either side of me unconsciously, give in to him completely. I open my legs wider, give him more of me.

His kiss takes on a feverishness, becomes aggressive, and I feel his tongue in my mouth, and I meet it with mine, but I can barely concentrate as he rubs me, as he plays me like an instrument.

I writhe in his grip, undulate, moan and whimper. He makes me feel so good, and already I can feel the pressure inside my belly growing. Oh, God, I want more, I want to come, it's like a blinding light on the horizon that I'm racing toward.

I break the kiss, look into his beautiful eyes, now darker with his desire.

"Make me come," I practically beg, and I feel his fingers speed up, feel his press harden, and I groan, pushing my head back onto his shoulder, my mouth open.

So quickly he brings me right there, right to the edge, and my body becomes tight as a tripwire. I tense up, squeeze, feel it in my belly, that growing pressure that's going to blow.

But then he pulls me back, and I turn accusing eyes on him.

"Stop it," I say, but then he's bringing me there again, and he pulls his other hand down my body, rings my entrance.

I'm in bliss when he pushes his finger inside me. I stretch around his thick finger, moan as he presses my front wall, makes me feel impossibly better.

I grip onto his legs like, and I feel his cock twitch against my back, and his lips and breath by my ear.

I'm his. He plays me. He controls me.

His rhythm speeds up, he fingers me faster and harder, and I feel my crisis racing toward me.

"Oh God," I groan, eyes shut tight, pleasure thrumming through me. The spring inside me is so wound up, coiling tighter and tighter.

I crunch my stomach, lean forward, inching closer and closer.

"Shit!" I hiss, white-hot bliss crashing over me as I come hard. I inhale deeply, hold my breath, squeeze around his finger. Pleasure explodes inside me, radiates down to the tips of my curled toes.

I'm soaring, in orbit, I feel so, so good.

I keep squeezing, he keeps going, and he makes it last, makes me feel this sharp pleasure for so long, and then it's waning, ebbing, and I shiver and shudder, the tsunami of ecstasy now turning to slow, rolling waves that thrum through my body.

I love every moment of this, being in his arms, him making me feel so good, being his.

I'm coming down, and my whole body feels wobbly and weak, and I suddenly feel so, so tired.

Duncan kisses my neck, pulls his fingers from me,

up to his mouth, and he sucks on them, sucks all my pleasure off them.

"I love how you taste," he says, and he claims my lips in his. I can taste myself on him but I don't care.

I'm a ragdoll, loose, panting, flushed, hot.

I grin, rub his thighs, reach around my back and feel his still-hard cock. I'm just about to turn around, to pleasure him like he pleasured me, when the pipes belch and the water hitches for just a second.

The shower dumps freezing water on us. The hot water tank has run out.

I scream, jump out of the shower laughing, quickly dry myself off with a towel. He seems unaffected by it, shuts off the stream and steps out. I toss him his towel, and we dry up in the steamy, warm bathroom, before darting across the hallway into my bedroom.

*

21

DUNCAN

Dee leans back on the bed, and puts a hand on my chest, pushes me back.

"I want to watch you."

Those words send my heart surging.

She runs a finger down my chest, leaves a trail of burning skin. Her finger roams downward, over the bumps of my tight abdominals.

I'm already beading pre-cum, so turned on by her. I can see her cheeks starting to flush red, and her breathing is quickening.

I begin to jerk myself off in front of her, slow at

first, watch her as she watches me, as her tongue wets her lips.

I never take my eyes off her as I pleasure myself, work myself right to the edge, then back myself off.

She sees it, the pleasure in my face, the desire and lust I feel for her, and her hand creeps down her body, and I watch her as she touches herself.

God, it's the hottest sight on Earth, and my cock gets impossibly harder, so hard it almost hurts.

"Come for me," she breathes.

I work myself faster, harder, never taking my eyes off her face. Her eyes narrow at her own pleasure, her mouth parts more, her breaths quicken more.

Her hand moves faster, and I hear a soft moan escape her lips, and I'm right there, right on the edge, and bliss thrills through my body, and my lust for her is like fire in my veins.

"Fuck, Dee," I groan, my thighs tensing. "Fuck."

I come hard, and the pinpoint of pleasure sears my senses, and I groan, pump myself wildly. I fire my load, it slaps the wall, and then my second, third, fourth.

I go to her, and she falls into my arms, looks up at

me and I crush my lips against hers, kiss her, love the feel of her hot breath on my face, so close, so intimate.

"God, you are sexy," I tell her, still hard, still ready. I can't imagine ever getting soft around her.

She kisses me again, bites my lip, then with a palm on my chest guides me around until I'm on the bed. She climbs onto me, straddles me.

She takes a condom from her bedside drawer, tears it open and rolls it down my manhood, and then I feel her fingers on my balls.

I put my hands on her hips, bring her over me, and groan as she lowers herself onto me slowly, as I feel myself enter her. She's so tight, makes me feel so good.

Dee bites her lip, scrunches up her face, eases into me slowly with a soft moan.

"You feel bigger than last time," she tells me.

I run my hands up her side, but she takes them and guides them above my head.

"Keep them there," she tells me, and she runs her fingers down my body, tracing the lines of my tattoos down my sides. "I like it when you put your arms above your head."

She begins to ride me slowly, shuts her eyes and she just looks all the more sexy for it. Her fingers go to my nipples, and she rings them, then puts her palms on my chest, and leans forward.

Her wet hair falls around my face, she lifts herself up slowly, brings me all the way out of her, and I groan at the sensation.

All I want to do is thrust my hips hard, bury myself inside her, but I get the feeling she's calling the shots right now.

And that's sexy to me. I like that.

A teasing smile parts her lips as she lowers herself back onto me, but just to my tip. She gyrates her hips, and God if it doesn't wind me up so completely.

I want to grip onto her, pull her hair back, lick a swathe of skin up her neck and bottom out inside her, fuck her crazily.

I lower one hand, but she slaps my arm.

"Don't," she says, continuing to tease me.

Her face bunches up in pleasure as my cockhead slides in and out of her, as I stretch her.

And when I can take it no more I wrap my arms around her, pull her toward me, claim her lips in mine and thrust myself all the way inside her.

She lets out a sharp moan into my mouth, but I don't let her go. I fuck her hard, fast, bury myself inside her over and over again.

Dee can't concentrate, can't kiss me, but I don't care, I just want her lips on mine, her breath on my face, her moans.

I grip her ass, drive myself into her recklessly, wildly, and the sticky slaps of our skin are loud, seem to echo in the room.

"Fuck," she says, her body growing tight in my arms, her back arching upward, her eyes clamping shut.

I fuck her for all I'm worth, slap her ass, grip her thighs. I reach in between us, find her stiff pearl, rub it fast just how I know she likes it.

"Ohhhh," she moans, and her body tightens more, and I know she's nearly there again.

I don't stop, I keep the same rhythm, and she drops her head onto my chest as I pound into her over and over again.

"Oh shit!" she cries. "I'm going to come!"

She opens her mouth, lets out a long mewl of pleasure as she climaxes, as ecstasy crashes over her like waves at a beach.

She shudders and shivers, her body a rigid snapshot of pleasure, and I feel her squeezing around me, so tight around me.

I groan, let go, and climax myself, emptying myself again, my balls tightening, my cock jumping inside her.

And then it's over, and she collapses on top of me, and I hold her tight, and our breathing is aligned, and it's like our hearts beat as one.

Her hand finds mine, and we interlock fingers. Dee's face is against my chest, rising and falling with my quick breathing, and I kiss her forehead, hold her harder against me still, and wonder at this feeling I now have inside my chest.

It's like a blooming, a firework exploding in slow motion. It's… I don't know how to put it into words, but I do know one thing. I can't imagine myself being with anybody else. She's all I want, all I need.

I never want there to be a day where I don't have

her, where I can't see her smile, smell her smell, taste her lips. Where I can't talk to her, laugh with her, be with her.

We lie together on the bed for ages, just her and I, alone in the universe, not sleeping, not talking. Our fingers talk, and our hands talk as we touch each other's bodies, and fuck if it isn't the best feeling in the world.

Eventually we fall asleep, her in my arms.

And I'm the happiest I've ever fucking been.

*

22

DEE

I wake up at a sudden, sharp sound, and rub my eyes. It was a door slamming.

I think nothing of it, roll over and find Duncan's body next to mine. He's sleeping flat on his back, one arm behind his head, and his eyeballs are twitching rapidly. He must be in a dream.

A smile spreads my lips. He even looks good when he sleeps, despite having messy bed hair.

It's odd how utterly still he is when he sleeps. I'm a mover in the night. I always wake up with the sheets tangled in between my legs, half the duvet on the floor, my pillow somehow vertical.

But he looks like he just crawled into bed, then turned to stone.

I sidle up to him, rest my head on his chest, and he stirs, pulled from his dream, and brings his arm down over me, holds me against him.

The blinking digital clock by the bedside reads five-forty-five, and internally I groan, wondering why the hell someone was slamming the door so—

Shit! Dad's back!

I sit up straight like I've just poked my finger in an outlet, and rub Duncan awake.

"Duncan!" I hiss, covering my mouth as I talk. "Duncan."

He rouses, blinks, sits up and rubs his eyes.

"Duncan, you have to go."

His eyes go to me, then the clock, and he gets out of bed, his naked body looking tighter in the morning.

"Wait, why?"

"Dad's home!" I say.

I don't know why, but I start grinning like an idiot. This is insane! My heart is pounding just thinking about the possibility of Dad knocking at my door, of him finding Duncan and me in bed together.

It's not even funny, but it's making me laugh.

I catch a glint in his eye, and a smirk pulls his mouth to the side. He presses his ear to the door, then looks at me.

"He's coming up."

"Oh shit!" I say, quickly climbing out of bed and rummaging for my pajamas.

I feel a hand on my hips, turn around and see Duncan. He runs his hand over my ass, dips lower, and I slap it away.

"Stop!"

I look down from his face, see that he's already got a boner. *Jesus!*

"You have to go," I say, retreating quickly from him, pouring myself a glass of water and gulping from it. I offer it to him afterward, and he takes a sip.

"Where? I don't have any clothes."

I spin around frantically, then my eyes settle on the window. I open it, squint down. It's not a long drop to the roof of the garage.

I look at him, flash my eyebrows.

Duncan laughs, then pinches the bridge of his nose and sighs. "Wow."

"Go," I urge, unable to stop a laugh from spilling out of my mouth. God, I can't believe he's about to jump out of my window naked.

He climbs up into the window frame. It's a tight fit, but he squeezes through.

"See you later," I say to him.

He blows me a kiss, and hops out. I hear him land before I reach the window, see him looking back up at me, wincing, rubbing the sole of his foot.

"You okay?"

"Landed on a fucking thumbtack!" he whispers.

I watch as he pulls the metal from the sole of his foot, chucks it away.

"You been throwing stuff out your window, Dee?"

I widen my eyes guiltily, nod at him. "Maybe! Hold on." I race around the bed, pick up his towel, and chuck it out the window at him. It wraps itself around his head.

I shut the window, pull across the drapes, and then jump back in bed just in time. Dad swings my door open without knocking.

"Dad!" I cry, pulling the covers around me. "You need to *knock*."

He leans in the doorway, looks around. "Everything is fine. Everything is sorted."

I blink, have no idea what he's talking about.

"With the other families!" he says grumpily. "After last night. I smoothed everything out. Just thought you'd like to know."

"Uh, okay."

"Mm," he hums, peering around my room. "It's been a long time since I've been in here."

I pull my blanket up higher around my neck, say to him, "Dad, I'm not ready yet."

He looks at me for a moment, then nods. "Of course, Deidre. You get up now, let's have breakfast together."

I wince. "Now? It's so early."

"Yes. Come on, get ready."

He disappears out of my doorway, and I hear him bump into Duncan in the hall.

They have a small chat, but only murmurs make it through the door. Dad's footsteps going downstairs reach my ears, and then there's a knock at the door.

I open it, and Duncan is standing there, grinning at me, a toothbrush in his mouth, towel wrapped around his waist.

"It's pretty cold out," he says, his voice a toothpaste slur.

"That was close," I tell him. I'm shaking a little, but it was kind of… fun, in a stupid, teenage way.

The condom!

It's the only thing in my trash can. Fuck, what if Dad had seen it?!

"You need to take the condom," I tell him. "I can't have it in here. Dad would go insane if he found it somehow."

Duncan pauses mid-movement, looks at me with a wrinkled nose.

"What, it's all *your* stuff, anyway!"

He shrugs, reaches into the can and pulls it out. And then he comes to me, pulls out his toothbrush and presses his nose against my ear. He smells me, and I feel the cool tip of his nose on my lobe.

"Go on, go!" I urge, pushing him in the butt. He swaggers out of the room, but at the last moment turns and looks at me.

God, he looks so fucking hot in just a towel.

"Go," I say, laughing. "Come on, Dad might come back."

He disappears down the corridor, into the bathroom, and I just shake my head, still my racing heart, and slow my breathing.

Too close.

Way too fucking close.

*

Things settled down after that. Duncan started fighting, winning, and I was there supporting him. They started calling him 'Creature' because he was so relentless in the cage.

I went to college, moved into residence halls, and Duncan got his own place using his winnings.

We no longer had to hide, and I split my time between his apartment and my room.

And time passed… and we were happy.

Dad… well, I could almost ignore him.

But it had to come to an end… a train bearing down on us in the night.

The rails were rattling, the horn was blaring, and we could feel the push of air.

That night by the pool started us down a path.

…The beginning of the end.

23

DEE

Dad is happy and that means something is very, very wrong.

Duncan and I both share a mutual look of confusion. We both know that if Dad is this bubbly about something, it means that it's good for *him*.

What's good for him is almost invariably bad for us.

The dining room is dimly lit. Dad brought out the candles, and their flames fall upward almost in an exact straight line, and I remember that he mentioned something about having the windows in the house resealed.

Dad's wearing a suit, charcoal grey, jacket open, tie a little too skinny for his wide body. His white shirt beneath is creased along the sides of his chest; it's too tight.

Duncan and I are dressed far more casually, and I wonder if we've both come underdressed for some big announcement.

"Tonight we celebrate," Dad says, lifting his glass of red wine.

We lift our cups of water.

Dad drains half the glass in one sip, then sets it down carefully, making sure to place it in the exact center of the square, cork coaster.

He smiles at each of us in turn. Well, maybe smile is not the correct word. His teeth peel thinly up over his lips, and his eyes narrow, and creases push into the leathered skin of his face, but there's not an ounce of warmth or even something relatable in his expression.

"Duncan!" he booms from nowhere, shocking me. I jump visibly in my chair, and I shut my eyes for a moment, feeling nothing but impatient frustration.

Duncan gives him a wry look. "Glass, what are we

celebrating?" he asks.

"You two," Dad says, shaking his head. "You both leave the nest, and never return to even visit. I have to call together a family dinner on a special occasion to see you two together."

I roll my eyes. I wish he would just quit with the woe-is-me melodramatics.

"What's the special occasion, Dad? I've got work I need to do tonight, so I'd like to get this over with as soon as possible."

Dad bristles, but, to my surprise, he bites his tongue.

"You ever heard of Conrad Butler, Duncan?"

I look across the table, see an expression of recognition fade-in on Duncan's features.

"Yeah," Duncan says slowly. "Fighter up in Canada. Best in the country, from what I've read. Very fast, very violent. They call him 'Manic'."

"He's agreed to fight you." Dad beams at both of us.

"And?"

"And he's the favorite!" Dad says, slapping the table with exhilaration. "Damn it, Duncan, nobody is going to bet against Manic Butler! Even you, no offense, lose on paper. He's taller, faster, and stronger. He's got more experience on you, and he's on a similar win-streak to you. The physicals alone make him the favorite, but when you take in his extremely effective moves, not to mention the fact that his trainer is a God damned heavyweight ex-champion… shit, we're going to win big."

Dad picks up a fork and knife, squeezes them both in his hands until his sausagey fingers go white. "We couldn't have asked for a better opponent."

I look in mild horror at Dad's gleeful expression, the excitement he has at the prospect of a fighter that not only matches up well with Duncan, but could beat him. Hurt him.

"I could lose, you know," Duncan says, his voice gravelly. "You're the bank, you take all the risk."

Dad points his knife at Duncan. "But you *won't* lose. You'll win. I know it, I can feel it. You're a better fighter, Duncan. You're tougher up here." He taps the sharp steak knife to his temple. "We'll get you ready for this one. The fight is in four days, and tomorrow I have some pro scouts flying in. They'll go over all of Manic's favorite moves with you, so you can learn to counter them."

I can see from Duncan's disinterested expression that he's not particularly impressed by this idea. How much he has changed since the beginning. At first, he wanted to fight, wanted to make a name for himself. He was determined to *do* something.

But now… now each fight feels perfunctory. The passion is gone. Duncan knows that to everybody, he's just a gladiator. Most gladiators were forced to fight against their will.

He meets my eyes for a moment, and I nod at him, telling him silently, *I know*.

"What, you afraid, boy?" Dad asks, glowering. His whole demeanor has changed, and his eyes might as well have turned red, and he might as well have sprouted horns from his forehead.

"I'm not afraid," Duncan says. You'd be hard-pressed not to believe him, the way he says it so casually. "Once I beat Manic, though—"

"There will be a few fights left, don't worry. I know for a fact Falcone is scouring Mexico for a fighter, and one of the other families has connections in Russia and they are looking there. There will be a few more big time guys they'll bring in, ex-pros and the like. You'll still have work. Then, once that well dries up, we just move to another. The pros. I'll get you into the biggest legit tournament and you'll run the gauntlet and come out on top. I'll put down numbers so large in just one event we'll make enough to live like kings for the rest of our lives. With something like UFC, it's not just national betting. It's *inter*national betting. We're playing with money from all across the world. Think about it, your children, *their* children will be set for life!"

Duncan remains non-committal, though, and I decide it's my turn to speak.

"How good is Manic?" I ask. When Dad opens his mouth to speak, I silence him with a wave of my hand. "I'm talking to Duncan."

My ears are burning, and I know Dad is staring bullet holes through me, but damn it, I get to speak at this table.

"I know him mostly by reputation," Duncan says. "I've watched a couple of his fights, that's it. He's hard and fast, likes to get dirty on the mat."

"What do you mean 'dirty'?"

"He'll tap your balls."

"Can't you wear a cup?"

"He pulls other cheap shit, too. Stuck his finger in a guy's ass once."

I frown in disbelief. "Are you serious?"

"Oh, yeah," Duncan says. "That's part of his reputation. It's not that uncommon, anyway. Just a moment's distraction, he locks you, submits you, and then doesn't stop. He'll tear your arm from your socket even after you tap-out. Manic's a little crazy."

Dad butts in now: "When you're on the mat, anything can happen. Just submit him fast. No need to draw this one out. He's too big of a name. He's been the top fighter in Canada for nearly a decade. But you've got the younger body! He may be strong, but he lacks your sheer athleticism, something only I know about. I've seen you squirm out of leg holds in ways that would have professional instructors asking for your secrets."

I watch Duncan as he seems to weigh the idea in his head for a moment. Soup is brought in, but none of us start eating.

"Fine," he says. "Let's do it."

I narrow my eyes at him, kick his foot under the table. "Duncan, are you sure?"

"I can beat him."

"Yeah, you might win the fight, but what could you lose in the cage?"

"An eye is always a possibility, especially with Manic." He grins at me, as if doing so can make my worries just evaporate away.

I fold my arms. "I don't like it. If people are already lining up to bet against Duncan, despite every win he's notched, then there must be something about this Manic guy. If he fights dirty, they'll no-doubt be whispering in his ears to do so."

"Of course they will, there's no need to state the obvious," Dad snaps. He turns to Duncan. "You may need to pull out a few tricks."

"I'm not fighting dirty," Duncan says. "Maybe you loaded your gloves, you know, a little *Plaster of Paris,* but I won't."

Dad is visibly taken aback, stammers, "I-I never once—"

"Whatever, Glass," Duncan says. "I'll fight him,

but I'll fight him clean."

I can hear Dad's teeth grinding against each other. "Good," he says through a strained voice. "Well, this wasn't a very pleasant dinner, was it?"

He gets up, tosses his napkin into his bowl of soup, extends a finger at Duncan. "I want you to win that fight, boy. Do whatever it takes. We're going to rinse these fucking fools who are going to bet against you, we're going to take everything they've got. For this fight, I'm bumping your share to ten percent. Don't say I never fucking took care of you."

Dad stomps out of the room, and we hear a series of doors slamming in the house.

"That was quick," Duncan murmurs, leaning on the table. He's taken an extra pleasure in getting a rise out of Dad recently. I know he thinks he's turning Dad on him, and away from me, but really all he's doing is putting us *both* in Dad's sights.

"You shouldn't have said he fought with loaded gloves."

Duncan shrugs, and so I get serious.

"You just make it worse for me when you do that."

He just looks at me for a moment, and there is no contrition in his features, but I know that he's measuring what I've said in his mind. After a moment, he agrees with me.

"You're right. I'll stop."

"Now, this fight."

"It'll be fine, Dee. I can beat Butler."

"Are you sure?"

He nods. "I'm sure, Dee."

"I want to study the film with you. I might see things you don't."

"Good, I was going to ask you."

"Is he dumb? Manic, I mean."

"He's no idiot, but he's not good at adapting from what I saw."

"So you'll have to surprise him, catch him off-guard."

"I was thinking about trying southpaw."

I push my lips together. Fighting left-handed? That's not a bad idea, would throw off the timing, make Duncan hard to predict, difficult to counter.

"Think you're good enough with your left?" I ask. I know I don't need to ask it – he is almost completely ambidextrous – but I want to know what his mindset is.

After all this time being with him, I know that leading with your strong arm – and while he can use both effectively, his right is stronger – is very risky.

"Yeah, I am, but I need to watch him fight a bit more first. He's a grappler, he'll want to take me to the mat. Do I try and grapple with him, use my angles, my agility, hope I don't get pinned? Or do I play defensive striker, turtle up and trade blows, try to wear him out?"

"I don't know," I tell him truthfully. "But if he has trouble adapting, then you need to be changing your style constantly. Don't let him get comfortable."

"Yeah," he says. "You're right."

I nod, and then lean forward over the table, and sigh.

"What is it?" he asks, his eyes darting toward the dining room door for a moment before he reaches across the table and takes my hand.

"I don't want you fighting anymore. I'm sorry, I know you don't want to hear that, but these last few fights…"

I trail off, thinking about all the people he's gone up against in the last month, since that night at the pool in the hotel. They've been tough opponents, and even though he's won all those fights, he's taking more hits. He's coming back home bruised, bleeding, and in pain.

I find nothing good in the idea of my man getting beaten up, even if he dishes out a worse beating up in the process. *You should see the other guy* is something that doesn't work when both men get fucked up, no matter how much he says it in jest.

And I don't want *my* man fucked up.

"I won't fight forever," he tells me. There's a soft certainty in his voice, and yet the pronouncement is vague.

"When?"

"Soon. Just a little more."

"But why?"

"I'm planning something, Dee. Don't push me on this one. I know when to stop."

"Are you sure you do? What if you leave this fight with a broken jaw? A torn ligament? Brain damage!"

"Then Manic will be in much worse condition."

"But I don't care about Manic!" I hiss at him, my temper flaring unexpectedly. "I care about *you*!"

That damn stupid tongue comes out of his mouth and wets his lips, and somehow it drains some of my anxiety away.

"I'm not going to get hurt."

"You got hurt last time."

"Just bruises, Dee. How can a fighter not pick up cuts and scrapes on the way?"

"Some fighters pick up paralysis on the way," I say, knowing it's unfair.

"Just a little more, Dee. Trust me."

"But why can't you just tell me why? It's clear you're not interested in the fighting anymore. It's clear you loathe Dad. I can see it in your body language. Don't think I can't tell, Duncan. I *know* you! You have to be honest with me, I deserve that. So why can't you tell me?"

"Because I'm not ready to, yet!" he says, his voice rising a little. "I haven't figured it all out yet."

I see now a kind of *un*certainty in his expression. Usually he's so assured about everything, like he knows the way life is going to unfold, and that he's going to be able to bend the creases the way he likes.

But this… this is something different. This is something that's scaring *him*.

"You can tell me, Duncan. Lean on me."

"I do, and I will," he says. "I promise you I will, but not now."

"Why not now?"

"I can't answer that."

I blink, shake my head in frustration. "What the hell kind of answer is that? After everything we've been through, now is when you stop trusting me?"

"I still trust you."

"So, tell me!"

"I can't," he says, his voice lowering to something guttural. I can see what's about to happen. I've been with him long enough to know when he's about to get all broody and introspective; shut me out.

"This is unfair to me."

"Damn it, Dee, I don't know how to say it."

"Just use the first words that come into your head."

"I already have. You need to just believe me, okay? A few more fights, I'll have everything sorted."

"Have what sorted?"

But he doesn't reply. We just sit in silence for a while, looking anywhere but each other.

"Excuse me," I say, and I get up and go to the washroom to pee. There, I check. Still nothing. I grip onto the edge of the sink, and look into the mirror. *Shit.*

My heart starts to beat quicker, and I feel a nervous shiver run down my spine. I'm late. It's only been a few days, but up until now I've always had very regular periods.

I tease my phone from the back pocket of my jeans and tap on the calendar app, count the days for the umpteenth time today. It should have come by now. It's been a little over two weeks since that night at the hotel, but that was the only night we had unprotected sex.

I tap my nails against ceramic, realize that I can't even keep a steady beat. My fingers are trembling. I've researched it all, looked it up online, but I only feel one of the early warning signs of pregnancy: My nipples tingle. Beyond that, I haven't been feeling unusually tired, and I haven't been feeling sick. I don't ache, and I'm not irritable. My appetite hasn't changed at all, either.

I sigh. They say morning sickness won't come for another two weeks. I'm almost afraid to buy a test. In my mind, maybe I can hold out a few more days. Maybe I'm just late, maybe I've just been too stressed at school. Maybe…

I can't be pregnant. Not now.

Not with him!

I'll wait. Just a few more days. I'll wait a week, and then I'll buy a pregnancy test. For a moment, just a fleeting moment, I think about mentioning this to Duncan.

But immediately I know I'm not going to. I don't know for sure, yet. I don't know anything, yet. I don't want to scare him.

I don't know what he'll think!

"What's wrong?" he asks instantly as I enter the dining room.

"Nothing," I say. "I'm tired."

He looks like he's about to press, and so I put up a hand, shake my head. "Really, I'm fine. I just want to leave this place."

"Then let's go."

We leave the house without saying bye to Dad, and I go back to his apartment with him. Both our moods are subdued as we no doubt consider the future.

Duncan likely wonders about his fight with Manic. He's probably going through the moves in his head, over and over. How to counter this, that, when to strike, when to turtle.

And me… well, I'm only thinking about one thing.

And it just goes round and round in circles in my mind.

I have no idea what I'm going to do.

*

24

DUNCAN

Where the hell is she?

I imagine her walking through that door, seeing those sexy lips smile. It's her smile and her deep, inky eyes that will take me aback first – they always do, even now. I get lost in them every time. I feel pulled to them, magnetized, and when she looks at me I can't look away, not even for a second.

My heart rate quickens, sends blood rushing south. The image of her in my mind is clear as day, every single detail.

Her lips are soft, generous, full. Those lips pressed against my own… she sets me on fire. Smiles come so easily to her, a reflection of who she is on the inside.

Somebody much better than me.

And with her standing in the doorway, silhouetted by the spotlights from behind, I'd let my gaze travel down her body, to the peek of silky skin I see at her collar bone that makes me lick my lips and swallow hard. To the swell of her breasts, the curve of her hips, those thighs and that ass…

My throat tightens, my heart pumps quicker still. My gut stirs, and I grow impatient.

She's late, and I need her.

I'm addicted to her, everything about her. That curvy body, that ass I want to hold and squeeze, kissing my way up the inside of her thighs, making her shiver.

I think about tracing my fingertips over the curves of her body, slowly, teasing her, making her squirm in my grip, making her look at me out of lust-laced eyes, her lips parted, panting.

She's waiting for me to take every hot, sexy inch of her, claim her as my own, and I'm going to make her beg for it.

I swallow. Hard.

But as much as I love her body, I need her mind with me. She stills the waves in me, quiets the storm. She makes me think about things from points of view I'd never considered before. She's opened up my mind to new things, made me, without realizing it, a better person.

But most of all she makes me feel happy, and even beneath the shadow of her father, even knowing… knowing that what we have can't last forever, it's her presence that makes me forget about all that. It's just so easy to lose myself in the present with her.

Dee… well, she's something else. Stronger than me, braver than me… I realize that I don't just treasure her… I admire her.

My imagination tricks my mind into thinking I can actually smell her wonderful scent, just behind her ears. Not perfume, nothing artificial. Her.

I wake up with that smell, cherish it every morning she's with me. I can't imagine not being able to kiss her neck, breathe in, feel her hair around my face, tickling, soft.

My imagination tricks me into thinking I can feel

her warm breath against me, see her lips parted, the peeking tips of her teeth, her eyes shut tight, her body tensed in my own, her moans in my ear. She's telling me not to stop. Never to stop.

God, I haven't seen her for just a day and already it feels like a lifetime. I'm hooked. She drives me crazy.

I shift my weight, feel a stirring in my gut, anticipation, desire. It's fight night, my biggest one yet, and I need her with me. It's like I'm thirsty but don't have water, like I'm hungry but don't have food.

I grunt.

Too bad I'm stuck with this fucking joker in front of me. He's meek, mild, and his back is curved instead of straight. It's like he's trying to retreat into himself, hide from me.

What the fuck for? It's not like he's climbing into the cage with me.

This fucker was the one who requested, over and over again, to get an interview with me. Now he finally has it, and he's fucking shrinking.

I don't have time for this shit. I have time for her, and I have time for the fighting. That's it. Everybody else, everything else, can go straight to hell. Soon, the fighting will go straight to hell, too.

Just a few more fights. I'll retire at the top, undefeated. I already know it's going to happen. I can't fool myself into thinking I haven't made up my mind. But I'm not there yet. Nearly, but not yet.

I have to make sure that she and I will have everything we need.

I'm in nothing but a towel wrapped around my waist, and I'm hoping the short, stout man won't see my bulge. I've been sporting it this whole time, a rock-hard boner that I'm hoping the voluminous fluffy fabric hides.

He's a fucking reporter or something. He'd have a field day writing about that for his magazine or website or whatever. Underground MMA fighter 'Creature' sits in his warm-up room, before the biggest fight of his career, with a hard-on…

But just thinking of Dee is all it takes to bring me up. Just a stray thought, and my mind goes from zero to one-hundred, and I'm imagining her in my arms, tasting her.

Since I started fighting, I've met a lot of girls.

They're all batshit fucking insane. They beg me to marry them – I've been proposed to after a fight. I'm there, blood dripping down my face, sweat leaving shiny smears down my body, and this chick is fucking holding a ring out for me, asking if I'll marry her. She's even down on one God damn knee.

People are fucking crazy.

The girls ask me all kinds of wild shit. Every fight night at least half a dozen ask me to have their children, to give them a baby.

A baby is something I want. I want to have a family, give my child something that nobody ever gave me.

But not with any of them. I don't want any of them. I never have, and I never will.

None of them compare to Dee.

Not a single one.

She is all I want.

"My name is Dan Peterson," the meek man opposite me says, sticking out a hand. I shake it, feel his grip turn to putty, and he seems mesmerized by how my hand just utterly swallows his up.

"You have really big hands," he blurts out awkwardly.

I pull my hand from his, give him a bored look.

"Mr. Marino said I could interview you."

"That's fine," I say, gesturing at him to just fucking get on with it.

"Are you in a hurry?"

"I need to start pre-fight," I say evenly.

"You mean your warm-ups?" he asks.

I tilt my head to the side. "Yes, my fucking warm-ups, stretching, etcetera. Pre-fight. This your first fucking time reporting on MMA?"

He grows flustered, his face goes red, his breathing hitches, and his hands shake. "No, I just wanted to make sure we're on the same proverbial page."

"We're not on the same fucking page," I tell him. "Use your knowledge, or leave. Do your job, or leave. But don't ask me dumb fucking questions. I don't have time for this shit. If you are going to ask me what fucking pre-fight is, then you can fuck off."

"O-okay."

I'm sitting on a sofa, elbows on my knees, and he's on a stool opposite me. The lighting is dim. For a few seconds, I see his eyes linger on my body, the bulge of my shoulders, the striations of muscle on my chest and abdomen.

"Hey," I say, snapping my fingers in front of him. "Focus."

I can see that he's terrifically uncomfortable, and I let out a slow breath of air. I can't believe this guy needs to be babied.

Fucking hell, why did they send someone so incompetent? Why the hell did Glass okay this? He's starting to live vicariously through my publicity. It's a little pathetic.

"Peterson, why don't you tell me who you write for?"

"Um," he says. "So, you know, I own arguably the most visited underground MMA website in the world, right?"

"I didn't know," I tell him. "But now I do. What's it called?"

"MMA-Underground?"

"I'll take your word for it."

I look over his shoulder toward the door, praying that any moment now Dee is going to walk in and I'm going to get to end this stupid interview, scoop her up in my arms, kiss her like it's the last kiss I'll ever have.

I'm going to see the curve of her hips, those thighs that I want to bite, her sexy, beautiful body, and I'm going to…

God, I can't get enough of her. I've seen, smelled, touched and tasted every gorgeous inch of her hundreds of times, and yet all I want is more. Every time I peel off her clothes, every time I run my hands over her soft skin, I feel like it's all new again, the first time again.

I can't imagine ever wanting anyone else.

"Okay, so I've got some questions here." Peterson taps his pad with his pencil. "But first I want to know if there's anything you consider, um, off-limits?"

"Fighting strategy," I tell him straight-up. "And my personal life."

That gives him pause. "All of your personal life?"

"Why don't you just ask me the questions," I say. "And if I don't answer, I don't answer."

"And that's the end of that?"

"You're damn right it is."

"Mr. Marino did say you would—"

"I don't fucking care what Mr. Marino said," I say.

"I'll answer what I want to. If you have a problem with that, you can take it up with me. You want to take it up with me?"

"Okay, okay," he says, stammering a little. "I don't have a problem with that. Really. Hey, we're all entitled to personal privacy, right?"

I narrow my eyes at him. "Was that one of the questions you wanted to ask me?"

"It was rhetorical," he murmurs.

"Don't waste my time. Get the answers you need, then get out."

"Hey, I'm just trying to form a relationship with you, okay?"

"I am uninterested in forming a relationship with you."

"I don't see why you have to cop an attitude."

Some backbone! Good.

"Let me fucking tell you something," I say, leaning forward. He sits back almost instantly. "In about thirty minutes I'm going to climb into a cage and fight a guy six-three, two-hundred and forty pounds of lean muscle mass. He's fast as hell, and is known for taking his submission holds too far. We're not just throwing punches, and you should know that. People have died in the cage, and permanent injury is common."

He whispers, "I know all of that."

"So what kind of state of mind do you fucking think you have to be in to get into that cage?"

"Um, I don't know?"

"Exactly. You fucking don't. But wasting my time beforehand is only going to make it harder for me to prepare that mindset. Stop fucking around. It's not personal. I don't care about you personally one way or the other. Take your ego out of the equation and do your fucking job so I can do mine."

He wilts some more.

I look past him toward the door again, wondering when Dee is going to arrive. I think of her clawing at my back, her legs wrapped around my waist in a vice grip, her—

"So you, Duncan 'Creature' Malone, are undefeated for thirty-three fights now, right?"

"Correct."

"Since you entered organized underground fighting, you haven't been beaten. What is it, do you think, that makes you a much better fighter than your opponents?"

"That's strategy."

"Why do they call you 'Creature'?"

"Read your own rag, I'm sure you've written about it before."

"But I want to get it from your perspective."

"I didn't fucking come up with the nickname," I tell him, looking into his small eyes. "I don't refer to myself as 'Creature'."

"Fair enough," he says, scribbling. "Would you say, though, that it describes your fighting style?"

"How the fuck would the word 'creature' describe my fighting style?"

"You know, you're relentless in the cage. Fast, aggressive, powerful. When you fight, you give off the impression that you're only barely under control."

I grin. "Barely under control, huh? People who lose their minds in fights are never good at fighting. You want barely under control, go to a bar full of idiots on a Friday night. Barely under control does not describe what I, or any of my opponents do. You should know that."

Peterson frowns. "Would you share with your fans any tips if they're looking to get into fighting?"

"Control, discipline, and mental toughness. Technique. Leave the anger out of it."

"Not physical toughness? Strength? Endurance?"

"You can have all the physical attributes in the world, but if you're not good up here," I say, tapping my temple. "You'll never be successful."

"I guess that's the same with anything in life," he says. "Why do you keep looking over my shoulder?"

"None of your business."

He raises his eyebrows for a moment, then sighs and accepts my answer. I'm controlling this interview and he should know it. It's high time he came around.

"You were raised in a group home, weren't you? In the poor city of—"

"Raised isn't what I'd call it, but I spent most of my childhood in the system, yes. In more than one group home."

"Do you think that helped you with your fighting?"

"Of course."

"Could you explain how?"

"There are plenty of articles on what life is like in the system," I say. "Do some research. Even the girls learn to fight."

"But what in particular?"

"Defending myself, obviously, especially against older boys."

"You were bullied by older boys?"

I meet his eyes again, and he somehow shrinks a little more. "Not bullied," I tell him. "Like I said, I defended myself."

"Did it help the mental aspect?"

"Of course."

"How so?"

"You've got to be tough or you won't make it."

"Won't make it?"

"You'll just move from one system into another."

"Are you talking about prison?"

"Of course I fucking am."

"But you were taken out of 'the system' by Johnny Marino, yes? At the age of sixteen?"

I nod. "That's right."

"He adopted you legally as his son."

"Correct."

"He trained you, became your manager."

"Yes."

"To be a fighter."

"Yes."

"When did your training start?"

"Informally, from when I was about eight years old. Formally, when I was sixteen."

"You mean Johnny Marino trained you to fight as a teenager?"

I nod. "Yes."

"You were sparring regularly as a teenager against adults?"

"Yes."

Peterson sits back, eyes-wide. "That could be construed as child-abuse, especially if he forced you to."

"Nobody put a fucking gun to my head," I growl. "I chose it. But if you want to write that about Johnny fucking Marino, go right ahead. See what that gets you. Gagged and tied to a cement block at the bottom of the lake is one possibility."

"I don't think I'll put that in," Peterson says,

offering a weak smile.

"I didn't think you were that stupid."

"You're quite well-spoken, if I may say so."

"Is there a question hiding in there?"

"Just an observation."

"And why is it a relevant one? Did you expect me to be some fucking moron because I'm a fighter? Or is it because I'm an athlete?"

"N-no—"

"Maybe it's my tattoos? Come on, Dan. What did you really want to ask me?"

"It's just unexpected."

"To who?"

"Everybody!"

"Then everybody can go to fucking hell."

He tacks in the wind.

"Um, there are rumors that you were trained out of the country? Is that true?"

"No comment."

"What about your love life? Any girlfriends?"

"You write for TMZ now?"

"Your fans want to know."

"I don't care."

"You don't care about your fans?"

"You want to quote me, go ahead and fucking quote me. I don't give a shit, I don't owe them anything."

"Arguably, you owe them your career," Peterson says. "After all, they come to these fight nights and put money into it, some of which reaches you. Are you trying to say you don't care about the hand that feeds you?"

I consider Peterson. Maybe there's more to him than meets the eye. He's got a soft body but possibly a sharp mind. Have I been lulled to sleep?

If so, I have more respect for this man than before.

"I don't control what other people do or think," I tell him, spacing my words. "I fight, I win. That's what I do, and that's all I worry about."

"What about the ethics? We all know underground fighting is illegal."

"Funny that you should report on it, make your advertising dollars or whatever the fuck off it. Off the backs of us fighters."

"I'm press, it's my duty to."

"You basically run a blog, one that champions the underground scene at that."

"The most popular blog," he says. "The readers belong to me. The fans." He tilts his head to the side, a challenge in his eyes. "Your fans."

"Dare to quote yourself?"

Peterson's eyes twinkle. "You know," he says, his voice now instantly more confident than it was before. "I can make you out to be anyone I want."

"Go on then," I say. "But you have an obligation to the truth. Compromise your own integrity for all I give a shit. I can't help you, and what you write about me will never matter to me."

"So what does matter to you?"

"Fighting and family."

"You mean Johnny Marino, your adoptive father?"

I hesitate. "Sure."

"Do you look up to him? Since he used to be quite a well-known boxer?"

"Well-known how?" I ask Peterson. "Why don't you tell me what you know of him?"

"He was considered talented, ahead of his time. Fast and strong, a physical specimen."

"And what else?"

Peterson frowns. "He was often injured, picked up the nickname 'Glass'."

I nod. At least he knows his fighting history, and I suppose he deserves credit for that.

"My career has already surpassed his. 'Look up to' is the wrong way to put it."

It couldn't be more wrong. I despise the man.

Just a few more fights!

"Do you not care that he helped to make you who you are?"

"I made me who I am. But of course I'm gracious for the opportunities Glass has helped to provide me." I staple on the standard answer.

"Doesn't sound like the correct sort of way to talk about your adoptive father?"

"We're getting into personal territory now."

"You said that all that matters to you is fighting and family?"

"Yes."

"What about the other member of your family, your foster sister?" He flips through his note pad, bunches up his brow. "Um, Deidre Marino?"

I regard the man. That was an act if there ever was one. Everybody who knows of Johnny Marino knows his daughter by name.

"What about her?" I ask, instantly feeling protective. What's this guy driving at?

"Is she in the business?"

"What business?"

"It's an open secret that Johnny Marino is a big-time mobster. Mafioso. That he owns half this town, north of the river. Do you also work for the mob, Duncan? Are you an enforcer? You'd make a good one, no doubt."

I grin. "Interview's over, Dan."

"Just one more question, Duncan."

"Get out or I throw you out."

He chooses wisely.

I glare at him as he leaves, and then lean back in the sofa.

I think about Dee, her beautiful face, her soft skin.

Dee, legally my sister, but I've never thought of her that way.

Dee, who means more to me than anything else.

Dee, the only woman I can ever imagine sharing my life with.

*

25

DEE

"He's *so* sexy."

The words float through the black speaker grill in the front of the limousine. Beside me, Frank grins.

"I love his eyes. They're so blue, like water at the perfect beach."

"Like sapphires!" another girl says.

I roll my eyes. Regular bunch of poets back there.

"Who are these girls, anyway?" I ask, jerking my thumb back toward the two-way partition glass that separates the back of the limousine from the front.

They can't see us or hear us up-front – it's just a mirror on their side – but we can hear everything they say, see everything they do. I peer back, and right now they're drinking champagne liberally from the limo's bar.

"And can we turn the speakers off?" I add.

"Sorry, Deidre," Frank says. He turns his ruddy face and sleepy eyes toward me, wears an apologetic expression. "Your father's orders."

"You have to *listen* to them? That would drive me nuts."

"I listen to everything," he tells me. "Re-re… I don't know the word."

"Redundancy. So who are they, anyway? Just some girls for Dad?"

Frank frowns, shakes his head quickly. "Not your father, no. They're for his friends. But don't worry, Deidre, they're here of their own choice."

I make a face. Usually, you wouldn't need that qualification. *Usually.* Dad swears he doesn't do prostitution, but I know that's a lie. He only says it because I'm a woman and he thinks I can't take it, thinks I'll burst into hysterics or something over it.

Like women haven't been living in this fucking world, too.

"You'd think they'd have something better to do. God, they're practically my age. Why do they do this?"

All of Dad's friends are *his* age… just the thought of it icks me out. I wonder again if these girls have a choice. Nobody has a gun to their head, but life is tough for a lot of people. The barrel is not always made out of metal.

Dad preys on those people specifically.

I glance back, look through the mirror. The girls, three of them, seem off. They're hyper, jittery, almost trembling, but not from cold. The limo's heated.

"They're really here to see *Duncan*, Deidre. You know that. They just entertain some of your Dad's associates, that's all. It's a transaction."

The girls in the back, three of them all dressed up – impossibly-high heels, tiny dresses, glittering jewelry – squeal with laughter. I wince as the speakers erupt into a static hiss.

"Damn it," I whisper, rubbing my ears, thankful I missed what they said. No doubt it was something about Duncan. No doubt it was something I wouldn't like to hear.

Words float through the speakers, but I try to ignore them.

"I don't think they're talking about anything important," Frank says, and he lowers the volume. He offers me a kind smile.

"Thanks," I tell him.

"They're obsessed with Duncan," he says before briefly clearing his throat. "All the girls are. Every fight now, they're all talking about him. More girls turn up to fights than guys now. Can you believe that? I shuttle more girls to these fights than I do guys. It's… I never would have thought it, you know?"

I raise my eyebrows. "Yes, I know," I say. I hate that they all come to watch him fight, call out his name, scream 'marry me' at him, flash their fucking tits at him.

I hate that they can't see me on his arm. I'm his, and he's mine. It's petty… but why can't I indulge in a little smallness every now and then?

"And yet," Frank says. "I never see Duncan bring one of them home. He's never cozying up with them, you know? He could have any he pleased, all at the same time if he wanted."

My eyes narrow, and I turn them on Frank.

"What?" he asks, shrugging, a guilty and dirty smile prying his lips apart. "What I would give to be his age again with all them girls after me like that."

"Frank, I *really* don't need to hear this."

But the truth is he's right. Duncan's practically a superstar. It's not just people clued in to underground fighting, either. Even middle-class people from the suburbs are starting to get wind of him. Dad really took underground fighting and blew it up big time.

Despite everything wrong with it – the corruption, the betting, the dirty money, the sheer violence of it all – it is the sting of jealousy that I feel the most. I can't stand all these girls rubbing their hands on Duncan's body as he leaves the cage after a win, walks back to his private room. I can't stand the thought of any other girl getting to *look* at him, let alone *touch* him.

They like to crowd around him, fancy themselves

groupies, cell-phone flashes going off as each tries to get a selfie, as each tries to strike a good pose *and* get a non-blurry snap.

It's completely ridiculous. They all look so stupid doing it. The selfie-sticks have only made it all worse.

I feel the indignation start to turn to anger, and force myself to just forget about it. There's nothing I can do. What, am I going to control what other people think?

To his credit, Duncan never entertains them. He never so much as looks at them. Their hands grope him and he ignores all of them, never lingers.

I got on him once about it before. I was in a bad mood and looking to start a fight. He asked me what he was supposed to do… lay hands on them, push them away?

He's right of course. He could never do that.

But sometimes I wish *I* could.

I take a flyer from my bag. Duncan's on it wearing nothing but his fighting shorts. The lines of his body are cut deep, and he's staring straight into the camera. His jaw is a sharp cut, shadowed, and his lips full, endlessly kissable. And then there are those striking, blue eyes.

The girls in the back are right, of course… his eyes are something else.

"Don't tell me *you* fancy him," Frank says. "That would be wrong. He's your brother."

Once again I look at Frank, now a growing feeling of unease in my belly. I correct him: "My adopted brother."

Frank grunts. "You know, little sisters… and he's more like a cousin or something, anyway."

"Don't tell me you're opening up to me about your own childhood fantasies, Frank."

He barks out a hoarse laugh. But little does Frank realize he's right on the money… he's always had a nose for these things.

I rub my belly absent-mindedly.

I turn my eyes back down at the flyer. They were handed out all around town the last few days. The biggest underground MMA cage fight of the year.

Duncan 'Creature' Malone versus 'Manic' Conrad Butler. Their nicknames aren't exactly oblique; they describe their respective fighting styles perfectly.

I sigh, wipe my eyes over Duncan's almost-naked body. We've been joined at the hip, inseparable, for so long. It's not been all good though, but what is? Ups and downs are a part of life. It's like a heartbeat monitor. No ups and downs means you're dead inside.

But now… now I've got to break the biggest news of his life to him… of *my* life, too. Something I only just found out for sure this morning. Something I only just worked up the courage to go through with.

Of course, I already knew. The body doesn't lie.

I fold up the flyer, put it back into my bag. I'm just going to have to come out and say it. It's not going to be easy, but I have to, no matter how worried I am about what he might think. I keep doubting myself. I keep telling myself, *Don't think you know him that well. Don't think you can predict what he'll say.*

I don't know why. Maybe it's just a way to protect myself. Dim expectations are a suit of emotional armor.

But I know what Duncan is like on fight nights. He's so amped-up, so psychologically prepared to beat a man to within inches of his life, to get him into a choke hold and black him out, or to take a twisted shoulder right to its limit before it pops out of the joint, or the same to a knee.

When he's that way, it's often hard to get through to him. He puts up a mental shield, becomes resistant to considering anything but the fight. His face will drain of emotion, become statuesque.

That's *his* mental suit of armor.

"We're here," Frank says a few minutes later. We drive toward a chain-link fence that swings open automatically, and then we're on a short runway for small aircraft. We drive to the end, where a narrow beam of light splits the foggy night. The huge, sliding doors to a plane hangar are slightly open. Compared to the size of the building, they look open only a sliver, but I've little doubt the gap is wide enough to fit an SUV through.

I pull out my mirror from my bag, check my makeup quickly, rub smudged eyeliner away under my eyes. I don't want Duncan to know I was crying earlier. Panic got the better of me, but only for a moment.

"You okay?" Frank asks. "You seem a little down tonight."

"I'm fine," I whisper back at him.

"Don't want to watch the fight?"

I shake my head. "Watch my… watch Duncan take punches so Dad can earn more money? Not really."

Now there's a stony silence, and I look at Frank, that uneasy feeling in my belly turning into nausea.

"What is it, Frank?"

"You been avoiding your old man for a reason?" he asks.

I freeze. "What?"

"Forget it. Not my place."

I swallow. *Does he know?* How could he possibly?

"What is this about, Frank? Don't clam up on me."

"Just you never come around the house anymore. He's worried about you, Deidre."

"No, he's worried about himself."

"Deidre, it's not like that. I…" Frank's voice trails off. "It's not my place. You get going, now."

I peer at him, decide not to push it so I don't look

suspicious, and then my gaze goes past him and out the driver's side window. The three girls are all walking toward the hangar, their steps wobbly, and likely not just from their insane ankle-breakers.

"You let them do anything in the car?"

"Of course not!" Frank says, instantly indignant. "Rules are rules. They just drank the champagne. They're on something, though, but it was before they got in."

"Great," I say, shaking my head. "Just great. Thanks for the ride, Frank."

"Don't sweat it. Hey, can I ask you something?"

"Sure."

"Tell Duncan I wish him luck."

"Sure."

Frank grins. "I put fifty-large on him tonight."

"Alright, Frank," I say.

I get out of the car, fix my bag over one shoulder, and walk toward the hangar in a perfume-drenched wake.

*

26

DEE

Two guards wearing black suits and earpieces approach me as I walk toward the open hangar door.

"Excuse me, miss," they say. "Do you have the—"

"Flyer?" I ask, pulling it from my bag.

But they've already seen my face, and they know who I am.

"Sorry, Ms. Marino," they both diffidently say in unison. They cast quick, nervous glances at each other.

"It's okay," I tell them, smiling.

"Just doing our jobs."

"Come on, it's fine. Don't worry about it, I won't

bite. Where's Duncan? I need to speak to him."

"There's a closed-off area down in the back," the guard on the left informs me. He's got an accent I can't place. Dad always liked to hire new immigrants; he says they're easier to control. "There's a guard outside, too."

"Okay," I say, nodding. "Thank you."

"Ms. Marino," the guard says, stepping in front of me when I move to enter the hangar.

"Yes?"

He hesitates, seems to be trying to figure out the most diplomatic words to use. Eventually, he just spits it out.

"Are you carrying a weapon?" He holds out a numbered tag. The number reads eighty-six. "If you don't mind."

"No," I tell him. I open my bag, let him peer inside. "Satisfied?"

"Do you mind if I look inside myself, Ms. Marino?"

I sigh, but give him my whole bag. He rummages through it quickly, before nodding and giving it back to me.

"I'm really sorry, but—"

"My father's orders," I say. "It's okay, I understand."

No weapons allowed inside. A wise decision, considering some people are going to lose a lot of money tonight when Duncan wins.

"Your father's orders," the guard echoes, nodding.

"It's okay. Really, you guys need to relax."

But I know they can't. Dad hates mistakes. Make one, and you are likely to end up in hospital with a cast around your leg.

Your second mistake puts you underground.

"One more thing, Ms. Marino."

"What is it?"

"Your father wants to speak with you."

A pang hits me right in the gut. Why would Dad want to see me?

"I'll speak to him later."

"He left specific instructions for you to see him immediately."

I sigh. "Thank you."

I have no intention of seeing him immediately. I'll see him when I damn well choose to.

I step into the hangar, and immediately wince, shielding my eyes from the bright spotlights. There is dust in the air, in the beams, and it looks like dripping liquid light.

The spotlights illuminate a steel-mesh cage sitting in the center of the enormous space. It's elevated on a platform about five-feet high, and facing each of its six sides are bleachers that rise up at a steep angle.

Already, the place is packed. I can faintly smell booze on the air. I cast my eyes around, studying the place. Toward the right wall of the hangar is the bookie's station.

I lick my lips, shake my head.

I hate this. I hate that they bet on Duncan like he's some kind of dog. They bet against him, want to see him beaten up, broken, lose.

When I first started going to Duncan's fights, I used to think it was cool. He'd be the winner, the star, and we'd celebrate together.

We'd drink together afterward and laugh and chat. And Duncan would never want to talk about the fights, and I always would. And Duncan would always ask me questions about what *I* was doing in college, as if it could somehow be more interesting than underground fighting with fucking senators in attendance.

But now I feel differently. The glamor has worn off. It's been getting that way for a while. The excitement has faded, and I'm starting to see it for what it truly is. Duncan is, to Dad, to the other mob bosses and attendees, nothing but an animal in a fight.

They all want to see blood and make money.

Now… now the fights are different. Now I see a man I care for with all of my heart taking punches, and sometimes it's worse when he throws them.

I've watched Duncan snap a man's leg in two, choke a man blue, turn a face to red and white mush in a flurry of punches.

I worry what it does to him.

What it's doing to me.

After thirty-three fights, after helping to clean his wounds, after watching him wince in pain just getting out of bed the next day… now I hate it.

I blink myself out of reverie, look around the hanger for where Duncan's private partition will be. Toward the left wall is the bar. Drinks are sold liberally, and you can even get a little something else on the side if you know how to ask for it. But guards walk through the area regularly. Anybody getting too rowdy gets thrown out.

I begin to make my way down toward the back of the hangar. I can see large, roofed partition, a building built inside the hanger.

A screech of laughter snatches my attention, and I see the same three girls that were in the limousine walk past me, arms linked. They're still wobbly, and they are moving in the same direction I am, flicking their hair, drawing attention to themselves.

I follow them slowly, all the way to the back room where Duncan is. A guard approaches them, and he puts his hands out.

"I'm sorry," he says, shaking his head. "You can't come back here."

"But we just want to talk to Creature," one of the girls says, her voice a drawn-out whine.

"Off limits," the guard says.

The girls all look at each other, and then turn big, puppy-eyes on the guard. They blink eyelashes at him, pout their lips.

"Please? We only want to wish him good luck."

"A kiss for luck!" one of the girls blurts, and they all descend into giggling. "Maybe something more."

I roll my eyes.

"You can see him later," the guard says, his voice growing sterner. "When he's fighting."

But the girls still don't give up, and I grow irritated. I walk around them with a sigh, and meet the guard's eye. He nods at me, swings open the door. The hinges grind.

"Why can *she* go in?" I hear one of the girls complain.

Another one hisses at her to shut up. *"That's Mr. Marino's daughter!"*

I turn around, meet her eyes. She gives me the best bitch-look she can muster as the door shuts.

And then I'm in darkness, and blink rapidly, seeing spots while my eyes adjust. A pair of strong arms wraps me up from behind, shocking me, and I feel warm breath against the back of my neck, feel lips against my skin.

"I've been waiting for you all night, Dee."

*

27

DEE

I turn in Duncan's arms, but before I can speak he crushes his lips against mine.

He's on me all in an instant, hands roaming, devouring. He lifts me up, carries me deeper into the room, and when I wrap my legs around his waist I can feel his bulge pushing into me.

"God, you smell so good," he growls into my ear before capturing my lips again and making them his, sending my heart racing, my breath panting.

I melt in his arms, want to push off him because I've got such big news to tell him, but find myself unable to.

When he breaks our kiss, I finally manage to say, "Wait."

He sets me down, concern on his face. "What's wrong? Did anybody give you trouble outside?"

"No," I say, seeing the flare of protectiveness in his eyes. "No, it's nothing like that."

Every fight night he's like this. Ultra-possessive, protective, as if the whole world is out to get me and he'll take them all on… and win.

It's silly, but I know it's a product of the mindset he has to get himself into. He spends the whole day preparing his mentality, so that when he's in the cage, the prospect of having bones broken doesn't scare him one bit.

It scares me, though. It always scares me.

"I think I need to tell you something," I say to him quickly, but when I see the look in his eyes I know he's not in the talking mood.

His tight body glistens in the dim light, and in between us his manhood is an iron bar pressed up against my abdomen through his towel.

I touch his face, feel his heat. He takes my finger into his mouth, bites it, and I touch his soft, full lips, trace my finger along the sharp line of his jaw, over his cheek bones.

God, he always looks so good before fights. I don't know why I like it so much, I just do. The sweat, the dim lights, the way he's so locked-in, the desire I see in his eyes…

I can smell him, too, from his pre-fight warm-ups. I love the way he smells, especially when I can detect a hint of his musk.

His eyes narrow, and there's a break in his expression.

"Nothing," I say, quickly. I realize that now is not the time to tell him. I realize that doing so will shatter whatever stony state he's in, whatever mindset he needs to be in to take a beating and win this fight.

I can't do that to him. I won't. The news will have to wait. He'll still be here after his fight, and so will I.

The fight won't last that long.

It can wait.

I lean back, look at his bulge, the outline of his need for me, and then back into his eyes.

"You look hot," I tell him.

A small grin parts his lips, and I see the tops and bottoms of his straight teeth. He pulls me close to him, wraps an arm around my waist.

"I've missed you," he whispers. "I want you."

I coil my arms around his neck, smile back at him. My heart is racing, there's so much going on in my mind at once.

But what floats to the top is the knowledge that I want him, too. That I've also been thinking about him all day. That after the first tears of panic, and last tears of joy, that I wanted nothing more than to be with him.

To be close to him.

God, why today, of all days? Why fight night?

"How much do you want me?" I ask him.

The lust for me that I see in his eyes catches fire.

Duncan pulls me in tighter, and I fold my arms around him, run my palms along his hard, broad back.

But he turns me around in his arms so he's behind me again. He likes to be behind me. He begins kissing the side of my neck. The touch of his warm, soft lips makes me hum, makes me crane my neck to the side so he can kiss more of me.

"More than anything," he growls. "I can't stop

thinking about the way you smell, the way you taste, the way you feel."

The sensation of his warm breath rushing against my neck is intoxicating, and his body heat radiates into me.

His hands run up my sides, and I feel a welling of anticipation inside me, a pressure. His touch, even through my clothing, is so electric, so possessive. It's like my body belongs to him.

"You're only mine," he says, his voice quiet. "I'm never letting you go."

He's like this normally, but on fight nights, it's dialed up to eleven.

I press back into him, feel his hardness against me, and reach behind me and cup him through the fluffy towel he's got wrapped around his waist.

"You're always so hard," I tell him, the thought turning to words effortlessly.

"You make me hard," he says, taking a fistful of my hair. He tugs it back, makes me look up at the ceiling, and from behind me he leaves a trail of hot kisses along my jaw, my chin.

"I spent the whole day imagining you moaning

onto me," he tells me. "With your arms above your head, your breasts against my chest."

"Is that all you think about?" I ask, letting a small smile creep across my lips.

I want to turn toward him, want to kiss him, let him claim my lips as his like he is my body, but he doesn't let me.

"Every fucking minute. It's been hell without you."

"Even while you were training?"

"Especially while I was training."

"Even while you were giving your interview?"

"I think he noticed."

I laugh at the thought, Duncan sitting there with an erection while getting asked inane questions.

"You must be frustrated, then," I say, gripping onto his manhood harder through the towel. I find the edge of the cloth, slip my hand inside, and there wrap my fingers around him.

"You have no fucking idea," he breathes.

I start to slowly caress him, stroke his cock. I can feel his pulse in my fingers… or maybe it is my own racing heart? I can't tell.

I bring my hand up and over his tip, feel a dab of wetness on my fingers. Slowly I rub my thumb against the back of it, and I hear him exhale slowly, know that what I'm doing makes him feel good. There's one rule on fight nights: He can't come. He says it helps his testosterone levels immediately before the fight.

"Do you enjoy doing this?" I ask him. "Even if you don't get to—"

"Every fucking second."

His hands move inward from my sides, cup my breasts, and I sigh as he massages them, kneads them hungrily. I feel the press of his teeth against the skin of my neck, the dab of his wet tongue.

"Some girls wanted to get in," I say slowly. "They said they wanted to give you kisses for good luck."

"Fuck those skanks," he says, his voice deep. "I only want you."

"Just me?"

"Just you."

"But for how long?" I tease. "What about when I get older?"

"Then I'll get old with you."

I smile, push my head against his. "What if I don't want you anymore when you're older?"

"Well, tough shit because I'm not leaving you."

He's more emotional today, I can pick up on it. Maybe he senses the news, somehow. Maybe, on some intuitive level, *he knows.*

"You still don't know what you do to me, Dee."

"I can feel what I do to you."

I take his hand, push it down over my belly, then lower, and he dips it below my skirt, brings it up, cups me.

I gasp at the heat in his palm. I feel it so acutely, and through my underwear he starts to rub me slowly, pull sighs and soft moans from my lips.

His body language, even just the aura of lustful energy he has speaks only of his desire for me, and it makes me feel so attractive, so wanted, makes me want him more in turn. He wants me bad… it's not just fight nights. It's every single night. Every waking moment.

I hear him inhale beside me. He always likes to smell me, right by my ear. I don't wear perfume on fight nights because he doesn't like me to. He says he loves the way *I* smell.

I know what he means. I love the way *he* smells, unmasked, unaltered, uncovered. I love to wear his gym hoodies… he thinks its gross because he sweats into them, but I like it. Maybe it is gross, but I don't care.

He starts to rub me faster, settles into a rhythm, and he pulls back my hair again, turns me so we're facing the full-body mirrors that line the wall.

With him behind me, his lips against my neck, his hand beneath my skirt, and all in clear view in the mirror… I never expected watching myself and him to be hot, but it is. It's really hot.

"Do you want me to make you feel good?" he asks.

I nod.

"Say it."

"I want you to make me feel good," I say breathlessly.

Already I can feel my knees growing weak. Already I'm starting to sag in his arms as he plays me expertly, his chosen instrument.

My breathing quickens, my temperature rises, and

in his arms I feel so safe, and in his arms I feel so wanted.

"Yes," I hiss at him, letting my eyes fall shut. He rubs me slowly, drags his tongue up the skin of my neck, squeezes my breasts, plays me so deftly, sends a mild and budding pleasure thrumming through my body.

I squirm in his arms, push my ass back against him so I can feel his hardness. I'm his willing captive, letting him touch me, and he pulls soft moans from my lips, makes me feel those hints of bliss, behind which is the promise of so much more.

"Mmm," I moan, and he bites the back of my shoulder, sends goose bumps erupting all over my body, and sends shivers shooting down to my toes.

I grin, lick my lips, grip onto him tighter behind me and start to jerk him off. He moves his body to the side, and I pull his cock out from inside his towel, and I can see him now in the mirror, see his hardness, feel him.

"Damn, you are sexy, Dee," he says, meeting my eyes in the mirror. We look at each other, him touching me, me touching him, giving each other pleasure.

And then when he can't take it anymore, he picks me up, pulling a yelp and a laugh from my lips, and he sets me down on the sofa, and pulls off my flats slowly.

He strokes my feet, makes me giggle and squirm, and then in between my legs he kisses each of my toes in turn, then the tops of my feet, and then makes his way up my inner thigh, leaves a trail of tingling skin.

I'm so wound-up already I almost want to hurry him on, but I know that on fight nights, we go at his pace. He made that clear the first time we ever did this before a fight.

His crystal blue eyes gaze up at me, and he lifts my skirt up, over my hips, and then with his teeth he hooks the elastic of my underwear and pulls down.

I grin at him, see him smirk back as he pulls it off with his mouth, baring me to him. He brings my panties to his nose, smells me, and for a moment I feel a flash of modesty, but the look in his eyes quashes that instantly. It's all hunger and lust, all desire.

He guides my legs up, so my feet are on the sofa, and presses his face closer to my sex, kisses me around my outer lips, teases me.

I feel his tongue dart out, touch my clit for an instant, and I'm jolted by sensation, a sharp hint of pleasure.

"You smell so good," he says, voice baritone, lust-laced. And then he pulls his tongue up my sex, and I moan and quake and tense my thighs as he starts licking me just the way I like it.

He settles on my clit, flicks it rhythmically with his tongue and I'm just lost in sensation, in heaven, leaning back against the sofa, wanting to stretch out like a cat and let him pleasure me.

I grip onto his hair, pull him harder against me, mash myself against him as he laps at me like he needs it to live.

"Oh shit," I hiss, feeling the temperature in my core rising, feeling that pressure in my belly. He works me so expertly, knows exactly how to bring me surging forward toward the edge.

"Yes!" I groan, gripping onto his hair harder, pulling him tighter onto me. I feel my body grow tight, lift myself off the sofa, right up against the edge.

And then he backs me off.

I grin at him, tut, shake my head. "You big tease. You always do that."

He smirks, keeps licking me, and I fall back into bliss as he rings a finger around my entrance, groan and squeeze as he pushes it inside me.

I moan as he slides in a second finger, feel myself stretch around him, and then he starts to finger me, pressing upward with each thrust, making me feel so good.

He groans onto me, and his laps grow feverish like he's starving for me, and his fingers fuck me harder, and again I feel that pressure inside me, feeling myself coiling tighter and tighter, ready to explode.

"Come on," I pant, practically begging him to make me come, to give me the release I want. "Fuck, yes yes, yes…"

I throw my head into the sofa, arch my back, grind myself against his face.

He brings me right there again, so close, and at the precipice, right when ecstasy is about to come crashing down all over me, there's a loud knock at the door.

I freeze. A voice that comes booming through the

door: "Fifteen minutes."

But Duncan doesn't stop. He keeps going, and remembering that the door is locked, my body thrills with pleasure again. I'm lost in it all again, climbing higher and higher. The pressure is building… I'm going to—

"Ooohhh," I moan as he drives me off the edge, as I crest. I'm soaring, in orbit, and I moan at him, "Don't stop!"

He doesn't, and as ecstasy grips me I squeeze around his fingers, and he makes my orgasm last for so, so long, I don't even know how he does it.

I'm shaking, trembling, mouth clamped tight so that I don't moan too loudly. I curl my toes, grip at his hair, tug him hard, so hard I'm sure it hurts.

He just makes me feel so, so good.

And then I'm coming down, the waves of pleasure no longer so intense. I'm bathing in a pool of bliss, humming, grinning.

I let out the long breath I was holding, and shiver as I grow too sensitive. Duncan pulls his fingers from me, plunges my pleasure into his mouth, sucks me off his fingers.

He tells me how good I taste, and his towel has come apart, and looking down at him in between my legs, I can see his hard cock jutting out from his crotch.

He leans forward, drags his tongue up my sex, and I shudder, pushing him off me.

"Wait a minute, okay?" I mewl at him, grinning. "I'm sensitive."

He kisses me furiously, crushing his lips against mine, and he takes my hand and guides it to his cock, and I grip onto him and jerk him fast and hard.

He climbs up over me, straddling me almost, his back curved. I push him backward, and once again I feel overwhelmed by desire.

I kiss him down his chiseled stomach, smell his musk, bury my nose in his trimmed pubic hair and smell my man.

I kiss my way up his shaft, lick up the droplets of pre-cum beading at his tip, and then I take it into my mouth, bob up and down on him fast, press my tongue against the back of his cockhead and jerk him to the same rhythm.

He leans back, his body tightening, and he runs his

fingers through my hair, tells me how fucking sexy I am.

I love the way he tastes, love the groans that leave his lips, love the way he looks at me while I suck him off, while I bring him closer and closer to the edge.

His breaths grow ragged, his thighs tense up, and when I get him almost there I pop him out of my mouth, and look up at him, grinning.

The look on his face is that of pure torture.

"God damn it," he growls, leaning down, kissing me. I push my tongue into his mouth, make him taste himself, and he just kisses me harder for it.

He lifts me up with an easy strength, one that makes me feel small in his arms, and I wrap my legs around his waist. His eyes bore into mine, and then flick down to my lips, and he kisses me again, like he can't get enough of me.

His cock is pressing against my entrance, and he lets me sidle down his body, and I gasp as he enters me, stretching me.

Slowly, his manhood inches into me, and I grip onto him as if for dear life as he fills me up, makes me feel so unbelievably, fantastically full.

I moan into his ears, only for him to hear because I know he loves it. He bites my shoulder, licks a stretch of skin up my neck, and then he pulls his hips back and thrusts all the way into me.

I dig my nails into his skin, moan louder into his ear, and he starts to fuck me standing. Our bodies slaps wetly together, and he guides my forehead to his so he can look into my eyes.

It's a struggle to be quiet – we have to be discreet – and he's making it so damn difficult.

"Duncan," I breathe, wrapping my arms tighter around his neck, pushing his face down against my breasts. I feel his tongue in between, and then he bites me.

"Your fight's starting soon," I say.

"I don't want to leave you." He thrusts more forcefully into me. I tighten up in pleasure, grip onto his waist harder with my legs.

"Lean back," he says, and he supports my weight with his arms, and I hold onto his neck with just one arm, lean back in his grip so that there's space between us.

"Come for me," he says. I know an order when I hear one.

I send my free hand down in between us, start rubbing my clit while he fucks me.

"Moan for me."

I moan for him, rub myself, bring myself racing to the edge, love how he makes me feel.

"You are so fucking sexy," he growls at me as I moan, let my eyes fall shut in bliss. "I love how tight your little pussy is around my cock. You make me feel so good."

He senses my nearness, thrusts harder and faster into me, and my thighs tense and that spring coils tighter and tighter, and then I'm right on the edge again, so, so, so close…

"Duncan," I breathe, bunching up my face.

He leans forward, takes my lips in his just as I climax, and I moan into his mouth, crest hard and tight and intense, so intense it almost hurts.

I shake and tremble. White hot bliss sears my senses, and I'm in heaven, and I never want this feeling to end.

He drives me through it, makes it last, and I'm limp in his arms, wracked by pleasure, barely able to hold on anymore.

I feel so damn good, so close to him, so intimate with him. Just me and him, alone.

And then I'm passed the peak, panting, sweating, clinging onto him.

His thrusts slow, and we stop moving, and he holds me tight against him, his cock still hard inside me.

He holds me for ages, refuses to let me go. His breathing slows, and he smells me, kisses me beneath my ear.

His lips find mine again, but this time the kiss is gentler. Our tongues dance, and I wish this didn't have to end.

I shudder as he slides himself out of me, and sets me down onto my feet. My knees are wobbly, weak, and I have to stand against him, lean my bodyweight onto him. He holds my face in his hands, looks into my eyes.

"Are you okay?" I ask, panting, stroking his face, feeling his stubble against my hand. "You seem different tonight."

Duncan shrugs. "Something feels different tonight."

Our intimacy seems to crack. We step apart from each other. I smooth my skirt, my top, fix my hair. Duncan pulls on his compression shorts.

He's still hard as an iron bar, and it's going to take quite a few minutes for that to slowly go way.

There's a silence between us. This happens before every fight, but this time… it feels more pronounced.

"Don't get too beat up," I tell him, taking my phone out of my bag quickly and checking it. "I can't stand watching you get hurt."

"I promise," he tells me. I go to him, let him wrap me up in his arms, and I hear him say to me, "I really want to know what you were going to tell me."

I feel a pang of guilt, but know I can't distract him during his fight with his toughest opponent yet.

"It's nothing," I say. I know it's a lie but it's the best thing to do. "I'll tell you afterward. I promise."

He nods, accepts what I say, doesn't push it any further. I love that about him… he knows when to push, and when not to.

He presses his forehead to mine, runs a thumb over my lip. "You are amazing," he tells me. There is only sincerity in his voice. "The best thing that ever happened to me."

Then, as if unable to stand that moment of gushiness, he separates from me, and walks around the changing room stretching. He begins his breathing exercises, thumps his shoulders and chest with closed fists, starts to psych himself up for the fight.

I find my underwear on the sofa, pull it on quickly, and then share one last look with him. He nods at me.

Already I can see the fire in his eyes, and that stony expression on his face. He's getting into his acute zone, that mental realm where he can beat a man to within inches of his life and not have it affect him.

To this day, I don't know how he does it. Duncan's never *not* returned from that realm, even if he sometimes gets a little punch-drunk.

"I'll be watching," I tell him.

"Then that means I'll win."

"Why's that?"

"Can't lose in front of the most beautiful girl in

the room." He smirks playfully.

"Groan," I say, rolling my eyes. "But you better win. Don't get hurt, okay?"

"I won't."

I leave him then, pick up my bag, and go back out into the fray.

The same three girls who were trying to get in to see Duncan mill about, shoot death-stares my way.

I ignore them, don't have time for that bullshit.

Duncan's all mine, anyway, and that's never going to change.

He'll now do his final warm-ups, and take his electrolyte-cocktail drinks that he mixes up himself. Fast-acting supplements to prevent cramping, boost overall oxygen uptake, get his balance of minerals right so water isn't pulled out of his blood and muscles and into his bladder.

He'll do his stretches, put heating strips on his major muscle groups to dilate the blood vessels there. He'll do breathing exercises, controlled hyperventilation to saturate his muscles with as much oxygen as possible prior to the fight, to prevent the initial burst of lactic acid build-up that comes with the start to every fight; they go zero-to-one-hundred in under a second in the cage.

I know it all by heart. I've researched the biochemistry, helped Duncan to formulate his cocktails. We've consulted with nutritionists, doctors, trying to find the perfect balance for Duncan's body.

His metabolism blazes, and he burns through energy reserves quickly. At just five-percent body-fat, he doesn't have enough free energy on his body to truly last him through a fight without him feeling fatigued, and we can't let his blood-sugar levels drop.

There's no stoppage in underground fighting unless there's excessive blood. There are no rounds, no breaks. It's fight until one falls, plain and simple. That means no rehydration. That means no fuel-uptake.

It's more complicated than the pros, in that respect. You have to get your body *more* prepared. In the event of stoppage because of too much blood, usually by then it doesn't matter anymore. If there's that much blood, somebody needs to go to the hospital.

Duncan will take some slow-release glucose pills to

keep his sugar levels up. He'll take beta-alanine to keep his muscles working efficiently and combat natural fatigue.

But really, in the end, these are all just the small bits that, from the outside, we *can* control. Most of the work toward winning a fight will be the physical work, something that can't be band-aided by supplements.

Duncan's simply going to have to fight better than Manic. I've seen the videos of Manic with him, scouted Manic's fighting style with him.

It's going to be Duncan's toughest fight yet. I hate to think it, but there is some flicker of doubt in me that he'll win this fight.

It's highly possible that this will be his first loss.

Losing is part of it, he knows it and I know it. This *Cinderella* run he's been on has been fantastic and entirely to his credit, but he's going to have to lose someday.

I'm worried about how he'll take it.

It will be a shock for him if he does. I know, psychologically, he can weather that storm. But to say he won't be bruised would be to say that he wasn't human.

And he's very, very human.

I make my way through the stands, go to the table where Dad and Frank sit with the other mob bosses. He beckons me to him, whispers into my ear, tells me he needs to speak to me privately.

"The fight's about to start," I say to him. Duncan's already walking out of the back, and the gaggle of girls are now around him, screaming and screeching, cellphone flashes blinding.

But Dad's expression is hard. He looks pissed about something. He gets up, excuses himself from the table, and pulls me by my elbow out of the bleacher-stands.

I cast a look over my shoulder, see Duncan walking around the cage. Any moment now he's going to look for me, but he's not going to find me.

God damn it, fighting is about routine! Dad is going to fuck this all up. Every fight has to be the same, same ritual. That means Duncan has to find me in the crowd. We *have* to meet eyes. He *has* to see that I'm there supporting him.

Duncan *needs* me.

"Dad!" I cry, trying to shake my elbow free of his grip, but he just holds me harder, and pulls me roughly toward an empty portion of the hangar, behind the bookie's table, and into a back room where all the betting money is collected and kept under-guard.

"Hey!" I cry, but his eyes shoots daggers at me. He whistles at the two guards, and they leave, shut the door behind them.

Now that we have some privacy, I let loose. "What the hell is wrong with you, Dad? Why are you being such a fucking prick tonight?" I rub my elbow. His grip was hard. "You hurt me, you know!"

He ignores what I say. "Is there something you want to tell me?" he asks, hands on his hips. He's huffing. His face is red, and I know the look of anger in his eyes when I see it. His gold teeth seem to glint a darker shade.

Inside my head, bomb sirens start to wail. I look around the room, see briefcases tagged, ordered, stacked on shelves. Duffel bags, paper envelopes. I spy one brown envelope with Frank's messy scrawl on the outside. His fifty-grand bet on Duncan.

"No," I tell Dad.

Dad pinches his brow, then rubs a hand over his gleaming, sweating bald dome. He's really worked up.

"Deidre," he says, his voice barely in control. "Don't lie to me."

I narrow my eyes at him. "What are you talking about?"

"Don't lie to me, Deidre!" he snaps, smacking his fist against the wall. I wince, step backward reflexively.

"Dad," I say, shaking my head. "What the hell is wrong with you? You're scaring me."

He takes a deep breath of air before asking in a low voice, "Are you pregnant?"

I swallow. I haven't told anybody, not even Duncan.

How the hell does he know?

*

28

DEE

Dad is scaring me.

"Sit down."

His tone is frosty, and he gestures at a stool in the room.

Great, I think to myself. I take the seat. What choice do I have? Dad's not going to let me out of this room.

Dad is not going to let me out of this room.

How fucked up is that?

The steel stool is uncomfortable, moves a little when I shift my weight. He puts his hand into his suit-jacket pocket and pulls out a ziplock bag. It takes me a moment to focus on what's inside it.

But when I see the thin, white, cylindrical object, panic sends my heart racing.

"I don't know what that is," I lie.

"I said *don't* lie to me, young woman," he barks. "It's yours. Don't try to deny it. There were others, too."

"How could you possibly know that's mine?" I ask a second before it dawns on me. I widen my eyes in shock. "You went through *my trash*? At my *dorms*?"

He throws the ziplock back onto the metal table beside me. The plastic pregnancy test pen rattles.

"I didn't personally, no."

"You made someone else do it?"

"Frank."

I'm speechless. The world is spinning. *Frank*? That's what he was on about in the limousine, acting all weird! But I know he was just following Dad's orders. The good soldier.

God damn it, Frank!

"Why?" I nearly shout. It feels like the ground is shaking beneath my feet. The indignity… I'm… I can't even put into words how I feel. "For how long have you been going through my stuff? My fucking *trash*? Did you do it when I still lived at home, too?"

I shake my head. I can't even… I can't even—

"Since you were a teenager," he says, waving his hand at me. "Don't act so surprised. It's for your own protection."

"My *protection*?" I cry.

"All of our protection. To make sure nothing sensitive gets out. You know how dangerous it can be in our situation. You know that we're constantly targets… the police, the other families. Anything they can get their hands on, they'll use against us. Against *you.* They will absolutely root through our garbage. It was for your own protection."

I shake my head at him in disbelief. Everything I've thrown away since I was thirteen was rooted through… seven years of my privacy violated, maybe more.

"Was it always Frank?"

Dad shakes his head. "Not always. But most of the time."

I bury my face in my hands. I can't believe it.

All these years.

It makes me sick!

"Get over it," Dad says. "Your trash is not that interesting. Nobody's is."

"You violated my privacy. Do you have any idea how I feel right now?"

He sighs, folds his big arms over his barrel-chest. He's put on comfort weight as he's gotten older, but beneath that is still a strong, ex-boxer's body.

I am physically afraid of my father.

That just makes me even sicker.

"I'm not going to repeat myself more than this last time, Deidre," Dad warns. "It was for our protection."

"You should have told me."

"Then you'd just hide things."

"I have the right to!"

"Not from me!" he yells, shocking me into silence. "Not from your father!" He points at the pregnancy tester. "Explain this now."

"What's to explain?"

"Who is the father?"

I lick my lips and lie: "Someone I met at a party."

Predictably, Dad's face morphs into shocked

judgment. He's so old-fashioned.

"I didn't raise you that way."

"You didn't raise me at all."

"Not this again."

"You think you were a good father? You never cared about me, especially not once Duncan came into the picture."

I know why I'm doing this, just to get him off-balance… anything to drive him off-topic. To not make it obvious that his surrogate son, the one he thought he could adopt and then shape into a better version of himself, the one he tried – and failed – to tame, is the father of my baby.

"What's the boy's name?"

I shake my head. "I don't know."

"You don't *know*?" he cries in disbelief. But then the expression on his face flattens. I can see the cogs in his mind whirring. He's starting to suspect I might be lying. He knows I wouldn't forget something like that.

"You're lying to me, don't think I can't tell." He lifts his hands up, claps them together, rubs them out of frustration. "My own daughter, my own flesh and blood, the daughter I raised, gave a good life. I spilled blood for you, and this is how you repay me?"

"You never once did anything *for me*!" I fire back at him. "You only did it for yourself, for your empire! You never hid how disappointed you were to have a daughter. You even went out and adopted a fucking son!"

"You watch your fucking mouth," he snarls. "That's not how a lady talks. And you're right," he says. "I regret that your mother couldn't give me a son. But that doesn't mean I wasn't happy to have you."

"Fuck you, Dad," I say, pointing a trembling finger at him. "You were never happy to have me. Not once."

"That hurts," he says, comically touching his chest. "You'd say that to your own father."

I shake my head, fold my arms. He's so fucking manipulative. "I'm not talking to you anymore."

"Why won't you tell me who the father is? If he's just some boy you… had relations with at a college party." He winces as he says the words. "Then why do you care?"

"I know what you'll do to him."

"What is it you think I'll do?"

"Have Frank pay him a visit, and then I'll be reading his obituary."

Dad sighs over-dramatically. He always was a bit of an actor. He always did think of himself as playing some kind of part in some kind of script.

Real life… never seems to be *real* to him. Especially when others suffer at his feet.

"I'll raise the child as my own," he says, voice stone-cold and resolute. "If it's a boy, he'll be my son."

"*What*?" I cry. "Are you insane?"

"You're not to tell anybody about this. I'm sending you to live with Aunt Ger—"

"You sure as fucking hell aren't!" I shout. "This is *my* baby, and *my* life."

He takes a deep, shuddering breath. "You will do as I say."

"It's my baby, and you have no right to tell me what to do."

Dad sighs, spaces his words. "You will do as I say. This is the family way."

"I don't fucking want to be in your family. I didn't ask to be in your family!"

"You will do as I say," he repeats. "Nobody knocks up Johnny Marino's daughter without my permission, do you hear me? If the other families get wind of this… if they know that *my* daughter is the type of girl to—"

"You care more about what they think of you than what *I* think of you. How sad is that?"

"Reputation is everything in this town. You know that."

I'm so disgusted. I want to hurl curse words at him but know it won't make any difference.

"You will tell me who the father of the baby is."

"No, I won't."

"You will," he says, and he steps forward. I wince, but he takes my hand, holds it. "You're my daughter, and you will because I love you, and I'm trying to protect you."

I tear my hand from his. "Don't try and manipulate me, Dad! I'm not a little girl anymore. You can't lie to me anymore. We both know why you're doing this. You don't want an illegitimate baby in the family. You don't want anybody to know… your precious *reputation.* God forbid your daughter have a baby out of wedlock! Oh, what will the other mob bosses think of me?" I sneer at him. "What century are you living in, anyway? Is a woman allowed to even speak in your presence, or does she need your *permission*, too, you fucking bastard!"

Dad sighs with melodramatic absurdity. "The father never sought my permission. He is not marrying you. The baby will be raised as my own. It is for the good of the child. It is the only way, Deidre."

I laugh, get up off the stool and back away from him. "You're so old-fashioned. No, it's not even old-fashioned, it goes beyond that, Dad. You're insane."

"Is it a boy or a girl?"

I shake my head at him, incredulous. "It's too soon for that, *obviously*."

"Well, then we can both pray that it will be a boy."

I freeze. The world comes grinding to a halt.

Pray that it will be a boy!

I see it now, I see why he's doing this. The reputation, the face, the name… that *is* all important to him.

But no, he sees this as a chance to finally have that son he always said he wanted. The son he wanted instead of me. The son that Duncan was supposed to be.

Of course he could never tame Duncan.

But now… now he can take my baby, and if it's a boy, he'll call it his own son.

No!

NO!

He's not going to get his dirty hands on my child. He's not going to steal my baby and make it his own.

I don't want my child growing up anywhere near this life. I want something better for my child than I ever had, than Duncan ever had.

"Why is it you never had another child, Dad?" I ask.

His face turns somehow harder. His lip twitches.

"Something wrong with you?"

"You'll not talk to me that way."

"I'll talk any way I damn well please!" I say. "But you know, I never stopped to think about it before. Why didn't you just remarry? Have another kid? Have your *own* son?"

Emotions I can't identify ripple across his features. "You think I have to explain myself to *you*?" he cries, laughing. "Tell me who the father is."

I mock-laugh back at him. "I won't."

I turn around, fling open the door. The two guards block my way.

"Try and stop me!" I yell at them, looking each of them in the eyes in turn. I push past them, hear Dad speak to them behind me.

"Let her go," he says. "She'll come around."

Like fucking hell I will.

I storm through the airplane hangar. Frank sees me, waddles up to me.

"Deidre—"

I turn to him, shake my head at him. I can't keep the tears from my eyes now.

"I trusted you, Frank," I say to him, my voice sticky. His face drops. "You were my friend! I liked you, you stupid, little man."

"Dei—"

I put up my hand. "Don't talk to me. I don't want to see you ever again."

I walk past him, past the cage. Duncan is in there,

fighting. He's dancing, skipping, so light on his feet, an artist on the mat.

I can't even watch. I can't bear the thought of meeting eyes with him right now.

Out of the corner of my eye I see him fake a jab, spin around on a pivot, elbow Manic in the jaw. Manic goes down like a sack of bricks, and Duncan clambers on top of him, gets him into a Pace choke; a submission hold that stops all blood from going to the brain.

The crowd is erupting. Duncan drips with blood; both his and Manic's. Tonight, they didn't stop at the sight of crimson.

Manic slips loose, though.

The fight will go on.

I start to run, push past people in my way. I get to the exit of the hangar, slip out through the crack of the two huge doors, and I run off into the foggy night.

I know what I have to do.

I have to save my baby.

And I can't let my mind linger on the fact that it breaks my heart to break another's.

Duncan's going to be looking for me after the fight, after he wins.

He has no idea he's the father of my child, has no idea I'm even pregnant, and now he can never know. I can't tell anybody. I can't let it out.

If Dad ever finds out, he'll send Frank after Duncan. He'll *kill* Duncan.

This is the only way to save us all.

I dry my eyes, walk out of the airfield toward the road. I find a waiting cab, climb in. There's not much time.

This is the only way.

I have to leave everything behind.

*

29

DUNCAN

Manic is on the mat clutching at his shoulder. I felt the ball pop out of the socket, followed by his labrum tearing. His whole arm jumped out like a jack-in-the-box.

He tapped out.

I spin around in the cage, look for Dee's face among the crowd.

I spot Glass at the table with the other mob bosses. He's looking at me proudly, clapping his hands.

Blood drips into my eye, and I wipe it away, ignoring the searing sting I feel from the fresh cut on my forehead.

Where the hell is Dee?

There's this feeling in the pit of my gut, like something has gone horribly wrong, like I'm about to fall through my own body.

My heart starts to race, and as the ref approaches me to declare me the winner, to lift my arm up, I push past him, throw open the gate to the fighting cage.

The crowd goes wild. Everybody gets up, girls rush toward me, rub their hands on me, try to clamber on top of me. Guys call me 'bro' and try to high-five or dap me. Men in suits just grin at me, counting the money they've made off my blood.

And Conrad Butler's blood.

I turn around, look back at him quickly in the cage. He's being tended to by the doc.

Glass' guards quickly come to me, start shoving people off me, and I spin around until I spot Frank, go to him.

"Frank, where's Dee?" I ask.

He looks down at the ground.

"Frank!"

He starts to speak, but stammers.

"Fucking tell me!"

"I don't know, Duncan. She left in a hurry."

"Was she upset about something?"

"Yes."

"About what?"

"It's not my place to say, Duncan."

I narrow my eyes, tilt my head to the side. *Not his place to say?* What the fuck does that mean?

"Where did she go?"

"She just left."

"The hangar? She left this building?"

He nods.

I weave myself around him, through the rest of the crowd, and into the back room. I throw on a t-shirt, pull up sweats, check for my car keys, and as I'm about to leave, I notice Dee's phone still on the table. She must have taken it out and forgotten it.

I grab her phone, then rush outside onto the airfield where all the cars are parked down the runway.

I find the Volvo, gun the puttering engine, speed as fast as the car can out of the area, onto the highway. There's this feeling of dread I've got, like a hole is inside me and sucking me into it.

It's not like Dee to just leave a fight, and with Frank saying she was upset about something… it just feels off to me.

Something is off.

My phone starts ringing, and I answer it.

"What?" I snarl. It's Glass.

"Where are you?"

"I'm going home."

"Why?"

"What do you want, Glass?"

"Why have you left? You need to get back here now. I want to introduce you to some of my associates. They're new in town."

"Not now, Glass."

I hear strain in his voice. "Get back here now."

I hang up, chuck the phone onto the dash. It rattles about. I might have broken it.

My heart is racing.

Nothing else matters.

I screech to a halt outside my apartment building, just in time to narrowly avoid a taxi pulling out. I take the steps up two at a time, throw open the door.

"Dee!"

There is no answer. I switch on the lights, look around. The apartment is empty.

I go to the bedroom, check the bathroom, then go back to the bedroom. Nothing seems out of pla—

The wardrobe is ajar!

I open it, and see half of Dee's clothes missing.

What the fuck?

I go back to the bathroom. Her toothbrush is gone, her deodorant, her bottles of cream and other toiletries.

The cabinet is missing band-aids, antiseptic cream. That one makes me *really* worry.

What the hell is going on? The first thought that crosses my mind is that she's been kidnapped by one of Glass' enemies, but there's no way they'd take her toothbrush or her clothes. They wouldn't care for her fucking *oral hygiene!*

No... Dee took them. Dee was just here.

I race back downstairs, get into my car, drive to Glass' house in Kenilworth.

There's nobody home here as well. I go into her

room, but it's been so long since I've been in here, I don't know if anything is out of place.

Where the hell is she?

I run my hands through my hair, feeling a growing fear and frustration. It's a ball inside me expanding. I'm going to explode.

I sprint back out to the car, call Glass on my phone. When he picks up, his tone is frosty.

"What the fuck is going on with you tonight, boy?"

"Where's Dee, Glass?"

"She left."

I blink. "Left?"

"I don't know, she left the fight."

"Why?"

There's a pause. "I don't know."

He's lying to me.

"Have you tried calling her, Duncan?"

"She forgot her phone."

"She probably went back to the college dorms."

The college dorms!

I drive up there, but am turned away by security at the entrance to campus.

"Can you please get a message through to Caroline Edwards, Moore Hall, third floor, room G," I tell the guard. Dee's roommate. "It's an emergency."

The guard stares into my eyes for a moment, considers me.

"Christ, I really need you to do this for me."

"I can't, sir," he says, his face stoic, his voice emotionless. "Not until I know who you are."

"Look, someone I know is missing, and was her friend and roommate. I need to know if she's seen her."

The guard, an older man, bearded and tough-looking, shakes his head.

"Not even a message?" I run my hand through my hair, turn away from the guard for a moment, collect myself. "Can't you just contact her residence administrator or whoever, check if she's here? She can come here to the gate, talk to me with you watching. I only need to ask her one question."

He considers me some more, and then relents. "Alright, son. Just hold on." He goes back into his office, clicks onto the radio.

I wait outside, pacing, and maybe ten minutes later

Caroline comes down.

"Duncan?"

"Is Dee here?"

"No," she says. "Are you two fighting?"

I lick my lips. "No. I just can't find her. She didn't come by here?"

Caroline shakes her head, shrugs. "Not that I know of, anyway. I've been in our room all night studying. We've got a mock quiz tomorrow."

"If she turns up for it tomorrow, will you text me? I just need to know if she's alright."

"Sure." She takes out her phone, punches in my number.

I thank her, jump back in the car, drive back to my apartment.

The lights are on!

Relief floods through my veins. God damn it, Dee's back home, and she gave me one hell of a scare.

I run up the stairs, burst through the door.

"Dee!" I cry. My voice almost breaks.

There's no reply.

I frown, check the bedroom where the light is on.

I notice her underwear drawer is open, and it was closed when I left here just half an hour ago. Most of her pairs of underwear are gone.

It hits me, a thump in the chest like I've been slammed by a cannonball.

She's left.

She came back because she forgot something. Maybe a passport she hid in that drawer? Fuck I wish I knew what it was she came back for, but I never, ever looked through her things.

God fucking damn it!

I suck in huge gulps of air, go back to the living room, and there I notice a small black object on the floor. I bend down, pick it up.

It's the mirror I gave Dee. It's cracked; she must have dropped it unknowingly.

I turn it over in my hand, watch the small cat wave.

"For fuck's sake, Dee, where the hell are you going?" I breathe.

...And *why* are you going?

*

30

DEE

The windows are weeping.

The plane arrives in heavy fog, but it's hot and humid outside, sub-tropical Hong Kong where I'm due for a several-day stop-over.

I can see the terminal building just outside from my window, a few meters beyond the extended arm of the gate.

They all drip with water; the air-conditioning on the inside must be at full-blast.

Getting off the plane is something of a new experience to me. I haven't been on a plane since I was a child, going to Thailand… with Dad. Since I first met Duncan.

Dad and I never did end up going to Paris.

Back then we were in first class… and it was great. Not this time, though. It's not like I'm about to complain about it. Sixteen hours cramped in a seat next to a man with smelly breath is a price I'm willing to pay if it means saving my baby, if it means giving my child a good life.

I'd gladly pay much, much more. I guess, leaving Duncan, I already have.

But the way everybody rushes to get off the plane… it just rubs me the wrong way. Why the hell is everybody in such a hurry?

I wait until I'm the last person — I can't be bothered to go at the same time as everybody else. Most of them push each other, hurry to get off the plane like a few minutes are going to make any difference.

I sigh, pinch the bridge of my nose and then rub my eyes. Chicago to Hong Kong was sixteen hours, and I had a seat right by the toilets. I didn't catch a wink of sleep. Even if it was quiet, I might not have slept at all. There was, and still is, too much on my mind.

The flight was full, too. Beside me sat a guy with death-breath, and next to him his wife and young daughter. The poor girl cried all flight because she couldn't equalize the pressure in her ears.

At least I had an aisle seat.

It made me think of my own child… whether it will be a boy or a girl… which I would prefer.

If I'm even *allowed* to have a preference.

Right at this moment, I feel an odd cross of emotions. I feel utterly alone, but also stronger than ever. There's a steely resolve that runs through my bones, vibrates inside me, keeps me on-course.

I don't know if leaving like that is the *right* thing to do, but I sure as hell know that it is the *best* thing to do for my child.

Distantly, I wonder what the difference is between the two. If it's best for my baby, surely it's right?

But I know I've wronged Duncan, and thinking about it even briefly threatens to unravel me.

The idea of being all alone, of not having him by

my side when he's been there for so long, supporting me…

…and then I think: What about him?

He's had me there by *his* side, supporting *him*.

He likes to think he's some kind of superhero who can take anything, *anything*. But… I know him better than that.

He's human, even if he's amazing to me. He's still human. I don't know how this is going to hit him. I don't know how it's going to affect him.

I could sit for hours just thinking about the possibilities, but I can't descend into that.

That's… that's a road that's now been wiped off the map.

Anyway, I can't risk my child, can't risk letting Dad get his hands on my baby. If it's a boy, he'll groom him into a fighter, just like he did Duncan.

God damn it, everybody that falls into Dad's gravity ends up suffering!

I don't want my child to suffer at his hands.

I want my child to do what he or she wants. I don't want my child to be brought up thinking there's only one way to live. I don't want my child anywhere near crime, the mob, the violence, like I was as a kid.

I can't stop Dad from doing what he does. I'm not under any illusion here. People might want to judge me, might say that I should have turned my own father in with the mountains of evidence I had access to.

But… he's still my father. *Family*. The only true thing he's ever said to me is that family is everything.

In the end, what else do you have?

Me…? I don't even *have* family anymore. I have nothing!

Damn it, the thought makes me feel weak.

I sigh. There's so much I could testify to. I've watched my father and Frank beat a man to a bloody pulp for not paying back a debt. His body was still, unmoving by the end of it. I was in the car with the inside lights on, maybe eleven years old. Dad told me to keep them on so I couldn't see outside.

Of course, I just cupped my hands around my eyes against the glass, and watched them. It was by the river, right in the middle of town, and before midnight. Nobody who passed by stopped. Dad's limousine, the license plate, *M4R1-N0,* was effective signage: *Stay Away.*

The guy lay there, in the winter night, out-cold, when Dad and Frank returned to the car. I never found out what happened to him.

He probably died by morning of hypothermia.

My thoughts invariably come back to Duncan. I wonder what he's doing right now.

I wonder if he's with Dad. I know he will have won the fight. He will have looked for me, searched up and down that hangar. He would have asked Dad where I was, would have asked Frank if he'd seen me.

He will have gone home to his — our — apartment, and not found me there.

Dad would likely call him in for a meeting the next day. He'd question Duncan. That's Dad, suspicious of everybody.

When he learned that Duncan had no idea where I was…well, that's when the hunt would begin.

I glance at my watch, it's still on home-time. Roughly twenty-two hours have passed since I left the fight.

It's only a minimal head-start, but I have a plan.

That plan involves changing who I am completely.

*

31

DUNCAN

Glass whirls on me, jabs a finger in my face. "God damn it, Duncan, is this your fault? Did you make my daughter run away?"

"No," I say. "Get your fucking finger out of my face."

His finger lingers there for a moment longer, but then he snaps it back and steps away. We're in the living room at his house – I've never called it 'home' – and perhaps he is remembering the time he tried to shout at Dee, and I got in his way, put a hand on his shoulder.

"You'll talk to me with respect, boy," he says,

starting to shake. "I made you. Without me, you'd just be some rat on the street, some fucking lowlife addicted to meth. Don't you forget that!"

I lick my lips, ball my fists, but control myself. "Are you sure she's run away?"

"Her bank account has been emptied, and her belongings from her room packed. She also stole about thirty-thousand in cash from my office safe."

"How do you know she packed her belongings? You went through her stuff?"

"When you have a child of your own, you'll understand," Glass spits at me. "Where the fuck did she go?"

"She can't go where she wants?"

"Not without my permission!" he barks, huffing, turning around and starting to pace up and down the room. "How do you think it's going to look? What about my reputation? Johnny Marino doesn't even know where his own daughter is."

"She's an adult," I tell him. "She can do what she likes." I say it because I'm indignant on her behalf, but deep inside it rips me apart that she left.

That she left *me*.

"That fucking girl stole what's mine!" Glass roars, slamming his fist down on the dining table. He drains his glass of brandy and with shaking hands pours another.

I don't know what he means by that… *stole what's mine.* Is he talking about the money? No… thirty-grand is nothing to him. This is more… personal.

"Did she say anything to you," I ask him. Glass' behavior is unsettling, and alarm sirens are wailing inside my mind. There's something else going on. It's time I fucking found out.

"No." he says.

I know he's lying right then and there. "I saw you pull her aside just before the fight."

"Oh, that was nothing, just a talk."

I raise an eyebrow. "About what, Glass?"

"None of your God damn business is what."

We stew in silence for a moment. I can hear Frank outside in the corridor shifting his feet.

"Did I ever tell you the story of why they call me 'Glass'?"

I meet his eyes. He's told me a thousand times. He wants to tell it again.

"Yeah, you have."

"I was going to be one of the best," he says, ignoring me. He mimes a one-two jab-cross, ducks left then right. "I had the best technique, was quick as a fucking gazelle. But I could hit like a fucking charging rhino, let me tell you."

I put my arms on my hips, pace up and down the room. I'm ignoring what he's saying, I know the story back-to-front.

My mind is on Dee. Where would she go? Why would she leave? I'm certain her father has something to do with it, but I don't know what.

I need to get him talking.

"I was going to go into the pros. Back then, boxing was all mob-controlled, not regulated like how it is now. You needed to get in with the big boys, you know what I mean? I started out as a scout for Accardo's outfit. Him, Giancarno, all them boys ran everything here. This was back in the sixties, you wouldn't know. They fixed the fucking election results for Cook County! I mean, these were big time gangsters. One day, he watches me get into a fist fight, and I just destroyed this guy. I was sixteen at the time, no older then when I found you."

Glass points a finger at me, and his gold watch slides up his wrist. "Remember when I found you? Plucked you off the street, gave you a life?"

"Yeah," I say.

"Accardo said I had what it took to be a boxer. He had some men train me, and I was going to be one of the best. By the time I was eighteen I was getting ready to enter the pros, to do my first real gig when—" His voice trails off.

"When you broke your leg," I say.

"Kicking a fucking football," he says with a sigh. "Toe hit turf, and the shock fractured my tibia. After that, it was just one injury after another. Tore my ACL when I was nineteen, Achilles when I was twenty-one. Ripped my shoulder out three months later, then broke my left femur clean in half on a fucking skiing holiday. Skiing, Duncan! Fucking skiing.

"I was so broken up that by the time I was twenty-four, I could no longer fight. I never put a string of wins together long enough to get me any notice. Accardo left me by the wayside, turned his attention to better, younger men in his stable, ones who could fight, ones who could earn him money. That's why they call me 'Glass'. Like I'm made of glass, you know?"

"I get it," I say.

He sighs again. This is his torture. This is all he cares about. "Fuck!" he spits, slapping the table.

I regard him, think to myself why now, of all times? Why did Dee choose now? I only needed just a few more fights, a bit more money, some wise investments, and we'd be living the life.

We'd have gone away together.

I'd have taken her anywhere she wanted to go.

But she left first. She left without me.

I ball my fist, dig my nails into my palm.

"So what could I do?" Glass shrugs, smacks his lips. "I went into business. I became a businessman. And… and I met Dee's mother. Boxing… boxing became boring after Tyson was done. The underground scene dried up, too."

But that coincided with the emergence of MMA, mixed martial arts, what I fight.

No… what I *fought*.

"I'm done fighting for you," I say after a moment. Just like that, there's a switch that's been flicked in my mind. "I'm not getting in that cage for you anymore."

Glass turns hard eyes on me. "You think so, huh?"

"I know so. I'm done, Glass. Finished. I've made you millions of dollars over the past two years. You got your money's worth out of me."

"You didn't fair too poorly yourself," he fires back.

"I fought for it. Spilled blood for it. Broke bones for it. I earned my share."

"I control you," Glass hisses, leaning forward. His tongue slithers out of his mouth. "I control your bank account, I control your *life*!"

"It's over," I tell him.

I've made up my mind. I'm done.

I'm finding Dee. I'm finding out just what the fuck is going on.

He's about to shout something back at me, but he stops himself, peers at me. "This is about Deidre, isn't it?"

"No," I lie. "I'm just done."

"Are you and her up to something? Are you running away together?"

I shake my head. *I wish.*

"You better not be fucking lying to me, Duncan, you ungrateful little shit. Because if you are I will hunt you down and I will kill you. And I'll fucking hunt her down, too! Are you the father?"

There's a pause. I blink. *The father.*

"What?"

"God damn it, Duncan, if you knocked up my fucking daughter I swear I'll—"

I lose it. I throw my chair backward. It thuds loud on the carpet. I rush around the table, faster than Glass can get to his feet, and then I rip him from his chair, pin him against the wall with my elbow against his windpipe.

"Get out!" I shout at Frank now frozen in the doorway. "Or I swear I'll crush his neck."

Frank reaches for his gun, but Glass yells hoarsely, "Don't fucking shoot him you idiot fuck, you'll hit me, too!"

Frank lowers his weapon, and I turn to look Glass in the eyes.

"What father?"

He doesn't reply.

"What fucking father, Glass?" I roar, picking him up and slamming him against the bookcase. "Is Deidre pregnant?"

"Yes, you little shit," Glass hisses.

I widen my eyes. "Dee is pregnant?"

"Yes!"

"Why did you say she took what's yours? Did she steal something from you? Apart from the money?"

"My grandchild!" The words bubble out of his mouth. "Nobody leaves my family. Nobody takes my family away!"

I shake my head at him. He wants Deidre's kid? He wants… *my* kid.

"You were never the son I wanted, Duncan," he spits at me. "You were never obedient enough."

I throw him against the bookcase again in disgust, step back panting, hands on my hips.

That baby is *my* baby.

He wants to take *my* baby.

Why didn't Dee tell me she had missed her period? Was pregnant? Why the fuck hadn't I paid attention? I was too focused on preparing for the fighting… too…

Fuck!

"You're the father, aren't you," Glass says, pointing at me.

"No," I lie.

"Then why do you care so much?"

"Dee was my best friend," I say. This time, it's no lie. "But she never told me."

"Women don't tell men these things," Glass says, shaking his head. "She didn't tell me, either."

I furrow my brow, cast an angry stare at him. "Then how did *you* find out?"

He doesn't answer me. Instead he says, "I'm going to get my grandchild back. And my daughter. I'll expect you to help me. She seemed to trust you."

Obviously not enough, I think.

"I won't help you, Glass," I tell him.

"I should have left you in that alley you rat fuck. You take my money, take my hospitality, and now you turn on me? Fucking typical."

"You got your return on your investment."

I catch the eye-contact between Glass and Frank, and whirl around, strike Frank in the side of the head with the back of my fist. He goes down, drops his gun. I pick it up and unload it then place it on the coffee table, scatter the bullets across the carpet.

"Don't send your boys after me," I tell Glass.

Frank groans on the ground, gets up. "Damn it, Duncan! Why'd you have to hit me so hard?"

I put my hand on Frank's shoulder, press on him. "I like you, Frank," I say. "But don't make me put you out."

Wisely, he sinks back down.

"You just signed your death warrant, Duncan," Glass spits impotently. "You're done for."

I look at the gun again, then back at him. "You want to threaten me now?"

"Fuck you."

I pick up the gun, point it at him, pull the trigger. An empty click, but he winces, and his whole body jolts.

My heart is racing.

"Next time it'll be loaded. Don't fucking come after me."

"Where will you go?" he calls to my back as I make my way out of the house. "You can't escape me! You hear me, you fucking shit! You can't escape Johnny fucking Marino!"

I ignore him, take the Volvo and gun it down the driveway.

I knew there would be a day when Glass and I would face up against one another… I knew it would be over Dee, too.

But I never knew it would be like this. Dee, pregnant with my child, all alone.

She took our baby, kept it a secret, disappeared. Now she's got her crazy father after her, and he has the resources to track her down.

I've got to get to her first. I've got to keep her safe. I've got to protect my family.

Maybe, just maybe, I'll also find out why she did this to me.

I tighten my grip around the steering wheel, grit my teeth together.

Why did you take my baby, Dee?

Why didn't you tell me?

*

32

DEE

Chung King Mansions. I've been outside the thirty-floor apartment complex for no more than five minutes, and already I've been offered weed, coke, meth, and sex.

I grimace, and pull my backpack tighter up on my shoulder.

The building in the Tsim Sha Tsui district of Kowloon, Hong Kong, is well known for being a hub of vice. Reading about it on the plane ride over, murders don't just go unsolved, but sometimes uninvestigated.

And here I am, a pregnant woman on her first

visit, and I'm about to go inside the dark, maw-like opening, and begin the climb up the escalators until they stop, before waiting for an elevator.

I have no choice, but I'm not that worried. This is also a tourist hot spot. They say you can get the best curry in Hong Kong here, according to my guide-book, anyway.

As long as I keep to myself, I'll be alright. I tell it to myself over and over.

I weave my way through mobile phone stores selling knock-off or stolen products, past clothing stores selling the same. As I make my way higher into the building, it becomes less crowded, and I realize, to my astonishment, that I'm already at a residential area. People live amongst the markets, sleeping in the back of their shop stalls on hammocks tied between steel posts.

Cage houses adorn the walls; literally men living in cages that would be considered inhumane for a big dog.

I see the weary eyes of the downtrodden. Kids younger than teenagers smoke cigarettes in the stairwells when they should be at school.

I reach into my bag, and pull out my mask with an air filter. They're sold all over, the only true way to ward off the smog that blankets the southern coast of China.

Once the escalators stop at the tenth floor, I wait for an elevator. The doors slide open, and I squeeze in. Surely we're above the weight capacity, but the elevator moves on upward anyway. I get off at the twenty-seventh floor.

It's just apartment units up here. I hear the cry of babies, the play of children, the scolding of mothers. I hear four or five distinct languages, maybe more. I walk down the hallway, hazy with smoke, looking for unit *2712*, and eventually find it.

The doorbell plays a tune. It's the British national anthem.

The door is buzzed open, and I step inside an air-conditioned and carpeted room. It's a small office, and far, far cleaner than the corridor outside.

"You can take off your mask," a young Hong Kong man says to me. He's tall and wire-thin. He speaks with an English accent, but from where in England I can't hope to tell.

"We have an air filtration system."

He offers me a seat after I take off my mask, and so I sit.

"I read your email. I tried to reply, but the email bounced."

"I deleted the account," I tell him.

"Very wise," he says off-handedly. "So you are looking for an Australian passport?"

"Yes."

"You are American?"

I nod at him.

"Very good, very good." He flicks through some sheets of paper on his desk, then pecks away at his keyboard for a moment. "Do you have a criminal record in America?"

I furrow my brow. "Why do you ask?"

"Our service is a trade-in one," he tells me patiently. "I cannot issue you a new identity without taking your old one."

"You want my American passport?"

"Yes," he says. His manner is perfunctory. "I need to know your background so I can measure how desirable your passport may be, and price it accordingly."

"Will you give it to someone else?"

He pauses, and slowly lifts his eyes to meet mine. "What do you think?"

I purse my lips. "No, I don't have a criminal record."

"But you want to change who you are?"

"Yes."

"Why?"

"Why should I tell you?"

"I didn't stay in this business for as long as I have without accruing information to trade. It is doubtful anybody will track you to me, but if they do, I intend to save my own life." He smiles. "I don't care about yours."

I sigh. "I'm running away from my father."

"Okay," he says, completely unfazed by that response. "And your father is a powerful man? Government official? Senator?"

"No. Mafia."

"Gangster, huh," the man says. He thinks for a moment, chews on the end of his pencil. "Okay," he says eventually. "I can work with this." He puts out his hand, but I shake my head at him, not knowing what he wants. "Your passport, please, and all other identity documents you have."

"No," I tell him. "Not until I see the passport I'm going to get."

He sighs, and gets up. "You foreigners… no trust. Wait a moment." He disappears into the back for barely a minute, then comes out with four passports in his hand. He drops them on the table, and gestures at me. "Choose a name."

I open them all up. Lydia Johnson, Yasmin Butani, Caroline Sax…

"This one," I say. I like the sound of the name Caroline Sax. It reminds me of my roommate.

"Now, your passport, driver's license, social security, everything, please. Fee is ten-thousand US dollars, cash only."

I swallow, and begin to rummage through my backpack. I take out everything he asks for, including the cash. I unroll the thick wad, count out ten thousand one by one in front of him.

Calmly, he takes the money and puts it through an electronic counter.

"Good," he tells me. "I need to take your photograph."

He guides me to the wall, and the flash blinds me for a moment.

"Wait here."

"For how long?" I ask.

"As long as it takes me," he throws over his shoulder before retreating into the back room.

I notice then that there are security cameras pointed at me, one in each corner. God, I hope this isn't going to be a bad idea.

Not thirty minutes later he comes out, and hands me my new identity. "Ms. Sax," he says.

I flick through it to the back page, see my photo inlaid perfectly. I run my finger over it… it's seamless.

"That was fast," I say, impressed. That's when I feel the microchip. "Wait a minute," I say, looking up at him. "This has a digital chip. It will bring up the photo of the real Caroline Sax at immigration."

"Relax," he tells me. "It's a custom chip, and will

inject a virus into the computer. It will show your picture, but I don't know for how long. One year, maybe. The security protocols are updated constantly."

"Are you sure?"

"Yes," he tells me.

"And what if it doesn't work? Do I get my money back?"

He laughs. "If you're not jailed, I'll happily return your money."

Somehow, I doubt that. "Who will you give *my* passport to?" I ask him.

"To whoever buys it."

"Will you do me a favor?"

He leans back, touches the tips of his fingers together. "I'll consider it."

"Give it to the first person looking for an American passport who walks in here."

"Hoping to put your father on the wrong track?"

"Something like that," I tell him. "Something like that."

I leave the way I came in, down the elevator, down the escalators. I politely decline, for the second time, some of the same people who tried to sell me drugs on my way up.

Dad will be looking for me, and he will be able to get my passport records. He'll know I came to Hong Kong, but hopefully somebody using my name to enter America will turn him back around.

Hopefully.

But I don't dare hope too much.

I pass the cage houses, see a man curled up, knees pressed against his chest, sleeping. He must be in his sixties, and he's thin as a rake.

The cages remind me of Duncan.

Have I left him trapped?

*

33

DUNCAN

Three fucking months… that's how long she's been gone.

Three long fucking months… it feels like three years, like a night that's never ended. I keep walking toward the horizon, hoping that the moon will disappear behind me, and that the sun will rise up in front of me.

Only it hasn't. Not *yet.*

She's got my baby, she's passed her first trimester, and she's all alone.

That fucking thought kills me. *She's all alone!*

I know she's strong, and I know she can do this,

but she doesn't *have* to. I know what it's like to feel alone, and I wouldn't wish it on anybody, least of all her.

One way or another, I'm getting Dee back, making her mine again. One way or another. But in this time that I don't have her, in this time that I can't reach over and touch her, kiss her… it leaves me embittered.

Every single fucking day I wake up and reach over instinctively, expect to feel her warm body, expect to hear her steady breathing, expect to be able to roll over, kiss her neck and smell her hair, sometimes watch her for a while. Treasure her, wonder at the chain of events in our lives that brought us together, like some kind of cosmic magnetism… destiny?

Every single fucking day my hand hits cold sheets, and I get out of bed with a soured mood to start the day.

A day of searching for the mother of my child.

It's been futile. All my leads are gone. There are no more breadcrumbs. Now… now I want to say that it's only a matter of God damned time. I never doubt that I'm going to find her, but what I do worry about is how long it'll take me to.

I'm faced with the idea of being unable to do something I want to do. It's not an unfamiliar feeling, but I haven't felt it in a while.

I *am* going to find her. I *am* going to get my family back.

But I can't trust in anything other than my own agency. I can't believe that our lives are drawn together the way our eyes are. If we really were like magnets, then what if, momentarily, we might have flipped over? How do I know that with each day I don't get pushed farther apart from her?

How do I know I'm even looking in the right fucking place?

How do I know that if I ever find her, that should the stars align and I find a person who is trying to hide in a city I don't know, trying to go unnoticed, that she'll then even welcome me back into her life?

Fuck, I don't even want to think about that. It's a well of frustration inside me, never-ending, like it digs down right through the Earth and pops out the other side, spilling my soul into the dark emptiness of space.

It's a black hole, sucking inward, right in my chest. I *feel* it in my chest. Usually all I feel in my chest is a good hit from my opponent, and the swell of happiness and anticipation whenever I saw or thought about Dee.

Nothing like this.

"Fuck," I whisper, rubbing my forehead, pinching my brows together between my forefinger and thumb. I clench my fists, force myself to calm, actually have to use the fucking breathing techniques I use during fights to keep my head screwed on straight.

Dee *needs* me. I tell myself that every single day because it drives me, keeps me going. I need her, too, but the thought that she's alone is what keeps shoveling coal into my furnace.

Everything else can fucking wait. Life is on pause. Nothing else matters.

Her old man is after her. Her old man wants our baby. She ran away because she was scared.

Why the fuck didn't she tell me?

I thump the steering wheel of my rental, gaze out of the window at the traffic slowly creeping by. The afternoon sun warms my arm, and I leave it hanging out of the car. My dark tattoos soak up all that heat.

"Dee," I whisper to myself. "Where the hell are you?"

I followed the breadcrumbs she unknowingly left. I went to Hong Kong, tracked down that slimy fucker who sold her a new passport. I made him tell me where she was going. His cries of pain still sometimes echo in my head.

He sicced the triads onto me. I only just got out in time. When I passed through passport control on my way out, I could see, out of the entrance of the departures zone, a group of mean looking men with dyed-red hair held up in ponytails, tattoos creeping up their necks, scanning the crowd.

It was a close call. They would have chopped me up, put me in garbage bags, and tossed me out to sea.

But after that it was a dead end. All I know is that she came to Australia, so all I can do is look where I think she may have gone.

It took three months for her face to surface on a camera in an identifiable location. Melbourne. The shiny RMIT college city campus behind her was like the city's fingerprint.

The email was sent to me anonymously from one of my fans. A lone security image at an ATM. How this fan hacked into that, I have no idea. Some people are just wizards.

But I'm glad, now more than ever, that I put out a call for help to my fans. That guy who interviewed me the night Dee left was right… if I didn't then, anyway, I owe my fans now.

All it took was one post to fan sites, and I had thousands of people offering me their skills. I was surprised to learn how many people regularly did illegal shit on the internet, and just how easy it was to gain access to places you shouldn't.

And how many people were willing to do it on *my* behalf, just some underground fighter.

Glass fucking Marino may have resources, he may have people in high places, he may have an army of enforcers on the payroll, but I realized that I have a militia of people who can hide behind IP addresses, who are able to track anybody by the digital footprints that they leave on the internet.

And *everything* is on the fucking internet these days.

A post on a message board looking for a job – young pregnant woman seeking teaching position at a kindergarten – a background check done on a *Caroline Sax,* a new bank account opened to the same name. A photograph of Ms. Sax at an ATM, withdrawing money.

Separate events linked through the network, time-stamped, recorded to exist forever. Traceable.

That's how I came to Melbourne.

Glass is old-fashioned. He'd never think to scour the online world.

That gives me a head start. Not a large one, but one nonetheless.

The sight of Dee's face, grainy, black and white and from a low angle, sent my heart surging. It made me feel a great longing for her, an ache that could not be dulled. The embers inside me burned brighter upon seeing her face, as if someone had just blasted oxygen at them. She looked well, had put on a bit of weight, no doubt because of the pregnancy.

And… she was so *beautiful.* Even in that blurry footage she took my breath away. Even just the fuzzy outline of her lips, her eyes… it kicked me into sixth-gear, because every single fucking day I long to see her, long to be with her.

I stared at that image for hours. I still do, every night. I boot up my laptop, open the image file, and I just sit there, a drink in my hand, and look at her. Nothing in my life has ensnared me so completely like she has.

When we were together, I never imagined not having her in my life. I had a vague plan, built on the resources I would have.

Just a little longer.

I only needed a little longer, another couple of wins, another few big payouts, and we would have been golden. We'd have had a way out, and could have bought ourselves secrecy, could have paid to drop off the grid. Nobody, not even the best private investigators could have found us.

We could have lived without Glass' shadow over us. We could have been happy somewhere together. I don't know if it was naïve to assume she'd say yes, go somewhere with me, disappear with me. All I know is that she ended up disappearing alone.

It was always going to happen… *always.* Glass would never let go of his greasy grip on her. The *only* way she could have freedom was to run, leave, vanish.

I just thought that it would be with me.

But when she did leave, I was a little surprised by how much it affected me. Maybe I'm not in touch with my emotions, maybe I don't understand exactly what I felt for her, how much I cared for her… how much being with her felt like plugging in the last piece of a jigsaw puzzle.

I would remember the times I would catch her staring off into the distance, lost in her intelligent mind, cogs whirring as she considered… well, I never knew what she was considering, but it was as if she was taking care of the universe itself.

But nobody is meant to be alone. Some like it, but they are self-destructive. Dee needs me. And God damn it I'm going to find her. She's not going to be a struggling single mother without a man. Our child is not going to grow up without a father.

She will *not* be alone.

I thump the steering wheel again, grip it so hard my hands hurt. Why haven't I found her yet? It's only a matter of time before Glass catches up. He may not be on the scent now like I am, but he'll get here sooner or later.

He wants that baby. He wants to take my fucking baby.

She stole what's mine! Glass' words echo in my head.

I didn't understand at first. Why would Glass call his daughter's baby his own? But it all pieced together, like a distant shape in the fog slowly growing sharper as it approached me.

I won't let him hurt her like that. I won't let him take what's not his.

That's him in a nutshell; he takes what he wants, thinks nothing of the consequences. Hurting his own daughter doesn't seem to matter to him.

How does a man get like that?

What kind of life does a man have to live to get like that?

I grew up with nothing, nothing but older boys trying to beat on my ass and steal my shit. I grew up with nothing but well-meaning social workers who went home at five. Us boys in the home, and the girls in the system, too, we ceased to exist after office hours.

It was a fucking free-for-all, and still I don't know how a man ends up like Johnny fucking Marino.

The snaking traffic finally starts to speed up, and I drive toward St. Kilda, into the parking lot of the complex where I'm renting a modest studio apartment.

I couldn't take much cash with me unless I wanted immigration to look at me funny, and I don't dare withdraw money from my account back home. No doubt Glass has eyes on that and he'll trace it. That ruled out setting up other accounts under my name, too.

But it's not like I need to live luxuriously. I prefer not to, anyway.

I climb the steps two at a time, open my door, and go straight to the corkboard I have mounted on the wall.

There's a map of Melbourne and surrounding suburbs, towns, and cities. I take a thumbtack and push into the map. Another school scouted, and another time there were no signs of Dee.

She would be a teaching assistant perhaps, or work in a less official capacity, but the timing of that message board post asking about openings in kindergartens, paired with the flight records for a Caroline Sax… it was always her dream to teach and work with kids. This is the only thing I have to go on.

I open the half-sized fridge and pull out a beer, cradle it in my hands on the balcony, watching life carry out on the street below.

That's seventeen schools I've looked into, searched their staff listings, sat outside of watching the faces of teachers.

It doesn't escape me, the risk I'm taking, staking out schools everyday… all it takes is one well-meaning person to notice me and call the cops, and they'll take me in, put me under investigation.

But what else can I do?

I feel a swell of anger, kick the railing. The metal rings, shakes, thrums. Why the fuck did she have to just up and run?

Why couldn't she wait? I would have been at her side. I would have dropped anything… *everything* then and there to go with her.

She's carrying my fucking baby and I don't know

where she is. I can't protect her… I can't protect our child. I can't help her, make it easier for her.

My family. The only family I've ever had, or will ever have. Of that I'm sure.

She's got nobody to turn to, nobody who can guide her, no maternal figure in her life to teach her what to expect. And how quickly will she have made friends she can trust here? Who can she rely on here? The comforts of online chat rooms populated by other expectant mothers looking for guidance are always cold and distant, squeezed through fiber optics.

It's nothing *real.*

I've sat in those chat rooms, too, even messaged a couple of Carolines… no dice.

But Dee's always been a paranoid person. She learned that from her father. My bet is she doesn't go online if she can help it. My bet is that if she's hiding, she's doing a damn good job of it, has thought of everything. *Everything.* Dee is too fucking smart to get caught, God damn it!

The thought of what Glass is doing to his own daughter makes my hands shake. Sometimes, I wonder how stupid I'd have to have fucking been to climb into that limousine with him.

Sure, he gave me the opportunity to get rich. I've got several million in the bank, sitting there doing nothing.

But to rub shoulders with a man like that… I'm glad I always kept a distance between us, a gap. I wasn't up to playing some fucking role, being his fucking surrogate son.

I *got* in it for the fights, for the chance to make something of a life that would have gone quickly nowhere. I'm not stupid, I knew what my chances were. I couldn't even fucking spell 'Deidre'.

No education, but I was no idiot.

I *stayed* in it because of Dee. There were times I thought about striking out on my own. I didn't need some motherfucker calling the shots for me. It was useful, but I could have become a straight mercenary, work for the highest bidder.

Five percent of the pot? I could have commanded ten, maybe fifteen. Unheard of for an underground fighter. It would force a change to the whole betting structure.

I was that good. Could have gone pro at a moment's notice and dominated.

But I couldn't leave Dee. There was no way I was going to. She… she was what I was fighting for. Those millions… all that money… what the fuck does a guy like me have to spend it on? I eat, I train, I fight; it's not expensive.

No, that was for *us*.

Perhaps I wasn't conscious of it at the time, perhaps I didn't understand it. But I was saving all of that for us. For our future. A future that only came to me in fuzzy outlines. A future that I couldn't peer into, because I wasn't sure how it was going to play out.

If only I'd planned it better. If only I'd talked to Dee, been honest with her about what I thought. But I wanted to wait until it was all there, ready for the taking. I wanted her to *know* she could leave, but not have to *wait* in order to do so.

Maybe I was stupid. How many times has she told me I didn't need to protect her?

God damn it, maybe I was stupid! Maybe I got it wrong! Did I drive her away? Did she leave because

I never commit as fully as I meant to?

Fuck.

That future evaporated, my last palm-full of water in a desert, when she took my baby and ran.

I put the beer down not even having taken a sip… I'm in no mood. I go back inside, stare at my map. I've sat on seventeen schools so far, each for several days at a time in case she's just working part-time. I never saw her at any of them.

There are plenty more to go, especially out in the suburbs, nearby places like Geelong. The schools, that she wants to teach, it's all I have to go on.

I'm full to bursting with frustration, recognize the need to burn it off before it robs me of another night of sleep.

I can't keep going on like this, sleeping for barely two or three hours a day. It's going to wear me out, burn me out, fuck with my mind. I don't have the body fat percentage to keep my energy levels up forever, and I'm not eating like I need to be. I've already dropped weight, most of it lean mass. Throw me in a cage now against the last guy I fought, and I lose easily.

Fuck. I'm coming apart at the seams.

I change, leave the apartment, jog toward the beach then turn left toward Brighton. I take an aggressive pace, force my heart to race, force my lungs to burn. I've sweated through my t-shirt, and I push harder, faster.

Maybe it's some stupid attempt to tire myself out so much that I forget about Dee tonight. But I know that's impossible. I'll look at that fuzzy ATM picture again. I'll stare at it until my eyes blur out and I fall asleep on the couch.

I race by the marina, hear the metal clangs of sail strings slapping masts. I pass a hidden beach, tucked away in an alcove of stone beneath a cliff face, and there I see nesting miniature penguins, no taller than a bowling pin. I heave past the mansions that belong to celebrities and the rich, with their swimming pools and servants and rare pure-breed accessory dogs.

And then I'm spent, panting, gasping. I double over, grip onto my knees. My white t-shirt has gone transparent, clings to my skin. I go toward a bench overlooking Brighton beach. Lining the beach are multicolored boat huts. They're painted in a variety of ways. One has a kangaroo on it, the other the colors of the local Aussie-rules team. One is painted in the colors of the Union Jack. I spy another one… the American flag.

My mind goes back to Dee. She's a foreigner all alone in this country. She's a woman carrying a baby who'll have to hold down a job to make enough money to live.

I see somebody walking along the beach in the distance. It takes a moment for my eyes to adjust as I'm pulled from my thoughts. Behind the person are two dogs, casually following.

Dee liked cats. That was one of the first things I ever learned about her. I grin at the memory, that cat t-shirt in Thailand. It was black, soaked up all the heat, and in that sub-tropical climate, no wonder she looked uncomfortable.

How it was *Sai*, that old village tabby cat, that finally got Dee more comfortable, that got us talking.

How much Dee changed! She didn't just become a beautiful woman with curves that make me swallow hard. But she grew a hard skin, found a spring of compassionate self-confidence that made her the brightest person in any room, pushed back at her asshole father, and started to finally do what she wanted to in life.

It was all getting better; we were on the right path. We were going to get out together!

I look away from the person with the dogs, stare out to sea, to where the world curves around. Hunting down Dee often feels like chasing the horizon. I've gotten nowhere in ninety days. Each day seems to move at half-speed. Each night slower still.

I hear the crinkle of a food wrapper. It's carried on the wind. I look toward the person by the shore, see now that it's a woman. She kneels down, pours something into her hands and then lets the dogs eat out of it.

They've got to be strays. Nobody feeds their dogs like that when taking them for a walk. Maybe a snack or two, but not a handful.

I wonder if Dee would have wanted to own dogs. I don't mind cats, but had my ideal life for us played out, we might have owned a dog, too. Maybe a rescued pit bull.

The woman stands up, and one of her hands goes to her belly. She rubs it. I wonder at it for a moment, turn my eyes away back toward the horizon and the setting sun. It's a huge lantern coming back down to—

I snap my eyes back toward the woman. She's still got her hand on her belly, and I see there a small bump.

My heart starts to race, blood thunders in my ears. There is no chance in hell… it could be *anybody!* How many pregnant women are there? There must be loads.

There's no chance.

"Come on," she says to the dogs. Her voice is carried on the wind.

Dee's voice.

I recognize it instantly.

Then I smell a hint of perfume.

Dee's perfume.

I recognize it instantly.

I stand up, start walking toward her. She hasn't noticed me.

As I get closer, her features become clearer.

I see her smile.

Dee's smile.

I recognize it instantly.

"Dee!" I shout, but a passing car drowns me out.

"Dee!"

*

34

DEE

I spin around on the spot after hearing my name called.

I recognize his voice instantly.

I see a huge man walking toward me, his broad shoulders swaying.

I recognize his gait instantly.

He closes the distance between us, his strides urgent, his hands outstretched. Slowly his face comes into focus, and I see the same face that stops people on the streets, only harder. I see the same eyes that could be mistaken for a wolf's in the night, only darker. I see the same lips, perfect for kissing, only thinner.

He takes my face, a little frantic, a little rough, cups it into his hot palms, and I feel them calloused where they once were smooth.

His kiss is nothing delicate, nothing gentle. I'm lifted off my feet before I even know what's happening, and I'm confused and wondering how he found me, and only after moments do I gather myself, find his lower lip, and kiss him back.

I recognize his kiss instantly.

It hasn't changed, but it's rougher around the edges, and his tongue seems restless, as though he wants to explore all of my mouth all at once.

He holds me tighter, breaks the kiss, then moves his lips to my ear where I feel him against my neck, where I hear him smelling me.

I press myself into him, want to be swallowed up by him. I don't know what I feel, but relief isn't the word. It's confusing, a hurricane of conflicting thoughts swirling around in my mind.

How did he find me?

Did he bring Dad with him?

The last one stings: *How much have I missed him?*

His hands are hungry, run up my sides, hold onto

me. It's like he never wants to let me go. I don't try to push back, I let him just hold me, smell me. His body shakes a little, not from tears, but from… I don't know what.

And then I find my strength. I feel my own surge. I grip onto him, as if for dear life, hold him tighter against me, cradle the back of his head as I sense the weight of his emotions from the drop of his shoulders.

It's my Duncan, and he's here… he's found me.

I look into his eyes. They've changed. He's changed. He's got new scars, but they aren't fighting scars. His hands are just as rough on the knuckles as ever, but now his palms are no longer so soft. They're harder; he's stopped taking care of them.

That means he's stopped fighting.

He doesn't say anything, he just looks at me, and his eyes travel down my body, to the bump of my belly.

He puts a hand there, kneels down, presses his face to my belly, holds me around the small of my back. His fingers slip beneath my sweater and he lifts it up, exposing my skin, and he kisses me softly, making me shiver, sending goose bumps erupting up and down the length of my body.

And then he *falls* back onto the beach. It's like his body has no strength, and I clasp a hand to my mouth, drop to my knees with him.

I see in his eyes… anguish.

Accusation.

"Duncan," I whisper, stroking his face. "How did you find me? What are you doing here?"

But he doesn't reply. He looks at me, his eyes darting everywhere, as if checking to see that it is really me. He turns my head to the side, studies me.

"What are you doing?" I ask, but still he doesn't reply.

His scent is strong, he's obviously been running. His t-shirt clings to him. He's lost a little weight; he's not as muscular as he was.

No longer training.

He's left it all behind!

"Is my father with you?" I ask. I hate to ask it, and I bunch my brow together as I do, but I need to know.

He shakes his head. Now in his blue eyes I see

more than just accusation. I see the flickers of anger, and pain.

"You sure he didn't follow you, Duncan?"

He folds his arms around his knees, ducks his head down for a moment. His chest swells as he draws in a huge breath, and then he lets it out slowly.

"I'm sure, Dee."

His voice even seems different. Deeper. Meaner.

Without warning he gets to his feet, holds out a hand. I take it, let him pull me to my feet.

"We have a lot to talk about," he says.

I nod, chew my lip. "We do. Do you want to clean up first?"

His tongue comes out, wets his lips. "No."

"Okay," I whisper. "My car's parked just over there. We should probably talk somewhere private. You can come back to my place? It's not far."

We walk in silence, shoulders rubbing. His hands are buried in his pockets, and he just stares straight ahead, his brow a permanent crease.

We don't talk the whole drive back… and that makes me nervous.

It's not fear I feel. Duncan has never scared me a

day in his life. He's never tried to, and he's never done it by accident.

But… but I feel trepidation.

It's all still as much of a shock to me as it must be to him.

How am I going to explain myself?

"You got a nice place," he says. "How can you afford this?"

I swallow. "The headmaster at the school I teach at… he owns some properties, he offered it to me for a good price."

Duncan's eyes stay fixed on mine. His voice is sticky… maybe a little afraid. "Are you and him…?"

"God, no," I say, shaking my head quickly. "No. There's nobody else."

I glance around the apartment. It is nice, though small. More expensive than I could afford on my pay if it went at market-price, though.

"That was good of him." The words leave Duncan's mouth slowly, but they are sincere.

"He knew I was pregnant, knew I didn't have anything to my name."

Duncan nods. "And those dogs?"

"Just some strays I feed every day after work."

There's just a flash of warmth in his face. "You like cats."

"Dogs are growing on me. Sit down," I tell him, gesturing at the sofa. "Cup of coffee?"

"Water," he says.

"That's right," I whisper. "No caffeine."

I feel so awkward around him. This is not how I imagined our reunion – if we ever had one – would be like. We look at each other just a moment too long, and I feel my ears burning.

I didn't anticipate this gap between us. It's palpable, like I can feel and touch the space between us, holding us apart.

I suppose I only have myself to blame for that. I did run away with his baby.

But it was *my* baby, too!

I set down the glass of water on the coffee table, take a seat next to Duncan on the sofa. There's a space between us on the sofa… that's a first. Usually we're always in physical contact when we sit together. Shoulder to shoulder, hip to hip, connected.

Usually… that's the wrong word now.

"You go first," I tell him gently. "How did you find me?"

He sips from the glass, sets it down, then squeezes his hands together. "Why didn't you tell me, Dee?"

That's him. Straight to the point.

I suck in air, don't know what to say. I shake my head.

The look in his eyes haunts me. When he turns them on me, I break. It all bursts out of me, a crack in a dam finally caving.

"He was trying to take our baby!" I cry, slapping the armrest before folding my arms. I fight back the tears but now I just feel so guilty. Now *I* feel like the bad guy.

Why is he making me feel like the bad guy?

Still, his hard eyes are on me.

"Dad said he would kill the father. He would put Frank on him! You'd have turned up face-down floating in the lake."

"You were trying to protect me?"

"Of course I was," I hiss, wiping my cheeks with a shaking hand. I collect myself, take a deep breath. "I never wanted this."

I can hear the enamel grinding together. Duncan's gritting his teeth, and the muscles in his jaw tense and relax.

"When did you find out you were pregnant?"

"That morning! For certain, anyway." I look down. "I couldn't tell you before the fight. It would have distracted you, you might have lost."

"I would have cancelled!" Duncan says, his voice rising a little. "We would have celebrated."

"No," I tell him. "We would have faced the reality. We were together in secret. We had a secret baby. We were legal brother and sister!"

"Were."

"Are. Dad would never have accepted it. He would have *killed* you, Duncan. He would have stolen our baby! Shipped me off into the countryside to live in the middle of nowhere with some old relative! Like they used to do with girls who had illegitimate babies."

"So you ran."

"So I ran," I say. "I couldn't think of anything else to do. I couldn't wait for you. I'm sorry. I didn't know where you'd stand. I didn't want to put you in that position. I didn't want Dad to put out a hit on you. Everybody back home knows your face, Duncan. You would have been dead before the next morning. I would *never* have gotten out of the country if you were there by my side. Your face was on flyers, for God's sake!"

Silence drapes over us like a wet, stifling blanket.

He doesn't reply, and that just makes me feel guiltier. He sits, broods, doesn't even sip from his water anymore.

"You need to see my point of view," I tell him. "Dad had just told me he was going to send me away, and when the baby was born, he said he would raise my child as his own."

Duncan's voice cuts in, low, slow. "Our child."

"Then he tells me he's going to kill the father. What if he found out you and I… all that time? You think he wouldn't have sent ten men after you? You know how he is."

He sighs, and again I see the muscles in his jaw tense.

"I had to protect myself, our child… and you.

Don't you see that? Don't you see that it was the only way?"

"It wasn't the only way. There was another way."

"Tell you before the fight?"

"Yes."

"I didn't want to distract you!" I cry. "If I had known Dad was going to pull me aside during the fight, I would have told you! But when I decided I had to leave, you were still in the cage, still fighting!"

"You didn't tell me you missed your period."

"I thought I was just late. I wasn't on the pill, Duncan! God, you *know* this shit. I know you're not stupid. And it's not like *you* noticed, either. I know you were busy preparing for your fight, but you still didn't notice."

"I should have."

"Damn right you should have!"

"I still don't understand why."

"What do you mean you don't understand? I just explained it to you."

He shakes his head. "Doesn't make sense."

"Why are you doing this to me? Do you know how hard it's been? On top of my crazy hormones, feeling sick all the time? Being stressed out of my mind all this time? I did this all alone. I've been all alone!"

"You didn't have to be."

I look away from him, start feeling angry. Why is he doing this?

"I was afraid," I tell him. "Afraid for the future. I had to do something. Maybe I didn't think it through, but it kept my baby safe, kept me out of Dad's hands. I don't regret it. I'm not sorry! I've been trying to do it all on my own, be strong."

"I don't expect you to be sorry."

"What the hell is that supposed to mean?" I ask. Was that some kind of attack on my character? "You think I can't see how this is? You think it wasn't hard for me, too? You think I wanted to leave you that night, knowing you'd come home to an empty apartment? I mean that, Duncan. *You*, in particular. With your history, the way you grew up, you think it never crossed my mind that I was abandoning you? You think that I don't feel bad about that?"

When he doesn't reply I grow fed up. I get up, go to the door, open it.

"You need to go," I tell him. "If you're not going to talk to me, *with* me, then go. What the hell has happened to you, anyway?"

His blue eyes pierce me. They shine a little, they're wet a little. He gets up, comes to me, but then turns and walks out the door, hands running through his hair.

I slam the door shut behind him, fold my arms, and lean against it.

I hear his footsteps disappear down the hallway.

What the hell is going on?

*

35

DEE

But I hear his footsteps returning, step back from the door. He opens it, comes to me, holds me in his arms and he kisses me. He lifts me off the ground, sits me on the kitchen counter.

"What are you doing?" I say, pushing him off me. "We are not on the same page."

"No, we're not."

His eyes exude a lustful intensity, but behind them is a fog of something else I can't identify.

"So what, you think you can just come in here and have me?"

"Tell me to go again."

I hesitate, and his eyes never leave me, like he can't bear to look away from me.

"You're mad at me still."

"I am."

"So why are you kissing me?"

"Because I've missed you, and I want you."

His fingers trail up my thigh, then beneath my blouse. When I feel his hot fingers on my belly, sidle slowly up to my breath, I suck in a breath of air.

"But we haven't finished talking."

"No, we haven't."

He pulls me toward him, jams his hard cock up against my sex, and despite myself I wrap my legs around his waist. It occurs to me that this counter is the perfect height—

"And we're not going to be finished talking in just one day," he growls, scooping up my face and bringing it to him.

He kisses me hard again, almost angrily, and pushes his tongue into my mouth. I pull back, bite his lip, and stare into his eyes.

"You think we can just sort this about by fucking?"

"Don't treat me like an idiot, Dee."

He claims my lips again, holds me against him, and with my hands against his muscular chest, I know I have no hope of pushing him off me.

"So what are you going to do?" I say, my breathing quick, my eyes unable to leave his amazing lips. "Just take what you want from me?"

"Tell me you don't want me to."

"If I did would you leave?"

"Yes. So tell me," he says, tugging me closer again, a little rougher. His hands travel up my sides, make me shiver, make me pulse.

I can feel his heat, smell him, and I know that in the blink of an eye I could just melt into his arms.

"Come on," he says. "Say it. Tell me to go again."

"Shut up," I say, leaning forward and taking his lips. His fingers come around to my blouse, and he rips it open, sending the plastic buttons spraying.

My whole body is jolted by the force, and he pulls it roughly over my shoulders.

"That was my favorite blouse," I say.

But he doesn't reply. He kisses my neck, leaves a smoking trail from my ear to my shoulders, makes me hold my breath as he nibbles on my skin, sets it afire with his tongue.

He unhooks my bra, pulls it off my arms, and then grabs each of my breasts hungrily, kneads my globes and thumbs my nipples.

"Hey," I say, grabbing onto his wrists. "Be gentle. They're tender."

I pull him into me tighter with my legs, weave my fingers through his hair and hold him close to me, my heart pounding, my temperature rising, at the same time both not wanting to do this and wanting to.

"You need to tell me how you feel," I pant, as he licks a swathe of skin down in between my breasts, takes my nipple into his mouth and sucks on it. "We can't just forget about it."

"Who says I'm going to forget?" he says, working lower still. He reaches my jeans, pulls open the button with his teeth, then pulls the flaps apart, forcing the zip down.

"You can't blame me for this."

"Who says I'm blaming you?'

His whole body is tense, and I see that lustful fire in his eyes.

"We can't just fuck it away!" I cry.

"We're not fucking anything away."

He steps back, rips my jeans down my leg, throws it carelessly behind him. His chest rises and falls rapidly.

"Duncan, just hold on," I say.

He pulls down my underwear, presses it against his nose, smells me, then jerks me forward on the counter so that I'm right on the edge.

He slaps my thighs open, spreads me, bares me to him. "God, I've missed your sweet pussy." He runs his tongue hard up my center, and I shiver, lean back, clutch at the edge of the counter behind me.

"Duncan, wait—"

He licks me again, up one side of my clit and down the other, and I'm feeling flushed, and I'm feeling it inside me, the anticipation building up, the pressure.

"God, you smell so good."

His tongue circles my pearl just the way I like it, and I moan and squeeze when I feel him slide a finger into me quickly, then a second.

"Oh my God," I pant, unconsciously bucking my hips forward to him, pressing against him.

Instantly he's sending hints of pleasure through me, making me feel so good, and he laps at me like a starving animal, like he's never needed to lick my sex more than he does right now.

"I've missed you," he groans. "The way you taste, the way you smell. God, why'd you run away?"

"I had to!" I say, taking his head, pressing it against me. I mash myself against him, gyrate against his face, lost in bliss, my eyes shut.

His tongue is fast and strong, and he knows just how to get me off. I'm surging forward, tightening up, feel so good and I'm getting closer and closer.

"Like that," I gasp as he rubs my front wall, massages it to the rhythm of his tongue. "Oh, shit, Duncan."

I squeeze, tighten, my whole body tense. I haven't felt this good in so long, since the night I left him. I've been so alone.

But he makes me feel sexy, now. He serves me as if that's the only thing he ever wants to do. He pleasures me like only he knows how, presses all my buttons, and I'm inches away from exploding in ecstasy when he pulls his fingers from me, sucks on them.

I sigh, feel myself backed off the edge, my whole body buzzing with electricity, every nerve ending inside me on fire, on the verge of going off, now cooling down.

"Are you punishing me?" I ask him, but again he doesn't reply, just looks at me.

My hands shoot to the elastic of his pants, but he pulls away from me. He removes his shirt, and his sexy body comes into view. He *has* lost a bit of weight, and it just makes him look leaner than ever.

He steps forward, takes my hand, runs it down his body.

"Tell me you don't want me," he growls.

"It's not about that," I say through quick breaths.

He lowers my hand still, into his underwear, and there I feel him, grip onto him, squeeze him.

"I never stopped wanting you," he says, closing the distance fast. He takes a fist of my hair into his hands and jerks my head back, and then he licks up my neck to my chin, aggressively, possessively.

His lips find mine, and he kisses me, sucking on my lower lip for a moment, before meeting my tongue with his.

I jerk him in his pants, feel his manhood, so thick and hard for me.

"You really want to know what I think?"

"Yes."

"I think you should have told me," he breathes.

"I wanted to tell you."

"I had a right to know."

"I know, Duncan!"

"Every single fucking day I searched for you."

He pulls in closer to me, still holding my hair, takes my lip again and bites it. I feel the sting, and it makes me shiver.

"And yes, I'm mad." He pauses, looks into my eyes. His blue orbs are magnetic, draw me into them. "But I'm still in love with you, and I'm never letting you go again."

Before I can reply he kisses me, and I wrap my legs around him frantically, pull myself to him. He lifts me up off the counter effortlessly with one hand, pulls his cock out with the other, buries himself all the way inside me in one motion.

I shut my eyes, rake his skin as he fills me up, makes me see white. He starts to fuck me hard and fast, buries himself in me to the hilt again and again.

All I can do is hold onto him hard, bite onto his shoulder, and as he thrusts into me ever harder, ever faster, I'm blinded, in the clouds, in oblivion.

His cock is so hard inside me, so thick, he makes me feel so full, so good.

"Oh God," I pant onto him, coiling my arms tighter around his neck. His frantic thrusting is slapping his pubic bone against my clit again and again and again, bringing me closer and closer to the edge.

"Don't stop," I say, gripping onto his hair, pulling it. He presses his forehead against me, looks into my eyes.

"Don't stop," I hiss.

I feel my body tighten up, feel my world turn white-hot, and just at the edge of my climax he claims my lips, and I moan into his mouth, squeezing and spasming inside me as my orgasm rocks my body, sets me on fire.

I cum hard, fast, shiver and shudder, moan onto his shoulder. I'm in heaven, feeling so damn fucking good, and then I'm passed the peak, coming down.

"Slow down," I say quickly, stopping him with hands on his chest.

He lifts me up higher on him, and I tremble as I feel him slide out of me a little. He takes me into the bed room, and then pulls himself all the way out of me, leaving me quivering and feeling empty.

"Lie down," he says, his cock jutting out hard as an iron bar, my pleasure all over him. I climb onto the bed, lie down, but he tells me, "On your side."

So I do, and I feel the weight of the bed shift as Duncan lies behind me, and then I feel his wide tip at my entrance.

"Hold on," I say, then gasp as he thrusts into me. "Wait!" I breathe, but he starts to fuck me wildly, and he takes my hair into his hands and yanks it, pulling my head back toward him.

He brings his face close to me while he fucks me, whispers into my ear, "Cross your legs."

So I do, put one foot behind the other, instantly making myself tighter, instantly feeling him so much more.

He fucks me ferociously, bottoms out inside me again and again, and I'm lost, can't even make a sound, as he licks and bites my neck and shoulder, as he takes the side of my lips into his, kisses me.

I feel his hand over my hip, and he finds my swollen bud, and starts to rub me.

I'm just overwhelmed. It's too soon! I'm not ready.

But he doesn't stop, and I find myself back on the runway, knowing he's going to make me take off again.

"Oh God," I groan, my voice a slur, my eyes shut tight, my mind lost in the wind.

I feel his body heat, hear his sweat at each slap of his pubis against my ass, at each powerful thrust.

He's making me feel so good again, so full, like he's touching me everywhere, like every nerve ending in my body is firing off at once.

"Come for me," he growls into my ear. "Squeeze your tight pussy around my cock, come all over me, Dee."

"Keep going," I hiss desperately, the agony of pleasure in my voice.

He pulls my hair tighter, and the stinging merges in with everything else I'm feeling. It's a heady mix.

"Harder," I beg him, and he drills himself into me, tightens his grip on me, bends my head back farther.

"Come on," I say through gritted teeth.

"Fuck, Dee," I hear him groan.

"Don't you dare come yet," I order him.

"Your pussy is so fucking tight, Dee," he says, voice husky. "God, you feel so good."

He doesn't stop, goes harder and faster, and I'm nearly there, climbing, so, so close…

"Ooohhh," I cry as climax crashes over me, wracks my body. I'm frozen, a tense snapshot of pleasure, and my senses sear, and I'm electric with bliss.

He drives me through it, and then I hear him groan, and I feel him tense up, and then his cock expands inside me impossibly more.

"Jesus," he grunts, emptying himself inside me, shooting his seed again and again into me.

We stay locked, stuck, spasming in pleasure. He's breathing hard, his chest slick on my back, and he wraps an arm under my neck, and holds me against him, kisses the side of my face.

"God damn I've fucking missed you," he says.

"Every day has been like torture for me."

I'm still coming down, am acutely aware of how hard he still is inside me. I buck my hips back, push him a little deeper, shut my eyes, savor him.

He stays inside me, and he forms his body perfectly to the shape of mine, holds me tight against him, smells my hair, behind my ear, kisses me, touches me.

His hands run up and down my body, grope every inch of flesh I have, run down to my sex and when he touches my clit I jolt, grin and hum, move his hand away.

He holds my thighs, traces the shape of my hip, pinches my nipples, kneads my breasts.

"I can't get enough of you," he says, taking my earlobe into his mouth, biting it.

I turn in his arms then, shudder as he slips out of me, and I climb on top of him, my hair falling down the sides of both our faces.

He kisses me, this time softly, lovingly, and we stay lip locked, and I realize just how much I've missed the feel of his lips, the taste of his tongue, everything about him.

"Duncan," I say. "We really can't just not talk about this."

"Okay," he says. "Let's talk."

"I know you've got questions."

"I do," he says. "Is it a boy or a girl?"

*

36

DEE

He lies on my belly, ear pressed against my skin while I run my fingers through his hair.

"It's a boy."

Duncan looks up at me, and he beams me the most joyous smile. "Really?"

"Yeah," I say, laughing. "I found out a while ago."

"Wow," he breathes, running a warm hand over my belly. "A boy."

"Yeah."

"You thought about what to name him?"

"I was thinking Thom… with an 'h'. What do you think?"

"I like it, Dee."

He starts moving his ear around my belly.

"What are you doing?" I ask. "I don't think the baby has started kicking yet. At least, I haven't felt it."

"You're at about twenty-weeks, right?"

"Yeah," I say.

"I read that sometimes you can feel the baby as early as thirteen weeks. The article said that you're more likely to notice it if you've been pregnant before."

"You been reading what it's like to be a pregnant woman?"

He nods. "Yeah, a bit here and there the last few weeks."

"Well I haven't felt a kick or even a movement yet."

He presses his ear harder against my belly, and suddenly I wish I could do that, too.

"What do you hear?"

"Squelching."

"Squelching?" I cry, slapping his head. "It doesn't sound that disgusting."

"Sounds liquid."

"That's the amniotic fluid."

"I'm listening for his heartbeat."

"You won't hear it this early. I can't even hear it through the fetal stethoscope."

"Turn over," he says, getting up and rolling me onto my side.

"What?"

He presses his ear to the small of my back, right next to my spine. "I read sometimes you can hear it from this position."

A few moments pass, and he sighs. "No, nothing."

"Try the stethoscope," I say. "It's in the drawer."

He stretches, opens the drawer and then pulls it out and places the diaphragm against my back.

"I just hear liquid sloshing. Sometimes there's a dull thud, I guess that could be Thom moving?"

"Could be," I say. "I hear thuds sometimes through that."

He sidles up the bed with me and holds me from behind, his hand on my belly, rubbing it.

"I wish I was there when you found out it was a boy."

I hold onto his hand, interlock my fingers with his.

"Do you want to see the ultrasound picture?"

"Of course I do."

I reach over to the bedside table, ruffle through some papers until I find the envelope. I open it, and slip out the small, post-card sized picture.

"Here," I say, handing it to him.

"I," Duncan begins, before his voice trails off. He turns it around, then back around, and then finally admits to not knowing what he's seeing.

"Here's the head," I say gently, tracing it with my finger. "See? Thom's little nose?"

"Yeah," he breathes. "I see it now." His lips pull into a broad beaming smile that makes me feel a pang in my gut.

"That's our son, Dee." His hands are shaking a little, and so I hold them in mine.

"That's our son."

"The doctor could tell it was a boy from this?"

"Here," I say. "That's his penis."

Duncan frowns. "Really?"

"That's what the doctor said."

"It doesn't look like one."

He stares at the picture for a while, tracing the outline with the tip of his finger, utterly mesmerized.

"Are you mad at me? Honestly?"

Duncan sighs. "Yes, but no. It's… I don't know. How can I be mad at you? You did what you thought was right. You were trying to protect our baby."

"And you," I say.

"And me."

"But you're still mad about something. I can feel it, Duncan."

"I'm mad I've missed this much."

"Do you blame me?"

"I wanted to," he tells me. The truth hurts, but I didn't expect a different answer. "But the more I thought about it, the more I trusted that you had a reason."

"But it bothers you."

"Dee," he says, leaning up onto an elbow and looking down at me. "Every day of my life I look forward. It was no different when I met you, and it's no different now. I'm here with you now, and I'm not letting you go again. I'm just looking forward."

"You can't just bury your feelings."

"I'm not burying anything. I'll work it out. We'll talk, don't worry. It's just… I can't just open all the doors and windows now, you know? I've kept it all shut. I'm not good at putting this shit into words."

"How did you find me, anyway?"

"I contacted my fans."

I blink. "What?"

"Some of them are magic with computers. They found out that you'd boarded a flight to Hong Kong, so I followed the next flight I could get out."

"You were in Hong Kong? When?"

"Two days after you left."

"Gosh, I was still there."

"I went to see the man you got your new passport from."

"He told you? That bastard. He warned me he'd talk, said he'd only do it to save his own skin."

"He didn't at first," Duncan says. "I had to make him."

"Was it bad?"

He sighs. "Yeah."

I nod, suck on my upper lip. "So what happened after Hong Kong?"

"I learned you came to Australia, but the guys who I had searching for you online couldn't get the flight records this time. So, I went to Sydney first. I figured you'd go there."

"I thought about it," I whisper.

"Thought you'd try to get to a big city, so it was a toss-up between here and there. I picked there and you went here."

"Then what?"

"One of my guys got a photograph of you through an ATM camera. He had some kind of algorithm running, searching through all the branches one by one. Everybody has to visit an ATM at some point, so it was only a matter of time. I figured out you were in Melbourne, came here, and started looking at the schools."

"But how did you know? I could have started waitressing or something."

"Figured you'd chase your dream, first. I mean, you needed something good after leaving everything behind. Plus there was a message board post from a Caroline Sax that my guy dug up. So I just sat on schools, just watched from my car. Most of them didn't keep updated staff records on their websites."

I frown. "That's dangerous."

"I know, but what else was I going to do? I didn't like doing it either."

"So how long have you been here?"

"Almost a month."

"A month," I echo quietly. "God."

"You know what the hardest thing was, Dee? The thought that I might overtake you on the road. Or that I might be walking down the aisle of a supermarket with you on the other side of the shelves. Or that I might be walking down the street, turn around at a sound, and then you'd sweep right past me, and…"

His voice trails off.

"Fuck all of that," he growls.

I hold him against me, rub the back of his head. "I thought about contacting you back home," I say. "But I knew Dad would be listening, too."

"He was," Duncan says. "For sure. I ditched my phone straight away. I told him not to follow me, but I was sure I was being tailed when I drove to the airport. I had to leave your mother's car somewhere else, duck through some alleys to lose them, and catch a cab the rest of the way."

"You took the car?"

"I didn't part with Glass on good terms."

"What happened?"

"I found out you were pregnant."

I grit my teeth together. That's not how I would have wanted him to find out… from fucking Dad.

We lie together in silence for a while, our bodies connected, but then he sucks in a trembling breath of air.

Eventually, I sigh. I have to say it. There's no point avoiding it.

"If you found me, then Dad will, too. It's only a matter of time."

"I agree," he says.

"He won't stop."

"So, we need to be ready. What?" he asks, reading the look on my face. "Yes, *we*. I'm not fucking letting you go again, Dee. How much money do you have?"

"I took some from Dad's safe," I say. I don't much like that I stole money, but it was the only way.

"But most of that is gone."

"Then we need money."

"I'm working part-time at the moment."

"It's not enough, Dee. We need an emergency fund, something that will buy us a quick exit."

"I don't want to run anymore. I'm tired, and I'm pregnant. It's already difficult physically for me, and it's only going to get harder."

"I don't want to run, either, but if your Dad is coming, he's coming with muscle."

"Frank."

"Maybe more. So if worst comes to worst, we have to be able to at least afford to leave. That means cash. I can't withdraw money, he'll trace it here. So, I'll fight."

I lean up, rest my head on my elbow. "What, underground?"

"There's got to be a gig somewhere."

"Duncan," I say softly, not knowing how exactly to broach it. "You're not in fighting shape anymore. You've lost weight, you're thinner now. You melted through all your muscle once you stopped training. I know you've stopped."

"I know," he says, licking his lips. "But I won't be coming up against seasoned guys."

"How do you know?"

"Come on."

"Come on, what? How do you know you won't face somebody who just wants to clean up with easy opponents? Somebody just like you, with experience? If you're thinking about doing it, isn't it possible others are? It's not just going to be inexperienced boys looking for their moment of dirty glory."

"Can you think of a faster way?" he asks me. "Because if you can, let's do that."

I shake my head slowly. "No, I can't."

"Then I'm fucking doing it. We need the money. Just in case."

"Yeah but what use is it to me if you get hurt?"

"I won't."

I think about it. It really is the best option we have, and I know he's dead-set on doing it. I'm not going to be able to change his mind.

"Then I'll be with you there at the fight," I say.

"Good, because I'll need you there."

"Did you beat Manic? In the end?"

He sighs. "Yeah, just. I looked for you after… I… I just knew something was wrong. We're going to need something else, Dee. We're going to need a way to protect ourselves."

"What are you talking about?"

"We just need resources. Now I need to know since you know him better than me. Are you sure Glass is coming?"

I nod. "Want to hear something scary?"

"Shoot."

"Last night, I got a text message from my email provider telling me someone had tried to re-open my account. I shut it down when I left. Dad's looking online for me, now. If that's how you found me, that's how he's going to find me."

"Can we move?"

"Where?"

"Into the country."

"And do what? It's easier to hide in a city."

"Okay," Duncan breathes. "So he's coming, and we have to be ready. We need a plan. I know a guy here, somebody who may be able to help us."

"A guy?"

"A fighter. I'll ask him for help."

I pinch my brow together in confusion. "How's he going to help?"

"That's what I'm going to find out. I don't want to get him involved, but I don't see it as us having much choice. Any help we can get, we take."

"Who is this guy, anyway?"

"He used to fight underground here. Stopped a while ago, I think he got tied up with the mob and had to retire."

"Is he a good guy?"

Duncan nods. "I think so. His name's Fletcher. We used to email back and forth, talk strategy. Fighter's stick up for each other, Dee. I think he can be trusted."

"Are you sure?"

"No, but I will be in a bit."

"Okay," I whisper. Then, I remember. "Oh, damn it, I was meant to go grocery shopping after feeding Lisa and Tammy."

"You named stray dogs?"

I nod, defiant. "So what if I did? I thought about taking them home once or twice, but I knew I'd never be able to afford all the vet's fees. Also, they don't allow dogs in this building."

"What do you need?"

"For what?"

"Groceries."

"Just something for dinner. Why, are you going out?"

"I have no clothes, Dee. I'll go by my place, pick some up, then do the shopping."

"No, don't worry about that, I've got some tinned spagh—"

"Damn it, Dee, don't eat that crap. Not now, not with… Thom. I'll go, it's no trouble. I'll talk to Fletcher as well, see what he says."

"Will you be long?"

"No. Be fast as I can. Trust me, I don't want to leave you."

"Why? Think that when you get back I'll be gone?"

"I don't think that's what is going to happen," he says, his face crunching up for a moment as if he's struggling to find the words for what he wants to say. "But it's a nightmare that plays in the background."

"I'll be here."

"You better fucking be here," he says, getting out of bed. "Because I'll never stop looking for you."

"I wasn't running from *you*."

"I know."

I watch him as he gets dressed, and I fold a robe around myself, take him through the apartment.

"One last thing, Dee," he says at the door.

"What?"

"If you haven't yet, forgive yourself."

I suck on my upper lip, whisper, "Hurry back, okay?"

*

37

DUNCAN

"Motherfucker!"

The man swaggering toward me is huge, obviously takes care of his body, trains a lot. His long arms are perfect for fighting, and his low waist gives him a great center of gravity; right in the mid-point.

"Duncan motherfuckin' Malone," the man says, clapping his hands together, shaking his head in disbelief. "What the hell are you doing in my gym?"

Everybody training – and I mean everyone, from the young teenagers at the punching bags to the young men hitting the weights – turn their heads to us. I see the looks of recognition on their faces.

Damn it, Pierce Fletcher always did like to make a scene.

"Hey," I say, sticking out two fists. He bumps them with his own, before taking my hand into his, gripping it tight and giving it a shake.

I see him check me out, the way a fighter sizes someone up. Traps, shoulders, neck, arms. Legs, feet, stance. Distribution of weight, balance, hands. Righty-or-lefty? Knuckles, how worn? Scars, demeanor. Confidence?

"I never thought I'd ever get to meet you." He pauses, cocks an eyebrow, then turns around to face all the members in his gym. "What the heck are you all looking at?" he barks.

They all go back to training.

"Come on, come in the back," he says, gesturing for me to walk with him.

"Nice set up," I tell him.

The gym is great, modern, spacious, and brightly lit. It looks totally legit, and most of the people working out are just boys, young teenagers.

Some of them look like they've seen some shit. I know the type. It's in the eyes. When they get older, they'll learn to recognize one of their own, too.

"Thanks. Most of it is quite new."

"You got a lot of kids in here."

He nods. "They need somewhere to be."

"All of them?"

"No," Fletcher says. "But a lot do."

"It's good of you."

"The training gives them self-confidence. You know, most won't keep at it forever, but for now it helps."

"I know first-hand."

Fletcher regards me out of the corner of his eyes. "I heard that it was rough for you growing up."

"Could have been worse."

He shakes his head. "Bad home?"

"Not good."

"But then Johnny Marino took you out, right? I read about that in an article."

"Yeah," I say. "Trained me."

"Good man?"

"No. I heard you retired from the underground, but didn't believe it. You were a force. Why'd you quit?"

"Shit got crazy in a real way."

"Bad enough to make you stop fighting?" I ask. It doesn't matter that he's not being specific. Being an underground fighter always seems to attract trouble… not that that's unexpected.

He regards me for a moment. "I wasn't alone anymore. I had—"

"Someone to protect."

He nods. "Yeah."

I lick my lips, wondering at the strange coincidence between us. Two underground fighters now both out of the game. Two with something to lose… something to save.

I notice then the fresh scar above Fletcher's eye. It's a fighting scar; he took a hit or a kick, and skin stretched and split on bone.

Then I pick up his slight limp. It's barely perceptible, but there.

It's part of my training to notice these things, the physical aspects of people, that it becomes second nature. I do it when I'm not in the cage. Everybody is measured up.

Fighters do it all the time, and they never miss it

when someone does it to them.

"I got shot," he tells me, understanding that I've caught on to the slight unevenness in his steps.

We meet eyes for a moment, and I wonder distantly what he got involved in.

"Any nerve damage? Ligament?"

"No. Went straight through, nicked nothing serious. Had to fucking fight on it straight after."

"Jesus," I say, frowning. Whatever trouble he got into was big if they shot him, then made him fight. But if there's anybody in the world who could do it, it's him.

Well, him and me.

We first started talking when I stumbled across one of his underground fight videos. His fighting style was haphazard and undisciplined, but fuck his natural talent was off the charts good.

After that, I started researching him, interested in what I could learn from his style. His first fight he danced around a man named Crazy Carl for twenty-two minutes, but beat him eventually.

A rook coming up against a seasoned fighter… the odds of winning are near nil.

Word quickly spread about him, and soon it was clear he was the best underground fighter in Australia, and one of the best in the world.

And if he ever decided to go pro, he'd be one of the best there, too.

But the pros aren't for everybody. There's too much bullshit to wade through.

Some people just like to fight.

From what I know, Fletcher liked to fight and fuck. Can't say I blame him; the girls are always everywhere, fawning, inviting.

In a different life, it might have been me. But Deidre always had me snared, from the first moment I saw her.

We go into his office at the back, shut the door. He opens his mini-fridge, pulls out a small plastic cup, unmarked, plain white.

"Here."

I smell it. "Homemade?" I ask him.

"Lipoic acid for glucose uptake, ginger root for focus and energy, sesamin for energy expenditure efficiency, and the usual shit, electrolytes, minerals, vitamins. Been using it for years. Give it a try, tell me what you think."

I take a sip. It tastes bitter, and spicy from the ginger.

"Sesamin?" I ask.

"A sesame oil extract, supposed to aid in more efficient energy utilization; the metabolism of glucose. Trials inconclusive, but I tried a month on and a month off and found a difference."

"Tastes like shit," I tell him.

There's a pause. Though Fletcher and I have conversed over email about fight tactics, and the evolution of MMA, we never really small-talked. It was always business.

"What brings you to Australia, Duncan? Specifically, to my gym?"

"A girl," I tell him.

"Fuck, it was a girl I got shot for."

"You know Johnny Marino, right?"

"By reputation. Both as a boxer ahead of his time, and also as a mob boss."

"He once told me," I say, remembering it vividly for some reason. "That girls unravel athletes."

Pierce shakes his head.

"Anyway," I say. "Something's come up."

"How can I help?"

"Marino is after me, after my girl, and after my baby."

Fletcher's eyes ice over. "Your girl and your baby?"

"Yes."

"Who is your girl?"

"His daughter."

"Your foster sister?" Fletcher asks without pause. It's curious to me that there's no surprise or disbelief in his voice.

"That's right."

"What does Marino want with your kid?"

"Does it matter?"

Fletcher pushes his lips together. "No. When's he coming?"

"I don't know. He could already be here in Melbourne."

"Has he got a crew?"

"What do you think?"

"Can you go to the police?"

"Absolutely not. Dee's here on a fake passport."

"Shit," Fletcher says.

"It'll get ugly. Storm's coming, I can feel it. And even if I'm wrong, and it's not, I still need to be prepared."

"Tell me what you need."

"A safe house in case we need it."

"I got a nice place, out of the way."

I nod my thanks at him. "Resources."

Fletcher shifts in his seat. "Like what?"

"I need a gun."

"Fuck, Duncan, I don't know if I can get you a gun here. This is Australia, not America."

"Can you try? Look, I'll be poking around myself, but I figure you know people, more than me. I just got here, man, and if I'm going to protect my family against Marino, I'm going to need one."

He takes a slow breath, and his brows pinch together. "Yeah. I think I got a couple of people who might be able to help you out. But I can't risk anything. You meet them on your own."

"That's how I would have it," I tell him.

"Do you want me to ask some of my boys to keep

a lookout for Marino? They know the streets here, and if you give us a photo—"

"No!" I say. "Not the boys, leave them out of it."

"Hey, I wouldn't be telling them to go hunting, just if they see him."

"Trust me, Pierce," I say, leaning forward. "If these boys are growing up how I did, they'll want to go looking. They'll think it's fun and cool. Don't get them involved."

Fletcher nods. "You're right."

There's a moment of silence between us.

"He wants to take my boy, call him his own."

"That's fucked up."

"You're telling me."

There's a camaraderie between fighters, even the ones you fight. In the cage, you're pit bulls trying to tear each other's throats out. Shit, even right before the fight, before you even step into the cage, you're enemies to the core.

But if one of us gets in trouble outside of the fight, it's the other fighters you can count on more than anyone else.

Not your agents, your managers, your handlers,

your whatever-the-fucks.

It's the other men like you who take a beating for a living, who can come within inches of taking a life every single time they win a fight… who can come within heartbeats of losing their lives every time they lose a fight. Who risk permanent injury or brain damage every time they climb into the cage.

When you live on the edge, the only people who really understand are others who do, too.

Make no mistake, fighting is a controlled sport, not just a science but also an art. But when you've got your opponent in a Pace choke, and you've cut off all the blood to his brain, you're a hair's breadth away from taking a life.

The life of a man with a mother and father, siblings, a wife, kids, friends. A whole network of people you could steal him from if you lose your cool, go too far… miscalculate.

No fighter ever forgets that. It's a weight on all our shoulders, something we try not to think about, like race car drivers try not to think about crashing.

Fletcher pulls a card from his desk, scribbles a number on the back.

"Get a prepaid, don't use your roaming as anybody can track that. This is my number, it's on twenty-four-seven. I'll keep it off silent, call me if you need anything. Write down where you're staying, I'll have somebody leave a location in your mailbox to get the gun. Text me in a couple of days, let me know if it all worked out."

"I appreciate it," I tell him.

"Is there anything else?"

"One more thing," I say. I sigh, pinch the bridge of my nose. "I need a gig."

"You're not out?" Fletcher gestures vaguely at my body. "You look like you haven't been training."

"I've lost some weight, yeah," I say. "But I need the money. Can you put me in touch?"

"I know there's an underground tournament coming up. Multiple rounds, some pretty seasoned guys but I think you'll have a good shot. Winnings for second and third placers, too. Interested?"

"Yeah."

"Okay," he says. "You call me on this number tomorrow, I'll have the details for you."

"Thank you," I say.

"Don't worry about it."

I start to get up when the door opens, and a pretty face appears in the crack.

"Oh, sorry!" she says, closing the door.

"Pen!" Fletcher calls.

She opens the door again and steps in. She does a double take at me, and then sticks out a hand. On her arm is tattooed a full sleeve; gnarled beanstalks disappear up beneath the sleeve of her t-shirt. I notice the same pattern on the top of her foot – she's wearing flip flops. It's intricate work, very impressive.

"You're *Creature*," she says excitedly, as if she's announcing it to me. "Pierce has shown me loads of your videos. He's a huge fan."

I grin at her, then look back at Fletcher.

"A fan, huh?"

"Wouldn't go that far, pal. This is Penelope Wordsworth."

I exchange greetings with her, then glance back at Fletcher.

So *this* is the girl he got shot for.

"Talk later, yeah?" he says to me.

"Yeah."

"If you catch some time in the future, come around the gym and spar with the kids. They'd love it."

"Shown them my videos, too?"

Fletcher shrugs. "It's an education."

"When I get everything sorted, I'll make it a point to."

As I leave, I hear Penelope's voice through the closing door.

"What was he doing here? You should have gotten his autograph to put up on the wall."

*

38

DUNCAN

It feels unreal.

I take the steps down from Fletcher's gym two at a time. As I sweep out onto the street, I see a white Mercedes pull out of a parking space. The bright, white LED lights blind me for a moment, and then it rumbles off, obviously a sport model.

I go to my rental, just a cheap and functional thing, and climb in, and sit in the car for a moment.

Unreal really is the word, and I'm afraid that at any moment I'm going to wake up, and this is all going to be a dream.

What are the chances? How… I shake my head. I can't even wrap my mind around it.

All I know is that seeing Dee… it didn't make me feel the way I expected to. I felt a surge of relief, and I wanted her, God, I wanted her. To be close to her, feel her against me.

But I thought I'd be crying tears of joy, and while I feel that, genuine joy, there is conflict. *It's not over!* Finding her wasn't just the end of the road. All this time, all this God damn fucking time I'd been thinking only up until the point that I found her.

I never thought about what we'd do *after* that.

But now I have her again, now she's mine again, and it's still not over.

Glass is still coming for us.

Fuck!

I do a quick grocery shop, pick up some chicken breasts to bake, some mushrooms and garlic to sautee quickly together as a side, and then some brown rice and broccoli. It may not be the most interesting meal, but it's healthy, nutritious, and that's the only way I know how to cook.

Dee greets me at the door, and I start setting up in the kitchen. She sits at the table, a basic wooden one, and asks me, "So what did this Fletcher guy say?"

"He's got a safe house," I say, filling up the sink and soaking the broccoli. "That we can use if we need to."

"That's good."

"And he said he'll send me the details for a gig. Just a small one," I say, shaking my head when I see her expression. "Nothing big or fancy. Small-ish payout, maybe thirty to fifty grand if I win all the rounds."

"A tournament?"

"I think it'll be five rounds with a bye."

"I can't talk you out of fighting, can I?"

"Why would you want to?"

"I just can't help but think you're out of practice, out of shape. You're not at peak conditioning."

"I don't need to be. I'll still win. I've got more to lose, anyway."

"Like that's a comfort to me."

"Anyway, I asked Fletcher about getting a gun."

There's a pause, and I start washing the broccoli heads.

"A gun?" Dee echoes slowly. "You're not supposed to have guns here."

"I know," I tell her, meeting her eyes in the reflection of the kitchen window.

"Aren't we taking a risk, then?"

"We'll keep it here. It's just a precaution. Look, would you rather need it and not have it?"

"No," she says, her voice quiet. "But I'd rather not need it at all."

"So would I, but your father's still looking, which means that we have to still be prepared. I've thought about it. I'll get the cash from the fights, we'll hide it here in the apartment, along with the gun. We pack a couple of small suitcases, park them by the door. We fill the trunk of the car with non-perishables. Canned food, that kind of thing."

"Sounds like a fallout shelter."

"Well, if we get wind of Glass, we're out of here straight away. Grab the bags, the money, the gun, and we hit the road to Fletcher's safe house where we lay low for a while."

"Why does he have one?"

"Leftover from his fighting days, probably," I say.

"And so, what, we just wait?"

"We can go now," I tell her. "You and me. I can

transfer all my money out of the States. We risk Glass tracking it here, but we think he's coming here, anyway. We take it, and go."

"And then what?"

I shrug. "The world's a big place, Dee. We could get lost, anywhere. All that money… all that fighting, that was for you, even if I didn't know it back then."

"What do you mean for me?"

"I think I was saving it all to buy you out."

"Buy me out of what?"

"Your father's grip. Remember? *Just a few more fights?* I figured we could go get lost. Who knows where… Asia if we want. Europe. We could just go traveling, move from place to place. Or we could find a place to settle down, change our names, leave no trail."

"We can't do that now," she says, rubbing her belly. "Not with Thom on the way. I trust my doctor here, and traveling would just put stress on my body."

"I agree," I say. "Things have changed, now. Now, you haven't just left home. Now you've left home with a baby, and that's what Glass wants. The stakes are higher for him, too."

"I can't believe he wants to raise the child as his own."

"I can."

"What do you think?"

"We don't know for sure Glass is coming *here*, not yet. If I access any of my accounts back home, he'll know from where exactly, and he's probably got connections out here."

"Probably."

"So," I say, leaning back against the kitchen counter, gazing down at the pack of chicken breasts. "I say we start exploring ways to get that money through a middle man if we want to use it to buy ourselves privacy. Or… or we just make do, say goodbye to it for now. I get a job, we try to do it here and hope Glass doesn't find us, but always have an exit strategy."

"Those don't sound like great choices."

"I don't want to live like that, either."

"I'm not letting Dad take my… take our baby."

"Then I'll get to work on the money. In the meantime, we go as usual, just together. Always together."

Dee nods at me. "Okay. If we get that money, then what?"

"Then we go anywhere we want. We just can't tip your father off."

"It's not that easy to hide, anymore. You found me through the internet and I changed my passport, my identity."

"Then we go somewhere where that kind of digital landscape is less robust. Where we're not going to be tracked by CCTV, by credit card receipts, by—"

"So, what, the third world?"

"Not exactly, Dee," I say. "But America, England, here… if you're worried about being tracked down, these are the places where it is most easy to be."

"So you're suggesting Thailand or something."

"Or something, yes."

"And what about Thom's education? What about his quality of life?"

"I don't have all the answers, Dee. I just know what we can do. We have one option we haven't explored."

"What's that?"

"Put a hit on your father."

She freezes. "No," she says after a moment. "And you don't have that kind of sway."

"I have several million dollars, and there are a lot of desperate people."

"Nobody would get close enough."

"We know your father's routine."

"No!" she cries, slapping the table. "I am not going to put a hit on my fucking father."

I lick my lips, meet her eyes. "I didn't think you would go for that."

"So why even bring it up?"

"Everything has to be on the table right now. We are working under the assumption that he is coming for you right this very minute. I won't ignore an option. In the cage, you—"

"Quit it with the damn fighting analogies, Duncan, I'm not an idiot. I get it. Try get the money through a middle man. See what you turn up, I'll talk to some people at work."

"Fine."

"If you get it, then we split, plain and simple. We go somewhere, change our names again, change everything, use all of that money to buy a secure future for our son. I don't need luxury, but I need security."

"I agree."

There's a drawn out pause, a moment of quiet where we both reflect, and where the tension between us is unusually high.

"You got any white wine?" I ask, knowing it's probably a long shot. Dee won't be drinking while she's pregnant, even if doctors say it's okay every now and then. She's thorough like that.

"You drinking now?"

"Sometimes, but it's a sauce for the chicken. I'm going to bake it."

"Yeah, I've got a bottle my boss gave me a while back. Hold on, I'll dig it out."

"The alcohol will boil off."

"I know."

She hands me a bottle of *Oyster Bay*, probably a little too good to use as just a cooking wine, but if it's all we have…

I season the chicken, salt, pepper, some diced garlic, whisk together the wine with a tiny bit of olive oil and then pour it over the chicken, cover it in aluminum foil, and pop it into the oven.

"We'll have a late dinner tonight," I say, looking at the clock. It's already half-past eight.

"You were really saving all that money for us?"

I meet Dee's eyes. They're wide, black, inky, and like the first time I climbed out of that limo and saw her outside her house, I feel like I'm falling into them.

"Yes."

"Why?"

"You were the only important part of my life. What the hell else did I have to spend it on?"

"Yourself?"

"I'm a simple person. I don't need to buy myself shit."

"So you thought I'd just run away with you, huh?" She grins. "We'd go traveling the world together? Go get lost together?"

"Yes."

"How did you even know if I would say yes? I was in college… I wanted a career."

"I didn't know."

"I might have," she whispers. "It was clear Dad wasn't going to loosen his grip."

"No," I agree.

"I never would have guessed it."

"I didn't talk about it."

"No, you didn't. You should have."

"Why?"

"We might have been able to go before all of… this. Before Dad found out about the baby."

"I wasn't ready yet."

"Ready for what? A few more fights gets you, what, a little bit more?"

"Ready to risk you saying 'no'." I grip the edge of the counter, for the first time admitting it to not just Dee, but to myself.

"You were scared?"

"Yeah," I say, voice low. I turn around, start washing the mushrooms, but feel Dee's hands snake around my waist. She rests her head on my back, and I wash and slice the mushrooms with her holding me in silence.

*

39

DEE

There's blood in his teeth, but it doesn't stop his smile from being so utterly infectious.

"Good job," I say, nodding, rubbing his shoulders. I look at him in the mirror. We're in a private room at the back of the basement. Everyone has filtered out now, and a lone man comes in and drops a duffel bag on the ground.

"Your payment," he says. "Stay down here as long as you like."

Duncan laughs. "Like hell we're going to stay down here."

"Suit yourself, mate. We got showers around the corner, fridge over there, take anything you like.

Good fights tonight. You kicked arse, mate."

"Thanks," Duncan says, his eyes returning to me in the mirror.

"You enjoyed that, didn't you?" I ask him. The fights were hard for him in his relatively untrained state, but he still ended up winning through sheer heart and skill.

He took his lumps, though. This fight was far more organized than I had expected... they had a doctor on site in case of injury, not the sort of thing you find usually in a dusty basement cage tournament.

"I did," he says. I appreciate his immediate honesty. "But not enough."

"No? You sure?"

"I'm sure, Dee."

"You were slow."

He rubs his jaw. "I know."

"Here as well," I say, pointing to the blotchy black-and-green bruise he's got on his ribcage where he took a violent knee.

"Yeah."

"And here," I say, bending over him to slap open his thighs. He winces, but as his legs come apart from each other, I see the bruise there, above his knee, from where he had to worm himself out of a leg lock. "These guys weren't just nobodies. Some of them obviously had training."

"Well, I won."

"You did," I say. "You did good."

"Come on, let's get the fuck out of here."

"You don't want to shower first? You've got blood all over you."

Duncan looks down at himself as if noticing it for the first time. "Damn," he says.

"Go on," I tell him, guiding him down the room toward the back. There are just a few showers side-by-side, nothing luxurious but they're clean at least.

I watch him as he stands beneath the faucet, water pouring down his muscled body. There's a weight to his shoulders, something that didn't used to be there.

He finishes, and I help him get dressed, pull a complaint from his lips: *I'm not a fucking cripple, Dee.* It makes me laugh.

Then we count the money. It's all there, fifty-thousand. It's not going to last forever, but it's certainly enough for an emergency fund.

"I'll take you out for dinner," I tell him. "Anything you want."

He smirks. "We living large now, are we?"

"You earned it."

Together we take the steps slowly up the basement. I can see that Duncan's in pain, even if it would take a two-hour interrogation session for him to admit it.

He tells me he wants a steak, which is pretty much what I expect, and so I take him to a nice place I know nearby my apartment.

The staff look at us funny, of course. Duncan's bruised visibly on his face, but nobody asks us anything out of politeness, which is good.

After an entirely too-large dinner – Duncan wolfed down his steak, and I settled for a bite of his and some soup and a salad – we leave the restaurant hand-in-hand. It's almost like we've forgotten that we're not yet at the end of it all. It's a nice moment of respite, though, just going out for dinner together. It's something we couldn't really do very often back home, lest one of Dad's men be watching us.

The night is chilly, and Duncan draws me into him

as we walk toward the car. "Sometimes," I say, looking up at him. In the harsh yellow street light, the cut of his jaw creates a straight-line shadow on his neck.

"Yeah?"

"Sometimes I feel like I could forget it all, you know?"

"I know."

I rub my belly, then pull my jacket closed over it. "Have you heard anything from your… *fans*?"

"No," he says, shaking his head. "I've got a guy trying to hack into your father's email right now, but he says it'll take time. Called it 'brute force' or something."

"Dad is good with numbers. He'll have a long password. It'll take forever to crack."

"Other than that, nothing. I don't really talk to them much because I don't want to be too active, you know? Draw attention."

"I can't believe I looked at your fan page on Facebook. I hated reading it."

"Why?"

"So many girls just… I don't even know how they

get the photos they have of you."

"They're photos from my fights," Duncan says. "Don't worry, I haven't been posing for private shoots in secret."

"I should hope not."

"Are you jealous?" he asks, teasing me.

"Wouldn't it make you jealous?"

"If some guy had pictures of you topless, I'd kick his fucking ass."

"Exactly."

"And then have a conversation with you."

"Ha. Don't worry, I don't take nude selfies and I never will."

"You could for me."

"Yeah… maybe not. I don't want my photos to live forever in the 'cloud' or whatever."

A loud shout pulls our attention forward, and we see a group of drunk boys walking toward us. They're swearing and laughing, just having a good time, but Duncan's grip on my hand tightens.

"Relax," I say. "It's a Friday night. You're still on-edge after the fights."

He sighs, eases the tension in his shoulders. "You never know, Dee."

"I hardly think they're goons my Dad sent. They look like they're sixteen!"

The boys pass us by uneventfully, spitting out a stream of swear words but otherwise doing nothing much of anything at all.

"See? You need to relax, Duncan."

"Trust me, I'm working on it. Hard habit to shake."

"Did you get the uh, you know…?"

"I pick up the gun tomorrow," he says.

"Will you be careful when you go?"

"It's all done pretty sophisticatedly. I drop money in a postbox, wait for the postman who is not really a postman. He 'collects the mail', then as he climbs back into his truck he drops a parcel. I pick it up, chase after the truck for a bit, and that's it."

"That much of a show, huh? Couldn't you just do it in a dark alley like most people do?"

"Fuck, this way I have deniability. I prefer it this way."

"Did you thank Fletcher?"

"Of course."

"Well, the next time you see him, thank him for me, too," I say.

"Maybe we can all go on a double date sometime."

He looks at me, and for a moment I think he's serious but then I see that corner of his lip creep up.

"Yuck, never a double date."

I hold onto his arm, and together we walk, and he's lost in thought about something now, but I don't know what.

A man stumbles out in front of us from around the corner. His eyes are glazed-over, and he almost falls forward toward us. His shoulder knocks mine, pulls a cry from my mouth.

"Watch where you're going, bitch!" he slurs.

Duncan steadies me, holds me up, looks me in the eyes. "You okay?"

"Yeah," I say. I turn and look at the drunk man still stumbling down the street. "Asshole."

I take Duncan's hand, squeeze it. I can see the expression on his face, and am desperately hoping he's not going to go there.

"I'm okay, really," I say. "He's just a prick."

But before I can stop him, Duncan's fingers have left mine. He charges down the street, a whirlwind, each step thunderous, and grabs the man by his collar and yanks him into an alley.

"Wait!" I cry, walking after him, shaking my head. I come to the alley and see Duncan has the man pinned against the wall.

He leans forward, says into the man's ear: "You just knocked into a pregnant woman."

"Fuck off, cunt," the man says, and I cover my mouth as Duncan winds up a punch and thumps him in the gut.

I rush forward, shouting "Stop!" and clawing at Duncan's arms.

But he doesn't let go of the man. He just keeps him pinned to the wall by the neck, and I swear he is actually *growling*, like some kind of feral beast.

I go to his side, try to pull his hand off the guy's neck, but I simply don't have enough strength.

"Duncan!" I cry, grabbing his face and wrenching it to the side so he faces me. His eyes are wide with a crazy anger. "Stop," I say, and I stroke his face softly. "You're overreacting. You're too on-edge. You need to go home and sleep it off. You get like this after fights sometimes, remember? You're punch-drunk."

There's a moment where he realizes it, seems to be in between two places, and then he lets the man go, his eyes lose their threat, and he's finally not seeing red anymore.

"Are you okay," I say to the man.

"Fuck off me!" he croaks, his voice a hoarse whisper. He rubs his neck.

"Let me see your neck," I say. I pull down his collar, see a bruise forming. "Can you breathe?"

"Yeah, Jesus," he gasps. "You need to control your fucking dog, lady."

Duncan is on him again in an instant, and I get in between them and push him off. I point at him. "Stop."

This time he listens. He ceases his advance, walks away with his hands on his hips, breathing hard.

I return my attention to the man who bumped me.

"What the fuck is wrong with him?" He tilts his head at Duncan.

"You knocked into me with your shoulder," I say,

"And you then called me a bitch, and you're asking what's wrong with *him*?"

He doesn't reply.

"He could have sent you to hospital," I say, narrowing my eyes at the man. "You owe me one."

Distantly, I hate myself for saying that. I feel like my father, collecting favors so I can call them in later.

The man snorts, slides against the wall out from under my now-hard stare. He disappears down the alley.

I turn to Duncan, and fold my arms. "What the hell was that?"

"He deserved worse," Duncan grunts at me.

"You just way overreacted, do you know that? What if there had been police? What if you were arrested for assault? You don't even know criminal procedure here, your rights. You're basically a *tourist*, for crying out loud!"

I lift my palms up, exasperated, shaking my head.

"You can't be acting this way! If you get arrested, then word might get back to Dad. Then what? Then he'll *know* where we are!"

But Duncan doesn't reply. He just stares off after

the man, nostrils occasionally flaring.

"For God's sake!" I shout, taking his arm and shaking him. "Are you listening to me?"

He turns to me slowly, and puts his hand on my shoulder. "Are you sure you're not hurt? What about the baby?"

"I'm fine! He hit my shoulder, that's all. And you need to control yourself better."

"Come on," he says, taking my hand again. "Let's go."

"I know you're just trying to protect me, but you don't need to get revenge. What made you so angry?"

"That I missed it."

"Missed what?"

"A few months ago I would have reacted to that before he hit you. My reflexes are shot. I haven't been training. I…"

"You're not a fighter anymore, you mean?"

"I'm distracted. I was thinking about babysitters."

I blink, shake my head. "Babysitters?"

"When we want to go out on a date, we're going to need to find a babysitter."

"And?"

"And so I missed him."

"He caught us both by surprise."

"That would never have happened before."

"Things aren't the same as before. What is with you?"

But he doesn't reply again, so we just walk to the car in silence, get in. Before he starts the car, I put a hand on his.

"Talk to me, Duncan. I know there's something more going on. Even before you wouldn't have just wailed on a guy in the street. What is it? Just come out and say it."

"I don't know, Dee."

"Are you still angry?"

"Not at you."

"Then what?"

Bright lights wipe over us, and I squint as a white Mercedes pulls out from the space behind us.

"Then what?"

"I've felt powerless before, when I was a kid. Then… then I had some power, control over my life. I could control my training. I could control your father, even, to an extent. I could win the fights. I could make you… happy, feel good, feel beautiful. Now… It's just difficult for me, this uncertainty."

"I know how you feel," I tell him. "But we need to take no risks. Nothing we don't have to. I know it's not ideal, but it's the way it is. You shouldn't be fighting people on the street, anyway. That's not *you*, Duncan. You're *not* just some street thug. Isn't that what you told my dad?"

"Something like that."

"Come on, it's fine," I say, slapping his arm. "Let's go. It's fine."

*

40

DUNCAN

The days blur by. Every day we grow happier together, find our groove again. Before we know it, a month has passed.

We've grown comfortable with each other, settled into a rhythm. I went with Dee to a pre-natal appointment, got to see Thom myself on the ultrasound monitor. It took my breath away, seeing that tiny head move ever so slightly, that little nose. It honestly surprised me even more than when I looked at the printout, just how formed the baby is at such a young age.

I fought a couple more times, too, just quick gigs, three or five rounds, always aiming to submit my opponent as fast as possible. Dee told me no bruises, don't get beat up, don't get hurt.

So every fight was technical. Take-down, submit. After those two gigs, people were trying to book me for bigger fights. They wanted to bring big boys in for me to fight, ex-pros, other underground fighters with some real training.

I declined. We had our cash, enough to make a good run for it if we ever had to, a nice emergency fund. I walked away with one-hundred grand, and promised Dee I wouldn't fight anymore. It would only draw attention to myself, anyway.

I look over at her in the car. She's staring out of the window, hand on her chin idly scratching. She's so beautiful when she's lost in thought, in a different place. I love everything about her, and I can't believe that, for a moment, it all hung in the balance.

What if I never tracked her down?

What if we never reunited?

She would be dealing with all of this on her own.

In fact, that was her plan all along. She took on all the responsibility, all the burden.

But I know she's no shrinking violet. She's as

strong as they come, and our son… Thom… he's only given her a greater reserve of strength.

Dee can dig deep, deeper than even I can, I suspect. Her spring of conviction is unmatched by any opponent I've ever fought in the cage, and that's saying something.

"We need to go for a shop," she says. The glass fogs up on her side. "We've got no greens at home."

I nod, pull us into the nearest supermarket to home, and park the car in the outdoor parking lot.

"You want to wait in the car?" I ask. It's cool outside, and a longish walk to the supermarket entrance.

"No," she says, undoing her seatbelt and getting out faster than me. "I've been sitting down all day."

"The kids don't make you run around?"

"Well, they make the teacher run around. As the assistant, I don't actually do all that much." She pats her belly. "Plus, they take it easy on me."

"The kids?"

Dee laughs, shakes her head. "No silly. The other teachers. Kids that age never take it easy on anybody."

Together we walk to the supermarket, hand-in-hand. I've spent a lot of time thinking about what Dee said when we were still living in Glass' house together, about how growing up in a group home or even in an inadequate foster-care situation doesn't prepare a child for life.

It certainly doesn't prepare them to one day be parents themselves.

Part of that makes me nervous. Most men probably start out with the sole intention of being a good father.

No, that's not the case. The fathers and husbands who left... the fathers like Glass… they don't care or don't know to.

But I care. I *want* to be a good father, but, deep down, I'm afraid that I don't know how.

She will give birth to this little, innocent life, one who will be shaped by us, will take from each of us a part. She'll form a bond with it instantly, something closer than any man can ever achieve.

But I just hope I'll form a bond, too.

I have to be able to protect my family when Glass comes calling.

And he's going to, that much is sure. We both know it, even if we don't vocalize those thoughts as much anymore. We're both as mentally prepared as we're ever going to be.

We've got the emergency equipment all set up. We've got supplies loaded in the trunk of the car, cash packed away in a duffel bag, the gun – even if we only have a single loaded clip. We're ready to leave at the drop of a hat, at a moment's notice.

But… this is no way to live.

I can't stand the thought of living like this, of Dee having to live like this. I put out some feelers to try and get a hold of Glass' location, to see if anyone can tap into his emails or his phone.

So far, nothing has turned up. If there's one thing a mob boss is good at doing, it's keeping under the radar.

Only, I've got this sensation that he's headed right for us… maybe not today, maybe not this month or the next, but *my* radar is pinging like mad.

I *need* to protect my family.

"What are you thinking about?" Dee asks me. I tell her the truth. "Of course you'll be a good father," she says, slapping my arm. "You just need to… adjust yourself a little bit."

"How so?"

"Well, you can't beat up another kid's dad because their kid bullies our kid, for example."

"Thom won't be bullied," I say.

"That was just an example. And, actually, he might be. You never know these things ahead of time. At the school I see kids bully each other all the time. They're horrible to each other. Sometimes, I think kids are more capable of cruelty to each other than adults are."

"It's innocent, though. They don't know better. That's what separates us."

"Are you worried about something in particular? I mean, all first-time parents worry. That's what all the women at school tell me, anyway. Everybody reads the books, wonders how to raise a child. You've got to feel through the dark your first time."

"I wonder if growing up without parents will make me a bad parent," I say outright. I have a feeling that Dee is going to keep probing, and she's the type of woman who when she wants something, she gets it eventually.

"You don't need to have had good parents to become a good parent," she says. "I'm going to be a good mother, and I can't even remember Mom. And Dad…"

"Bad parents have to come from somewhere. There's enough of them around."

"Don't be so cynical, Duncan," she chides. "Come on, let's change the subject."

"We can't get complacent," I tell her as we walk through the sliding glass doors to the supermarket.

"I know," she whispers back. "He won't stop."

Bright headlights momentarily illuminate us from behind, and I turn over my shoulder, see LED headlights of some expensive car.

The car's red brake lights are now all I can see, and it drives out of the parking lot. I wonder if I'm starting to get too paranoid.

"What is it?" she asks.

"Nothing," I say. "Just… feel like we're being followed sometimes."

"You're as bad as I am."

I grin at her. Together, we shop, load up a trolley. The fighting money has allowed us to buy better foods, allowed Dee to stick to a healthier diet. For the baby.

I eat the same things she does, pretty-much, though a lot more protein. It helps her stick to it, and eating healthy is something I'd do anyway to keep my body in fighting-form.

But even so, I don't have access to the facilities, the supplements I used to. Already I can feel that I'm losing some of that razor-sharp edge, that my quick-twitch muscle fibers are less springy than they were.

It's amazing how quickly the body strives to achieve homeostasis; the tendency to return to a stable, efficient baseline.

I've had to adjust my eating, limit my energy intake, since I'm not burning three-thousand calories a day training anymore.

It's been an adjustment, like everything else.

We do our shop, get Dee a treat that she's earned, some vegan tofu ice cream. She says she's had it before, that it's not as nice as the real thing, but in a pinch as a healthier alternative that is as good as it gets.

We leave, load the car, and even if only for a moment, Glass becomes just a distant worry. We *are* getting comfortable. We're settling in to life together.

I always wanted this, a life alone with Dee where we could both be happy, where we could both be, in a way, out from under the shadows of our pasts.

But when I spot a white SUV, I'm only reminded of the Mercedes. The feeling of comfort, this time, is short-lived. I continuously check the rear-view mirror until Dee asks me what's up.

"Remember a white Mercedes?" I ask her. "Those LED headlights? The really bright ones?"

She shrugs. "Kind of, I guess. It's familiar, anyway."

"Yeah," I say, nodding slowly. "I've seen that car a couple of times already. I think I saw it tonight."

Dee tenses up. "Are you sure?"

I grind my teeth together, shake my head. "No, it was dark, and before I got a good look it was driving away."

"Damn," she says, looking over her shoulder out of the rear windshield.

"I can't see if we're being followed," I say.

"There's too much traffic on the road."

"I wondered why you took this route. It's quicker to go around the park the other way."

"I wanted to hit a four-way crossing," I say, slowing down for a red light. But I see a break, gun the engine, and take the turn across traffic. It's reckless, I know, but it's one way to be sure.

"Jesus," Dee says, clutching onto her seat in between her legs. "Tell me you're going to do that next time!"

"Sorry," I say to her. "I only just saw the gap."

She turns around. "No other car followed."

"Think we left them behind?"

"I don't know. You really think we're being tailed?"

"This is your father we're talking about, right?"

She nods.

"Then it's possible."

I drive us back to her apartment, but steal another resident's parking space, one that's covered under shelter.

"Why are you parking here?"

"Just want to hide the car more. They can't see it

from the road from here."

"You're pretty spooked."

"It's just a feeling," I say. "You know… You go on up first, I'll get the shopping."

"Geez, I can carry a *bag*, Duncan. Don't forget, I have to carry kids at work."

"No, go get changed, get comfortable. I won't be a minute. I want to look up and down the street anyway."

"Okay," she says, getting out of the car. I watch her from my seat. She's got a habit of rubbing her belly as she walks, almost as if she's trying to soothe baby Thom. I wonder if he is aware of it.

I reach into the back seats, pull out the shopping bags, and start walking toward the gate of the complex.

It's not that I expect to glean anything looking up and down the street. If anything, it's an attempt to calm myself so I don't project my paranoia, so it doesn't stress out Dee.

But I notice a white convertible parked on the street outside the complex. Tinted windows, and some custom work done to the body, the three-pronged star on the hood.

I can't be sure if it's the same car, and digging into my memories I can't get a picture if the previous cars I saw had four doors or two.

But nevertheless, I've never seen that car parked on this street before, and it's already dark. I set the bags down onto the ground, move out of line of sight of the gate, and then jump and pull myself up the brick wall surrounding the complex.

I see the bright orange burn of a cigarette through the front windshield.

I watch the car, alert, a sixth sense inside me going off like mad. It's *definitely* the same car.

A moment later, the car pulls out, drives off down the street, it's sleek visage at odds with the deep rumble of its powerful engine.

Shit! He must have seen me.

I drop down from the wall, sprint up the steps.

I burst through the door. Dee is standing at the kitchen counter, rolling some rice that she's taken out of the fridge.

"I thought we could make some sushi with the left-over rice," she says over her shoulder. "Just add some white vinegar to it, and—"

"Dee!"

She spins around. "What's wrong?"

"Get your suitcase."

Her eyes widen, and without saying a word, she drops everything she's doing, goes straight to the bedroom.

I reach under the sofa, pull out the pistol. It's loaded, safety on. I push it through my belt at the small of my back.

I take two four-liter bottles of water from and line them up at the door, then open my duffel bag to check the cash briefly. I throw in a change of clothes, and Dee comes out of her room, small two-wheeled luggage in tow.

"He's here? My father?" Dee asks.

"I don't know," I say. "I saw that fucking car again."

"Are you sure?"

"They drove off when they spotted me watching them." There's this moment where a ripple of panic crosses her face, and I go to her wrap her up, kiss her head. "We're getting out of here tonight, okay?"

"I'll call Pierce," she says. "Give me your phone."

I toss it to her. "Keep him on the line."

I shoulder the duffel bag, take Dee's suitcase, and scoop up the bottles of water into my arm.

Together we're out of the house, and I haul the suitcase up and take the steps down two at a time. I throw it all into the back of the car, wait for Dee to catch up.

"It's ringing out!" she says.

"Try again."

We get in, I gun the engine, leave the complex.

"I need directions!" I say to Dee.

"He's not picking up."

"Dial again!"

"Pierce!" Dee says urgently into the phone. "Duncan needs directions to the safe place. No, we're not being followed."

Bright white headlights blind us from in front of us, and I swerve the car into an alley.

"Actually, yes we are! Navigate us. How can we lose them?"

*

41

DEE

"Left," I say to Duncan, my voice an urgent whisper. I listen to Pierce on the phone. "Then right at Fitzroy Street. Blow through the lights, he says traffic is slow there and it's not a patrol route."

Duncan obeys, takes the left. We come to a set of lights, he accelerates, pushes us through the intersection onto the far left. We cut across traffic, but it's slow enough for Duncan to weave us neatly through.

"We're going to Geelong," she says. "That's a city north-west of Melbourne, a bit of a drive, but he says if we take the back roads we can lose our tail. It'll take longer, though."

"Okay," Duncan says, his voice a rumble. "But this shitty car is not going to outrun that one."

I turn around, see the Mercedes right on us. *Damn it.*

"What do we do?" I ask him.

"How many people in the car?"

I turn around again. "I think it's just one. I can't really see."

He reaches behind him, pulls out the gun.

"What?" I cry. "No! We're not going to fucking shoot him! We don't even know who he is."

Duncan just emits a low growl. He jerks the car over, pulls us into a multi-story parking garage. We take the u-turns hard, and I'm thrown against the side.

"Careful," I shout, holding onto my belly. "The baby, Duncan!"

He stops the car, looks over at me. "Get out, run, hide somewhere. I'll get him."

I exit the vehicle, run as fast as my feet will take me down the parking lot, sticking to the shadows.

I hear the roar of the Mercedes' engine, and I duck down behind a parked truck, look through the windows to where Duncan is.

The parking garage is mostly empty, and there are only a few cars dotted about, occupying spaces.

Duncan is still parked, and I can see his silhouette sitting in the car. The Mercedes stops behind him, perpendicular to his car so he can't reverse out, and stays put with the engine chugging.

What the fuck is he doing?

I hear a door open, and from the Mercedes a huge man steps out. He's easily taller than Duncan, wide as a mountain, and the suit jacket he's wearing can't be closed around his barrel-chest.

Another car door opens, Duncan steps out, gun drawn.

"Uh-uh, big guy," he says. His voice echoes down to me. "Keep your hands where I can see them."

The big man doesn't move. I look around wildly, see nobody else, and then come out from my hiding spot, start walking toward Duncan. A crack of thunder jolts me, and outside I hear it begin to rain.

"Who are you?" Duncan asks.

The man doesn't respond.

"Why are you following us? Who sent you?"

I approach Duncan, and he guides me behind him.

He's gripping the gun tight, and his finger is on the trigger.

"Duncan," I say, touching his shoulder. He's angry, I know he is, but he can't squeeze that trigger by accident.

I don't even know if he can squeeze the trigger at all. We can't become fugitives here!

The sound of tires turning pulls all our eyes toward the entrance ramp to this floor. The front end of a limousine appears, makes the tight turn. Duncan puts his gun down by his side, glares at the huge man.

We all wait for the limousine to slowly roll by around the corner, before Duncan raises the gun again.

"Is Johnny Marino here?" he asks. "Did he send you?"

The big man still doesn't speak, but he's starting to look uncomfortable. His hand veers toward his waist, but Duncan steps forward, shouts, "Don't!"

The big man stops his hand.

"Do you understand me?" Duncan asks. "Can you understand me?"

Finally, the big man gives us a response: He nods his head.

"Is Johnny Marino here in Melbourne?" Duncan barks, stepping forward again, pushing the gun out farther.

"Maybe he can't speak English," I say to Duncan. "Or maybe he can't say. Maybe Dad's holding something over him." He looks, to me anyway, like he's stuck. "He could be afraid."

"Afraid?" Duncan spits. "I've got a fucking gun pointed at him, Dee."

"You!" I call to the man, get his attention. "Is my father forcing you to do this?"

His expression changes for an instant, and his brows furrow quickly before flattening out.

"He didn't tell you I was his daughter? He's trying to take my baby." I pat my stomach. "He wants to steal my baby."

Now the big man speaks. I can barely understand him through his thick accent – he's from somewhere in Eastern Europe. He says, "I have family."

I turn to Duncan, meet his eyes for a moment,

realization like a wind blowing away a fog of confusion.

"He's got your family, doesn't he?" I ask him. "He's holding them hostage somehow."

The man doesn't respond.

"What is it? Money? Do you owe him? Are you doing this because my father threatened your family?"

He doesn't move an inch, but his eyes flick to me for an instant.

"I'm trying to protect *my* family," I say. "My baby."

I hear the sound of a car engine, turn around. Down the empty parking space behind me, I see the same limousine, headlights off.

"Duncan," I whisper as it dawns on me. Why the hell didn't I look twice at a fucking *limousine*? It's totally Dad's style.

"What?"

I try to tell him, but a big hand wraps around my mouth, jerks me back. The limousine screeches forward.

Duncan turns, sees it, jumps out of the way but the front bumper catches his legs, sends him spinning head-over-foot in the air, and he lands with a sickening thud against a concrete pillar, before falling down toward the floor.

I struggle against my captor, throw an elbow behind me, hear a grunt, feel a heavy body. But the hand doesn't leave my mouth, and he wraps an arm above my belly, lifts me up off the ground.

I slap at his hand, horrified that he's hurting the baby. Teeth clamped around his finger, I bite down hard, taste bitter metal, and then his hand is free of me, and I scream, "Not so hard! I'm pregnant!"

The man drops me, I turn around and see Frank.

"Frank, you asshole!" I shout, trying to slap him, but he grabs my wrist, spins me around so that my arm is wrapped around my front, and then pulls me back toward him. He grips onto my hair, and when I open my mouth to scream he shoves something inside it, a cloth.

I try to breathe, but in my panicked state barely can.

"Calm down, honey," he says into my ear. "Breathe through your nose, and stop struggling. Don't hurt yourself. Don't hurt your baby."

You fucking asshole!

The limousine door opens, the driver's door, and I see a bald dome. Dad steps out, looks angrily at the huge man who gets back into his car.

Those angry eyes swivel straight to me, and he shakes his head as he approaches me.

"You thought you could get away from me?" he asks, slapping his chest. He tilts his head to the side. "You're family, Deidre. Family don't abandon family. I would have hunted you down to the end of the Earth."

Hunted.

I throw a heel at his shin, but he just steps backward, deceptively light on his feet. His old instincts never vanished.

He touches my face, and I try to recoil, retreat from his hands, but I can't.

"I've missed you, Deidre. My own daughter ran away from me." He shakes his head. "I've obviously done a bad job raising you."

You're damn right you have!

"You never did understand," he says, now turning around and walking toward Duncan.

My eyes go to his body, limp on the floor, chest rising and falling quickly.

"Good, you're still alive," Dad says. "I've got something special planned for you. Put her in the car, Frank."

I try to push back against the huge bulk urging me forward, but I can't. A hand shoves my head down, forces me into the back of the limousine.

"Take her to the school," Dad shouts.

Frank gets in the limousine, starts the engine, takes us carefully around the u-turns down the exit ramps until we reach the ground floor.

Pellets of rain pelt the windows as he drives us into the night.

The last image I have of Duncan is Dad leaning over his body, grinning, his gold teeth flashing.

*

42

DUNCAN

Dull pain throbs through my back, my legs. I hear the limousine drive off, but my head is spinning from hitting the ground. Blood drips off my chin.

The hardest hits I've ever taken in the cage don't compare to this, but I've got to get up. I've got to find a way to get back to Dee.

I roll over, see Glass kneeling beside me. He takes the gun out of my hand, unloads it in front of me, then pulls back the slide. The bullet in the chamber is spit out, clinks on the concrete floor.

Then he smiles nastily at me, flashing gold teeth.

"Is this the first time you've ever been on the

ground with your opponent above you, Duncan?" he asks. "I don't recall ever seeing you in this position. It's sad. Such a short fighting prime."

I try to get up, wince, rub my rib cage.

"I wouldn't move," he says. "Don't know if you've broken any bones. Broken rib might pierce your lung, kill you right here."

I control my anger, and instead focus on my body. I shut my eyes, listen to the pings of pain pulsing up my nervous system.

I wiggle my toes, move my legs. Nothing feels wobbly, out of place. Then I suck in a breath of air, rub my hands down one side of my ribs and count. I do the other side, count. Nothing broken. Nothing misaligned. Everything is there where it should be.

I touch my head, feel the cut, my hand comes away sticky and red.

"Don't worry, it's not deep," Glass says, taking a fistful of my hair and jerking my head to the side. He reaches into his pocket, pulls out a handkerchief, and presses it against the wound. "But we should stop the bleeding."

"Where did you take Dee?" I ask.

"Don't worry. She'll be safe. She's my daughter, Duncan. Family is everything. I would never hurt my own daughter."

I grimace, push back from him, sit up against the pillar. I see the glint of gunmetal. He's taken out his own gun. It's a huge revolver.

"This'll take your head clean off," he says, jamming the barrel under my chin. "Your neck will just be a bloody stump if I pull this trigger. I'll keep your head, too, put it in a jar of that preserving liquid, keep it in my office, you fucking prick."

I look into his eyes, force my racing heart to calm, then give him a big, bloody-mouthed grin. "You said you had something special planned for me, Glass?"

"Oh, yes," he says, sneering at me. "After all I did for you, Duncan. Look at what you've become. I should have known it would all be a waste. But now I'm going to have a grandson. I don't need you anymore."

I widen my eyes.

"Of course I know it's a boy, you dumb fuck. You think we couldn't get to a fucking obstetrician? I also know you're the father, as if that wasn't obvious. You defiled my daughter under my own roof after I rescued you, you fucking mongrel," he says, venom in his voice. "You fucking dog, you fucking dirty piece of shit. You put shame on my family; you gave me no choice."

"You shame yourself," I say.

"There is one consolation. With my genes in the bloodline, and yours? My grandson will be a champion fighter. I'll make him the best there ever was."

"You can't outrun your history," I tell him. "You'll always be the prize-fighter who couldn't. Your legacy can never change."

"Youth!" Glass barks, looking toward the white Mercedes. "So fucking stupid. Come on, get up."

He steps backward, gestures at me to get to my feet with the gun. I climb up slowly, back against the pillar. My chest feels like it is on fire, like I've been drowning in boiling water.

"Good, good," Glass says. "You're still in fighting shape."

I narrow my eyes at him. *Fighting shape?*

It clicks. The huge man, *something special planned.*

Glass is going to make me fight the brute, and in this condition, I'll probably lose.

"One last fight, eh?" Glass says. "For old time's sake."

"Nobody betting on this one."

"Oh, it's not for me. Well, that's a lie. It is for me. But it's for Deidre, too."

I nod, calm myself down even more. *Good.* If he's going to take me to her, then that just simplifies things. It's a long shot, but I have to play it.

"You're going to make her watch?"

"Bullock over here is from Ukraine. He's something of a legend over there. I can't pronounce his real name so I gave him that nickname. I was going to call him Bruticus, but then I realized he kind of looks like a fucking bull, doesn't he?"

"He probably prefers his own name, Glass."

"Big fucking head, might as well have horns. Bullock." He nods, sucks on his upper lip for a moment. "What a good name. I'm proud of that one. And his balls! This man has some big fucking balls on him. He ain't afraid of nothing."

I turn to the huge man now sitting in the

Mercedes. The two-door sports car looks comically small around him.

"He'll break you," Glass says. "He'll snap every bone in your fucking body. He'll tear your vertebrae from each other. Then, while you're still barely alive, I'll fucking kill you. The last thing you see will be my face before you go to hell for what you've done to my daughter."

I lick my lips, grin at him. "The devil will be a welcome sight compared to your ugly mug."

Glass bursts out laughing. "You always were a little crazy, you know that, Duncan? I liked that about you." He points toward the Mercedes. "In the back."

I walk around, wary of the huge revolver pointed straight at my head, and open the passenger side door. I move the seat forward, climb into the tiny back seats, and Glass gets in after. I've got to lift my legs up onto the seat.

"To the school, Bullock," he says. "We have an audience waiting."

The drive is short. Glass takes me to some high school in the suburbs. Once we stop, he meets my eyes in the rearview mirror, and a flash of lightning makes his shine like a demon's.

"It's so hard to find a good fighting surface in the streets," he says, sneering. "We're going to do this right."

I'm ripped from the car by Glass, and I hold onto my chest, each breath sending throbbing pain right down to my toes. The cold rain is refreshing, and I look up for a moment, let some of it wet my eyes.

I shake free of his hand, and he raises the gun and points it at me. Rainwater pours off the tip of the barrel. "Walk."

"Where?"

"Inside the school."

I look at the front entrance, and there see the glass inlaid in the door shattered. *Frank.* I push open the unlocked door, and we walk down a school corridor – something only distantly familiar to me – past lockers and classrooms.

"Find the gym," Glass orders. "We'll need some space."

I look up at the hanging signage, take a right turn, and then we step outside briefly before coming to the gymnasium. It's two indoor basketball courts side-by-side, with bleachers surrounding them.

Where is Dee? I blink my eyes rapidly, adjusting to the darkness, before I spot her at the far end, sitting on the bleachers, Frank right behind her. He's got a gun pressed into her back.

I grit my teeth, feel my blood boil.

"Move!" Glass barks.

Dee meets my eyes. They're wide, shiny, scared. Her eyes go from me to Bullock, and it dawns on her what is about to happen. I stare into her eyes, shake my head a little. I hope she knows the message I'm trying to convey to her.

Don't do anything stupid! Protect the baby!

Glass gestures at me with the gun to walk into the middle of the nearest basketball court. So I do, stand at half-court.

Bullock starts to remove his jacket, unbuttons his shirt and takes it off. He's wearing nothing underneath, and when I see the disciplined lines of his body, I realize he's built like a tank.

There's no fucking outmuscling this guy.

"Fight," Glass says to me, gesturing at Bullock.

The huge man drops into a stance, starts to circle me. I watch him, then look back at Glass.

"I said fight!" Glass shouts, and he pulls the trigger on his gun. The bang is deafening, bounces around the gym, and the bullet splinters wood three feet from me.

"Damn it, Glass!" I roar, advancing on him, but he lifts the gun to my head. I stop in my tracks.

"Fight," he says. "I'm eager to see you lose for once."

I turn around, see Bullock approach me, skipping lightly on his feet. He's leading with his right – he's a southpaw. A left-hander. I've only fought two really good left-handers before, and they were tough. The timing is different, the positioning, everything.

I'm in no fucking state to fight.

I take off my jacket and pull off my shirt, throw it all onto the hardwood. The last thing I need is to give him something to grab onto, to tug me around by, to strangle me with.

"Come on you big bastard," I growl at him, lifting my hands, getting into my stance. I can't think of anything else to do at the moment. I'll beat this fucking brute into the ground and then I'll get after Glass. At least it'll be one less man to deal with.

"You come," he says to me.

He curls his fingers in front of me, beckons me. I straighten up, get out of my stance, laugh at his cockiness.

Bullock takes the bait. He lunges, a double hop, left foot out like a cobra ready to strike. I slap his foot, use my upright stance – my body-weight imbalance – to lead my spin around him. I almost fall, my body at forty-five degrees as I pivot, but regain my balance and throw an elbow into the back of his head.

That's a big no-no in the cage, even in underground, but fuck fighter's etiquette.

He stumbles forward, holding onto his head, turning his neck left and right. I hear his vertebrae click as pockets of air between his bones are released.

"You come," I say to him, beckon with my fingers, flash him a grin.

"Get him, Bullock!" Glass shouts. He's circling us manically, baring his teeth. The prospect of a beat down obviously gets him excited.

Bullock approaches me more carefully now. He's dancing on his feet, shifting his weight back and forth in quick rhythm. He does it so he can easily switch pivot foots to dodge or counter, but I turtle up, lift my hands protectively, gaze at him from the gap between my two arms like a boxer.

Glass should recognize this, the fucking bastard.

"Get him!" Glass yells again, forcing Bullock to charge.

Bullock tests a jab, I sidestep it. He tries again, again, this time feints but I see it coming. His right jabs, his left swings wide for a hook. I dodge the jab, duck the hook, thump him in the gut with a quick one-two, then send a heel right onto his kneecap.

He drops to one knee, and I lift my own, trying to catch him on the chin, knock him out. But he sees it coming, forms a net with his interlocked fingers to catch my knee, then twists.

I slap against hardwood, my whole body pivoted like I was a mere fucking garden rake. Fuck, this guy is strong.

He tries to clamber on top of me, tries to get his arm around my neck, but I twist out, roll backward over my head onto my feet, and I'm up faster than he is.

I swing a kick at his head; he takes the full impact. Any other fighter and he'd be out, but Bullock just grunts, gets to his feet, rubs blood from his mouth.

I mimic his move, double-hop, except this time *I* go southpaw. I hop with my right, kick with my left, he doesn't anticipate it.

He takes it on the other side of his head, right against his ear, and his brain's automatic response to the impact is to relax every muscle in his body. His legs give out, he falls back down, and I clamber on top of him, get his neck into the nook of my arm, hold on to my fist, and pull.

Bullock throws elbows wildly behind him, catching me in the ribs again and again. I wince, hold on, and when he tries to get up I stab my heel into his calf over and over, numbing the muscle so he can no longer use it.

"You lost this one, you big fuck," I growl into his ear. I heel-kick his other calf muscle, then aim for his ankle on the one leg he's carrying both of our weight. It gives, bends grotesquely to the side, and he flops over. I wrap up his legs in my own, pull his legs back, stretch him out, leverage his own bodyweight against him, tightening my chokehold.

I choke him with all the motherfucking strength I have left in my body. He's gasping for air, his eyes are bloodshot, his lips are turning blue.

He's tapping the hardwood rapidly out of habit, but this isn't a fucking cage fight, and I'm not going to let go of this fucking beast.

"Fuck you," I breathe. "I'm going to fucking kill you."

The world is white-hot around me. My skin feels on fire. Something distantly is telling me to let go or he's going to die, but all I want is to choke this motherfucking cunt, choke the fucking life out of him for threatening my family, for—

His words echo through my head: *I have family.*

I let go, throw him away from me in disgust. He lies, curled up on the floor, sucking in lungfulls of air.

He's not the one I should be fighting. He's only being made to do this, just like me. Glass is holding *his* family above his head, just like me.

I get up, rub my side. I'm sure he cracked a rib

with one of those thunderous elbows.

"There," I say to Glass, who looks astonished. His eyes are wide and his mouth open. His gold teeth glint. "One last fight, right?"

I start moving toward him slowly, knowing that I have to close the distance between me and him, knowing that I need to get myself to within arm's reach of that fucking gun.

I glance up at Dee, meet her eyes. She's signing me something with her fingers. She lifts her thumb up, extends her forefinger, then darts her eyes toward her side.

No! I shake my head at her, hope to God she can see my eyes, see what I mean: *Do not try to get Frank's gun!*

"Stay, boy," Glass says, lifting his revolver again, pointing it at me.

I freeze on the spot, not having come close enough to him yet to even attempt to reach for the weapon. I know I'm quicker than Glass, and I know I could do it, hold it down, if I was just a few feet closer.

"You thought you could find someone better than me, Glass?" I taunt him. "You thought, what, that I wouldn't fight the best I ever fucking fought when you've got a gun to the mother of my child?" I bellow the last words at him, and I see his whole body jolt.

He looks past me at Bullock, and I turn to follow his line of sight. The huge man is getting up, rubbing the deep-purple bruise on his neck. He is one tough son of a bitch.

I hear the sound of metal, snap my head back to Glass to see him holding a butterfly knife. He lifts it up in front of me. "Remember this, Duncan?"

It was the knife I took from Danny, which Glass then took from me. It was the very first time I met Johnny fucking Marino.

It was the day that changed my life, that led to me meeting Dee.

He tosses it to Bullock, who catches it mid-air, then carefully opens it up.

"Fight," Glass says.

"You dirty fuck!" I bark. "This ain't no fucking fight anymore."

"Fight," he tells me, pointing the gun at my left leg. "Before I decide to handicap you even more."

*

43

DEE

The hard metal barrel jabs painfully into the small of my back. I wince, shift my weight, but Frank's strong hand grips my shoulder.

He leans forward, whispers into my ear: "Sit still, Deidre. Don't make this difficult."

Rain slaps against the windows, and the crack of thunder booms, echoes in the room. Dad is pacing around Duncan and the huge man. He's jittery, screaming at them.

"Get him, Bullock! Tear him up!" His voice is shrill, excited. He gets off on this stuff. He's sick.

"Frank," I whisper. "Frank, don't do this."

"Deidre," he says. "I always liked you. I always

treated you like my own niece. But you need to shut up right now."

"Frank, listen to me," I hiss hurriedly. The words are rushing out of my mouth. I can't keep up with my thoughts.

"Dei—"

"Frank!" I say, turning around, catching his eye out of the corner of my own. "How long was my father making you go through my trash?"

He doesn't reply.

"How long, Frank? Years? Did that make you feel good? Did it?"

"Of course not," he says quietly.

Duncan grunts as Bullock thumps him in the gut, doubles over. The knife sings through the air, but Duncan spins out of the way at the last minute, but fails to dodge the cutting counter-swipe. He grabs his face, backs away from Bullock, and his hand comes away stained red.

"God damn it, Frank!" I growl, breathing hard. "He's going to kill Duncan. Damn it, Frank, Dad is trying to steal our baby! Do you know why?"

"I said shut up!" Frank snarls into my ear. He

pushes the gun harder into my back.

"I know you won't shoot me, Frank. I know you can't. You know I'm pregnant. Isn't this breaking your heart, pointing a gun at a pregnant girl? At someone you thought of as your own family? I always trusted you, Frank. Whenever Dad had it out at me, I always came to you to talk. Don't you remember? We used to sit in the garden, you'd tell me all about your day. Don't you feel responsible? Don't I matter to you?"

He meets me with silence.

Duncan dodges another swing of the shimmering knife, spins, pivots on his heel and lands a thunderous elbow into Bullock's sternum. The huge man staggers backward, winded, gripping onto his chest and struggling to breathe.

"Frank, this baby is mine. Dad only came out here when he found out it was a boy, right? Am I wrong?"

No reply, which means I'm right.

"He wants the son he never had! He wants someone he can train, someone he can tame! He wants to make *my boy* into the fighter he could never be! Don't you understand? All he cares about is *legacy*!"

"He's the boss," Frank says stonily.

"So you're just following orders? The good dog you've always been?"

"I'm no dog," Frank growls.

Finally! Some pride! Some backbone! God damn it, how deep had he buried it? How long had it been missing? I need to take that thread, and I need to pull on it. I need to do so without snapping it.

"Damn it, Frank, then don't let him do this. You know this is wrong. This is too much, even for my father. He can't steal my kid from me! You're not his dog, right? You have a conscience, right? Are you going to blindly follow Dad everywhere, do *whatever* he says? Aren't you your own man?"

I feel the press of the barrel in my back weaken.

"Save us, Frank. Save Duncan. You always liked him, didn't you? He always had time for you. He was never rude to you. He's a good man. You're a good man, too. Somewhere inside, there's good in you. Save us."

"Shut up," he says, but his voice cracks.

"My son's name is Thom," I say. "Thom. You hear me? Thom!" I repeat the name, over and over. "He has a name. He's innocent. He should be able to choose his own life. Would you want your child to grow up like me? Like you? Do what Duncan does? Do you want him to suffer like all of us, Frank? Look at Dad, he's lost. He can't be saved. He's fucking crazy. But you! You can do this. You can save us!"

"Please stop talking, Deidre. Please."

"For fuck's sake, Frank!" I growl, shaking my head. "My son's name is Thom. He is innocent. Don't let Dad take him away from me. Don't let Dad ruin him!"

"Deidre," he whispers. "He'll kill me."

"Not if you kill him first."

Still silence.

"Fucking hell, Frank!" I whisper hoarsely, gripping tight onto the metal bleachers. "He's going to take my fucking baby!"

The gun barrel leaves my back. I feel Frank stand behind me.

"Enough!" he bellows.

Dad, Duncan, and Bullock all turn their heads to us.

I take my chance, and run toward the exit, flail open the door before closing it behind me. I find the fire alarm switch I noticed on the way in, slam my palm against it, break the glass.

Sprinklers spray, emergency lights flash red, and bells ring..

I poke my head up through the window in the door to the gymnasium. Bullock is now on the ground, knife sticking out of his thigh and arm broken, bent disgustingly between wrist and elbow. Duncan only needed a second's distraction.

Dad hasn't moved. Duncan stands, looking at me, blood dripping from the slice on his face.

I inch the door open.

"It's over, Dad!"

"Like fucking hell it is, you ungrateful bitch!"

I calmly approach Frank, touch his shoulder. "You're doing the right thing," I tell him.

He's panting, and he's sweating, and I'm worried he's going to give himself a heart attack for how nervous he is.

He says to Dad, "You shouldn't be doing this to your own daughter."

"It's for her good!" Dad yells back, but Frank just shakes his head.

"Put down the gun."

Slowly, behind Dad, Duncan creeps forward, each step as silent as a cat's.

"Never."

"Put it down, boss," Frank says, his voice rising.

To my astonishment, Dad raises his gun, points it at Frank. Frank flinches a little, but keeps his weapon trained on Dad.

"I can't shoot him, Dee," Frank whispers to me.

I summon up the courage to bring myself to say it: "You have to, Frank. You have to kill my father."

But Frank doesn't move. His finger is down the side of the barrel, not on the trigger.

"Damn it, Frank!" I shout, grabbing hold of the gun, trying to get my finger on the trigger.

The loud bang pierces my ears, sends pain throbbing into my skull. I jump back, look toward Dad, see his revolver smoking.

Frank drops to the ground, his body limp, his eyes open but dead. There's a hole clean through his chest.

Dad turns the gun on me.

*

44

DEE

Duncan floats in slow-motion.

He grabs the gun, holds the hammer, and then kicks Dad's knee. It's the hardest kick I've ever seen, and I watch as Dad's knee gives, bends out to the side.

Dad wails, falls to the ground, clutches at his lower leg that hangs limply from the knee, foot facing out the side instead of the front.

Duncan snatches the gun, points it at Dad, and then brings his foot down on Dad's thigh. I hear the loud crack of bone, and Dad's scream echoes in the gym.

It just took two seconds, and I'm still frozen to the

spot. I look down at Frank's still body, see the gun, and immediately bend down and pick it up.

"You motherfucker," Duncan growls, pushing the barrel under Dad's chin. "Give me one reason not to blow your fucking head off. You threaten the woman I love, my family? You piece of shit."

"I should have never rescued you off the street you rat fuck," Dad says, his words labored. "You were never any good for her. You turned my daughter against me!"

"You did that yourself!" Duncan roars, jamming the gun deeper into Dad's neck.

"Don't kill him," I say quickly, staring at my broken father on the floor, then flicking my eyes up to Duncan. "Please."

Duncan throws a wild look my way.

"Please. I need you. You can't kill him. The police are on their way."

He pulls back the gun, throws Dad to the ground. Dad just holds onto his leg and whimpers.

And… and I'm surprised that I feel the way I do. I never expected that I would. I thought that seeing

Dad stopped, knowing that my baby is now safe, would flood me with relief.

Instead, I'm more heartbroken than I ever have been. The sight of my fractured father on the floor tears at me. I never wanted it to come to this. I never wanted it to end this way.

Duncan rushes to me, holds my face, asks me if I'm okay.

I barely hear the words. I feel shell-shocked. I'm just looking straight at Dad, the man who was supposed to be my protector in life, the man I was supposed to be able to look up to, admire, moaning on the ground, his legs broken by the man that I'm in love with, the father of my child, Dad's adoptive son.

I touch Duncan's hand, nod at him. He puts his arm around me, holds me and kisses my head. "I was right on the edge."

I tap him on the chest. "I know. You okay?" I pull his head toward me, see a gash along the side of his jaw where Bullock got him with the knife. The wound on his forehead has opened up as well. "Damn it."

"It's fine."

"You ungrateful little shits," I hear Dad groan from the ground.

I step around Duncan, go to him, kneel down beside him. His face is contorted by the pain, but he looks up at me out of savage eyes.

"Why, Dad? Why couldn't you just love me and take care of me? Why couldn't you support me?"

He doesn't reply, just lets out a snarl.

"Why?" I ask, raising my voice. "Tell me why!" I slap him hard across the face, hear his head thump against the hardwood.

"Why?" I cry, slapping him again and again. I hit him harder, faster, and each slap stings my palm.

He just takes them, doesn't say a thing, and then I feel Duncan's arms around me, and he lifts me up, pulls me away.

"I hate you!" I scream at Dad. "I fucking hate you!"

"I wish your mother had never died," he says, his voice slurry. He spits out a wad of blood. "So she could have given me a son."

Duncan turns on Dad, points the gun at him. "You shut your fucking mouth right now."

"You were always a disappointment, Deidre."

"Shut up!"

"I needed an heir, not a fucking—"

Duncan kicks Dad in the mouth. I look away, but too late, and the image of Dad's flying, bloody gold teeth is seared into my mind.

I go to the bleachers, sit down, and Duncan comes toward me, his whole body tense like some kind of tornado, and he holds me, and I want to cry, I feel like I'm so pent up, like I just need to burst, but I can't.

Nothing comes out.

I just look at Dad, can barely feel Duncan stroking my hair, can barely hear him telling me it's over.

But after a moment I tell him, "It's not over. It's in my mind." I touch my temple, then lie against his shoulder. "I hope I don't lose you. The police are coming."

The fire alarm bells have stopped, and the sprinklers peter out. I can hear their sirens now, wailing in the distance, growing louder by the second.

"You won't. We'll be fine. We just have to tell the truth."

"How does it look?" I ask, nodding at Duncan's hand. He lifts up the revolver, then drops it to the floor in disgust. "Your prints are on the gun that killed Frank."

He sighs, pinches his eyebrows together in his fingers. "Fuck. I had to take it."

"I know."

"God damn it."

I peer into my own hand, realize I'm still holding Franks gun. I look at Dad, then Bullock, then Frank's limp body.

We can't count on Bullock, and I realize, my mind whirring at a million miles an hour, that I have to take this into my own hands.

"It's cold," I tell Duncan. "Go put on your top."

He listens to me, gets up, picks up his shirt and jacket off the floor. He squeezes into his t-shirt, and then looks at me and asks me the question I was waiting for.

"Are you cold?"

"Yes."

He gives me his jacket, and I worm my arms into it, then find the inside jacket pocket.

"Go check on Bullock," I say.

"Why?"

"You need to see if he's dead. We need to know what to expect when the police get here."

Duncan goes to Bullock, kneels down by him, and when his back is to me I shove Frank's gun into the jacket's inside pocket.

Duncan returns to me, and looks down at the revolver on the ground. He opens his mouth to speak, but at that moment the door to the gym opens, and we see a yellow fire helmet.

The fireman steps into the gym, looks at Duncan and I in turn, then sees the bodies and the gun on the ground, and he throws himself back out of the door.

"Be ready," I say.

Duncan bends down, picks up the gun.

"What are you doing?" I ask, widening my eyes. "Put it down, don't hold it."

It's too late. The cops come in, weapons raised, shouting at Duncan to get to his knees. He holds the gun out, lets it hang off his finger, and then falls to his knees.

He looks at me, says, "The gun had to be in *my* hands, Dee."

The police circle Duncan, handle him roughly, and I shout at them, tell them that he was just protecting me, that I'm pregnant, that we were held at gunpoint.

But they clear out, carry out Bullock and Dad, and then I see a lone detective walk into the gym. He's old, wiry, but his eyes shine. He sits down beside me, and asks me one question: "Are you the daughter of Johnny Marino?"

"Yes," I say.

"I'm going to have to take you down to the station."

"Am I under arrest?"

"Yes."

"I want to be read my rights."

"You will be."

"But I need to see a paramedic first. I'm pregnant, and they weren't gentle with me." I rub my belly, and the detective's eyes go to it, fill with compassion for a moment.

"There's an ambulance outside. Come on."

I get up slowly, shake off his helping hand.

"I can do it myself."

We go outside, and there I see Duncan being forced into the back of a police car. He's cuffed, and he swings his head over his shoulder, and I meet his eyes for a moment before he disappears.

"This way," the detective says, guiding me with a hand on the small of my back. He's holding an umbrella out for me, and rainwater wets his long trench coat.

"How did you know to come?" I ask, looking around, seeing just one fire truck but a barrage of police vehicles.

"We got a tip from someone out of Hong Kong," he tells me. "That a man on the FBI's most wanted list was entering Australia. We maintain a cooperative relationship. We've been following your father."

"You could have fucking got here sooner," I say.

"He lost us in the rain."

I shake my head, watch as Duncan is driven off.

"What's going to happen to him?"

"He's under arrest."

"Charges?"

The detective shrugs. "We'll hold him while we analyze the crime scene."

We reach the ambulance, but the paramedics are busy dealing with Dad's knee and Bullock's knife wound.

"I think there may be someone else," I say. "A fourth man, the driver of the limousine."

The detective stiffens, pulls out his weapon.

"Here? At the school?"

"Yes, one of my father's men."

The detective rounds up the officers to sweep the area. In the commotion I take the gun from Duncan's jacket and throw it down a sewer grate.

It's been raining so heavily all night, I can hear the water surging.

The cogs in my mind are whirring, and I'm hoping I'm not making a terrible mistake.

When the detective returns, panting, he tells me that they searched the school but found nobody, asks me if I'm sure.

"I don't know," I say. "I think I'm in shock. Are you going to handcuff me?"

"Not if you don't resist."

"Then I'll come willingly," I tell him.

I just hid a piece of evidence. I've got to get this exactly right!

*

45

DEE

The man who walks into the room is not the media stereotype of a cop. He's well-dressed, clean-shaven, in good health for a man in his fifties.

The detective has cleaned up after getting wet in the rain. He obviously keeps a change of clothes at the office.

He smiles warmly at me as he closes the door to the interview room behind him.

I've been sitting in this room for four hours, but they've put the radio on in the room to keep me awake. It's now nearly five in the morning, and I haven't been able to catch a wink. I know they do it for a reason, to get you tired so you might blurt something.

There's water and food on the table, and I've helped myself liberally. If they're going to keep me up, then I need to keep my strength up.

"Ms. Marino," he says, looking down at his file and then back up at me. "Deidre Marino?"

I nod.

"We found an image of the real Caroline Sax."

"Am I being charged?" I ask.

"Not yet."

"Am I being detained?"

He pauses briefly. "Yes."

"For how long?"

"Eight hours, but we can get that extended to twelve."

"And how long can you question me for, legally?"

The man sits down opposite me, and gives me a curt smile. "Four hours."

"You're required to give me your identity."

"Detective Inspector Mike Grayson," he says. "Would you like to see my identification, Ms. Marino?"

I nod. "Yes."

He sighs, reaches into his back pocket and pulls out a worn leather wallet. He flips it open, and there I see his badge. He pulls out his identification card and slides it over the desk to me.

I look at it – it's him.

"I have the right to be told what I've been arrested for, Detective Grayson."

"Ms. Marino, you should know that being hostile is only going to make this last longer."

"My right to know what I've been arrested for, please," I say. I try to keep my face as calm as possible on the outside, but inside my heart is racing, and my nerves are threatening to undo me.

I remember reading about the process of events when you're arrested in Australia when I first got to Melbourne, but four months later, my memory is hazy at best.

"Accessory to murder before the fact."

I swallow. *Murder*. They must mean Frank.

"What is the maximum sentence?"

"Life imprisonment," he says. "In Australia."

"Will I be extradited?"

"You haven't even been charged yet."

"So I'm being interviewed as a suspect?"

"Yes," he says. Then, almost awkwardly, he adds, "Formally."

I ponder the addition. What's his angle?

"Then I have the right to be given a reasonable chance to communicate with a lawyer."

"You do," he tells me. "But Ms. Marino, I think you should let me speak for a moment."

I nod slowly. I don't have to say anything if I don't want to.

"You, Duncan Malone, a man who we cannot yet identify, and Johnny Marino were all arrested tonight. We've got video surveillance from the school sports hall, however, that will be entered as evidence should any one of you be charged with a crime."

I blink. Video evidence. The gym had cameras!

"Nobody has been charged yet?"

"No."

"Not even my father?"

Grayson raises an eyebrow. "Why are you concerned with him in particular?"

I shrug. "He's my dad. What daughter wouldn't be?"

"Look," he says, clasping his hands together on the table in front of me. He wears a silver wedding ring. His hands have the texture of weathered leather. "The truth is I don't think you had anything to do with this. I think you were the victim here."

"Oh yeah?" I ask.

"Yes. We have you entering Australia with a false identity presumably under duress. You are pregnant, obviously, and soon after Duncan Malone entered the country, followed by your father and the big bloke, who we learned about after a tip-off. It doesn't take a rocket scientist to figure out you were running away. The question is, from whom?"

My eyes widen. Do they suspect Duncan of anything?

"Did you watch the tape?" I ask.

He nods. "Of course."

"Then you know Duncan and I were both the victims."

"Let's talk about you," he says. He gets up, walks to the door, and then pokes his head outside. A few moments later a television is wheeled in. He thanks the man who brought it in, then shuts the door.

He empties his pockets then, onto the table.

"What are you doing?"

"In my pockets I have my wallet, a stick of gum, and my mobile phone." He picks up his phone, unlocks it, then holds it out in front of me. "Please turn it off."

I would think that he's just trying to get my fingerprints, but they already printed me. I'm too on-edge, too paranoid. My mind is racing through every possibility, but I can't figure out why he wants me to touch his phone.

I reach out, turn off the phone.

"As you can see around the room, you are not being watched, listened to, or recorded. There are no cameras in here as this is just an interview room. No two-way mirrors. It's not like the cop shows on telly."

"So?" I ask.

"In my pockets I have no recording devices, and my phone is off."

"You could be wearing a wire," I say, but it sounds stupid even as I say it.

He doesn't laugh at me, to his credit. "You're

right. I can take off my shirt if you'd like."

"Just get to the point," I say.

"Right now what you say to me can be admitted as evidence. However, I am not recording you, as a gesture of good faith because I believe you are a victim."

"You can still testify against me."

"Which is why I'm going to ask you a series of yes-or-no questions. You simply nod your head or shake it. That testimony would not stand."

"Why are you doing this?" I ask.

"I'm only interested in catching the bad guys, Ms. Marino. I have no desire to see innocent people charged incorrectly." He gestures at my belly. "I have three children myself, and I can remember the first pregnancy like it was yesterday. I know how tough it's been for you. I'm only interested in the truth."

I let his words roll off me. I don't trust him.

He flicks on the television, and the recording of the gym buzzes to life. It's black-and-white, more blurred than sharp, but it is unmistakably the events which occurred just earlier tonight.

The camera is obviously positioned behind us. I

can see Frank… and myself sitting just in front of him. I can see Dad, too, his pistol gleaming with reflected light. Farther out in the image are Duncan and Bullock, standing opposite each other at the half-court line of the basketball court.

"Is this you?" he says, pointing at me.

I nod.

"And this is your father? Yes? Okay. Frank, Duncan, and the big guy, right? Good."

I take in a breath. There's no harm in identifying them.

He plays the video. I watch Duncan and Bullock fight, and wince at the narrow misses as Bullock swipes his knife at Duncan.

Grayson pauses it. "Does this man, the big guy, have a weapon?"

I nod.

"Is it a knife?"

Nod.

"And is Duncan being forced to fight?"

I nod again.

"By your father?"

Nod.

"Are you being threatened?"

Nod.

Detective Inspector Grayson scribbles down some notes in a pad. "These are just for me, personally, to remember your responses. They will be inadmissible."

He plays the video again. I watch as Duncan and Bullock fight, as Dad paces the floor, gripping onto his gun, eagerly watching.

Then Frank stands up. The camera, from its position, only shows Frank's back. There's no way to see what is in his hands.

Grayson pauses the video. "Is Frank telling your father to stop the fight?"

I nod.

"Does he have a gun pointed at your father?"

I meet Grayson's eyes, but don't give a response.

"Did he have a gun pointed at you when he was still sitting?"

I… shake my head.

Grayson plays the video again. I watch Dad's arm twitch. I watch Frank hit the floor dead. I watch myself sprint away. Duncan whirls on Bullock, takes him down, stabs him in the leg then breaks his arm.

Frank's body is lying away from the camera, and we can only see him lengthways. Still his gun isn't visible. My sigh of relief exits through my nose.

The sprinklers start, muddy up the image, but I see that I come back into the gym, and then Duncan moves on Dad, and I kneel down beside Frank.

Grayson pauses it again. "At this moment, are you feeling for Frank's pulse?"

I nod.

"And did you do anything else?"

I shake my head.

"Did he have a weapon?"

I shake my head.

Grayson leans back in his chair and regards me. I struggle to keep myself as calm as possible.

I just lied to the police… I lied to get Dad locked up. If I tell them that Frank had a gun, then Dad will have been under duress, self-defense, whatever.

Dad's going to go to prison for a long time because of me.

"So are you telling me that as soon as Frank stood up and asked your father to stop – I presume that's what he's doing – your father shot him without provocation?"

I nod.

"He murdered Frank Marsh in cold blood?"

I take a deep breath, and nod again. A tear leaves my eye, and I wipe it away quickly, but I'm unable to stop my lips from trembling.

I don't want to cry right now, but it all seems to be trying to come out right now. I don't want to give myself away first and foremost, but I also don't want to regret this decision.

I had to do it. I *had* to.

"Will you testify to this?"

I consider it, then shake my head.

Grayson sighs. "Let me tell you how this will go down in court. The jury will see this video, will see your father shoot Frank. In the absence of any mitigating factors, your father *will* be convicted for murder charges, and will be sentenced to life imprisonment as per sentencing rules in Victoria. Or, if he is extradited, he will likely serve a similar term in the United States."

I nod, showing my understanding.

"If Frank had a gun," Grayson says, leaning forward. "And if you took it, then you are liable to charges of obstruction of justice. *You* can go to jail for that. If you lie under oath, you risk yourself to charges of perjury, which you can also be jailed for."

I nod.

"If Frank had a gun, your father will have been acting under provocation, and possibly self-defense. You understand that he can be acquitted of all charges in that event?"

I nod.

Grayson pinches his brow, sighs, then taps his pad idly with his pen. "You're free to go, Ms. Marino. Stay in Melbourne, please. We'll contact you if we need to."

I blink. "I can go?"

"We won't be pressing charges." He rubs his brow. "I see no reason to."

"You believe me?"

"I believe you were a victim. As for the events that transpired tonight…" He shakes his head. "I don't know."

"What about Duncan?"

"He's free to go as well," the detective says. "All he's guilty of is trespassing, but that was under mortal threat." Grayson walks to the door and opens it. "We'll be in touch."

I get up, walk past him, and in the hallway see Duncan. I rush to him, and he to me, and he wraps me up in his arms, kisses my forehead.

"Are you okay?" I ask him, my voice wavering.

"Yeah," he says. "They stitched me up. Come on, let's talk outside."

Together we leave the police station, and Grayson watches us all the way out, chewing on the end of his pen.

*

46

DEE

We walk outside into the cool morning air. The sun is rising on the horizon, casting an orange glow across the waking city.

Duncan pulls me along with him, throwing glances over his shoulder.

"I don't think they're following us."

"Did he ask you about the gun?"

I look up at him, and nod.

"Did you take it?"

I nod again.

"Why?"

"It was the only way to put Dad away," I say. "He had it coming. It was eventually going to catch up to him, anyway."

I say it with conviction. I believe it.

"It was the only we to protect our son." I take his hand, put it on my belly.

"But you could have been caught."

"But I wasn't," I say. "Was I?"

"That was a huge risk, Dee."

"I know."

"What if they had found out?"

"Then I could just say I was in shock, didn't know what I was doing."

"Would that even hold up?"

I shake my head. "I don't know, Duncan. It's over now, okay?"

"Okay," he says. "Remind me never to mess with you."

"I know what I'm doing," I tell him. "Most of the time, anyway."

"Where did you put it?"

"I just dropped it into the sewer. It had been raining all night, right? It'll have washed away somewhere."

"Did you wipe the handle?"

"No," I say. "But in the sewer? With that much rain?"

"It's a risk," he whispers.

"I don't think they're going to be pulling any *CSI* shit on us, Duncan. They've got all the evidence they need to put Dad away… that video is enough! The detective seemed to want to help me, too. What did *you* tell them about the gun?"

"I said I didn't know if he had one, it was too dark to see."

"But you did know, right?"

He nods.

"How did you know to lie?"

"I saw you holding it, and then you weren't. At first I thought you had just put it down somewhere, until they asked me about it."

He pulls me around a corner, then he pins me up against the wall, kisses me hard. I wrap my arms around his neck, hold onto him, and he kisses my neck, my shoulders, and we hug each other tight.

We don't let go. We hold each other, breathe slowly together.

"We're a team," Duncan says. "Always."

It's dawning on me now that I'm finally free of Dad. He'll go away, and Frank – who is the only other person who knew about my pregnancy – is dead. If Bullock was going to say something, he would have already, but they'll have nothing on him. He was forced to fight, and he's obviously not pressing charges against Duncan for sticking that knife into his leg.

Duncan and I can disappear, live the life we want to in peace. "I can't believe everything that's happened," I whisper into his ear. I bury my face in his neck, inhale his smell, and even though it's sharp after a long night, I love every bit of it.

"You're okay, right?" he asks. "Did you get hurt in any way?"

"No."

"The stress levels can't have been good. All that adrenaline running through your body, it will have made its way into the fetus, right?"

I blink, then shake my head. "I don't know, Duncan."

"We need to make an appointment with your doctor. I saw the way Frank held you."

"Will you come with me?"

Duncan's whole face creases up for a moment, bunches together. "Of course," he whispers. "I wouldn't miss it for the fucking world. I'll be with you every God damn step of the way, Dee. Every moment, every second, I'll be at your side." He smirks. "Even when you don't want me around."

"You can get a bit much sometimes," I say, grinning.

He looks worn, frayed at the edges. I'm not surprised, either, since he took a good beating. The bandaging on the side of his head that covers the slice up his jawline is already starting to show blood through it, and the white gauze on his arms are also spotting crimson.

"Damn, you got fucked up," I say. I don't know why, but this great big grin spreads on my face, and then I'm laughing with him, and we're laughing together.

And then I'm crying, and I don't even know why. It's just a flash of emotion, there one moment, gone the next, but it leaves me teary-eyed in its wake.

"I'm so tired and so hungry," I say. "Let's go get some breakfast."

Duncan wipes the tears from my cheeks, and his own eyes shine red.

"Now let me see," I say, turning on the spot, wiping my nose quickly. "We're in St. Kilda, I know a good place where we can get some delicious oatmeal. It's all organic stuff and they put cinnamon on it and—"

Duncan makes a face.

"What?"

"Oatmeal?"

"It's healthy. For the baby."

"I think you've earned a treat."

"Full-fat breakfast?"

He nods. "Yeah. It'll be alright."

I don't even need to think it over. A full breakfast sounds great, something I haven't had in ages… since before I found out I was pregnant. I've been sticking to all the healthy foods, trying to give my baby the best nutrition… but I can't think of a better time to get some food for my own soul.

"I know a cute café in Brighton," I say. "They do

the best scrambled eggs. I don't know what they put in it, but it's magical."

"Maybe opiates."

"Stop it," I say, slapping his shoulder.

"I read about it. Some noodle shop somewhere in China. They were putting opium in their broth to keep people coming back."

"I doubt that's the case here."

Duncan waves down a taxi, and we get in. He turns to me, wipes smudged eye-liner from under my eyes.

"It's going to look like we had one hell of a night out," he says.

*

Epilogue

DUNCAN

Fletcher's.

I take the steps up to Pierce's gym two at a time – it's on the second floor – and push open the heavy, wooden double-doors.

There I see a group of young boys huddled in a semi-circle on the floor. In front of them is a large flat-screen television. They're watching an MMA match, and Pierce is standing next to the television, explaining the moves.

He catches my eye for a moment, ignores me, and keeps instructing. As I get closer, I realize that he's playing one of my matches.

I'm not doing too well in this one. I remember the

fight, it was tough, and I almost got pinned when I let my opponent get on my back and get a hold of my leg.

"You roll your body," Pierce says, pausing the video. "Like Creature does here. Use your forearm for leverage, twist, then pull."

He's teaching them how to get out of a leg lock. You have to get your opponent off-balance, so that they can't exert force in the proper direction. It's all about angles and leverage. Get the right angle, get leverage, and you can outmaneuver a man twice your strength.

"Watch how he uses the movement as momentum, to spin himself up to his feet."

One of the boys says, "It's like a kung-fu movie."

Pierce waits until the sparse laughs die down. "This move requires a lot of core strength. That's why I'm always telling you boys, work your core." He slaps a flat palm against his stomach. "Here. Where else?"

"Back," one of the boys says.

"Correct. Where else?"

"Obliques."

"Good," he says, pointing at the boy who answered. "Now, where else? You're all missing a big one."

The boys don't answer. They look at each other, confused. And then one of them spies me, does a double-take, and I hear him whisper to the closest next to him, "Holy shit, it's Creature."

All the boys start murmuring, and as they turn on me, I see familiar looks in their eyes. These are at-risk kids.

Some will live in group homes, others in foster care, and most are likely latchkey kids at low income households.

Some are older, already out of the system, already young men, looking for something to work toward in their lives, something to help them build self-confidence.

"Hey!" Pierce cries, clapping his hands together, snapping their attention all back to him. He's got a natural authority over these kids, and they listen to him. He's doing good for these kids. They all don't look at me even once more. They're well disciplined.

"Where else constitutes your core?" he asks.

"Which major muscle group?"

"Your butt!" one of the kids shouts. Everybody snickers.

I see a smile on Pierce's face. "Correct. Your glutes are very important for stabilizing your body. They are one of the most important muscle groups in your body. Stretch them for twice as long as any other muscle, got it? Ever wonder why so many people have back pain? It's because they have tight asses."

Again, everybody snickers.

"I'm telling you the truth," Pierce says. "Ask any physiotherapist. If everybody just stretched their ass a bit more, they wouldn't get so much back pain. You see, the tight glute muscles will pull against your lower back." He turns around and rubs a hand just above his tailbone. "This worsens your posture, and you are forced to use other muscles to compensate. Remember, every muscle in the body affects every other. That is why we emphasize core strength, and conditioning of the major muscle groups. Having big guns…" He lifts up his arm, flexes his strong bicep. "Is useless. You need strength here." He motions at the trunk of his body. "Got it?"

Some of the boys nod.

"Got it?" Pierce says, raising his voice.

"Yes," all the boys say together.

"Now go on, split off into pairs. Get into this leg lock," he says, tapping the screen. "No strength, this is just practice. Work the angles, see how you can slip it. I'll come by in a bit to check on you."

He jerks his head, and the boys immediately get up, pair off, and then he walks toward me, his brow creased.

"Everything alright? I didn't hear from you for a while."

I nod at him. "Yeah, things got a bit crazy. Just been cooling down."

He sticks two fists out, and I tap them. Fighter's tradition.

"This fight got pretty hairy, eh?" he asks, looking back at the television.

"You know, I honestly thought I might lose that fight. I was a little off that night. When he got on my back… Where'd you get that video, anyway?"

"MMA-Underground dot com," he says.

I grin. "Dan Peterson's website."

"Yeah, you know him?"

"Nah," I say, shaking my head.

"Bullshit. I read the interview."

"What did it say?"

"Usual fluff piece. Oversold you."

I laugh, look around the gym, see brand new punching bags. "Doing well?"

"We just got a donation, actually."

"Really?"

"Yeah. Anonymous, but it was enough to buy some new equipment for the boys."

"It really helps them?" I look at the boys now all lying on mats, practicing – and mostly failing – to properly get out of a leg-lock. It's a technique that takes weeks of practice to even perform semi-competently. Pierce is setting up long-term goals for these boys.

"They have a ways to come," Pierce says, noticing their form with me. "But yes, it really does. Most of these boys came in scared, bullied at school. They didn't know how to stand up for themselves. They didn't believe that they had inherent worth. This helps them to build their confidence, and teach them the value of hard work. I'm sure your training helped you. It did me."

I nod. "Yeah, of course."

"So," Pierce says. He looks me up and down. "Damn, you got pretty beat up. What's that?" He points at my jaw.

"Got sliced by a knife. Stitches just came out a few days ago."

"Fucking hell."

"At least I wasn't shot."

He laughs. "I got a tattoo around that scar on my foot."

"Yeah?"

"Only time I've ever had something go right through my body."

I push my lips together. That's definitely one way of looking at it.

"Scratch that off the bucket list, I guess," I say.

"What is it, Duncan?" he asks after a moment. "Just tell me."

"I came to say thanks, for helping out."

"Didn't do much."

"Thanks, anyway. I appreciate it."

I hear the sound of drilling, frown, look around.

"We're expanding," he says. "Onto the floor above." He looks up. "Penny wants to get some girls in the gym, you know, girls like these boys."

"Yeah?"

"Teach them fitness, good health, get them exercising, maybe even have me do some light fighting training with them. It's going to be really cheap, she's managed to get some sponsors, women's organizations who will help out. We've got physical trainers who have volunteered to work with the girls for free, all women of course."

"That sounds… really fucking good, Pierce."

"We're starting to make waves, man. People are donating in small amounts regularly. We're doing a little light merchandising, selling sports drinks that aren't all loaded with sugary crap, or stimulants like caffeine or yohimbine."

"Fletcherade, huh?"

"That's right."

"Seems like you're doing well. I'm glad."

"You know, with the extra space upstairs, I'd love to take on more boys."

"Yeah?"

I see the look in his eye, the smirk at his lips, return it.

"Guy like Duncan 'Creature' Malone would be a real attraction."

"You think so?"

"Can't pay you much, but I'm pretty sure you've got a lot tucked away from that thirty-three-to-nil streak you went on."

"Good guess."

"Interested?"

I look around. I could work with these boys. Help them, guide them. Give them something I never had enough of in my youth.

"It's not just the fighting or the training," Pierce says. "It's more.... What's the word Penny used? Wholesome?"

"Holistic."

"That's the one. Damn, Creature, so you're not just a dumb fighter after all?"

"Wouldn't go that far. It was a buzz word for a

while for the social workers at my group home."

"Anyway, we tell these kids straight up that most of them aren't ever going to make a living fighting. We discourage underground stuff. This is just so they can be good at something, take that mental discipline to whatever else they choose to do. We do picnics, outings, activities, things to build their sense of self-worth, to improve their social skills, allow them to see a little more of the world. We take them to fancy restaurants, teach them how to use the cutlery properly, how to order, how to address service staff. All kinds of things. You know, social worker stuff, but unburdened by bureaucracy.

"We're not trying to help everybody, just everybody we possibly can, so we're not stretched too thin. I even have a university professor on the payroll as a consultant. She's all clued up on the social work research, helps design programs for these boys."

"Yeah, that sounds good," I say. "Real good. Your speech was good, too."

"Hey, fuck, I got to be a salesman half the time now. We don't charge these kids anything. So, you interested? I could use another partner. Penny and I are starting to get overloaded, and her tattoo shop is getting big, you know. She's picking up a new client every day almost."

I think about it, even though I don't really need to. "Count me in," I say.

A broad smile erupts on his face. "Great. How about all that stuff with your girl's old man?"

"That's all done," I say. "He's back in the States, awaiting trial, no bail. Police received a tip on financial records kept at his house in a hidden safe. His crew is getting picked up one by one."

"Bet they're all flipping upward, now, aren't they?"

"Of course they fucking are," I growl. "Bunch of spineless fucks, all of them. When the dust settles, I wouldn't be surprised if he goes away for consecutive life sentences. He has a lot of fucking skeletons buried and they are going to get dug up."

"Nothing will follow you back here?"

I shake my head. "Shouldn't, but if it ever does, I'll be out of here." I pause. "You know, for the boys."

"Okay, good. Hate to make a point of it, but they're my priority."

"It's fine," I tell him, waving a hand.

"Hey, I got to get back to it. You come by Monday morning, half-seven, I'll show you where everything is. Going to need all your tax info and that stuff as well if you have it. Say 'hi' to your girl for me."

"Yeah, thanks."

Pierce mimes a pregnant belly. "Everything going well?"

I grin. "So far so good. We're going for an ultrasound next week."

"That's fantastic. It's a boy, right?"

I laugh, can't keep myself from beaming. "That's right."

"Got a name?"

"We're naming him Thom. With an 'h'."

"It's a good name, man. I'm happy for you." He leans into me, and is now wearing a smile that's more pride and joy than anything else. "We just found out. Penny's pregnant, too."

"No shit," I say, clapping him on the shoulder. "That's fantastic. Were you trying?"

He shakes his head. "But we're going to roll with it."

"Get a chance to fall in love all over again," I murmur.

"I don't know why they call you Creature," Pierce says. "You're all sentiment."

We shake hands, I leave.

I went to Pierce's gym to ask for a job to work with the kids, figured he'd do a fighter a favor. Just as well he was looking to hire, anyway.

Dee will be pleased.

I climb into my car, receive a text, and pull out my phone. The bank transfer went through. The several million I had earned with literal blood and sweat are now in Australia. Going to have to find someone to help me invest that, look into getting a bigger place.

The clock in the dash reads half-past three, which means I've got thirty minutes to get across town.

Plenty of time for just one more thing.

*

DEE

All the kids have been picked up, and together with the other staff I check all the rooms, tidy up, make sure nothing has been left behind.

"Caro— sorry, Deidre, go home."

I look at the headmaster of the school, an older man with white hair and thick glasses and the sort of kind smile you only ever see in movies.

"It's fine, Jack."

"I keep calling you Caroline."

"You'll get used to my real name," I say, winking at him.

"But, really now, go home," he says. "I'll stay to tidy up. Your belly is getting bigger than mine!" He rubs his beer belly, looks at it forlornly. "Except mine won't ever go away."

I smile. "You know, they say losing the pregnancy weight is pretty tough as well."

"You're young, you'll manage. Go on, see you on Monday."

"Thanks, Jack," I say, climbing up from my knees slowly, my hand instinctively going to my belly. I'm nearly at six months, and due to start maternity leave fairly soon.

"And thanks again," I say. "For giving me a contract."

"I've seen you with the kids. You're a natural. We'll get you some more specific training after things settle down. But I think it's good for the school to have a young, American teacher, anyway. To be exposed to different cultural elements at a young age."

"You really think so?"

He shrugs. "I try to hire not just Australian teachers, in case you hadn't noticed."

"I had."

"I think it's good for them. Attitudes towards

people that are different from us is something I believe kids pick up at a young age, and it just gets progressively harder to correct. The kids here at the school will have a head-start, in that regard, even if it's an unconscious one."

"I hadn't considered that before," I tell him. "I was going to do a module on diversity education and exposure for children… back at college before I was forced to leave."

"Well, if you're ever interested, I'm subscribed to all the journals. I could talk your head off."

"Thanks," I tell him.

"How will everything be, if I might ask? To take care of the baby?"

I sigh. "To be honest with you, Jack, I haven't even begun thinking that far ahead. After everything that's happened…"

"It's okay, Deidre. I didn't mean to pry."

"When I figure it out, I'll let you know?"

"No worries," he says. He nods at me, shuffles his feet for a moment, then continues down the hallway outside.

I gather my things, say bye to everybody, receive

no less than four rubs of my belly, and then go outside. It's warm, the sun is shining, and I soak it all up in my black sweater, feeling a little like a cat.

With a hand over my eyes, I look around for the car, see it parked a small ways up, and start walking. Duncan's leaning against it, reading a book.

A book.

I don't think I've *ever* seen him read a book.

"Hey," I call, smiling. He snaps the book shut, comes to me, holds me and kisses me.

"I missed you."

"Yeah right," I say. "I saw you eight hours ago. What are you reading?"

He opens the door for me, and I climb into the car, and then he hands me the book.

The Happiest Baby on the Block.

I turn around, look in the back seat, and see piles of books on parenting, on what it's like being pregnant, on giving birth.

He gets into the car beside me, and I say to him, "Someone went on a shopping spree today."

"Well, we're getting closer," he says. "Things have calmed down now. I've got some catching up to do."

"I've got some books at home, Duncan."

"I know," he says. "I've read them all."

For some reason, that makes me laugh.

"What, were you reading in secret?"

"Just while you were at work."

"I don't think it's going to be that complicated. I mean, we'll manage."

"I want to give our son everything I never had, Dee. Everything you never had. I grew up without parents. How can I possibly know how to *be* one? Now is the time to learn whatever I can."

"You're over-thinking it," I tell him. "Nobody knows how to be a parent the first time. People manage by following their hearts. Parenting is instinct, you can't just read a book and then follow some sort of blueprint."

"I know it's not a blueprint, Dee. I'm not treating this like fighting training."

"Are you sure?"

"I'm sure. But in my mind, over-thinking it is probably better than under-thinking it. At least I've read about other people's experiences. I mean, Dee, I never *had* parents. I was never once told off by my mother, never kissed goodnight by someone I cared for, never been shouted at by someone I didn't want to let down. I never had a father to look up to, to learn from. I never felt a soft touch when I was upset. These are experiences people draw on when they become parents, and it influences how they behave to their children."

I suppose I can't really disagree with that.

"It's not just the baby stuff, changing diapers and all that. I'm worried about discipline, communication, all that stuff. How to form a bond." He shakes his head, and his voice trails off.

I pat his arm. "It's fine, I was only teasing you. Read everything you want to."

"Fuck if it hasn't just made things more confusing, though, I'll fucking tell you. Competing theories, contradictory advice. Fuck me…"

"I can tell you one thing for sure."

"What?"

"You'll need to start swearing less."

He laughs, but agrees with me, then pulls us out into the lazy afternoon traffic.

"The money came through."

"Good," I say. "That's one less thing to worry about now."

"I figure we should find someone to invest it. Someone we can trust."

"I'll speak to my colleagues at work," I say. "You can talk to Pierce about it? Surely he's had to have someone money-wise around him to start that gym."

"I went to see Pierce today, actually," he tells me. "He offered me a job working with the boys."

"What did you say?"

Duncan looks at me briefly. "I said yes."

I smile. "That's really great. I'm happy for you. What will the hours be like?"

"Mostly after school to early evening. You know, that's the time to keep them occupied so they don't get up to things. A lot of them are latchkey kids, and some of them live in homes."

"That's perfect," I say. "It means you're free when I'm at work. To take care of Thom."

"Means I'll see you less."

"Like I said, we'll manage."

We drive in silence for a while. I consider everything he's said. The money coming in is great, we're going to need it. It's a lot, something I'm happy for if only because it provides stability for the future as long as we use it right.

I was surprised to find out how much he had saved up from all those fights. It had simply never occurred to me that it was sitting in a bank account all this time, collecting practically no interest, or at best, something equivalent to a fine layer of dust.

"Do you want to work for Pierce?" I ask.

Duncan chews his lip for a moment. "Yeah. You know, I think, if there was a place like that *I* could have gone. One that wasn't overloaded, one that wasn't so lacking in funding… things would have been different."

"We might not have met."

He shoots a look at me. "Nah, we still would have met."

"Why do you say that?"

"It's what I choose to believe."

"What, like destiny?"

"Do you believe in fate?"

I shake my head. "No."

"Me neither," he says.

"So how can you choose to believe it?"

"The alternative is worse."

"Isn't that like sticking your head in the sand?"

"Yeah, but doing so about some fake alternate reality doesn't bother me so much."

"Well, as long as working at the gym is something you want to do, Duncan, then I'm all for it. You'll need to keep yourself occupied, anyway."

"I agree. There's something else."

"What?"

He pauses for a moment.

"Just say it," I say.

"I got a call from the district attorney back home. He wanted to know if you'd changed your mind on testifying. He said if you don't want to, he won't pursue it, but he's eager to get everything he can on Glass."

I shake my head. Damn it, why does the DA keep bothering me with this? "I already said 'no'," I tell Duncan. "And I meant it. I still mean it. What's his name, Windhorst? Windham?"

"The second one."

"I don't see why he doesn't just leave it alone."

"He could get a court summons."

"How does that even work internationally?"

Duncan shrugs. "Something to look up, I guess."

"Well, anyway, I'm not testifying against my father."

"After all he did to you?"

"He's my father, Duncan. I… you know I can't. That whole business with the gun… I've done as much as I can already. I don't want to be there in court to put the final nail in his coffin. It's not about him… it's about me. *I* don't want to do it."

"That's fine, Dee. You know I'll support any decision you make."

"They've got enough on him to put him away until he dies of old age, *anyway.* They don't need my testimony. I'm not going to add needless years to his sentence. Anyway, speaking of Dad, I got a letter from his lawyer."

"Yeah? When?"

"This morning."

"I thought they weren't supposed to be in contact with you."

"It's not related to the trial."

"What did it say?"

"Dad wants me to come and visit him some time. I mean, in prison. He knows he's not going to get out of this, and I'm sure none of the other families are willing to lend a hand. They all hated him. Dad rubbed people like that."

"Are you going to?"

I sigh, shrug. "I don't know. Not yet, anyway. I won't ever forgive him, but he's going to be an old man alone in prison, with enemies on the inside. With all his henchmen giving him up for their own deals… snakes, all of them. But he's going to need somebody."

"If you ever go, I'll come with you," he says. "If you want me there, I'll be there."

"Thanks. Honestly, I don't think it's going to come to that."

"But you considered it."

"Of course. He's my dad. Let's change the subject. How was Pierce?"

"Penelope and him are going to have a baby."

I scrunch up my face. "What, really?"

"Yeah, he told me today. They just found out."

"Huh. We can be new mothers together."

"She'll probably look to you for advice, since you've got a head start."

"Fair enough," I murmur, and put my hand on Duncan's thigh. We don't talk much more on the way home, and I just watch the world go by outside the car.

It's oddly calm, and I'd be lying if a small part of me didn't almost… almost *miss* the thrill. My whole life, I've been a mob boss' daughter. I've had a bodyguard shadow me, I've had people cower when they found out who I was.

I ran away, lived life for several months constantly looking over my shoulder. It was draining, tiring, consumed every last ounce of strength I had.

And we almost lost it all… Duncan almost died. I came so close to certainly having my baby taken from me.

It's crazy, now, that everything is so still. I feel like there needs to be some wind, some rustle.

The therapist tells me that's normal, that there's an adjustment period. I was glad when Duncan said he'd absolutely go with me to therapy. I almost expected him to scoff at the idea, or act all macho about it, but he was receptive at once.

When I asked him why, he said it's because he trusted me. If I thought it was a good idea, then he did, too.

I'm glad because there are a lot of things that have happened, and it's affected us in ways we don't realize. I don't want to be carrying around any emotional baggage… for the baby. I need to get it all out, get it all sorted out in my mind, and he does as well, before we start raising a child.

Duncan was never great at examining his own emotions. I don't blame him, he's had to keep them locked up tight for most of his life.

But now is the time to figure all of that out. We need to put everything behind us, and look only onward. We can't be distracted by the past when the future weighs on us heavily.

We've got a kid to raise, and we've got to raise him right. We've got to give him a good life, but not spoil him. He's got to be our total focus. One-hundred percent.

How could we do that if we were still battling our

own issues? I know it's not impossible, but we don't need a handicap. I personally feel it's vital for the health of our family.

The therapist says we'll need to stay in therapy together for at least a year, and likely more. She says that it's important we work through it together. She says, in Duncan's particular case, that he needs to let me know if he still feels anything residual… about me running away like that.

It's a process, the therapist says, but a good and necessary one.

When we get home, Duncan pampers me. It's sweet, and makes me laugh, because the baby, the prospect of family has changed him so much.

Truth be told, if you took me back in time to when he walked through our front door, didn't take his eyes off me, told me he was going to be the best fighter ever, kissed me in the gym room, then talked back to Dad… I would have never thought he could be tamed, least of all by me.

We are both still so young, and yet it feels like we've lived a lifetime. I've seen things in my youth that people don't ever see in their lives, and for him it's the same.

He brings me a hot cup of lemon water, my book, and a blanket. I lie on the sofa, read for a while in the afternoon. He's said he'll cook dinner tonight; he's going to try making homemade sushi. No raw fish, just cucumber, egg, teriyaki chicken, and smoked salmon sushi.

Not only is it not exactly authentic, but it's going to be disastrous… I'm fairly certain of that. He's still working on his cooking skills – all he knows how to do is brown rice, broccoli, and chicken. But even I tried it once myself, and it didn't taste like the real thing at all.

And after dinner, we watch television together. It's something so banal, so domestic, and yet it is something that makes me surprisingly happy. And when the episode of *Game of Thrones* finishes, we turn the television off, and Duncan still kisses me like he used to. He tells me how gorgeous I am, and with soft dabs of his lips on my neck and shoulder, he makes me shiver and hum, and then he climbs under the blanket and he makes me shudder and moan.

We go to bed together, and we make love, and then he holds me tight, and I know that he's never going to let me go. It's like this every night. I've never felt so secure, and yet that is not enough to stop me from sometimes second guess myself.

Did I do the right thing, running away, taking the baby, keeping it a secret? If I hadn't have done that, then Duncan might not be here with me now. Dad would have had him killed.

Before bed my mind kicks into overdrive, like it does most nights now, and I consider how at one point, not so long ago, I thought that I'd have to live out the rest of my life on my own. That I'd have to be a single mother, and that I'd have nobody to turn to.

That I'd have to be endlessly strong, that I wouldn't have somebody to rely on, to let my guard down around, to protect *me* and my child in the warm embrace of his arms when *I* wasn't feeling up to it, when *I* wanted a break. When *I* couldn't be that iron woman, forged in fire, that somehow I feel I'm expected to be.

Duncan falls asleep first, unburdened at night in

the same way that I am. He's so well-trained to sleep as soon as he shuts his eyes, from all the naps he used to take throughout the day after heavy training sessions so that his body could recuperate. I sometimes envy him.

But his slow breathing, his arm around me, and knowing that he'll be there for me, really *knowing*… I couldn't ask for anything more, I guess.

It all sort of worked out. We saved our baby, saved our relationship. We've got money, lots of it, and we've got jobs. Duncan's not fighting anymore, and Dad's not in the picture anymore.

It's crazy, insane, really. It could have so easily *not* worked out.

But it did work out in the end.

Duncan rolls over, half-asleep, and murmurs, "Stop thinking so much."

"Go to sleep," I tell him softly.

"Don't worry," he says. "Things are only going to get better."

"I know," I tell him.

He wraps a leg around me, as if somehow trying to make even more of me his. "I love you more than anything, Dee. I think we're going to be fine."

And like that he falls asleep again, and when he sleeps his body is perfectly still.

I slip my fingers in between his, force myself to stop thinking, to shut my eyes.

I think we're going to be fine, too.

THE END

Also by Emilia Kincade:

UNCAGED

Fighting and fucking — that's all I know.

Win the fight. Pick a girl. Screw her brains out. Rinse and repeat.

Every night ends up the same, with my opponent tapping out and a smoking-hot girl in my bed.

Until Penny.

I want to tangle her hair in my hands and taste her lips, make her scream my name all night long. Every single night.

She's mine… until the mafia takes her.

To get her back, I make a deal with the devil… one last fight.

This time, she's the prize.

*

Bad boy...cage fighter...stepbrother.

Pierce Fletcher is naked from the waist down. He came into my shop demanding a tattoo, and I've got to do it.

It's already *very* clear just how much he wants me.

He looks at me like I'm already his property.

One peek at his body and I'm hooked. One arrogant smirk and I'm ready to have his rough hands all over me.

Why do I let him unravel me? It doesn't matter, anyway.

The mob wants to use me to get to him... but he's not going to let that happen.

And neither am I.

1

PENNY

He's talking about his dick. *Again.*

What can I say? I'm not even a little bit surprised.

"What is it?" I ask, tattoo machine in my hand. I'm going over the shadowing of a fluffy white rabbit tattoo on my client's arm, but already he's screwing up my concentration.

"I want a Prince Albert."

I lift the compact needle off her skin, watch as her reddened flesh depresses slowly. I don't bother looking up at him. I know the expression he's got on his face without needing to see it. A cocky smirk, as though he thinks he's so funny, so clever.

He's already got me completely annoyed.

A Prince Albert? Is he serious? He can't just come to my place of work and mess with me like this. But it's not the first time he's done it, and I'm certain it won't be the last.

I push my lips together. My temper frays. "Please don't disturb me while I'm working."

But he doesn't move. He just stands by the leather-bound reclined chair my client is sat in. He shouldn't even be in the back room where we administer the tattoos. But things like regulations, closed doorways, heck, even mere manners don't stop him.

At the bottom of my vision I can see his lower legs up to his knees. He's wearing jeans, but I see straight through the dark denim.

Tribal-inspired lines coil around his shins and calves. On his left knee he's got a ram's head with huge, gnarled horns, and on his right knee he's got an owl with ram's horns. The two look scary, unreal in a monster-in-the-dark kind of way. The first time I saw them, I was extremely impressed by the artistry. The eyes on each beast look straight into you, no matter which angle you look at them from.

Of course, I should know about all his tattoos. I'm his new favorite tattoo artist, apparently.

"Sorry," I mouth to the girl in the chair, scrunching up my face with an apologetic look. This is unprofessional, and she, the client, shouldn't have to deal with Pierce's uncontrollable and childish impulses.

She says *no problem* with her eyes, and then offers me a quick but confused smile. I'm not sure if she knows what a Prince Albert is.

"Can you do it?" Pierce asks me. In his baritone voice I can hear just a hint of playfulness. He's definitely trying to rile me up, trying to get under my skin. And if there's one thing he's good at, it's being a splinter.

With deliberate slowness I pull my eyes up his body. I don't see his clothing or his skin, but instead see his tattoos. I know them all because I've worked on them all.

I filled in the trawling tentacles of the jellyfish on his leg, redid the outline of the coiled serpent-slash-dragon on his chest and stomach. I darkened some of the fading ink on the snarling, salivating white wolf he has on his right shoulder. I added a line to the tally he keeps on his wrist – his fighting wins – and I did the fifth numeral on his fifth knuckle. I have no idea what the numerals mean.

"No," I say, finally meeting his eyes with as stony a stare as I can muster. He doesn't blink, doesn't shift his focus, doesn't grow uncomfortable in the slightest. He looks right at me with a sparkle of amusement. I hate that he always seems at ease, confident, unburdened by awkwardness, embarrassment, or shame. I hate that he still messes with me.

Truth be told, we've been through too much together. I thought he had grown up.

"I can't, and I won't. Please leave," I tell him curtly. The last thing I want to do is make a scene in front of this client. His eyes seem to flash, grow hot not with anger but with... competitiveness. It's the only way to describe it. He thinks everything is a competition. He thinks every situation has winners and losers, and God forbid he ever lose.

Pierce's eyes are this shade of light grey that always surprise me. Looking into his eyes is like looking into a shaken-up snow globe. They almost seem to glow. Sometimes, his eyes remind me of a wolf's in the night. They have a shine to them, something intense.

"You sure?" he asks. His thumb slides beneath the waist of his jeans, and he adjusts it, showing a flash of trimmed pubic buzz.

I roll my eyes. "One-hundred percent."

"You *don't* want to… *pierce* my dick?" He's in full-on smug mode now, and he has an eyebrow raised as though he just made the witticism of the century.

"I'm not trained," I tell him in a matter-of-fact manner. I do my best to sound bored. "I'm sure you can appreciate the… *dangers* involved if I were to attempt to give you a Prince Albert."

His lips curl to the side, a little off-center within his granite jaw. "Amen to *that!* Don't want to damage my junk, do you?" He pauses for a moment. "Go get training, then."

I wear my annoyance freely on my face. "Go get *training?*"

"Yeah."

"Just go away, Pierce. I don't want to see your dick."

His full, endlessly kissable lips pull farther to the side in what I can only describe as the most smug and conceited smirk ever. He's so full of himself. Why have I gotten myself into this mess? He's a walking whirlwind of trouble… it seems to seek him out.

"You know," he says, voice dripping with sarcasm. "That's not what you said last ni—"

"No!" I bark, glancing quickly toward my client. I pinch the bridge of my nose, and lower my voice, steady it. My client is stewing in the awkwardness. "We don't do piercings here."

"You could do *this* Pierce."

He grins, I glare.

"I only trust you to do it," he says. "Besides, you and I both know you wouldn't mind getting your fingers wrapped 'round my junk again."

I groan and look away. Why does he insist on calling it his *junk?* It's disgusting.

"No, okay? I can refer you to someone who is qualified, though."

"I don't want anybody else touching my cock, Penny. Just you. You know it's all yours."

The girl on the chair clears her throat. "Maybe I'd better go into the waiting room."

I nod at her. "Sorry, Maya. This will only take a minute."

"Take your time, honey," she says, and she gets up. She looks Pierce up and down. He licks his lips and flashes his eyes at her, and I'm certain I see her knees wobble.

I feel it in my chest: The white-hot burn of unwanted jealousy.

Even worse? *He* sees it in my eyes.

"Oh, don't worry, Pen, she's not my type. You are."

"Please go away."

"Come on, sis," he whispers conspiratorially.

"Don't call me that. It's Penny. And I'm not your sister."

"Stepsister."

"No! Not yet I'm not."

Pierce grins. "I read up about it on the internet, the cock piercing, I mean. They say there can be complications, but that it's unlikely."

"There can," I tell him. I'm leaning back on my stool now, and clasping my hands in front of me, elbows on my knees, hoping I look as irritated as I feel. "But it's unlikely as long as you take good care of it."

"What happens if I don't?"

"Infection is most likely, but a relatively low risk. Urine cleans the cut somewhat."

"How big is the risk?" he asks. His face grows serious. I can't tell if he's still messing around or not. Sometimes he's so hard to read.

"What do you think, idiot? You're sticking a ten-gauge metal ring through the skin on the base of your penis, and passing it *into* your urethra. It's not exactly something the body is used to, so of course there's a risk."

"Ah."

I narrow my eyes at him. "With as much as you like to talk about and use your prick, are you sure it's one you're willing to take?"

"That's why I want you to do it. I trust you. I know you and Tina run a clean shop." He grins. "Also, you know how to handle my ju—"

"This is Tina's shop, not mine." I focus on my vials of ink instead of him. "And she doesn't do piercings here."

"What's the difference? Your shop, her shop… why not branch out? Attract a new clientele."

Now my patience has officially been torn to tatters. "What is this really about, huh? Do you *really* want a Prince Albert, or are you just trying to find some new way to annoy me? Especially after everything that happened? You're going to do *this* to me now?"

I'm huffing, really on the verge of just losing it, but he just laughs it off. It's insanely infuriating. He flops down into the reclined chair, let's out a sigh, and puts his arms up, gripping onto the top edge. It creaks beneath his weight.

His tight t-shirt strains against his body. He's a heavy guy; all muscle, whipcord tight. He said he was close to two-hundred pounds at six-two.

"You can't just come into my place of work and harass me like this, Pierce. I thought we moved past this immature posturing."

"Hey," he says, feigning innocence. "I'm a client."

"You're not booked for today."

"I want an unscheduled consultation."

"On dick piercings?" I cry, slapping my thighs

with frustration. "You're really annoying the shit out of me, and Tina is going to be back from lunch at any moment. You're going to get me in trouble!"

Pierce levels his eyes at me, except now they've gone hard. "You left this morning without saying bye. You were cold and distant all night last night."

"And this is how you address that, is it?" I ask, scowling at him. I throw the tattoo machine down onto my equipment tray, and fold my arms across my chest. "You said we'd talk about it last night. You said we'd talk about what happened. Don't you think we need to talk about it?"

He raises his eyebrows, challenging me. "It takes two to fuck, which is all you seemed to want to do."

I feel my temperature rising. "I *told* you not to do that fight. I *told* you that you were getting mixed up with the wrong people. It was too close!"

Unbelievably, he just shrugs. He's silently saying *whatever*.

"It would be nice if you took responsibility for once."

"Responsibility?" he asks, eyes narrowing. "You know why I had to do that fight!"

"Right, of course. How could I forget? Look at you! You're all fucked up." I point at the eight stitches in the cut above his eye. I then look down at his foot. "They fucking shot you in the foot, Pierce. What the hell are you even doing walking around?"

"I'm fine."

"Oh? Didn't the doctor tell you to stay off your foot?"

"Fuck the doctors."

"What about your fractured rib? All the bruises on your body? The black one on your thigh?"

"It's not like you were worried about that last night." He licks his lips. "While you were screaming my name… scratching my back."

The image of his hot, sweaty body pressed up against mine, his hips thrusting into me, flashes through my mind. I scowl at him.

"You're losing me, Pierce. I'm telling you, I've had it up to here. I'm ready to walk away."

"No you're not," he says, and he gets up off the chair. It creaks and cracks again. He's comes to me, closes the distance fast in just two hard strides.

I put my hands out, but he moves them aside, turns me around, and wraps me up from behind. He buries his nose into my neck and inhales.

"God, you smell sexy."

I feel a pang of self-consciousness. The last time I showered was yesterday morning, and we got very sweaty the night before. If only I hadn't overslept!

"Pierce…"

"Pen," he says, and I don't fail to notice his right hand sidling ever lower over my belly.

"*Pierce,*" I hiss. "Not here, not now!"

He takes my earlobe into his mouth, gives it a nibble. Goosebumps explode all over my body, and still his hand is creeping ever lower.

"Why not?" he asks. "There's construction on the road. Traffic is bad. Tina won't be back for a while."

"Tina *walks,*" I say, my voice barely a whisper. "And she'll fire me if she catches us. This is unhygienic."

"Well, you *can* be pretty dirty." Before I can reply, he lowers his voice, and says: "I need to taste you."

"Pierce."

"Right now. I'm going to make you come."

*

2

PENNY

"No," I say, but I find myself wrapping my hands behind me, around his ass. I squeeze, feeling firm, compact muscle.

He starts to plant soft kisses on the back of my neck. I can feel his warm breath, smell the leftover of a mint candy. It's intimate, heady, and a part of me hates myself for not stopping this right now, right this moment.

I crane my neck to the side, let him kiss me more, let my eyes fall shut.

"Why do you do this?" I ask.

He doesn't answer, but just keeps kissing me. I feel the dab of his tongue on my shoulder, then feel the press of his teeth.

"You smell so good," he whispers. "Get up on that chair."

"We can't."

"Why not?"

"Pierce…"

His finger dips beneath the elastic of my underwear. His huge hand is so warm, it leaves my skin aching and hot. Fingers thread through my pubic hair, and a ball of energy, pure longing, starts to grow in my gut.

"Really," I say, half-heartedly trying to pry his hand out. "Not here." My voice is barely a whisper.

"You want it," he tells me. He turns me slightly, makes me look at him. I stare into his light, ashy eyes. They're determined, full of lust, full of wanting.

I go to shake my head, try to say 'no', but as I part my lips he claims them in his, and he kisses me with crushing force. His tongue is in my mouth, and he's taking from me what he wants. His finger dips into my folds, and I moan softly at the fleeting hints of pleasure.

"You do want me," he says as he breaks the kiss. He presses his forehead against my own, pulls his finger up to my clit. It's already a hard stub. "I can feel it."

I open my mouth again, let him kiss me, let him

bite my lower lip, let him send his tongue inside to dance with my own.

"Oh," I breathe, turning in his arms, wrapping my own around his neck. He lifts me off the floor easily, pushes me up against the wall. Photographs of tattoos previously pinned to the corkboard scatter onto the floor. His arms aren't shaking, and his hands are groping my ass.

The press of his bulge is against my inner thigh, and I look down his body to see it, prominent through his jeans. I send a hand down, cup him, feel his hardness, rigid as steel. Longing, lust, it blooms inside me.

No, more like it booms inside me, a firework going off. Oh, God, I want to pull him out, wrap my fingers around him.

No! I can't believe I'm letting this happen. I can't believe I'm unraveling like this. At my place of *work!* This is so unprofessional.

That's when it clicks. He's no good for me. I'm supposed to be here trying to make a name for myself, trying to start my career as an artist, and I'm being derailed by him. He's already gotten me into enough trouble!

Jesus, we both almost lost our *lives!*

But fuck if he isn't sexy. Fuck if I don't want him,

every inch of his hot-as-hell body. Fuck if he doesn't make me feel like the most beautiful, most desired girl on this planet, the way he devours me, plays me like an instrument. He knows my every button, and he wants to push them all. He wants to pluck every single string.

Somehow, he knows how to uncage my desire. He only needs to draw me close to him, promise me the pleasure I know he's good for, to pick that lock.

I hate that, to him, I'm so seemingly easy to conquer. I hate that it seems like I have no defenses, no walls or barricades. He melts through them all, sees straight through me.

Why do I always let him get what he wants?

Pierce sets me down, spins me around, and holds my hips and pulls them into his own. I feel his hardness on my ass, and his other hand goes to my breast and squeezes hard.

In a flash he's undoing the button to my jeans, and he pulls down the zip before I can stop him, and his whole hand is inside my underwear, and I'm throwing my head back against his shoulder while he kisses the top of mine.

I feel his fingers slide down my sex, and my whole body buzzes with anticipation, a heady thrum, and I know in my heart that I'm ready to give in, to let him take from me every single thing he wants… right here and right now.

He plays with my pearl, rubs it in circles, teases me. He pulls strands of bliss from my core. He winds up my spring, tighter and tighter, and that ball of energy inside me keeps expanding, a pressure in my abdomen.

My heart races faster, my breaths draw quicker, and our bodies writhe together synchronously as one. He pushes a thick finger inside me, and I clench my jaw to stop from moaning. He rubs my front wall, turns my legs to jelly, and then his lips are at my ear again.

"I need you," he tells me.

I press my ear into his lips, want him to kiss it, want to feel the bite of his teeth on my lobe.

He's guiding me to the chair, the one my client was just seated in. He pushes me into it, I flop down into the cotton cushioning, and hear the crackle of the sterile wrap that gets replaced for each customer.

My eyes go toward the doorway that adjoins the tattooing room to the waiting room. It's just a curtain, a sheet of fabric that hangs down from wooden rings set into the frame.

"Wait," I gargle, trying to push him off me, but his hungry hands are having their way with me. I realize that he's in control. I realize this is all about him today.

He pulls up my tank, rolls it over my breasts, and with one finger tugs my bra cup to one side.

"Pierce," I whimper, but I find myself lifting my breasts to meet his lips. He sucks on my nipple, gives me a small bite, and then grins playfully up at me, my hardened bud in between his teeth.

Anticipation… urgency… longing… it's all coursing through me, all egging me on, all telling me that I *have* to let him do this to me, here, now, because I can't possibly resist.

Because I don't want him to stop.

"Damn it," I hiss, and I hold his head against me, savor the feel of his wet, insatiable tongue ringing my nipple. I yelp when he bites me again, and I push him off me, finger on his forehead, and wag it at him.

"Not so hard."

His eyes bore into mine, and I can see his lust for me playing out in every feature on his face. From the way the muscles in his jaw twitch, to the way his eyes won't ever leave my body. He wants me. No, he *needs* me.

"You are so fuckable," he growls, dipping his head to smell me behind my ear. Expecting a compliment that isn't crass from Pierce is like expecting diamonds to rain from the sky.

He's back at my jeans, and now he's tugging them down my legs. I know I shouldn't be doing this, but I help him by wiggling out of them. Now I'm in the seat, just in my underwear. All thoughts of modesty evaporate when I see the look in his eyes.

He settles in between my legs, tugs my underwear to one side, and before I can protest he drapes his hot, wet tongue over my sex.

I jolt in the seat, already so sensitive, and then he's licking me wildly, like some kind of starving dog. All I can see is his head bobbing slightly in between my legs.

I throw my head back, clamp my mouth shut. Making a sound is something I just don't dare to do. My client is right outside. She could walk in at any minute.

Not to mention my boss…

"Jesus," I mewl softly. He's settled into a rhythm on my clit, flicking it left and right with his tongue. He's going fast and hard, trying to make me peak, trying to bring me racing toward oblivion.

And I've no doubt he can do it in under a minute.

He's holding onto my thighs, gripping them hard. I can see his fingers digging into my flesh as he feasts on me, as he plucks strings of pleasure deep within my core.

I'm panting, heaving, and I'm mentally begging him to bring me there, faster, sooner, harder.

Pierce puts a finger at my entrance, rings it slowly, teases me while he laps at my pearl. I pull at my nipples, and my eyes are shut tight. I lift my hips to meet him, press my sex into his face, grind myself into him. The sounds of him pleasuring me are all I can hear.

He pushes his finger inside me, rubs my front wall, right there, right at the spot. I'm drowning in bliss, waiting for him to take me there.

I'm climbing, ever higher, getting closer to the edge, waiting for him to heave me off.

I'm waiting to soar.

"Yes," I whisper, holding his head against me, pushing myself harder into his mouth. His deft tongue works me so expertly. He pushes in another finger, draws a quiet but extended moan from my throat.

"You taste so good," he groans. The vibrations of his voice thrum through me. "I could eat your pussy forever."

"Make me come," I beg. I'm so close. The ball of pressure in my belly is so big. I feel like I'm going to explode.

It grows and grows, gets tighter, tauter.

"Oh, shit," I gasp. "Oh, yes… oh, yes!"

I'm nearly there. So, so close.

But then he backs me off!

"What?" I say a little too loudly, exasperated, panting. My face is flushed, and my eyes are wide, accusing. Why did he do that? Don't tell me he came here just to tease me!

He grins at me, pulls his two fingers from me and sucks on them. "You taste good, Pen." He walks around to the side of the chair. His bulge is visible through his jeans.

"Unzip me," he commands. I reach out my hands, but he stops me with two fingers on my head. "With your teeth."

There's a pause, just the space between two heartbeats. But then my teeth are around the metal zip, and I'm pulling it down. His hands weave through my hair, and when I've unzipped him, he tips my head up so I meet his eyes.

"Together," he tells me.

I gulp and nod. He pulls out his cock from his boxer briefs. Even though we've been together before, I'm still surprised by how big he is.

He guides me to his manhood, and I take it into my mouth. Still gripping onto my hair, he pushes himself into me, and I struggle for a moment to open my throat for him.

That's when I feel his fingers on my folds again. They dip inside me, and he uses his thumb to rub my clit.

He begins to finger me hard and fast, rub my pearl in just the perfect way. I'm instantly overwhelmed, thrust back onto the runway, pushed back toward the precipice.

I can't concentrate on his cock, can't focus on pleasing him. I notice his hand go to his shaft, and he begins to pump himself, jerking off into my mouth.

"Come for me, Pen," he growls, leaning over and taking the top of my ear in between his teeth.

He's got me right there, so close again. I feel the pressure. I let my eyes flutter shut, focus on his fingers, squeeze around them. I'm so, so, so fucking close…

It explodes, white-hot, blinding. I groan loudly onto his cock, feel my body thrown off the edge. I come hard. It's intense, so intense, and he drives me through it, keeps it going, doesn't let up with his dancing fingers.

Pleasure overwhelms me, and I clench tight around him, cresting so hard. My body is a rigid snapshot of ecstasy.

"Fuck," he says hoarsely. I feel his body stiffen,

see him get to his toes, and then he's emptying himself into my mouth, firing his hot seed into me over and over again. I only barely manage to swallow it all.

"Damn, Pen," he says, winding down. "You are good."

I've become too sensitive, and I jolt as he pulls his fingers from me. He examines them, and I see my pleasure on them. He sucks off each finger, pulls his cock from my mouth, and then his hand is cupping my chin.

Pierce guides my face up to his, and he kisses me hard, pushing his tongue into my mouth. I can smell and taste myself mixed with the smell and taste of him.

It's… gross and sexy at the same time.

He breaks the kiss, pulls away, and tucks himself back into his trousers with some difficulty. He brings me a box of sanitized wipes from the counter, and watches, lips at a slight curl, while I wipe my mouth and chin.

"Damn it, Pierce," I say after a moment, breathing hard. "We could have been caught." But I feel so good, so relaxed. I needed that.

I quickly yank my jeans back up my legs, and get out of the chair. My tank top is sticking to my back. I notice that Pierce's neck is shining.

He always looks so good when he sweats.

I sigh, and shake my head. "You really should go."

But he doesn't. He smirks at me and asks, "So, will you pierce my cock?"

*

3

PENNY

If a pin dropped, we'd hear it.

I push off him, flustered and frustrated, and quickly zip up my jeans and do up the button.

"Go!" I say with venom, pointing toward the curtained doorway. "Leave. God, do you *ever* stop messing around?"

"I'll pick you up after work," he says. He grabs his crotch and adjusts it to exaggerated effect, and I can only look away, shake my head.

"No you won't."

"We can talk more about my cock piercing then."

"I'll cut it off," I say. I make a pair of scissors out of my index and middle finger.

He winces. "Ouch. See you at six."

Before I can reply, he's left the curtain flapping in

his wake, his finger in his mouth, and a cocky swagger in his step.

I part the curtain, and catch him wink at Maya in the waiting room. I clench my jaw.

When she comes into the back, sidling past me, she stops, seems to sniff the air. Dread fills me. Can she… *smell* it?

"I like his cologne," she tells me a moment later.

"Mm," I sound, turning around and taking a moment to collect myself.

"Not too strong."

"Yeah."

"Smells expensive."

"Sure."

"I've smelled it before. I think it's—"

I cut her off. "You ready?"

Maya looks stung. I'm being too short with her, and it's unfair. She has no idea, and she's also my client. Wrong. She's *Tina's* client, and damned if I'm going to lose her because I couldn't put on a better bedside manner.

"Sorry," I say.

Maya sits in the chair slowly, lowering herself onto the crinkling wrap. I wipe a hand across my sticky forehead, wonder if she can feel how warm the chair still is.

"Are you okay, Penelope?"

"Yes," I say, tucking hair behind my ears and taking a deep breath. I touch my cheeks with the backs of my hands. They're boiling. I'm sure Maya will notice.

"Trouble?"

"You could call it that."

"Is he a client?"

I sigh, and give her a polite smile. "Yes. Hold out your arm again, please." I pick up the tattoo machine, but my fingers are still trembling a little, so I put it down and shake them a bit. I've still got Pierce's taste in my mouth, and so I go to the sink and run myself a glass of water.

"What's a Prince Albert?"

I almost spit the water out, but play it off like a cough.

"You don't know?"

"Well, from what I gather, it's a piercing on a, uh, man's…?"

"Yup. It's a piercing on the underside of the penis, beneath the glans, and into the urethra. The ring is pushed through one of the thinnest membranes on a male's body, into the urethral passage, and actually comes out of the urethral opening. It's relatively simple as far as male genital piercings go, and is one of the most popular."

I recite it off the top of my head. It's a way to distract myself, and hopefully Maya. I know a lot about body art and piercings.

She scrunches up her face. "That's kind of disgusting. Doesn't that hurt?"

"Typically people say it hurts more than an ear piercing and less than a nipple piercing," I tell her. "Some guys say it doesn't hurt at all, but I don't believe that. Four-to-six weeks healing time."

"Why do they do it?"

I shrug, and then sit down on my stool next to her. "It's not like I *have* a penis. People report they have heightened sexual pleasure. Some say they like the sensation when they urinate. Some women say that, in certain positions, the piercing can actually enhance sex for them."

"Really?" she asks. "Huh. I wonder what positions?"

"Use your imagination," I deadpan.

"Why does that guy want one? Doesn't he know you don't do piercings here?"

I laugh. "Oh God, to tell you the truth, I don't know. I don't think he even knows why *he* wants one, or if he truly does, or if he's just winding me up."

"He's hot, though."

I push my lips together, stare daggers into her arm. I try not to squeeze it too tightly. "Yeah, he is."

"Great body."

"Yeah," I say, contemplating pushing the needle into her arm a little deeper than I should.

"Who is he, anyway? Your ex or something?"

I shake my head slowly. "No, not my ex. He's Pierce Fletcher."

"Pierce Fletcher," she echoes. "I've heard that somewhere before."

"He's an underground cage fighter."

"Yeah, my brother talked about him. Something like one of the best ever in the scene."

"That's what they say." My tone lacks any semblance of enthusiasm. "He's also about to become my stepbrother."

"Oh," she says. I see it on her face. At first, there's polite acknowledgment, and then confusion: *Weren't they just talking about his cock?*

"And," I say, sighing, drawing out the word. "We're sleeping together."

She covers her mouth.

Silence swallows us.

*

4

ONE MONTH EARLIER…

PENNY

"I'm moving to Melbourne."

It is a statement of fact.

My father looks up from his paper, and his cornflake-filled spoon hovers in between the bowl and his mouth. His sea-green eyes narrow and his crow's feet deepen.

"Are you telling me or asking me?"

I flash him a quick smile. "We've talked about it before, and I've made up my mind. I'm moving to Melbourne, and I'm going to apprentice for Tina Azume. She's already granted me an interview."

Dad gives me a slow blink. Out of nowhere, he looks like he's aged ten years. "Oh."

"Rose lives out there and she's got a spare room and says that I can move in with her. Tina Azume is my favorite artist and one of the best on the planet." I offer a small shrug. "It's what I want to do."

"You're *serious* about becoming a tattooist?"

I hold my breath, wait for that hint of passive-aggressive judgment to rear its ugly head, but it doesn't, so I nod at him. I should give him some credit this time.

"Yeah, Dad. I really am. And actually, we prefer to be called tattoo artists."

"We?" he asks.

"I'm going to become one, Dad, and I'm going to be good. And I'll be honest, nothing you say will stop me from chasing this."

His bushy brows bunch, and he looks hurt for a moment. "I can see you're on the offensive."

I lick my lips. I won't lie, I'm nervous. Butterflies are raging in my stomach, and I'm desperately hoping he doesn't say no. I want to go with his blessing. I don't want to disappoint him.

"You're confident you can do this, Penelope?"

"You've seen how well I can draw. I'm going to be good, Dad. I really am. I have a good hand, and a better eye."

"I know you do. I've seen your drawings. You've got great perspective and lines."

I feel a blush in my cheeks. "Thanks. That means a lot coming from an architect. And from you, Dad."

"But, Penelope, body art, really?"

"Do you have any idea how hard it is to draw well on skin?"

"I can't say I do," he admits.

"It'd be really great if I could get my father's support on this."

He sighs. "You know, you get that manipulative streak from your mother."

"I'm not being manipulative. I'm just being honest."

"Your mother was appalled to find out you got another tattoo." He gestures at my wrist. I have a silhouette of the Chicago city skyline there. I did it myself with my *left* hand. I am a little ambidextrous, and so I've been training it.

"Well, frankly, I don't really give a shit what Mom thinks," I tell him. She burnt her bridges with me long ago. It's just me and Dad now.

He grows cross in an instant. His tone is deep and disapproving. "Penelope."

"What, Dad? Come on, we don't get along. Heck, even *you* couldn't bear to be with her. And after what she did to you? I can't—"

"She's still your mother, and I don't want you using that language at the table."

"Yeah, well I chose *you*. And sorry for swearing."

He can't help but smile. "You know, I always thought it was fathers and sons that had troubled relationships. Not mothers and daughters."

"Shows how much you know."

"Evelyn and her daughter have a good relationship."

"Not everybody is the same, Dad. Besides, did Evelyn break her daughter's father's heart?"

He frowns. "You shouldn't hold on to that, darling. It's not healthy. I'm past it, and I don't blame your mother, either."

"Any time you cheat, you deserve to be blamed."

"It's not always that simple."

I fold my arms. "I know, I know, you grow distant, the passion fades, whatever. You still don't do it. You either sit down and talk like responsible adults, or you break it off. It may be black and white, but that's how I see it."

He sucks on his upper lip for a moment. "Just, consider not throwing away your relationship with your mother, okay? You'll regret it when you're older."

"Fine," I say. "I'll consider it. So, will you give me your blessing? To go to Melbourne?"

He sighs. "I guess it's not like I can stop you, huh? You always did do your own thing."

"No, you can't stop me. This is my *dream*, Dad. I've got the money grandpa left me, and I can afford to buy the ticket. I've already got my interview set up, my appointment to get my visiting tattoo artist apprentice license, and a meeting set up for my visa."

"I see that you've planned it all without me."

I frown. "Dad, you were the one who told me to give this serious thought, and to get the legwork done. I've done my due diligence. This is not some wishy-washy idea. I'm serious."

"Forgive me for not being overly thrilled."

"Hey, all the other kids who just graduated are all going to Hawaii or Mexico to get drunk, do drugs, and have sex. I'm going to Melbourne to start my *career*. As an *artist*."

"Okay, fine, I'll concede that point," he says. "Penelope, I admire your ambition, I really do. But why don't you try it out here first? In Chicago?"

"It's *Tina Azume*, and she's looking for an apprentice!"

"I really don't know who that is."

"Only one of the most famous tattoo artists in the

world! She's got this amazing style, and she's extremely humble. She's not super exclusive or a snob or anything. She's really cool, Dad. She's, like, a role model. I've got posters of her work up in my room."

"Those? They just look like normal tattoos."

"And the *Mona Lisa* just looks like a normal painting."

He pushes up his lower lip with a finger. "Okay, but I don't like the Mona Lisa, anyway."

"But you see where I'm coming from, right? I've already made up my mind."

"You're only nineteen."

"And that makes me an adult."

"I'd be an irresponsible father if I just let you waltz off for God knows how long."

"Would it be any different than if I was going to Australia for college?" I ask.

"Yes," he says. "You'd be getting an education. There would be responsible adults around you. You would be in an academic community focused on learning, self-betterment."

"I will *still* be getting an education," I cry, throwing my arms up, exasperated. "I'll apprentice and learn more about body art and techniques. And as for your slight on the community, tattoo artists and people that get tattoos are just as human as anybody else, and believe it or not, shock horror, are for the most part responsible adults, too. They also, believe it or not, value learning and self-betterment. Don't go stereotyping them because of your own narrow-mindedness. Just because someone's got a full-sleeve doesn't mean he's a bad person, just like how not having tattoos doesn't automatically make you a good person."

He blinks, rubs his red eyes. I notice then that his hair seems to have grayed more in the last week alone, and he's looking a little thinner.

"You're right, Penelope. I'm being judgmental."

I wince. Somehow it almost hurts to hear Dad admit that he's wrong to me. "You're looking tired, Dad."

"Things have been crazy at work. The Dubai project of course came to a stall once the economy flat lined, and we're in a legal battle to get our owed fees."

"That sounds boring."

"It is."

"But you know what I'm chasing, right? What if somebody told you that you couldn't be an architect?"

"My father wanted me to work at the bakery."

"Grandpa? Really?"

"Yeah. Said I had great hands, but bread wasn't my thing."

"See, so you still went off on your own! You

chased your dream."

"It involved seven years of architecture school, sweetheart, in an ultra-competitive environment."

"And I'll likely be apprenticing for years as well, and it's *just* as competitive. Come on, don't patronize me."

He lets out a deep, shuddering exhale, and I know he's relenting.

"I'm going to miss you," he says.

I won't lie. It hits me right in the gut. It's just been me and him for a few years now, and since he works so much, we're like a team. He takes care of me in some ways, I take care of him in other ways.

"Will you be okay alone?"

He laughs. "Come on, Penelope. Of course I will. I'm only a fifty-two year old man."

"Really? Because I've seen the way you eat when I don't prepare dinner. It's unhealthy."

He clears his throat, and sidesteps the issue. "How long are you planning on staying there for?"

"Oh, jeez, Dad, it's not like I'm leaving forever. I'll be back! I think my visa only gives me one year, anyway, with the option for a second."

"And it'll be legal for you to work there?"

"Yes."

"And it'll make you happy?"

"Yes!"

He puts the spoon down, and it clinks against his bowl. "Fine. But I expect you to email me at least twice a week. And call me once a week. A *proper* telephone call, not just the hi-dad-bye-dad bullshit that kids do these days. Actually, I want it over Skype as well. I want to be able to see your face. Anyway, I need to put the new laptop to good use. I haven't even used it once, you know?"

I grin. "Okay."

"And I want the telephone number of Rose and her mother or father or guardian. I'll want to have a talk with both of them first."

"No problem."

"And I want you to write me out a plan. I want you to list out exactly what you're going to be doing, how you're going to do it, and anything else that entails. I want to know how you'll get a license to tattoo, where this Tina person is. I want to know how you'll sort out your taxes, driving license, everything. I want you to be on top of everything, and I expect it by tonight when I get home from work."

I nod rapidly. "I can do that." I've got this broad smile on my face, and I reach across the table and take his hand. "Thanks, Dad."

"You know," he says, giving my hand a squeeze. "I

never thought my beautiful daughter would become a tattooist. Sorry, tattoo *artist*."

"What did you think I'd be?"

"I don't know. Graphic designer? Something safe."

"Try and be a little more open-minded."

"Wait until you get to be my age with children of your own, and let's see how open-minded you'll be then when they ask you if they can do insane things."

"It's not insane."

"Well, maybe it's just because I'm your father, but the idea of letting my nineteen year-old daughter live alone in a different country without any real supervision sounds insane to me."

"You can trust me. I'm not a partier. I'm not interested in that stuff. Heck, I've never even tried a cigarette."

His expression hardens. "I should expect not."

"You have to trust me, Dad."

"I do trust you. But if you disappoint me—"

"I won't," I promise him. "I swear it."

"Okay."

"Hey!" I say after a moment of silence. "You can use this as an opportunity to see… what's-her-name more!"

"Her name is Isabelle," he says sternly. "Isabelle

Fletcher." Then his face lights up. "Hang on a minute." He pulls out his phone, and starts going through his messages.

"What is it?"

"Melbourne, right?"

"Yeah."

"Well, Isabelle has a son, and he spent his teenage years in a boarding school in Melbourne. I think he's still there."

"Really?" I ask. "That's a coincidence."

"Indeed. His name is, um, Pierce."

"Oh. Like the James Bond actor?"

"Different spelling, I think. I've got a photo of him somewhere. Isabelle sent it to me."

I watch as he manhandles his phone, punching the on-screen buttons the way he pecks at his keyboard.

"Ah, here we go," he says.

He turns the phone around and shows it to me. There's a photograph of Isabelle. She's looking uptight and well-dressed as usual. And standing next to her is…

"That's him?" I ask.

"Yeah. Why?"

I say nothing, just shake my head.

The guy is hot as hell.

*

Untamed
An Bad Boy Secret Baby Romance

By

Emilia Kincade

* * *

* * *

50382020R00418

Made in the USA
Lexington, KY
13 March 2016